The H

Steven A. McKay was born in Scotland in 1977. He is the author of two previous series of historical fiction, following Robin Hood and the warrior-druid Bellicus in post-Roman Britain. He plays the guitar, is the co-host of historical aventure podcast *Rock, Paper, Swords!* along with author Matthew Harffy, and lives just outside Glasgow with his wife and children.

STEVEN A.
McKAY

THE
HEATHEN
HORDE

1C CANELO

First published in the United Kingdom in 2023 by

Canelo
Unit 9, 5th Floor
Cargo Works, 1-2 Hatfields
London SE1 9PG
United Kingdom

A CIP catalogue record for this book is available from the British Library.

Print ISBN 978 1 80436 548 9
Ebook ISBN 978 1 80436 549 6

Look for more great books at www.canelo.co

Printed and bound in Great Britain by Clays Ltd, Elcograf S.p.A.

1

To Yvonne, Freya, Riley, and Lianna.

PROLOGUE

Northumbria, AD 864

It had been a clammy night and King Aelle had slept fitfully. He was forced at last to give up his bed as a vicious storm rent the night air. The rumble of thunder, drumming of rain on his roof, and, most alarmingly, the crack of lightning as it lit up the sky, had all combined to bring him fully awake.

He looked out onto his lands being battered by the harsh weather. It was almost as if God was sending him a sign. But how was he to interpret the sign? Was it a good omen, or bad? Aelle knew he would have to seek out his priest when – if! – the sun finally came up in the morning, and ask the old man's advice.

Father Hyglac would give the king the answers he needed.

Aelle winced as a particularly loud clap of thunder pealed directly over his house and muttered a prayer that lightning wouldn't follow and set fire to the thatch on his roof. After a time it seemed the storm was moving on eastwards. The rain lessened and the frightening rumbles faded into the distance.

He could see something burning not too far away in a field, despite the rain. A tree perhaps, or a barn. Men were running towards it already, shouting at one another to fetch buckets of water and extinguish the blaze. If it was a barn Aelle hoped that any animals inside were freed in time. Christ knew his people could not afford to lose any more cattle since the Danish raiders had killed so many of them already.

The sea-wolves had been ravaging Northumbria for seventy-odd years now. Pillaging, raping, killing men, women and children or carting them off into slavery. Aelle shook his head and sighed. 'Maybe it will end tomorrow,' he muttered, and began stripping off his bedclothes. He must have been staring out the window for longer than he realised as the eastern sky was already beginning to lighten with the approaching dawn.

'Are you not coming back to bed?'

Aelle glanced across to see his wife Aethelthryth watching him from beneath her blanket. He smiled and shook his head. 'No, my dear,' he said. 'I must prepare for what's to come.'

He lifted a jug of water and poured some into a silver cup. It was stale, but helped moisten his mouth as he continued to pull on his clothes and sword belt. He wanted to look his best, his most impressive, on this great day.

Aethelthryth had fallen back asleep by the time he was ready. Aelle went out into the morning and headed for the nearby church. The walls were strong, and the doors had been replaced after the raiders had smashed them open the previous year. From the outside at least, it looked like a worthy place to worship God. Inside however, it was but a shell of its former glory. The Danes had stolen the magnificent golden cross from the altar along with anything else of value and destroyed any furnishings they didn't think worth carrying off.

The people had done their best to tidy up and rebuild the broken altar, but Aelle felt the rage rise within him again, as it did every time he came here. He had only been king for two years, since his predecessor, Osberht, had been deposed, and in that time the Danes had truly seemed to be a punishment from God.

It would end today, the king hoped.

'Brother Hyglac!' he called out softly. The priest was on his knees with his back to Aelle, but it was obvious from his brown robe and tonsured hair who it was. The man made the sign of the cross, quietly spoke the end of his prayer, and got stiffly to his feet.

'Is it time, my king?' the priest asked, and there was a determination in his tone; a hardness which was unusual for the man of God.

'Just about,' Aelle replied. 'First, pray with me, brother, and help guide me in what must be done this day.'

By the time they were finished the sun was fully up and streaming through the empty windows which the raiders had shattered the previous summer. The colourful glass would not be replaced for a long time, but the sunlight was welcome after the terrible storm of the night before.

Together, they went outside. A crowd was already forming near the edge of town, expectant and excited for the coming entertainment, their eyes shining almost as bright as the sunshine. They bowed deferentially as king and priest passed by, calling encouragement and demanding justice.

'Are you sure that's what the storm meant?' Aelle asked as they approached the low, stone building that was their destination. 'That we should do this? I wondered if, perhaps, it meant we should be merciful…'

Hyglac gave him a haughty look. 'Of course not, my king. The storm merely showed God's fury, which we all share. The fact that the morning has dawned clear and bright proves this.' He spread his palms and gazed out at the fields in the distance. 'It's a perfect day for our Lord's justice.'

Aelle accepted the priest's words gladly, for he wanted nothing more than to send a message to their enemies.

'Bring him out,' he said to the spearmen guarding the house. 'And drag him to the field, there.'

Aelle and the priest did not wait for the orders to be followed, walking down the slope towards the empty ground that had been cleared specifically for what was to come.

The king climbed the steps onto the wooden platform which had been built there the day before. The timber was damp from the downpour but the sun was quickly drying it out, and steam rose as Aelle made his way to the simple wooden chair in the centre of the platform. Hyglac stood by his side, hands clasped, a small smile on the priest's face.

The townsfolk lined the way towards the platform, chattering with excitement. Their voices rose as the prisoner appeared from the house that had been his prison since he was captured the previous day.

The man was not young, perhaps approaching sixty summers as his bristling, grey beard attested, yet he was still large, well-muscled and heavily scarred. A true warrior. His hands were bound behind his back, and he was roughly made to walk past the jeering townspeople, many of whom spat and shouted the vilest of insults at him. The prisoner moved on towards Aelle with a blank, almost indifferent look on his face, as if their hatred could not touch him.

At last, the warrior stood before the platform, staring at the king. Aelle nodded and one of the guards slammed the shaft of his spear against the backs of the prisoner's knees, making him fall, face-first, onto the road.

Cheers and laughter erupted and the guard grinned savagely, as if he'd performed some mighty feat.

Aelle waited until the prisoner was looking at him again. 'King Ragnar "Lodbrok" Sigurdsson. You and your heathen kin have ravaged my lands for long enough. Today, I will make sure you never rape another woman, or kill another child, or burn another man's home.'

The people broke into venom-filled shouts and jeers again. Every single one of them had suffered in some way at the hands of Ragnar's pagan followers who, although generally known as Danes, might more accurately be termed Northmen as they came not only from Denmark, but also Norway and Sweden, to take whatever they wanted from Aelle's lands.

'Shave his head,' Aelle commanded and the guards moved in, one kneeling heavily on Ragnar's back, another on his legs, while a third took out a dagger and used it to chop away their captive's long, grey hair. Ragnar did not fight back, merely stared fixedly at Aelle as he was shorn like a sheep until only dozens of tiny spots of blood remained on his scalp. Then he was dragged onto his feet again, to stand and face the king who was sitting in judgement over his past actions.

'Strip him,' Aelle ordered.

Again, the guards moved in, with two gripping the prisoner in case he tried to fight back, but he did not move as his tunic was ripped off and his trousers roughly cut away leaving him standing naked before them all. For a man of his age, and considering the life he had led, he looked healthy enough, with only his many scars, and the sagging chest and gut, marking him as an older warrior.

'If you can make it to the banner there,' Aelle said, pointing along the road, between the gathered townsfolk. 'I will free you. Do you understand me?'

The Dane turned his head, eyeing the white banner with a great red wolf's head on it. He looked at the howling mob lining the road, many of them holding sticks, and faced the king again. He never uttered a word or showed any sign of fear, despite the gauntlet he would be forced to run if he wanted to live.

'Do you understand, dog?' Aelle demanded, slamming his hand down on the arm of his chair, making the whole platform shudder.

Ragnar did not reply, although his upper lip seemed to curl slightly in contempt.

'You can remain silent, Dane,' the king cried, voice carrying over the crowd who hushed to hear his words. 'I know you understand me, for we've met before when I paid you to leave our lands alone, and you took our coin.' He stood and glared down at the naked captive. 'Yet you returned to defile our lands, and my people, even after being paid to leave. You have no morals, and no honour. You are worth less than the shit I will take after the feast to celebrate your demise.'

The mob roared in delight at their lord's crude words, enjoying every minute of this revenge on the man who'd led the heathen hordes against them.

'You could not be stopped in Francia, and you could not be stopped in Ireland, or Mercia, but God ended your evil at last by wrecking your ship on our coast. Do you have anything to say, Ragnar?'

The Dane stared at him, bound, naked, head-shaved and bleeding, yet somehow he still stood proud. Even so, he could not face his death silently like this, although he probably knew what the answer would be before he asked, 'Can I have a weapon?'

Aelle laughed shortly. 'I know it's your pagan belief that to die without a weapon in your hand means you will never reach Valhöll—'

It was Ragnar's turn to laugh mockingly now. 'That is not quite what we believe. Óðinn knows of my bravery. My place at his side is assured.' He looked back at the townsfolk. 'I simply wish to kill a few more of you fools before I die.'

His words, predictably, brought howls of rage from the people, and Aelle, who had been planning to prolong his captive's suffering for some time longer, gestured to his soldiers.

'Run, dog,' one shouted, hitting the shaft of his spear against Ragnar's back. The Dane stumbled forward and the crowd roared, eyes blazing, teeth bared in a hatred cultivated over generations. This heathen warlord, this king, Ragnar 'Lodbrok', would feel their suffering a hundredfold.

'You may kill me,' the Dane shouted, addressing everyone there to revel in his pain and humiliation before turning to look at King Aelle and the priest, Hyglac. 'But my sons will hear of this and come to avenge me. Halfdan, Ubba and Ivar shall lay waste to your lands, with iron and fire, until none in Midgard remember this place, or any of you, ever existed.'

The common townsfolk could not make out what he was saying, but Aelle could. Hyglac could too, and he paled as he made the sign of the cross. 'Kill him!' the priest shouted, wiping beads of sweat from his tonsured head. 'Kill him!'

The king stood and furiously repeated Hyglac's command, drawing his own sword as if he might leap down from the platform and run Ragnar through himself.

Now Aelle saw the first hint of true fear in the Dane's eyes as he hesitantly took a single step towards the incensed mob, then was dealt another blow in the small of his back from the spear. Forcing a lupine grin onto his seamed face, Ragnar began to run towards the banner.

They had not severed the bonds on his hands so he could not even attempt to defend himself as he reached the first of the gathered Northumbrians. A fist glanced off his skull. Feet lashed out against his legs. He staggered, but ran on, ducking and trying to dodge the many attacks aimed at him.

He did not get far before something hard, a cudgel or hammer, shattered his shoulder and he screamed in agony. Still, he struggled forward, staring at the banner as blow after blow rained down on him. At last, he could take no more and fell to the ground with a cry.

Aelle and Hyglac watched in grim satisfaction as the people swarmed over the fallen Dane and made an end to him. They were so overcome with bloodlust that they were fighting with one another, pushing and shoving just to get close enough to land a kick on the prone heathen. By the time their rage subsided and the king's guards moved them back Ragnar was barely recognisable as a man.

'It is done,' the priest shouted happily, raising his hands to the sky. 'By God's grace, it is done!'

Aelle stared at the shredded remnants of their enemy and considered the man's last words. The king knew of Ragnar's sons, and he shuddered at their names. They were notorious for their cruelty, particularly the one known as Ivar the Detestable, and the thought of them coming to wreak vengeance on Aelle's lands terrified him. As if the Norse raids hadn't been bad enough already...

'God be praised,' Hyglac was crying. 'It is finished!'

A cloud passed over the sun and Aelle shivered. It was not finished, he feared.

It was only just beginning.

PART ONE

CHAPTER ONE

Mercia, AD 868

Autumn

'Look out, Alfred!'

The rider heard his brother's warning just in time to raise his shield and the linden boards took the brunt of the axe which had been heading for his skull, splinters flying as the wood shuddered, pain lancing through his arm. Baring his teeth in rage, Alfred swung his sword down, catching his attacker's hand just as the axe had been about to strike again. There was a scream of pain as fingers were torn through to the bone and then Alfred's horse was past and cantering away from the battle.

'Back,' he grunted, tugging on the reins and bringing the horse around quickly. His heart was thudding in his chest and he felt light-headed but it was almost a joyful sensation. He was afraid, aye, but he was also excited, and eager to get back to the fight. He could see the axeman who'd tried to kill him, grimacing and eyeing his mangled hand as if he feared he might never hold a weapon properly again.

Alfred was charging back into the fight before he knew it, battle fever overtaking him at the realisation that he'd almost had his skull caved in. He headed straight for the axeman. The man had transferred his weapon to his left hand but could only wield it awkwardly and his wide eyes told of his fear at being forced to fight in such a manner. Alfred's horse came alongside the Dane's and, screaming an incoherent battle-cry, the young warrior smashed the edge of his blade into the enemy's neck. The sheer force of the blow was enough to throw the man off his horse's back despite the Dane's long, mail neck guard. He lay on the ground, unmoving, as his mount bolted and the pounding hooves of the other combatants' animals swirled around him.

Alfred grinned savagely, knowing that, if the Dane had somehow survived the attack and the fall, he wouldn't last long before the weight of a horse crushed the life from him.

God be praised, one less sea-wolf to ravage Anglo-Saxon lands!

Before the young nobleman could engage another of the enemy warriors there was a shout from their leader, and they broke off the fight and started running towards the fortified town that lay not far to the east of their position.

Alfred looked to his older brother, Aethelred, and saw him smiling in grim satisfaction.

'Let them go,' Aethelred shouted, watching as their enemies retreated like scolded dogs towards the high, timber walls of Snotengaham. There were fifteen or so of them, while a similar number lay dead or injured on the grass around Aethelred's mounted warriors.

Alfred, noting the unprotected backs of their beaten foes, felt a sudden urge to kick his heels into his horse's flanks and give chase. They would be such easy targets for his blade, and God knew, the bastards deserved death for all the trouble they'd caused in these lands over the past three years.

'Brother.'

Alfred turned away from the fleeing Danes to see Aethelred coming towards him shaking his head slightly, as if he knew what the younger man was thinking.

'Let them go. We've given them a lesson here today.' Aethelred, King of Wessex, took off his helmet and shook out his long hair, which was damp with sweat. He looked at the bodies on the ground, but not all of them belonged to the enemy. 'No point in more of us dying. Let them run back to cower behind Snotengaham's walls. They'll starve eventually.'

Blowing out a long breath, Alfred nodded and jumped down, thudding onto the grass beside one of the fallen Danes. He wiped his sword blade on the dead man's cloak before sliding it back into its scabbard and then looked up to the sky, closed his eyes, and mouthed a soft prayer of thanks for their victory.

'What about the survivors, my lord?' someone asked the king. There weren't many of them, but a handful of men from both sides were lying around groaning in pain or begging for aid.

Alfred could tell there would be no helping some of the wounded. Those with severed limbs or similar, severe injuries, could not be saved. His brother knew it too.

'Make our own comfortable,' he commanded.

He looked every inch the victorious king from high atop his horse, thought Alfred, who viewed his brother as something of a father figure. 'Kill those of the heathens who can't be helped and take the rest as slaves. They can work off their debt to our people. Make themselves useful for once in their miserable lives.'

There were cries of terror and pleas for mercy but they were soon silenced as Aethelred's warriors went about their grim task. Within moments another three of the enemy were on their way to the afterlife while the rest were disarmed and being forced to stumble back towards the main camp of the West Saxon forces.

'My lord!'

Alfred saw one of his own comrades lying on the ground, a pool of blood soaking the grass beneath him.

'My lord,' the man repeated desperately, and Alfred hurried across to kneel by his side.

The man's injury must have been grievous for so much blood to have spilled from him and the prince took the man's hand in his, gripping it firmly.

'I'm dying,' the warrior said and there were tears in his eyes. He was only young, perhaps a little older than nineteen-year-old Alfred himself. Barely a man yet. Alfred could not bring himself to lie to him, to tell him he would be all right.

'You fought well,' he said instead, and then he fell silent for he did not know what else to say. This was his first real experience of warfare and, now that the battle lust was wearing off, he found himself shocked and filled with sorrow at the carnage that had just taken place.

This was merely the beginning too, for the Danes were not likely to go anywhere for a while. Snotengaham was surrounded by a wooden palisade wall encircled by a deep ditch, offering great protection to those inside. The sea-wolves were safe for now, and they knew it.

'My lord,' the downed warrior muttered, gripping Alfred's hand convulsively. His complexion was fading from a healthy pink to grey, and his breathing was becoming uneven and ragged. 'My lord, is there a priest nearby?'

There was not.

Alfred reached inside his mail vest and drew out the pendant he wore on a leather thong. It was a simple, silver cross with four arms of equal length. He showed it to the man and smiled encouragingly. 'Join me in prayer, my friend,' he said and started to intone the words of the first thing that came to mind, a favourite of his.

> 'We walk in the light of this bountiful day
> in the great strength of the most high God of gods,
> in the favour of Christ,
> in the light of the Holy Spirit,
> in faith of the patriarchs,
> in the service of the prophets,
> in the peace of the apostles,
> in the joy of angels,
> in the splendour of the saints...'

Alfred paused as he felt the grip on his hand lessen and saw the man's eyes glaze over as a soft gurgle came from his throat. The prince stared, knowing the warrior was gone, and then he recited the rest of the prayer to the end, finishing with,

> *'In this is the way of all who labour for Christ,*
> *who led the saints into joy forever after their deaths,*
> *that they might listen to the voices of the angels,*
> *praising God and saying:*
> *"Holy, holy, holy."'*

A shadow fell over them then and Alfred glanced up to see his older brother watching him still gripping the hand of their dead soldier.

'Who needs a priest when you're around, eh?' Aethelred said with a sad smile. 'You did well today. In the battle, and in easing that man's passing.' He put out his hand and helped Alfred onto his feet. Together they watched as the rest of the warband went about their business. Very quickly their dead or injured comrades were transported back to the encampment a short distance away, while the stripped corpses of the defeated Danes were left to rot where they'd fallen. Alfred knew their enemies normally buried their dead with the possessions they believed they would need in the afterlife: weapons, armour, jewellery, and occasionally horses and even slaves were sacrificed and inhumed or cremated with the deceased warrior.

They would receive no such honour here, unless their kinsmen inside Snotengaham wished to try and retrieve the bodies. Instead, crows, jackdaws, foxes and perhaps wolves would come to feast on their flesh. Alfred could only wonder how those men would appear in their so-called Valhöll when the beasts had left their bones picked clean of flesh and scattered about the countryside. It was ludicrous, and a stark contrast to his own wondrous image of Heaven.

'Are you all right?' Aethelred asked protectively, perhaps noting his brother's pensive look. This was the younger man's first real taste of battle on such a large scale after all.

Alfred nodded. 'I am, brother. This all just seems like such a waste.'

Aethelred grunted agreement and headed towards his horse. 'It is, God knows. But until the heathen raiders are gone from these lands forever, we must fight them with everything we have. Come, let's get a drink and remember those who fell beside us this day.'

Grasping his saddle, Alfred nimbly jumped up onto his own mount's back and nudged it into a trot behind the king's. He turned one last time to look at the walls of the nearby town. Snotengaham was supposed to be a Mercian settlement and, he vowed, so it would be again, soon. They just had to starve out the besieged Danes and, God willing, put them to the sword, just as they'd done to the foragers who'd thought to sneak out to hunt that day.

'Conceited whoresons,' he said as he caught up with Aethelred. 'To think they could just ride out, with our army and the Mercian army both camped right outside the town they're hiding in.'

Aethelred nodded grimly. 'True, but that's something you'll learn about the Danes soon enough. They think themselves warriors without peer, and it makes them act with the arrogance we saw today.' He shrugged. 'It's a weakness we can sometimes, perhaps, exploit.'

They were almost at the West Saxon camp now, the red banner of Wessex with its golden dragon flying high over the king's tent, and the cooking fires with their aroma of roasting meat filling the air and making Alfred's stomach rumble loudly. He was surprised to find himself famished for, as he'd been praying over the dying man, he felt like he might never regain his appetite. It was amazing how quickly one adjusted to the trials and tribulations of life in this warlike age. He reached up to touch the cross around his neck and realised it was still out, rather than safely tucked beneath his mail shirt. He gripped it and gave thanks to God for their small victory, and the roast pork he was about to enjoy, then slipped it away again.

Almost before he and Aethelred had dismounted they found mugs of ale thrust into their hands with their fellow soldiers, and the thanes who led them, praising their valour and leadership.

The pleasure that Alfred had felt during the battle returned in that moment, and he grinned at the adulation of their subordinates. He swallowed a huge mouthful of his ale, grinning and laughing along with the other men, and Aethelred joined in too with the revelry.

'This, little brother,' called the king over all the noise. 'This is living! Make the most of it, for it might be you or I left out for the crows next time we meet the Danes in battle.' With that, he hoisted his mug and downed its foaming contents. A second was in his hand before he even had time to fully swallow the first.

Alfred laughed. He knew Aethelred was right, it could be one, or both of them feeding the battlefield birds soon – hadn't they already lost all three of their older brothers, along with their father and mother? Life did not seem to last very long within their royal family. With that gloomy thought, he too drank the last of his ale and reached for a refill. Tonight they would feast and make merry, and tell tales about the brave warriors who had died by their side, and then, Alfred thought, with a stirring in his loins, he would fall into bed with some willing serving girl.

Perhaps more than one…

Aye, this, brother! he thought, raising his mug once more and joining in with the victory song his men had struck up. *This was living!*

CHAPTER TWO

Alfred winced as men shouted greetings outside the war tent, and the clattering of servants bringing food and drink for those inside seemed like the pounding of Norse war-hammers within his head. He reached again for the ale mug on the table before him, feeling fragile and nauseous after the previous night's drinking and...

His loins twitched as he remembered the firm, naked bodies of the two girls he'd had in his own tent just a few hours before. How beautiful they were, and how skilled. He could smell them now, their musky sweat still on him...

God, punish me for my sins, he thought, wishing the bulge in his trousers would not get any bigger as a pretty serving girl came across to pour him some more ale.

'What are we going to do about these bastards?' His brother slammed his own mug on the table, making Alfred jump.

'Starve them out,' said Burgred, King of Mercia. It was his lands the Danes had occupied, and he who asked for aid from his brother-in-law Aethelred when the invaders had taken control of Snotengaham. 'Now that we have your army with us, we can keep them penned inside the town.' He smiled grimly. 'You showed them yesterday that riding outside the walls to forage for supplies was a foolish idea. I don't think they'll try that again.'

'How much food do they have stored in there, though?' Aethelred asked, nodding his head in the direction of the town. 'We can't sit around here forever, my lord.'

Burgred looked away and Alfred could see the Mercian king didn't want to answer the question.

'If there's even a couple of weeks' food stored within the walls we can't starve them out,' Aethelred said. 'We'll starve before they do!'

A warm glow was making Alfred feel more like himself and he nodded agreement with his older brother's assessment of the situation. 'Winter approaches, King Burgred,' he said respectfully. 'The fields need harvested. The meat slaughtered, salted and stored.' He stood up and walked to the tent's entrance, pointing out towards Snotengaham. 'Stored,' he said, 'in there.' He was repeating things he'd heard Aethelred's commanders saying but it was all true, and the Mercian king understood his position all too well.

'What else can we do, then?' Burgred asked almost plaintively. 'Those animals have wrecked half the settlements in Mercia. They're like locusts! A Biblical plague!'

His analogy struck Alfred deeply for he loved the story of Moses, but he could see no way they could force the Danish leaders to leave the protection of Snotengaham's walls and come out to meet them in battle.

'Either we storm the town,' Aethelred said, more to his brother than Burgred, 'or we leave here, as unsatisfying as that may be.'

Alfred met his gaze and an understanding passed between them. Wessex's king would not throw away their men's lives by trying to storm that towering palisade wall with its deep ditch. It would be pointless and result in nothing but carnage for their own army.

They would need that army, for there was nothing more certain than that the Danes would continue to move from place to place once spring arrived, destroying and taking whatever they wanted. As much as Aethelred and Alfred wanted to help Burgred, Wessex would surely require every last one of its warriors in the coming months.

'I'm going to have to pay them to leave, aren't I?' the Mercian king whined. He sounded like a beaten man and

Alfred wasn't surprised. This was becoming a pattern for the Danes, where they would turn up someplace, take whatever they wanted, then be offered silver to move on, leaving a trail of death and destruction in their wake.

Aethelred nodded. 'That seems the most prudent course.' He reached out and patted Burgred consolingly on the arm. 'At least Snotengaham still stands, mostly intact, and you yourself haven't suffered the same fate as King Aelle.'

Burgred shuddered at that, and Alfred's brows drew together as he remembered the stories of the battle that had taken place the year before. The heathen army had met the Northumbrian forces led by Aelle and Osberht and the Danes had easily won the fighting. Osberht was killed, mercifully, during the battle, while Aelle…

'Is it true?' Alfred asked with youthful curiosity. 'That the Danes tortured Aelle before he died? What do they call it?' He looked at his brother, trying to recall the name of the horrific execution method the sea-wolves were said to employ at times.

'The Blood Eagle,' Aethelred said grimly. 'When they cut open the individual's ribs and lay out their lungs on their back, like wings. All while the victim is still alive.'

Burgred shrugged. 'It was said that Ivar the Detestable killed Aelle by that method,' he said. 'They even poured salt on the poor bastard's bleeding flesh to add to his pain, as if it wasn't bad enough. All to gain revenge on Aelle for killing Ivar's father, Ragnar Lodbrok.' He pursed his lips thoughtfully. 'I have no idea how true the stories are. Perhaps there's an element of truth to them. Me? I've never seen a man survive long under such punishment and I doubt one could, without passing out at least. The pain would be too great, surely, especially for one as old as Aelle. He would have died long before they'd sawed all of his ribs apart and reached in for the lungs.'

'Just a story then?' Alfred asked hopefully. 'I liked Aelle, and the thought of him suffering so much has haunted me. I prayed for his soul often.'

'As I say, I don't know how much of the story is true. I doubt Aelle was given an easy death, though. Ragnar's execution is what brought the great heathen army here after all.'

The three noblemen sat in thoughtful silence then, thinking of all those who'd been killed by the invaders over the past few decades. The people taken as slaves. The towns and villages burned to the ground. The wealth stolen. Yet the Danish army that had arrived three years before was the biggest yet, and seemed unstoppable.

'It's ironic, isn't it?' Alfred mused, gazing through the open tent flaps at the camp outside. 'That we should face these barbaric invaders, when our own ancestors did much the same things when they first came to these lands.'

Aethelred made no reply, and Burgred simply grunted. The older men were not much inclined to look at the past, although, given the state of things now, looking to the future wasn't very appealing either.

'You've spoken with the heathen war-leaders?' Aethelred asked. 'They'll be receptive to a bribe?'

Burgred nodded. 'Oh, aye. They'll be glad of it. They'll take my silver and simply march to some other poor bastard's kingdom and do it all again there.'

'Maybe not,' Alfred said, trying to be cheerful. 'Winter will slow them, as it usually does. They'll find someplace to see out the bad weather, and leave us all alone for a few months at least.'

'Good,' Burgred muttered sourly. 'As long as they leave Mercia in peace for a time. Maybe when they next come here they'll find us better prepared.'

Alfred doubted that, for it seemed to him that none of the Anglo-Saxon kings were learning any lessons from their battles with the Danes. Or perhaps it was simply that none of the kings lived long enough to gain from their experiences. All who stood against Ivar and his brothers, Halfdan and Ubba, seemed destined to die soon afterwards. As Aelle and Osberht had done.

'Be sure and tell them not to come to Wessex,' Aethelred said to Burgred seriously. 'Send them north.' He saw Alfred looking at him and sat back on his chair almost defensively. 'What? We don't want the bastards coming to our lands for winter. We have to take care of our own.'

Burgred nodded firmly. 'Agreed, my lord. Now, I suppose I should go and find an emissary to carry my terms to the Danish leaders, but, before you men journey back south to Wessex, I have a proposition to make.'

Aethelred smiled knowingly. 'Oh? What's this, Burgred?'

'We'll discuss it later,' the Mercian king said, laughing. 'Make yourselves at home here, for now, my lords. I'll have more meat and ale sent in and hopefully be back soon to share it with you.'

'Good luck,' Alfred said, draining the last of his ale and helping himself to more. He felt much healthier now that he'd had a couple of mugs. 'Don't be away too long, for I'm thirsty and plan on doing my best to get through your supply of drink.'

Aethelred frowned at his brother's jocularity but he ignored it, saying to Burgred, 'Don't offer that whoreson Ivar too much silver, you might need it if they decide to come back in a few months. And don't stray too close to Snotengaham's walls, in case one of their archers gets you.'

The Mercian king did not reply to that, merely went outside muttering to himself about God striking down Ivar, his brothers, and the heathen hordes that followed them. When he was gone Aethelred shook his head.

'What?' Alfred asked plaintively. He never liked it when his brother was angry at him.

'We're not here to drink ourselves into oblivion, and plant our seed in every willing girl in Mercia,' Aethelred said sternly. 'You're not a carefree aetheling with no real responsibilities any more, brother. You're my deputy, and a commander of the West Saxon army, despite your youth. You must start taking this more seriously.'

Alfred held his brother's stare, but his eyes soon dropped and he looked into the ale mug he held. It was half empty already, even though he'd just refilled it moments before.

Aethelred was only four years older but had been given much more responsibility in his earlier years than Alfred. Witnessing his first charter when he was only nine years old, and acting as an underking for three years before he succeeded their brother, King Aethelbert, to the throne, Aethelred had been groomed for power from childhood. He also tried to act as a father figure to Alfred, keeping the naïve and occasionally irresponsible prince in check when he could.

'I...'

Aethelred smiled and shook his head as Alfred's sentence trailed off almost before it began. 'I know,' the king said kindly. 'You never wanted this responsibility. You never expected it, being the youngest of so many brothers.' He sighed and sipped some of his own ale, staring into space. 'This is how it is, though, and you need to accept it. God forbid, if something happens to me, you'll—'

'Don't say that!' Alfred broke in angrily. 'Nothing's going to happen to you.' He flushed, embarrassed by his reaction to Aethelred's words. Forcing a smile, he said, 'It's bad enough being the heir apparent, never mind a king.'

They both laughed and the somewhat tense atmosphere lifted as they slowly supped their drinks and listened to the bustle of the army going about their business outside.

'What d'you think Burgred meant?' Alfred said eventually. 'What proposition is he going to make?'

'I've no idea,' Aethelred replied. As he said it, he hid his face behind his ale mug, but he couldn't hide his eyes. They twinkled with merriment, making Alfred suspect his big brother knew rather more than he was admitting. When questioned, however, the king would admit nothing, and when a servant brought more food and drink, they set about it gladly. Alfred was left to wonder what Burgred and his brother were up to.

CHAPTER THREE

The Northumbrian was roaring a battle cry, eyes bulging in fury as he thrust out his spear. His angry expression changed to one of glee when he felt the leaf-shaped point slide past the links of mail his target wore and into the soft flesh. Then his head exploded in a spray of bone and brain matter as Halfdan's axe smashed into it.

The Danish jarl felt a moment of satisfaction and hoped his attack had been in time to save the warrior next to him, but he had to raise his shield as yet another spear was aimed at his face and he was forced to knock it aside. Taking a moment, he stepped back and glanced along the front line of his army.

The man pierced by the Northumbrian's spear was already dead, but the Danes were winning quite comfortably. Although he'd expected victory, it was always good to see an enemy force whittled away by the relentless unstoppable power of one's warband.

At the very last second he saw something hurtling towards him in his peripheral vision and ducked. It was a hatchet, and it missed Halfdan by a hair's breadth, only to batter into the helmet of the warrior behind him. The man fell, stunned, possibly concussed or dying, but there was no time to help him, even if Halfdan had the skill. His talents lay elsewhere; in dealing death, not preventing it.

'Keep going!' he bellowed, pushing his way into the battle once more. 'Leave none alive. Their women and children will be enough to serve us once we take the town.'

His words brought ragged, breathless cheers from the men in the shieldwall beside him, and a renewed sense of urgency. Axes, swords and spears were all brought to bear with a savagery the Saxon defenders had never known before, but they fought back desperately, for their lives and the lives of their loved ones.

It was futile, however, and that fact became clear when one of the defenders looked over his shoulder at the town walls and saw a Dane smiling back at him.

'By Christ!' the Northumbrian screamed in panic. 'They've taken the town! We're done for!'

More of his comrades looked back instinctively, seeing the walls – their walls – filling up with more and more Danes.

Halfdan took advantage of the momentary confusion and hammered his axe into the Saxon in front of him. It shattered the man's collar bone but the scream of agony was cut off as the axe came down again, and again. The other Danes in the shieldwall were pushing forward too, following their jarl's lead, and the Saxon line, which had fought gamely until now, disintegrated. They ran towards their town, wanting the safety of the walls and knowing they'd have to somehow defeat the laughing warriors standing on top of them if the day wasn't to be lost completely.

Of course, that point had already passed and, as the men of Loidis flowed towards the town gates, a barrage of arrows rained down upon them. That first volley caused numerous casualties and those who survived the missiles stormed into their streets only to be met by more Danish shieldwalls. And these were fresh troops the Saxons faced, not the ones who'd just given everything outside the walls. These newcomers were from Ubba's warband, and must have broken into the town from the other side.

Halfdan heard the men of Loidis calling out for guidance from their commander but he'd taken a savage blow to the side of his face and could offer no leadership. Loidis had been attacked a number of times in recent years by Danes like

Halfdan, and every time many of the most capable soldiers were killed or taken into slavery. Even before the Northumbrian leader's head wound he hadn't been a true military man. Halfdan guessed he must be nothing more than a merchant who somehow found himself in charge of Loidis's pitiful defence force which amounted to less than a hundred men. Or at least it had this morning. Now there were fewer than half that number still standing, and they were beset front and back by Halfdan and his brother Ubba's warriors.

'Put down your weapons,' Halfdan called, striding through the ruined gates of the settlement. They'd been destroyed during a previous raid by his men and the Northumbrians had never repaired them. Why bother? They did little to stop the heathen invaders. 'Drop your weapons,' Halfdan repeated. 'And you may go about your business. We will need people to bake our bread and butcher our meat for us this coming winter, so...' He smiled beatifically, as if he was some benevolent liberator rather than a conqueror. 'Go about your business. No, not you.' As the greatly relieved Saxon defenders put down their weapons and hurried away to their homes, their barely conscious commander, who managed to tell Halfdan his name was Cenric, was taken prisoner.

It was a measure of the fear the people of Loidis held for the Danes that none of the defenders spoke up for their leader. They simply melted away into the streets with barely a backward glance. They did not want to share Cenric's fate. Whatever it was to be, it would not be pleasant.

'Why did you fight us?' Halfdan asked the ealdorman. 'You must have known we would beat you easily.'

Cenric stared at him, dazed. 'We had to protect our town,' he said, and his words were slurred, like those of a drunk man. Halfdan suspected he *was* drunk; many warriors downed ale or mead before battle after all. The combined effects of the potent drink and the terrible head wound were making the Saxon a less than interesting conversationalist.

'You did not know we had another hundred men coming through your northern gate while your little "army" came out to face us in the south, eh?' He laughed, but he was feeling little satisfaction in this. There was no glory in besting such men. Still, he had to make an example of the Saxon leader. That was how the Danes did things – strike fast and hard, and leave the few survivors with horrific tales of the invaders' brutality so that any future enemies thought twice before trying to stand against them. 'I do not take pleasure in killing you,' Halfdan said to the pale ealdorman. 'As much as you Christians think all us Danes are vicious animals. You people started this by murdering my father, Ragnar, and now you will pay.'

Cenric merely stared at him, slack-jawed and drooling.

'Ach, take him to the town centre,' Halfdan commanded his men. 'And fill him with arrows. Make sure the people of Loidis see it.'

'Is that it?' one of Halfdan's hersir asked, and he was clearly disappointed, even irritated.

'Aye,' the jarl replied, staring at his subordinate. 'The fool is half-dead already. Would you have me perform the blood eagle on him? By Óðinn, these people are already utterly beaten. Making this wretch suffer will do nothing but make them hate us even more, and we shall likely spend the winter here and return again in the future.'

Halfdan ignored the hersir's muttering as he and a dozen of his warriors took Cenric away. He knew the man feared his elder brother, King Ivar, and he and Ubba, too much to protest any further. 'And remember!' Halfdan called after them, pitching his voice loud enough that everyone around could hear. 'No raping or killing anyone else now. The battle is over, and it is time to live in peace.' He was simply repeating the orders he'd given his army before the attack. They could have slaughtered everyone within Loidis, but why bother? The winter would be far more comfortable with servants and enter-tainment within easy reach. There were stocks of grain and salted meat within the town's walls, and plenty of women willing to open their legs for a few coins.

Halfdan's men did not lack coin. They had already taken a fortune in silver from these lands after all.

The jarl walked along the street towards the centre of town. Many of the houses and workshops lay empty, their inhabitants killed either today or in earlier raids by his people. That was good, the buildings would provide sturdy, warm homes for the army when the snow began to fall. Winters here were not as severe as his warriors were used to back at home in Denmark, Norway or Sweden, but it would still be cold and, more annoyingly, wet. A strong, wooden house was a more comfortable place to bed down at night than the tents Halfdan and his army were used to for most of the year.

He reached the middle of the settlement just in time to see Cenric being made to stand, swaying, before the archers. A few inhabitants of the town watched in consternation and, as the hersir barked his command and the arrows hammered home in the Saxon's torso, there were cries of sorrow and outrage. The ealdorman fell without a sound and Halfdan knew they had actually done Cenric a favour, for his wound would surely have killed him within a few days. At least this way was quicker and relatively painless. Halfdan hoped the men and women of Loidis appreciated his benevolence, for Ivar or Ubba would not have been so merciful.

'My lord.' The hersir in charge of the archers was approaching, and his eyes were glittering for he recognised the building his jarl was standing beside.

'Time for a drink,' Halfdan said with a grin, shoving open the door and heading into the tavern, the smells of sweat, sawdust, ale and vomit assailing him.

'Aye, a drink,' the hersir agreed. 'And then we can empty our balls. I remember this place, and the whores that work in the back rooms!'

Some of the Danish army were already inside, downing ale, mead and wine as the terrified landlord, an old man long past his fighting days, looked on. The warriors cheered as they saw their superiors stepping into the gloomy interior and within moments drinks were in every hand and a victory song was being roared out. In contrast with their savage reputation the Northmen's music was much more than an uncouth cacophony. Some of the warriors carried flutes and the men had rich voices which harmonised well with one another thanks to a great deal of practice.

'Not much better after a good fight,' Halfdan shouted to the hersir as they watched their men bellowing out the victory hymn, 'than a drink and a song.'

The man nodded and poured the last of his ale down his throat. 'Aye,' he agreed, eyeing a woman in the corner who was quite openly displaying her cleavage. 'And don't forget a good fuck. Get me another drink, my lord. I won't be gone long.'

Halfdan laughed and joined in with the music, his powerful, deep voice blending with the others as they praised Óðinn, the glory of battle, and the spoils of war.

CHAPTER FOUR

The music swirled around the hall and men and women danced and supped drinks, eyes shining in pleasure and relief. Ivar's great heathen army had left Snotengaham, no doubt to join his brothers Halfdan and Ubba wherever they were, the town was back in the control of Burgred, and the Mercians were celebrating the 'victory' along with their West Saxon allies in the king's hall.

One of the Mercian ealdormen, Mucel of Gegnesburh, had been sent to parley with Ivar. When he'd returned safely with an agreement from the Danish king the emissary had been greatly praised for his courage. Not all who dared walk into a Danish stronghold were lucky enough to come back out in one piece, after all.

As the musicians played their flutes, lyres and drums, Alfred approached Mucel, who was seated at King Burgred's own long table.

'How did it go, my lord?' Alfred asked, dropping onto an empty seat next to the Mercian ealdorman. 'With Ivar, I mean.'

Mucel turned and dipped his head respectfully to the West Saxon prince. 'Considering the fellow's reputation, it went all right.' The ealdorman swallowed a piece of roasted meat and wiped the grease on his fingers onto a rag. 'In truth, I think the Northmen were happy to take our silver and go. They're masters at raping, pillaging and plundering, but they're even better at avoiding a fight that isn't on their terms.'

Alfred nodded, sure that the man was right. He had stood with Aethelred that morning and watched Mucel walk, alone, through the gates of Snotengaham to speak with the leader of the invaders. The ealdorman was in his forties, with neatly trimmed grey hair and goatee. He was chief of the Gaini tribe, but did not look like a warrior, and that was probably why King Burgred had been happy to send him. Mucel was not threatening in appearance, although he did not come across as weak either. There was a keen intelligence in his eyes and Alfred felt completely at ease chatting to him. 'Where do you think they'll go now?' he asked.

'North,' Mucel said with certainty. 'We know they've already crushed most of the resistance against them in Eoforwic, or Jorvik as the bastards have renamed it, and the surrounding towns as well. I expect they'll head there for winter.'

'And Burgred can spend the months preparing Mercia for the next time they return.'

Mucel glanced at him, raised an eyebrow, then looked back at the men and women dancing drunkenly between the tables in the hall.

'You don't think so?' Alfred asked, somewhat surprised at the ealdorman's lack of support for the king.

Mucel shrugged, then shook his head. 'It's not so much that Burgred won't prepare,' he said. 'It's just that, well, it doesn't seem to matter what we do, the Danes are simply too strong. Their tactics are hard to defend against and, let's be honest, Burgred is not much of a warrior.'

Alfred nodded agreement. 'What we need are proper standing armies, rather than individual fyrds. And better fortified towns,' he said. 'And a system of watch towers. Maybe even better roads.' He tasted his ale, fully intending not to get as inebriated as the night before. 'It's amazing to think the Romans had all these things in place, here in these lands. Yet, five hundred years after they left, we can't replicate their achievements.'

Mucel looked at him, clearly surprised to hear such thoughts from the young aetheling. 'I suppose so,' the ealdorman conceded.

Alfred smiled. As the youngest of five brothers he'd been far removed from ever taking the throne of Wessex, so he'd been allowed to enjoy the carnal delights with more freedom than his siblings. Perhaps that was why the likes of Mucel underestimated him. But Alfred was now the aetheling, heir apparent to the West Saxon throne, and not stupid. Indeed, he valued learning and education a great deal. He was also not drunk enough to take offence at the Mercian ealdorman's apparently low opinion of him. 'Tell me what happened when you went in to speak with the heathen king,' he said. 'I've never had to do anything like that. It took courage, and I admire you for it.'

Mucel sat up straighter, obviously pleased by Alfred's praise. He thanked the aetheling and poured some more ale for them both. 'Well, I've spoken with Ivar before,' he said. 'In Loidis. A similar situation, actually, where we had to pay him and his army to leave.' He watched one young woman in particular, her close-fitting dress showing off her figure as she danced with a tall, beardless warrior.

Alfred had noticed the same girl and forced his eyes away from her, urging Mucel to continue.

'I walked through the gates here this morning,' the ealdorman said, finally returning his gaze to the aetheling. 'And Ivar was waiting for me, as were many of his men. They shouted insults, laughed at me, mocked my hair, my lack of weapons, my beard…' He snorted mirthlessly. 'They're like children really.'

Alfred put down his cup, wiping his mouth as he nodded hearty agreement. 'I've always thought that. Their entire culture seems to be childish, from their simple way of life to the gods they worship. It's like the whole thing was dreamed up by a youngster who just wants to fight, drink, and bed women all night!'

'Indeed,' Mucel said, raising his voice as the music came to an end and everyone clapped and cheered their appreciation. 'And yet, for all that, Ivar is not a fool. I have no doubt he's a mindless animal on the battlefield, revelling in inflicting as much pain and death on our people as possible, but he's deceptively clever when you talk with him.'

'Is that why you agreed to pay him so much?'

Mucel flinched, clearly surprised again by Alfred's questioning. His face flushed red, but he did not immediately reply, instead thinking for a moment and framing his words so as not to show his irritation. 'I agreed to pay him what I thought was a sensible amount. I had King Burgred's authority.'

Alfred nodded, impressed by the man's self-control. It was clear why Mucel had been chosen as the emissary, for a 'true warrior' might have reacted with anger at such a damning assessment of his conduct. 'I'm sorry, I meant no offence,' he said. 'I'm young and have little experience in these matters. My father didn't think it worth me learning about such things, yet I find myself fascinated by them now that I've become a close advisor to my brother.' Honestly, Alfred thought Mucel had paid Ivar far too much to leave – as the ealdorman had noted himself, the Danes *wanted* to leave Snotengaham rather than being besieged within its walls – but the prince saw no point in antagonising the Mercian. His friendship and good will might be useful one day.

The ealdorman accepted the apology with good grace, perhaps thinking the very same thing about Alfred. 'I did not offer Ivar as much as Burgred wanted me to. I'm quite happy with what we paid to get rid of the Danish bastard.'

Alfred laughed dutifully as Mucel grinned at him and they both looked back towards the people singing and dancing to the new tune the musicians were playing. The girl with the tight dress seemed even more attractive to Alfred now as he continued to down ale. Yet she was undeniably pretty, he thought, whether he was drunk or not. Her long, brown hair was tied back, and she wore a narrow circlet of gold around her head, marking her as one of high birth. She looked about the same age as Alfred himself, or perhaps a year or two younger at most and…

The girl suddenly looked directly at him and he hastily averted his eyes. When he looked back at her she was still staring at him and they both smiled, but the moment was broken as the man next to her drunkenly nudged her, almost knocking her over. He caught her, they laughed, and the dancing continued.

'Who is she?' he asked Mucel.

The ealdorman turned and gazed at him. 'My daughter. Ealhswith.'

'Oh, really?'

'Are you all right, brother?'

Alfred tore his gaze away from the dancing girl and saw Aethelred, and their sister, Aethelswith, who was also King Burgred's wife, standing over him, grinning.

'I'm fine,' he replied, flushing. 'What d'you mean?'

'You seemed to be in a trance,' Aethelred said, still smiling. He took a drink from the cup of mead in his hand and nodded at Ealhswith. 'Enjoying her dancing?'

'She's very attractive,' Alfred muttered, acutely aware of the girl's father's eyes upon him.

'That's good,' the king said, and he too was watching the girl dance with the big drunk warrior. 'I've been talking with Burgred and Aethelswith, and Ealdorman Mucel there.' He nodded respectfully to the Gaini chief then turned his attention back to Alfred. 'We all thought it would be a good idea to cement the alliance between Mercia and Wessex.'

'Of course,' Alfred agreed, not seeing yet where the conversation was going. 'Especially since the Danes are still around.'

'Then it's settled,' Aethelred said, slurring slightly from the mead. 'You shall marry Ealdorman Mucel's daughter, Ealhswith, and further strengthen the bonds between our lands.'

Mucel reached out and took the stunned Alfred's wrist in a warrior's grip. 'Congratulations, my lord. I'm sure this will be a great marriage for all my people, and particularly for you and my daughter. I trust you'll take good care of her.'

Alfred's head was spinning and he reached for his ale, swallowing a long draught before he felt like speaking again. So, this was the 'proposal' Burgred had mentioned to them earlier...

And Mucel, diplomat that he was, had managed to keep it a secret during their conversation today.

'When?' he asked at last. The idea of refusing to wed the young lady never even crossed his mind; the two kings had agreed it would happen, and that was how things worked. Besides, Ealhswith was very pretty and Alfred could think of worse marriages he might have been forced into for the sake of an alliance.

'Three days,' Aethelred said. 'No point in wasting time. We'll travel to Gegnesburh with Mucel's warband, have the wedding feast, and then get back home to Wessex before the winter blocks the roads.'

'Three days!' Alfred gasped. He'd hoped to have at least a few more weeks as an unmarried prince, drinking and whoring. 'But I don't even know her,' he said lamely. 'Shouldn't we get acquainted, at least a little, before the ceremony?'

'But you do know her,' Aethelswith said. She looked very like Aethelred, with similar shoulder-length brown hair, although she was the oldest of all the surviving siblings at thirty summers. 'You two met as children, more than once, when you visited Gegnesburh with Father.'

Aethelred drained his cup and wandered away towards King Burgred, who was seated a little further up the table. 'Go and speak with her, Alfred,' he said over his shoulder, nodding towards Ealhswith. 'Dance with her. I'll tell Burgred we've agreed to his proposal.' He patted Mucel fraternally on the shoulder as he passed, and the ealdorman's eyes shone, for this arrangement was a great honour for his family.

Alfred watched his brother go, and saw the two kings conversing, looking in his direction and raising their drinks towards him in happy salute. He returned the gesture and then, pushing himself up from the table, he smiled at Aethelswith, and Mucel – his future father-in-law – and went forward to join his betrothed in a dance.

'My lady,' he said, holding out his hand to Ealhswith. The big warrior she'd been dancing with glared at Alfred but just for a moment, quickly recognising the West Saxon aetheling and deferentially backing away to find either another partner, or at least more drink.

Ealhswith accepted Alfred's hand and smiled in such a way that he suspected she'd known about their coming betrothal for some time. Longer than he had at least.

'Are you happy, my lord?' she asked as the musicians began a lively jig and the people danced and swayed in time.

'I think so,' he replied, shouting over the noise in the hall. 'I've to wed a beautiful young lady, and the Danes have been sent northward for the winter. God be praised, things have turned out very nicely!'

–

Aethelred shook his head, bemused. 'I thought you were happy to be betrothed to Lady Ealhswith?' the king asked. 'You certainly seemed to be when you spent all last night dancing with her.'

Alfred winced and rubbed his head. He felt like he might vomit, and eyed the jug of ale that a servant had placed on the table for them. It was a sign of just how hungover he was that he hadn't already helped himself to some of it, fearing anything he swallowed might come straight back up.

'What's the problem?' Aethelred asked, clearly becoming irritated as he watched his little brother suffering from his own self-inflicted woes as usual. 'A marriage with Ealdorman Mucel's daughter is ideal for Wessex. And Ealhswith is lovely! It's not like I'm marrying you off to some worn-out old widow.'

Alfred retched and now he did take some of the ale, pouring it with shaking hands into an empty cup and then sipping gingerly at first before quickly downing it. 'I *was* happy when you said I was to marry her,' he said, breathing heavily and wiping his mouth. He belched and refilled the cup before sitting down again, shivering as if he was cold. 'But that's because I was drunk. You could have told me I was to marry Ivar the Detestable himself and I'd have happily danced the night away.'

'Drunk.' Aethelred glared at him, and even placed his hands on his hips just like their father used to do when he was angry. 'That's the problem, brother,' he spat. 'You're drunk all too often. We spoke about this the other night. You have to accept your responsibilities, and drinking ale from the moment you wake up until the moment you fall asleep in some wench's bed is not how an aetheling should behave!'

Alfred sighed and took another long draught. 'I like living this way,' he said defensively. 'I'm young.'

'Well, you can't go on like this anymore, Alfred,' the king scolded. 'This is exactly why you're to wed Ealhswith. She's a clever girl, sensible and God-fearing. She'll make a good wife, running your household properly, and you'll have a warm bed to share every night without behaving immorally. She'll calm you down a bit.'

Alfred's nausea was passing now and so was his anger at the betrothal he'd had no say in. He knew his brother wanted the best for him and, had their father been alive, he'd probably have been wed years ago, and to a much less attractive girl.

Aethelred took some of the ale too and sat down, looking out through the open tent flap at the drizzle that was turning the ground slick and soft. 'Why *do* you feel the need to indulge your carnal desires so much?' he asked. 'I mean, we all did, when we were young, but you take it to excess, and show no sign of ever growing out of it. Why?'

Alfred met his gaze and thought about the question. 'I don't really know,' he said. 'I feel lonely. I think I have ever since Mother died, and then our brothers, and father... And then you became king and it felt like I hardly ever saw you anymore. What else is there to do, but hunt and drink and bed women?'

Aethelred watched him as he spoke, a sad expression on his bearded face. 'Do those things take away the loneliness?' he asked.

Alfred smirked, and opened his mouth to make a glib reply, but then he paused, sighed, and shook his head. 'Not anymore,' he admitted.

'Well, there you go then,' Aethelred said. 'Marry Ealhswith and start a family of your own. Have enough children and you'll never feel lonely again. Besides, you'll enjoy making them, trust me. You'll have no energy left for serving wenches or whores once you're married and looking to grow a family!'

They laughed then, the tension between them dissipating as it always did eventually. Aethelred had one son so far and had been trying for more with his wife, Wulfthryth. He often 'complained' about how tiring it was trying to create more heirs.

'I don't know how you do it,' Alfred said. He felt good now, not sick at all. Instead he felt bright and alert although... 'I feel like there's a lot of expectation on me these days, and I'm only the aetheling. It must be unbearable for you.'

'It is hard,' Aethelred admitted. 'But being king is also a great privilege. God has chosen me for this. Besides, even the lowliest ceorl has weighty obligations heaped upon him: feeding himself and his family; paying his taxes; working every day; and joining the fyrd to march to war if called upon. Would you swap your position for theirs, brother?'

Alfred shook his head emphatically. For all his complaints and doubts about his suitability for the role that had been thrust upon him, he enjoyed his elevated position in society.

'What you need,' said Aethelred, 'is someone to share your responsibilities. To take some of the burden from your shoulders. Ealhswith will do that for you, as my wife does for me.'

Alfred frowned. 'When you put it like that,' he replied, 'maybe Ealhswith should be the one complaining about our betrothal!'

They laughed again, and the king said, 'She's been brought up with this in mind. I'm sure she's looking forward to marrying the Aetheling of Wessex and taking up the duties she was born to do.' He became more serious then, reaching out and patting Alfred paternally on the knee. 'Trust me, Ealhswith will be a fine companion, and I know you'll be kind to her. You two will make a good life together. I would not have agreed to your betrothal if I didn't believe that.'

They met each other's gaze and for a moment it felt to Alfred like they were children again, sharing a quiet moment together. He nodded.

'It's settled then,' Aethelred grinned, raising his drink in salute to the coming union.

'Aye,' Alfred agreed, lifting his own cup and clattering it against his brother's. 'It's settled. And I'll take my responsibilities more seriously,' he promised. 'No more drunkenness.'

He felt genuinely excited. Aethelred's words had stirred something inside him, and he found himself greatly looking forward to the coming years with Ealhswith by his side.

CHAPTER FIVE

Alfred felt like the wedding was passing in a blur. Despite his promise to Aethelred, he'd woken with yet another hangover and, to remedy it, had downed some wine, but not until he'd already vomited. In truth, he wasn't sure if it was only the drink that was making him feel sick – marriage was a big step after all. It frightened him.

His days as the carefree young aetheling were over. His world was changing, and he would be expected to act as more of a right-hand man to his brother, King Aethelred; take on more responsibility, be a leader, a man.

And today, a husband.

The wine he'd drunk didn't just help his hangover, it made him feel somewhat numb throughout the ceremony. His nerves did not cause him any problems once it came time to stand up in front of everyone and take Ealhswith as his wife. The fact that she looked so lovely helped, of course. Going into this new life with her was made much easier by that fact and, when he vowed to be faithful to her, he genuinely meant it. Or at least, he would genuinely try to stay true to it.

She stood on his left and he glanced at her, drinking in the sight of the young woman who would soon be his wife. Her blue, woollen gown came down to her ankles and was drawn in around her neat waist by a girdle. The gown had white silk bands on the sleeves, embroidered with blue decoration, and was open at the top to reveal a necklace with rings of silver wire with a gold and garnet pectoral cross. On her head she wore a white headdress and a veil edged with gold braid.

Alfred breathed in and smelled the scented, floral water which Ealhswith had bathed in that morning, as well as the flowers that were placed all around the room, bringing vibrant colour to the occasion. Overall, the prince's senses were quite overwhelmed, and he knew this moment would live long in his memory.

When the bishop pronounced them man and wife, Alfred kissed his new bride and they went off to celebrate, which was just as well for the prince as the wine was beginning to wear off and the earlier sickness was taking hold again. The general feeling of anxiety that often accompanied his hangovers was also bubbling to the surface. It was almost as if he'd gone into battle and the focus that danger brought had held his nerves in check but, now that the most difficult part was over, his mind was running free and not in a healthy way.

It didn't help that he was the centre of attention, with every eye on him, watching to see how he conducted himself on this important occasion. Perhaps he was imagining that, for Ealhswith looked so radiant that surely the men there would rather look at her than the aetheling, but telling himself that did not ease Alfred's stress. Only drink could do that, he knew, and he eagerly grasped a cup of ale from a tray carried by a serving girl as she passed, swallowing it in just a few long gulps.

'Are you all right, husband?'

He looked down at his new wife, seeing her smiling, but he wondered if there was a note of disapproval in her tone as he held the empty cup like a talisman, looking around for a refill.

'I'm fine,' he replied, replicating her smile as they reached the centre of the long table in Ealdorman Mucel's great hall. The place of honour, normally reserved for Mucel himself, but today set aside for his daughter, Ealhswith, and his new son-in-law, Alfred. Even Aethelred, King of Wessex, and Burgred and Aethelswith, had been shunted sideways to let the happy couple take the centre seats, and Alfred nodded at his sister as he sat down.

Happily, a servant came along to fill their cups and the prince downed half of his immediately.

'Nervous?' Aethelswith asked softly. She had a reassuring smile on her face as she leaned in against Alfred. 'Don't worry, you'll be fine. Ealhswith will make a good wife.'

The bustle and chatter of the other guests meant their conversation could only be heard by the two of them yet, even so, Alfred kept his voice as low as possible as he replied. 'I've a bastard of a hangover. I'd like nothing better than to get drunk but…'

'Not a good idea,' his sister said sympathetically. 'Finish that one, but go easy on the ale after that. We don't want the lords and ladies of Mercia thinking the Aetheling of Wessex is a hopeless sot, do we?'

Alfred heard the warning in her tone, and nodded. 'Don't worry. I'll remain clear-headed.' The wedding guests, the great and good of Mercia along with the few thanes and ealdormen of Wessex and Northumbria who could make it there in time, appeared friendly and supportive of Alfred. He knew they were like the crows who encircle a battle, however, waiting for their chance to swoop down and feast on the dead and dying. Neither he nor his brother could afford to show any weakness in front of such powerful men.

Mucel appeared then, beaming, and no wonder, for he was now part of the West Saxon royal family. Alfred was sure nothing would ruin his new father-in-law's day; not even Alfred getting roaring drunk and starting a brawl would sour Mucel's happiness.

Soon enough the guests were seated and happily feasting on roast meat, vegetables, fresh bread, and salmon or herring caught in the River Trent whose sparkling waters were visible from the hall. There was not so much talk during this phase of the celebration, as everyone devoured their portion with gusto and gladly accepted second or even third helpings from the continually moving servants.

Alfred thoroughly enjoyed his fish, which smelled wonderful and was prepared somewhat differently here in Gegnesburh to what he was used to at home, with ginger and thyme. The local cabbage was also delicious and he ate almost as much of that as the salmon, washing it all down with one more cup of ale. He felt quite bloated and heavy by the time his trencher was cleared but content, and rather more relaxed than he'd been at the start of the meal. And then someone called out, 'A speech! A speech from the aetheling!' and Alfred's stomach seemed to leap into his mouth as the call was taken up by all those gathered beneath Mucel's rafters.

Aethelred was grinning, as were Aethelswith, Burgred, Mucel and everyone else. Alfred turned to Ealhswith and a flare of deep, sudden affection filled him for she alone seemed to notice the anguish he was feeling. Her brow was furrowed, and she took his left hand in hers, meeting his eyes as if trying to impart some of her strength to him.

He felt ridiculous. He was the Aetheling of Wessex, the heir apparent! Son to a king, brother to kings, and he had even met the Pope himself when he was a boy. Yet the thought of standing here, before these people, and giving a speech, made him feel like all the rich food he'd eaten was bubbling back up his throat and about to explode out of his mouth.

There was nothing for it, however, he knew he would need to get up and mumble a few words about how happy he was. His right hand gripped his ale cup and he forced himself to stand, staring out at the wedding guests as sweat beaded his brow and his tongue seemed to swell in his mouth. He coughed, and then a sudden, searing pain tore at his guts and he doubled over, gasping.

'Brother!' Aethelred jumped to his feet and placed a protective arm around Alfred's shoulders, and Ealhswith squeezed her new husband's hand in alarm.

Alfred gritted his teeth and could not stop a low moan escaping from his lips as the pain seemed to grow in intensity.

'What's the matter?' Mucel demanded with such force that, even in his agony, Alfred knew the ealdorman feared his cook had poisoned the food. 'Is he unwell?'

'Alfred,' Aethelred hissed, pressing his mouth close to his brother's ear. 'What in God's name is wrong?'

'I don't know. My guts feel like a red-hot seax has been plunged into them.'

'Take a moment,' the king murmured, still gripping him firmly by the shoulders. 'Breathe. It will pass.' He sounded uncertain, as if he did not really believe his own words but desperately wanted to. This was not how the king had hoped the day would go.

Alfred did not need to look up to imagine the disdain that would be written plainly on the guests' faces. Their mockery of his weakness.

The pain was not dissipating, and he let out another groan, louder this time, and higher pitched. 'I have to get out of here,' he begged. 'I must lie down, or throw up, or...' His mind was reeling and he genuinely believed he was about to die. It could not happen like this, in front of all these judgemental bastards! 'Please, brother, take me out of here.'

'Come.' It was Ealhswith who took charge, gently pulling Alfred away to the left as Aethelred continued to support him. She led the way towards the main doorway, glaring at the guards there who opened the door for them to pass through, daylight spilling in and framing the trio in its yellow radiance as they went outside.

Alfred sucked in huge, deep breaths of fresh air. It felt so good, smelt so clean after the acrid cooking smoke that swirled perpetually around Mucel's hall. Yet the pain was still there and he snarled like a wounded dog as he was half-carried past a couple of workmen who were repairing a damaged roof on a nearby hovel. They gazed at him, disdain as clear in their eyes as it had been on the noblemen's within the hall, and shame filled him.

'What the hell is wrong with you?' Aethelred demanded again, clearly frightened. 'Has this happened before?'

'Never,' Alfred gasped, relief filling him as they came to the house that had been set aside for him and Ealhswith to spend their first night of marriage. There would be no-one here to stare at him, to judge him, to smirk and share knowing glances with their fellows. 'God is punishing me,' he said, and he knew it to be true.

A while ago he had visited the shrine of Saint Gueriir in Cornwalas and prayed that the painful growths in his backside that he'd suffered with for years would go away. And they had, praise the Lord! But only to be replaced with this new, much worse affliction, it seemed. As Ealhswith unlocked the door and threw it open to let Aethelred bring him inside, Alfred knew that this would be his lot from now on. He would suffer with this pain for the rest of his life; it would be his punishment from God for indulging his carnal vices.

The bed was before him then, cool and soft and inviting, and he collapsed onto it, lying on his side with a whimper that shamed him more than anything that had happened so far. Yet, as Aethelred left the house with promises of sending a healer, Ealhswith lay down next to her new husband and her presence was incredibly comforting. She did not speak, merely placed her body against his, arm gently around him, and he took her hand in his and they lay like that for what seemed like forever.

--

Aethelred went back to the hall with his thoughts churning. Concern for his little brother was paramount, but there was also an irritation with him. He'd warned Alfred not to drink too much, but the fool must have ignored him again and now this was the upshot. Mucel would not be impressed, but neither would the rest of the lords, and word would travel fast of Alfred's weakness. Within days, even the kings and nobles at the furthest ends of the isle would have heard about the West Saxon aetheling's crippling pains.

And, of course, the Danes would hear of it too.

It was not the best start to a marriage, and it reflected badly on the entire royal family of Wessex, including Aethelred.

Already people muttered of bad omens and bad luck following the line of Aethelred and Alfred's grandfather, King Ecgberht. In the forty-odd years since the old man's death his descendants had not fared particularly well, and the rumours would go around now that Alfred was another of the line destined to die at a young age.

It made the rulers of Wessex appear weak, and there would be other noble families just waiting for a chance to try and stake their claim for the throne. Aethelred could really have done without today's unfortunate events so early in his kingship.

He strode into the hall, straight-backed, head held high, stonily meeting the eyes of any who looked at him.

'How is he, my lord?' Mucel asked, coming towards Aethelred and offering him a cup of ale. 'What's the matter with him?'

The king shook his head and smiled broadly, hoping the expression looked real. 'I think he must have eaten too much, or something disagreed with him. The spices used to flavour the salmon perhaps.'

Mucel looked aghast, so Aethelred patted him on the shoulder consolingly.

'It's not your fault, the food was delicious, if perhaps a tad rich for my brother.' He took a drink and looked around the room, somewhat relieved to see that his smiles had gone some way to make the wedding guests relax once more. 'Do you have a healer around, Lord Mucel? A leech?'

'I've already summoned one,' the ealdorman nodded. 'He will go directly to your brother.'

Aethelred thanked him for that and added, 'And a priest too. Have one of your servants send a priest to see Alfred as well, if you would.'

Mucel blanched. 'A priest?'

'Don't worry,' Aethelred laughed, much louder than was necessary. 'He's not dying, but my brother *is* extremely pious. The presence of a man of God will go some way to help ease his… discomfort, I'm sure.' He noticed Alfred's captain, Wulfric, nodding towards him then, before striding along the hall in the direction of a tonsured man in a dark robe.

'Never mind, I see Wulfric is fetching the priest. Come, Lord Mucel, we have a wedding to celebrate. Set your mind at ease: Alfred will be fine, and your daughter will be very happy with him.'

'Do you really think so?' Mucel asked with fatherly concern. Alfred's sudden illness had visibly worried him. 'Do you believe they will be well matched?'

Aethelred understood the ealdorman's apprehension; anyone with eyes and ears must have noticed his brother's insobriety over the past few days. 'I know what people are saying,' the king said to Mucel. 'But Ealhswith and Alfred will be good for one another. It's true, my brother is immature and, at times, intemperate, but he's a good man, and he'll settle down now that he's married, trust me.'

His words settled the Mercian ealdorman's fears somewhat. 'I'll trust you, my lord,' he said with a shallow nod.

Aethelred smiled. 'Our families have become one today,' he said, placing his arm around Mucel's shoulders. 'And strengthened the bond already forged between the people of Mercia and Wessex when my sister married your king.' He raised his cup, looking around at everyone there and they followed his cue, lifting their own drinks in a toast. 'To Wessex,' he cried, watching as Wulfric and the priest hurried by. 'And Mercia!'

The guests cheered, and gulped down their drinks, fully intending to get as drunk as possible that night, whether the newlyweds managed to consummate their marriage or not.

Aethelred thought he too might as well drink himself into a stupor. His jovial performance appeared to have calmed the situation, but he feared Alfred's show of weakness would come back to haunt them. How, he was not sure, but as he looked at the faces of the thanes and ealdormen filling Mucel's cosy hall

Aethelred imagined them as the faces of hungry wolves and scavenging crows.

God, let this illness of Alfred's pass, he prayed as he emptied the cup of ale into his mouth. *And let him stand by my side as I rule Wessex for many years to come!*

CHAPTER SIX

Wessex, AD 869

February

Winter deepened and Alfred grew into his new life as Ealh-swith's husband. The newlyweds had journeyed from Mercia to Wessex in October, just as the weather was really beginning to turn cold and the harvest had been gathered in. The Danes had remained a threat during those months, but only to those settlements closest to where their army had settled further north. Eoforwic and Loidis were firmly under the heathens' control, but those towns were a good distance away from Wessex and Alfred did not greatly fear any attacks from Ivar the Detestable's forces.

That winter had been a time of great peace and pleasure for Alfred as he learned how to be a husband. The West Saxons were mostly content with King Aethelred for he'd managed to keep the Northmen at bay and there was enough food to go around. The people further north, in Mercia and Northumbria, were surely not faring so well. The fact that Burgred, Mucel and the rest of the lords in those lands had pressing matters of their own to deal with meant Alfred's bout of illness on his wedding day seemed to have been mostly ignored. Of course, he was not foolish or naïve enough to think it would ever be completely forgotten – there would always be gossips looking to spread vile rumours about those in power, and ambitious ealdormen marking their rivals' weaknesses – but, during those early days of marriage Alfred and his wife were content.

Lady Ealhswith, Alfred discovered, did not share his passions for hunting, drinking to excess, or making love at every opportunity, but he could find willing companions for those pastimes easily enough. Especially in winter, when there wasn't much else to do. His wife did enjoy Alfred's more cerebral hobbies, however, such as reading, and listening to poetry, and the pair spent many pleasant hours together beside the fire in their hall. They would also, weather permitting, take walks or ride around the estate King Aethelred had granted them in Ceodre, and chat about their childhoods and hopes for the future.

Unlike many couples who were wed for political reasons, Alfred and Ealhswith were content with their lot, and made the most of those quiet, chilly months.

During a sunny morning in February the pair were within their hall listening to a priest read from the bible. The worst of the cold weather seemed to have passed but an icy wind still blew across Wessex and Alfred had ordered the fire be built up while they relaxed. Their dwelling was a large, timber construction with thick pillars to support the thatched roof and even an upper level for the servants. Weapons, painted shields, and tapestries depicting battles or hunting scenes decorated the walls which, along with the blazing fire, provided a little colour. Tables ran the length of the building and they would be occupied in the evening by the thanes and warriors of Ceodre, but they were out working or patrolling the surrounding lands for now.

The door burst open and a huge warrior of about thirty winters came in, holding a hand up as if by way of apology as a cold draught blew through the hall.

'Oh, no,' Alfred groaned, recognising the newcomer and knowing the grim expression on the man's face could not mean good news was about to be delivered.

'My lord,' the soldier said in a deep, baritone voice that filled the hall with effortless power. He made a shallow bow yet, even so, still towered over everyone gathered there, including Alfred who got to his feet to welcome their guest.

'Ealdorman Wulfric,' the prince said, tilting his head upwards that he might meet his captain's steely blue eyes. 'What's happened?'

Wulfric was clad in a tunic of undyed wool, with a red cloak over his shoulders which was held together by a round, silver brooch. If there was any doubt as to his profession the mail shirt which showed beneath the neck of his tunic, the fine sword at his waist, and the helmet in the crook of his left arm made it obvious. He had a scar on his right cheek but was ruggedly handsome, tall and athletically built, although the padded gambeson he wore under his mail made him seem bulkier than he really was. In short, Wulfric was a hugely impressive man, which was just one reason Alfred had made him captain of his personal guard.

'The Danes, my lord,' Wulfric said in reply to the prince's question.

'They're here?' Alfred demanded, his own hand dropping to the seax he wore on his belt as he felt a momentary rush of panic.

'Aye, lord,' Wulfric said. 'But they claim they're just passing through our territory. Nothing to get too alarmed about, yet, I think, but the king has sent word for you to join him in Ragheleiam with the fyrd.'

In Wessex, each ealdorman or thane commanded the warband – the fyrd – within their own lands, and, when called upon, they would take their soldiers wherever the king commanded, and join together into one great fyrd. This was how the West Saxon army worked, and it was a system that had been in place for generations, although it was not perfect, relying heavily on the loyalty and good faith of each individual fyrd's commander...

Alfred frowned, realising the journey to Ragheleiam would take five or six days once he'd gathered his warriors. He turned and hurried across to his wife, bending to put an arm around her shoulders and give her a kiss. 'I must go and deal with this, Ealhswith. Hopefully it won't take too long.'

'Get your thickest cloak, my lord,' she told him, and her eyes betrayed her concern. They hadn't heard much word of the Danes since the previous November but they'd all known this day would come eventually.

'I shall,' Alfred smiled, nodding to her before he turned to the priest who was still holding the bible he'd been reading to them from. 'Help Lady Ealhswith look after things, Brother Oswald.'

The priest made the sign of the cross and uttered a soft blessing on Alfred before the aetheling headed for his quarters at the far end of the hall to gather his weapons and warm clothing. Wulfric followed although his eyes lingered on the crackling fire, no doubt wishing he might stay right there for a while and warm the chill from his numb fingers.

'Have you eaten?' Alfred asked over his shoulder as they moved away from the heat and into the deeper shadows.

'I had something on the ride here, my lord,' Wulfric admitted.

'Go back to the fire and have one of the servants heat some wine for you,' the prince said kindly. 'And more food if you like. We have better than the simple soldier's fare you would have eaten on the road. I can dress myself while you rest for a few moments.'

'Thank you, lord,' Wulfric grinned. 'I'll be ready to leave when you are.'

Alfred simply waved without turning and continued walking. He always liked to treat his soldiers well, for he was one himself now, and he knew how important morale could be when it came to a choice between supporting one's commander or running from a fight with a horde of Northmen. Besides, he genuinely liked Wulfric and felt the man deserved whatever decent food his house could offer.

The prince went through the partition that separated his royal quarters from the rest of the hall. It was chilly so far from the firepit but he knew exactly what he wanted and he began gathering it together as his breath steamed in the air. He lifted a gambeson, mail shirt, blue tunic and a heavy fur-lined cloak of a lighter blue, then put them all on with practised ease, leaving his other clothes in a pile on the floor. A servant could collect them later. Then he took his sword and buckled the belt around his waist. Finally, he changed his soft leather shoes for a sturdier pair of boots, and took down the helmet that sat on a shelf of its own. It had been a gift from his father: a fairly simple iron skull cap with nose and cheek guards, and brass crests which formed a cross on the top of the helmet when viewed from above. A curtain of mail known as a camail was attached to the back to protect the wearer's neck. The helm was based on a much earlier design and Alfred always felt like a true soldier when he wore it.

There was a small, polished steel mirror on the shelf and Alfred stood before it, dressed for war in the dim light coming through the open doorway. He nodded in satisfaction. He might not be as big as Wulfric, or as experienced as Aethelred, but what he saw reflected in the mirror was still impressive.

Removing the helmet, he gave the marital bed a last, lingering look, wondering when he'd next be able to sleep within those thick, comfortable blankets, then headed back to the fire where Wulfric waited. Brother Oswald was no longer within the hall, but Ealhswith was, and she frowned upon seeing her husband decked out in full battle dress. Her expression was fleeting though, and she smiled dutifully as he approached.

'Be careful, Alfred,' she said quietly. 'The Danes have killed enough of our people already without adding you to that sorry list.' She held his hand in hers and squeezed it, and the depth of emotion in her eyes struck him deeply. This was the first time he'd ridden to possible war since they'd been wed, and she was evidently frightened by the prospect.

It warmed him to know he was cared for so deeply and he drew her into an embrace, breathing the heady scent of rosemary in her hair, before kissing her once on the lips and grinning confidently. 'I'll be back before you know it, my lady,' he said, gesturing towards Wulfric. 'I have him to protect me. Even the Northmen can't stand against him.'

She smiled back, but she did not look reassured by his words. Wulfric was a ferocious fighter, she knew that from the stories told about him, but the Northmen could not be stopped by one man. 'Just be careful,' she said. 'It's easy to think ourselves safe down here in Wessex, but if the Danes are in these lands they can't be taken lightly.'

'I'll take care,' he said. 'Will you look after the estate while I'm away?'

Ealhswith arched an eyebrow and smiled. 'While you're away? I run the place even when you're here, Alfred.'

He laughed, knowing she spoke the truth, then kissed her again and nodded before bidding her farewell and looking to his captain. 'Are you ready to go, Wulfric?'

'I am, my lord,' the big warrior replied, quickly downing the last of the warmed wine he'd been given and placing the cup on the table for the servants to clear.

'Lead on then, man,' Alfred said, and the pair left the hall to gather the fyrd and ride out to face the raiders who'd arrived in West Saxon lands.

CHAPTER SEVEN

Aethelred's expression was grim as Alfred rode towards him. The king had spent the past two weeks in Ragheleiam, and the stress showed plainly on his face.

'Brother, what's happening? Danes, here in Wessex?'

'Well met, brother,' said the king, reaching out to grasp his arm in greeting. 'Ealdorman Wulfric.' He nodded to Alfred's captain and then pointed to the south. 'Danes, aye. Four ship-loads of them down at the beach.'

Alfred blew out a heavy breath and glanced at Wulfric in consternation. 'So many?'

'Must be about two hundred of the whoresons,' the king said. 'How many men did you bring with you?'

'Fifty, my lord,' Wulfric replied. 'We didn't think it prudent to leave our own lands undefended.'

'Fifty is enough,' said Aethelred. 'I have two hundred gathered here myself, although the sea-wolves have not attacked any of our settlements. So far.' His horse moved ahead, riding towards the sea which could not be seen from their position but was only a few miles distant.

Alfred followed and Wulfric gestured for the fifty soldiers ranged behind them to do the same. Frightened locals watched as the fyrd passed, probably wondering how long it would be before the gulls were feasting on slaughtered warriors.

'Why are the Danes here?' Alfred asked coming alongside his brother's horse and shading his eyes as he gazed at the horizon. 'And why didn't they attack when they arrived, before you had time to muster the army?'

'I've spoken with their leader,' Aethelred said. He gave his brother a sideways glance. 'It's Jarl Ubba.'

'Ubba!' Alfred felt a moment of fear at the name. If Ubba was here in Wessex there was a good chance his older sibling Ivar, and the other brother, Halfdan, would turn up eventually. The two hundred men that were already here might be supplemented any day by two, three or even four or five times that number. It was not a comforting thought.

'He says they're not here to cause trouble in Wessex,' Aethelred said somewhat gloomily. 'They're merely gathering in this location before moving on.'

'To where?' Alfred asked.

'And to what purpose?' Wulfric muttered darkly.

The king shrugged. Like the other two men he was clad in full war-gear and looked every inch a leader of men. But Alfred thought his brother appeared older than the last time he'd seen him. Perhaps it was just the light, but for a man in his mid-twenties Aethelred appeared ten years older thanks to the bags under his eyes and the harried expression he wore. 'Ubba wouldn't tell me any more, and I wasn't in a position to force the issue, since he had as many men at his command as I did. We just have to hope he spoke the truth, and they'll move on soon.'

'A Dane speaking the truth?' Wulfric growled. 'That'll be a first.'

It didn't take long before the sounds of the gathered armies could be heard over the hooves of their horses. Aethelred's two hundred men were encamped some distance away from the beach, where tents had been set up and fires burned, heating pottage and meat to keep the men fed. It was not yet spring after all, and with the spray from the sea it had been a cold and miserable time for the king's men.

The longships of the Danes were drawn up on the beach, animal or even dragons' heads on their prows, colourful shields draped along the sides. They were hugely impressive in both construction and design, appearing both serviceable and attractive, or even frightening, depending on the observer. Alfred could see the men there, wandering about as if these were their lands. No doubt they would be hunting nearby and – if it came to it – stealing food from the nearest settlements, unless the West Saxon army forced a battle. But the Danes were so well used to an even colder climate that the weather would not be the annoyance it was to Aethelred's men.

Their homelands must seem like hell to them, Alfred thought as he stared out at the glittering sea. *The sun is said not to rise at all on some days – no wonder the* vikingar *spend so much time here in our lands.*

Yet the harsh conditions they were used to certainly stood the Northmen in good stead, for they were hardy fighters, tall and strong, and steeped in a tradition of warfare.

They neared the Danes' camp and Aethelred turned to Wulfric, slowing his horse. 'You take your fyrd and have them settle in with the rest of the army.'

The ealdorman bowed to the king, and then to Alfred, and then he brought his mount around and roared a command to the soldiers behind them. As he rode by the whole troop turned and followed him towards the main Saxon encampment.

'He has them well trained,' Aethelred noted.

'He knows his business,' Alfred agreed with a proud smile. 'I'm lucky to have him. Where's Sicgred?'

Without raising his hand from the reins Aethelred pointed a finger and Alfred swivelled in his saddle to see the king's captain riding towards them.

'My lord,' said the man as he reached them. He was older, perhaps forty-five, with thinning brown hair, and a moustache. His complexion was a ruddy pink, weather beaten from a life-time of campaigning, and it contrasted with the blue tunic he wore over his mail shirt.

'Well met, Sicgred,' Alfred said to him, nodding. He'd known the man his whole life, as he'd been a West Saxon ealdorman and a warrior in service to the royal family for years. Bluff and dour, Sicgred nonetheless had a fine military mind and the heart of a lion, making him the perfect bodyguard and advisor for the king.

'Shall we go, gentlemen?' Aethelred said without any further greetings or small talk, and kicked his horse into a trot towards the shore.

The ships of the Northmen were larger than Alfred was used to seeing. He guessed each one could carry fifty or so men and a sudden vision of the vessels burning came to him. His eyes shone as he imagined it, a fire sent by God, to sweep the sea and the land clean of these brutal invaders. One day, he vowed, that vision would come true.

'Why are all the Danes so big?' Aethelred asked as they rode past the first of the Northmen in the camp. 'Hardly any are smaller than me, and most are rather taller.'

'Their homelands are useless for farming,' Alfred said. 'So, they eat a lot more meat – beef, pork, mutton – than we do. It makes them bigger.'

Aethelred grunted. 'No doubt you read that in some book of yours, but I wonder if it's true or just some philosopher's idle speculation.'

Alfred looked at the Danes as they passed through them unimpeded, heading towards the large tent near the centre of the camp. He did not know if his claim about their diet was true or not, but *something* made the bastards taller and burlier, on average, than the West Saxons, Mercians, Northumbrians, and other people of these lands whose diet was based more on grain than meat. He also wondered if riding like this into the Danes' camp was wise, but, so far at least, no-one seemed too interested in them.

'Have you met with Ubba before today, then?' he asked, trying not to think about what would happen if the sea-wolves suddenly drew weapons and closed in upon them.

'I have,' Aethelred said. 'A few times. Tried to get him to become a Christian, but he merely laughs when I mention it.'

Sicgred looked disgusted and the king laughed heartily.

'He thinks we should just attack them,' Aethelred told his brother. 'Diplomacy is not Sicgred's strong point. Here we are.' He pulled up his horse and dismounted gracefully outside the large tent which had two stocky guards positioned at the entrance. Both held great war-axes that looked like they could smash a man's ribs to pulp with a single blow, but they nodded amiably enough to Aethelred and the one on the left gestured with his palm for the Saxon king and his companions to go inside.

They did as they were instructed, instantly feeling the chill within the shadowy tent. The thing itself was well constructed, with a frame of ashwood and oak which was carved with serpent heads over the door, and a thick linen covering that would keep even the heaviest of rain at bay. Alfred was struck by how sturdy it all was, and by the intricacy of the carvings and decoration on the wooden sections. They might possess many faults, but the Danes had apparently mastered the art of timber construction. His gaze fell on a warrior seated on a chair in the centre of the tent.

The man wore a linen undertunic, long-sleeved red shirt with embroidered neckline and cuffs, and blue trousers with bindings around the calves. Rings of gold and silver were on his fingers and arms, and a heavy amulet depicting Þórr's hammer, Mjölnir, hung around his neck.

Ubba.

'You again,' the Danish jarl said, and his tone was neutral, betraying neither annoyance nor pleasure. His light blue eyes glittered however, and Alfred thought the man happy enough with Aethelred's visit, or perhaps he was simply a little tipsy on the mead that sat on a table nearby. 'And you've brought your little brother! But who's this? Your grandfather?'

'I might be old,' Sicgred retorted coldly. 'But I'd still take you in a fight, sea-wolf.'

Ubba laughed and stood up. It was not a threatening movement – he was simply going to fill the horn in his hand with the mead – but it allowed Alfred to get a better look at him. The jarl was not as tall as many of his followers, under six feet, and slim too, but, like his brothers, Ivar and Halfdan, tales were told about Ubba's viciousness. Stories were told by the scops about all the Northmen's leaders of course, and none more than Ragnar Lodbrok, but Alfred doubted many of the stories were true. Still, he would not underestimate the intelligence, or at least the cunning, of the young jarl who was their host at that moment.

'Drink?' Ubba held up the jug of mead and, although the Saxon language was not the same as the Danes' it was similar, and based in a common root. Plus, as nobles, the men in the tent had all taken the time to learn something of the other side's tongue so, by speaking quite slowly and clearly, there was no major confusion.

Aethelred nodded and reached out for the cup – not a horn, that seemed to be solely for the jarl – that he was handed by Ubba. Alfred gladly accepted one too for he enjoyed the strong drink the Danes favoured, especially on a cold February day.

'You, old man?'

Sicgred did not look amused by Ubba's insults and he took some of the mead with poor grace, merely offering a grunt and a scowl by way of thanks. The jarl, of course, found this amusing.

Alfred thought the Dane irritating and looked forward to leaving the enemy camp. 'Why are you in our lands?' he asked, not waiting for his brother to begin the serious conversation.

Ubba's mocking smile faded, replaced with a shrewder look as he took in the West Saxon aetheling. There were only about eight years between them, but the jarl had seen many more battles than Alfred and commanded great armies in a variety of locations. 'You do not waste time in getting to the point, do you?'

'It's cold,' Alfred answered, returning Ubba's stare. 'I'd like to get back to my estate and prepare for the coming spring.

Instead, we've been forced to ride here to deal with you. So, again I'll ask: Why are you here?'

Ubba seemed taken aback by the younger man's bluntness and he looked at Aethelred, the mocking smile slowly returning to his face. 'You should take a lesson from your baby brother,' he told the king. 'No attempts to make me renounce Óðinn and follow your nailed god-man. Just a simple question. I like it when people are direct.' He was smirking as he turned his attention once more to Alfred, but the mirth did not reach his eyes, which were as hard as iron. 'We are merely gathering here, my lord. We're not here to attack your people.'

'Well,' Alfred said, sticking his head out through the tent flap and peering theatrically from side to side. 'It looks to me like you're all gathered, so you can be on your way. North, or east, I would suggest, away from Wessex.'

Aethelred did not seem displeased by his brother's questions and he watched Ubba, waiting for the reply. When it came, it surprised all three West Saxons.

'But we are not all gathered,' the jarl said softly, sipping his mead while continuing to stare at Alfred. 'We are awaiting the arrival of another ship.'

'Another ship?' Sicgred demanded, and his face betrayed his anger and alarm. Indeed, he made no attempt to hide it as he looked to Aethelred for the king's own response.

To Aethelred's credit he managed to mask his surprise, but Alfred could tell his brother was not expecting Ubba's answer, and it had frightened the king. Another ship full of Danes? Perhaps fifty or more men? If such an army did decide to move westwards, into Wessex, there would be carnage.

'Do not be afraid,' Ubba said soothingly, as if speaking to children. 'Once our comrades arrive in the final ship we will move on, as you ask, to the northeast.'

Aethelred and Sicgred appeared greatly relieved by this, and, although Alfred was also happy that the Danes would be leaving Wessex, he knew what it must mean.

'You're going to attack East Anglia.'

Ubba did not reply immediately, merely looked at the aetheling and continued to take sips from his mead horn, and then he said levelly, 'Would you prefer us to attack *your* lands, my lord?'

'When will your final ship arrive?' Aethelred demanded, and his tone revealed the relief he felt upon learning the Northmen would be moving on to raid and plunder another king's lands.

Ubba shrugged as if he didn't care about the answer very much. As if he was quite happy to remain on this windswept West Saxon shore forever. 'They should have been here days ago. Must have been blown off course.' He sat down in his chair, grinning as he stretched out his legs to get more comfortable. 'Perhaps they will turn up soon. Only Þórr can say.'

Alfred frowned, noticing the Dane's teeth for the first time – deep horizontal grooves had been filed into them, and those were coloured bright red with resin. The aetheling shuddered, touching his tunic where it hid the cross around his neck, and Ubba eyed him knowingly. It was a strange scene as his brother, king of the lands they were in, stood, while a Dane sat comfortably sipping mead and looking insolently at them.

Sicgred was not as tactful, or as patient as his superiors. 'You'd better be gone from here soon, Northman,' he growled, resting his hand threateningly on the pommel of his sword.

'Or what?'

'Why don't you come outside, in front of all your heathen lackeys,' the ealdorman said. 'And I'll show you *what.*'

Ubba roared with laughter at that. 'Do you hear this, my *vikingar*?' he called to the guards outside. They turned and looked in, grinning at their jarl and Sicgred, whose normally pink face was flushing red with barely controlled rage.

'You are a coward,' the ealdorman spat. 'Frightened of an "old man".'

'We will meet one day, on the field of battle,' Ubba replied, the infuriating smirk never leaving his face. 'And we will see who's the coward. Until then, I've been told not to antagonise the king and great lords of Wessex. As I said to you, Aethelred, we are not here to attack your lands.' He flashed a lupine smile. 'Not yet, at least.'

Sicgred practically thrummed with rage, and it seemed he might attack the Dane where he sat until the king laid a warning hand on the ealdorman's arm.

'My brother tells me he was trying to make you give up your pagan gods. Þórr, Óðinn, and so on,' Alfred asked.

Ubba nodded at the aetheling's question. 'He's wasting his time. We Danes have no interest in your weak God and his teachings of love and forgiveness. Our gods are strong, and appreciate the strength of a true warrior.' His voice grew hard, and his mocking smile disappeared. 'Your Christ would have me forgive the people who murdered my father, Ragnar, but I am here for vengeance, not forgiveness.'

Alfred shrugged. 'One day, Jarl Ubba, your people will all be Christian. It's inevitable. And one day we will drive you and your brothers from our shores, back to your frozen hell of a homeland.'

Ubba was nonplussed by this turn in the conversation, but, before he could say anything one of the guards outside poked his head into the tent.

'Lord,' he said in a rumbling voice. 'Our final ship has been sighted.'

King Aethelred drew himself up straight and glared down at the jarl. 'Good. Your comrades have finally arrived. We'll expect you and your men to be gone within two days. Farewell, Ubba.'

He stalked from the tent, followed by Sicgred and Alfred, but the Dane could not resist getting the final word in.

'Farewell,' he called jauntily, raising his mead cup in a mocking salute. 'Enjoy a peaceful summer, my lords, it might be your last…'

CHAPTER EIGHT

East Anglia, AD 869

November

'What should we do with him?'

Ubba grinned savagely, but his oldest brother, Ivar, held up a hand.

'I can guess what you want to do to him,' said the Danish king, who had well-earned the nickname of 'the Detestable' with his many acts of viciousness. 'Let Halfdan speak.'

The middle brother, Halfdan, was the tallest of the three and the least sadistic of them, with a great love of poetry and song. He was also a warrior, however, and knew the power of sending a message to their enemies just as well as Ubba or Ivar. 'We must execute him,' he said simply.

'Well, yes,' Ivar retorted. 'Obviously. We're not going to let him simply walk away and go about his business after he's caused so many deaths of our men.'

'We hardly lost any of our own warriors,' Halfdan noted with a glint in his eye. 'Edmund's pitiful army was no match for our brave *vikingar*.' He looked out at the battlefield, which was littered with East Anglian corpses being feasted upon by raucous crows. 'But still, we should kill their king, so the next place we raid knows what happens to their leaders if they oppose us.'

'But *how* should we kill him,' Ivar asked irritably. 'Hurry up, brother, it's threatening to snow again.'

'I don't care,' Halfdan said, smiling. 'Hang him. Drown him. Behead him.' He shrugged as if they were discussing what the weather might be like the next morning. Behind them the defeated East Anglian king, Edmund, watched their conversation with a terrified expression. When the Danes spoke slowly, as Halfdan had just done when naming his suggestions for methods of execution, Edmund was able to understand them.

'My lords,' the king said tremulously. 'If you let me go I'll make sure you're given double the number of horses we gave to you those three or four years ago when you first came—'

'Shut up, fool,' Ivar said, and Edmund immediately fell silent.

'I could do with some archery practice,' Ubba said thoughtfully, eyes scanning the terrain around them. 'Why don't we tie the royal dog to that big tree and see who can get the most arrows in him?'

Edmund visibly sagged as his legs threatened to give way, but, to his credit he did not moan or beg for his life. In truth, he appeared somewhat relieved by Ubba's suggestion. Dying in such a manner would hardly be pleasant, in fact it might be quite agonising depending on where the arrows struck home, but the Danes had worse ways of killing their enemies. The so-called Blood Eagle that King Aelle had apparently been subjected to, for example... An arrow to the heart would be a mercy compared to such unimaginable, monstrous torture.

'On second thoughts, that doesn't sound like much fun,' Ubba muttered, walking over to stand before Edmund and staring into the king's eyes. 'Considering the trouble he's caused us. And we did swear an oath, my brothers, to take bloody vengeance on the people of these lands for murdering our father.'

'I had nothing to do with that,' Edmund replied and it seemed that knowing the manner of his impending doom had strengthened his waning resolve. 'I was only trying to take care of my people. You would have done the same.'

Ubba's amused look suggested otherwise.

'Maybe archery would not be much *fun* for you, brother,' said Halfdan. 'But it would make for a good sacrifice to Óðinn. We should give offerings for our victory here after all.'

Ivar nodded. Of the three siblings, Halfdan was the one who always made sure the correct rituals were carried out before and after a battle. Even prior to eating, or hunting, or anything else the Danes considered important, Halfdan would make offerings to Óðinn or Þórr or whichever of the other gods and goddesses he thought suitable. Although they did not have a widespread, organised caste of spiritual leaders such as the Christian priests, or the earlier Britons' druids, the Northmen took their deities seriously, and made great efforts to please them.

Killing a highborn prisoner taken in battle was one of the greatest sacrifices a warrior could offer to the one-eyed war god, Óðinn.

'All right,' Ivar said, stretching up to his full height of over six feet and rolling his head to loosen neck muscles beginning to tighten after the battle. 'Tie him to the tree. Halfdan? You can do the honours.'

Without complaint or requests for mercy, Edmund allowed himself to be dragged backwards by the arms, towards the tree Ubba had selected for the execution.

Halfdan nodded in appreciation as the East Anglian king was slammed hard against the trunk with a loud thump. 'It is an ash tree,' said the Dane, looking up at the spreading branches and the pale brown bark which was almost grey in places. 'Like Yggdrasil.'

'That's why I chose it,' Ubba said, and it was true, for the Northmen were renowned for their knowledge of trees. They were greatly skilled in building halls and especially ships from timber, thanks in part to their knowledge of the strengths and weaknesses of various tree species. Yggdrasil, the Norse 'World Tree', was supposedly the very centre of the entire cosmos, with its branches and roots containing the Nine Worlds, which were populated by snakes, deer, squirrels and even a dragon. It was a tree synonymous with Óðinn, who was said to have hanged himself upon it, and pierced his side with a spear in a quest to discover sacred runes. Halfdan in particular often noted the similarities to the Christian Jesus's death upon the cross.

Somehow this ash tree near Theodford seemed the ideal place to spill the blood of a king who served that Christ.

There was real, naked fear in Edmund's eyes again and for a moment it seemed as if he might panic and either try to fight off his captors or begin sobbing and pleading to be released. In fact, he did neither, pulling himself together instead and staring straight out over the lands that had been his for the past fourteen years.

'You're younger than I thought,' said Halfdan softly as he came forward and peered at the king. 'How old are you?'

'Twenty-eight.'

'Same age as me,' the Dane grunted. 'Have you spent those years wisely, my lord?'

'I've done my best,' the king said through gritted teeth.

Halfdan nodded thoughtfully. 'That is all any of us can do. Your part in this saga has come to an end, however, and you shall go to Valhöll to serve our fallen warriors.'

Edmund laughed shortly at that, almost convulsively. 'No, I'll find my place in Heaven, with my own people, not in your heathen drinking hall.'

Ropes had been wound about the king's ankles, waist and chest by now, securing him firmly to the tree and making it impossible to move, never mind escape. Halfdan bowed his head slightly. 'I wish you luck on your journeys in the afterlife, lord.'

Edmund merely stared at him.

'Óðinn! All-Father!' Halfdan moved back, away from the tree with its captive, raising his hands in the air as he called out. 'We thank you for our victory this day, mighty god of war!'

His brothers and the rest of the Danes stood in silence, watching and listening as a breeze stirred the bare branches of the ash that was to serve as their sacrificial 'altar'.

'We give you the blood of this man.' Halfdan pointed at Edmund. 'This great king. As an offering. As thanks for your favour.' He held out his hand and accepted a hunting bow and a handful of arrows from one of his hersir. Nocking the arrow to the string, he raised the iron-tipped missile and aimed it at the victim. 'Are we ready, my brothers?'

His shouted question was directed at all the men holding bows, maybe twenty of them, including Ivar and Ubba. They shuffled forward, forming a horseshoe shape with Halfdan in the middle.

'Do not make his death a quick, or easy one,' Ubba cried out. 'Óðinn will want to savour this king's lifeblood slowly seeping into the ground and the roots of the tree.'

A gentle rain had started to fall making the air even colder as Halfdan looked from left to right at his fellow archers and said, 'Loose!'

The bowstrings snapped and there were thuds as the arrows tore into Edmund's torso. Most of the missiles found their target and the king gasped in shock at the pain, and the weight of the iron-tipped arrows, the wooden shafts of which were as thick as a man's finger. He had been allowed to remain fully clothed, and even still had his shirt of mail on, but it could offer only scant protection against this onslaught.

Ubba laughed in delight as Edmund groaned, but the archers were not done, releasing another volley into the unfortunate king, who slumped against the ropes holding him up. He was obviously dead, pierced by dozens of arrows, and no longer made any sound or movement, head bowed down.

Ivar put his bow on the ground and made to walk ahead when there was another snap and thrum of a string and a final arrow tore through the air, just past Ivar's ear, to hammer into Edmund's skull.

'By the gods, Ubba!' Ivar bellowed, rounding on his brother who shrank back, bow raised as if in apology. 'No more.' The Danish king glared along the line of bowmen, meeting their eyes, and then he strode to the tree, drawing his axe as he went.

Halfdan drew in a deep breath and called out once more. 'Óðinn, you have our offering. Grant us your favour in the coming winter months, All-Father.'

The Danes cried out to their war god and, with that, Ivar raised his axe and brought it down on the already-dead East Anglian king's neck. It took more than one blow to remove the head from the body, which shuddered against the ropes holding it in place.

When Ivar, forearms and face splattered with blood, raised the severed head in his left hand the Danes cheered, laughed, and finally started to sing one of their victory hymns.

The battle was over. Theodford, and all of East Anglia, belonged to Ivar's great heathen army.

CHAPTER NINE

Aethelred was pale as he listened to the report from Wulfric. The ealdorman had been sent to Theodford to find out what was happening in the war that had been raging throughout the summer between the Danes and the East Angles. He'd just returned that afternoon, but had been allowed time to bathe and rest until night fell and the king was ready to grant him an audience. They were in Wichamtun, at one of the king's royal palaces, and Alfred was there too.

The prince had already spoken with Wulfric and heard most of the tale the ealdorman was telling again now, but, even so, Alfred's teeth were gritted and his face was almost as pale as his older brother's.

'You saw this?' Aethelred asked during a pause in Wulfric's recounting of the events he'd witnessed in East Anglia. 'With your own eyes?'

'Aye, my lord,' Wulfric confirmed, shoulders back, chin up, gaze fixed straight ahead. He was the very image of the perfect soldier and the story he was telling only backed that up. 'From the top of a nearby hill. There I saw what the sea-wolves did to King Edmund.'

Aethelred glanced at Alfred and the pair shared an outraged look. No words were needed to convey how they felt about the report they were hearing.

'Tell me again,' the West Saxon king said to Wulfric. 'What they did to him.'

Drawing himself up and taking a breath, the ealdorman repeated his story once more. This time he responded to questions Aethelred asked at various points looking for some clarity, although the simple facts always remained the same: Edmund had been tied to a tree, used for archery practice, and then beheaded, all in the name of the pagan war god, Óðinn. Wulfric had been too far away to hear what the conversation had been before the execution, but the shouts praising the one-eyed deity had carried far and wide.

A log split in the firepit, sending a loud crack reverberating off the smoke-blackened roof struts and making many of the men gathered in the hall flinch. Wulfric did not move, and the king took a drink, wiped his mouth and then said, 'What happened after that?'

'The sea-wolves kicked King Edmund's head about the grass for a while,' Wulfric reported, drawing murmurs and shouts of outrage from the thanes and ealdormen. 'And then they went away to Theodford, no doubt to celebrate their victory.'

'I can imagine their celebrations,' Aethelred spat, staring into the firepit. 'Heathen scum.'

Alfred spoke up then, calling to his captain over the angry mutterings. 'Tell them the rest, Wulfric.'

The king dragged his gaze from the flickering flames, frowning in surprise and gesturing for silence. 'The rest? Something more happened?'

Everyone looked to the ealdorman, tall and proud, the scar on his right cheek seeming redder than usual in the firelight. 'Aye, lord king,' said Wulfric. 'When the Danes wandered off, one of them remained: Jarl Halfdan. He lifted Edmund's head from where it had been kicked, a good distance away from the tree they'd used to execute him, and he carried it back to place it on the ground beside the body.'

Aethelred's frown deepened, and he glanced at Alfred before nodding for Wulfric to continue.

'Then Halfdan turned and looked up the hill, to the very spot where I was hiding amongst some bushes, and he held out his hand towards Edmund's remains before hurrying after Ivar and the rest of the Danes.'

Everyone digested this strange and unexpected twist in Wulfric's tale.

'He knew you were there,' Aethelred said. 'Yet he allowed you to live. Interesting. What did you do after that, Lord Wulfric?'

'I waited until I was sure they were gone, then I returned to my men. We rode to the tree and collected King Edmund's... remains. I carried them away, to a chapel a few miles south of the battlefield, in Hægelisdun.' He bowed his head and blessed himself. 'They promised to see the king had a proper Christian burial. If – no, *when* – the Northmen are driven off from those lands for good, perhaps Edmund's people can give him a funeral befitting his station.'

There were respectful nods and murmurs as many of the noblemen repeated Wulfric's pious gesture, marking Edmund's death with the sign of the cross and a quick, soft prayer.

'That's not all,' Alfred said. 'Word has been coming in from other parts of Edmund's kingdom and it's not good. The heathen host have started attacking monasteries.' His head dropped as the men cried out and then he forced himself to continue despite the obvious pain his words caused him. 'They've burned down the minster in Medehamstede,' he muttered. 'Reduced it to nothing. Killed the monks, and... decapitated old Abbot Hedda.'

The morose atmosphere in the hall gave way to righteous fury, and there was a clamour as everyone demanded vengeance for the murdered Christians. Aethelwulf, Ealdorman of Berrocscire was particularly vocal in his calls for action.

'We can't let this stand, my lords,' he said in a powerful, confident tone as he stared around the room at his peers. Everyone there knew Aethelwulf and respected him, for he was widely regarded as the greatest military commander in Wessex, having proved himself countless times in battle. Being average in height and build, with thinning straw-coloured hair, he did not look especially impressive, but when he spoke, others listened.

'You all know I would like nothing better than to seek vengeance for what Ivar and his lackeys have done – are doing! – to the people of East Anglia.' Aethelred stood up and, although he was not wearing a sword, he had a seax in his belt and rested his palm on the handle as he gazed out at the men on the benches. Their faces were wreathed in cooking smoke, and flickering shadows from the firepit and the torches set in the walls, but their grim expressions were easy to read.

'What are we going to do about it then?' one of the younger thanes called out.

'What would you suggest, Lord Diuma?' Aethelred asked, directing his gaze to the man who now stood up.

'Well,' Diuma said, looking somewhat embarrassed as every eye turned in his direction. He could only have been around eighteen or so, broad shouldered but lean, with straight, dark hair and a wispy beard. He probably regretted opening his mouth now that so many more experienced lords were waiting to hear his sage advice. 'Why don't we just attack them? They won't be expecting it.'

Alfred sighed and waited for the inevitable, harsh responses, which didn't take long to come.

'Attack them?' a greybeard near the front of the hall demanded, hooting with laughter which many of his nearby companions joined in with. 'Idiot boy, don't you think people haven't tried that?'

'In winter?' Diuma demanded, face quickly turning scarlet, especially as his question only roused more laughter, even from the king.

'Sit down, lad,' Aethelred said, grinning at the young thane's ludicrous suggestion. 'We do not campaign during winter, surely your father, Ealdorman Wealdmar, told you that? It's simply too treacherous to move men, and horses, and supplies, when it might snow at any time.'

'Not to mention it's no fun freezing your bollocks off in the middle of a field,' someone added.

'And even worse trying to fight in a flooded plain, when your fingers are so cold they can barely hold a sword or a spear.'

This was met with a chorus of 'aye's but Diuma, perhaps to his credit, Alfred thought, would not be put off so easily.

'Well, it never seems to stop the Northmen,' the thane argued. 'They sometimes raid in the middle of winter. Our people don't expect it, so they aren't ready to defend against it. If the Danes can do it, why can't we?'

Aethelred's humour had faded now and he shook his head irritably. 'Sit down I said, Diuma,' the king called over the chattering nobles. 'It's already been explained to you why we don't fight until the warmer weather is here. Now be silent and listen to those of us who know what we're talking about.'

The young thane sat down, embarrassed and angered by his humiliating dismissal. The other men resumed their grumbling about the heathen Northmen and their continuing rape of Britain, many pledging men and supplies to Aethelred for the coming spring's battles.

Eventually talk of war faded and the ealdormen and thanes spoke in smaller groups, of simpler things, such as farming, the weather, women, and the quality of the meat and drink the king was serving them that night.

'I don't think it was wise to dismiss Diuma so publicly, brother,' Alfred said to Aethelred as they sat at the high table watching their men enjoying the evening. 'His father's lands in Brycgstow are vast, and one day Diuma will be ealdorman of them.'

The king merely laughed and shrugged his shoulders. 'Even his father, Wealdmar, would admit that the boy's suggestion was a foolish one.'

'Was it?'

Aethelred turned to his brother in astonishment. 'Yes, it was. There are many good reasons why we don't go to war in the winter. Not unless forced into it, at least.'

Alfred stared out at the inebriated, laughing men in the hall. Most of them were over thirty. Many were over forty, with some being considerably older. 'Men such as these want an easy, comfortable existence,' he observed, nodding towards a red-faced, bald man who wore jewel-encrusted rings that glittered in the firelight. 'Bishop Deorlaf does not want to be anywhere on a December night, other than safely in his hall in Hereford, fire blazing, his dogs and wife by his side, and servants bringing platters of cheese and roast meat.'

'Deorlaf has earned that right,' the king retorted. 'He's served Wessex well enough over his sixty-odd winters. Would you have him standing in a field in the howling wind, fingers turning blue with frostbite, in an attempt to draw the Danes out from behind the walls of Theodford? You know those walls will have been fortified by the time we would get there, and the Danes, damn them, are masters at building things with wood!'

'Then let Bishop Deorlaf remain in his hall with his dogs and his platters of meat, counting his wealth,' Alfred said levelly. 'His fyrd can be commanded by one of us.'

Aethelred stared at his brother for a long time and then, at last, turned away, shaking his head. 'That's not how we do things in Wessex. It never has been, and never will be. It would be folly. The Danes are used to the cold weather.'

'It's cold in Wessex,' Alfred argued. 'We should be used to it too.'

'You're being disingenuous now, brother,' the king said, reaching out to lift a piece of buttered bread from the trencher before him. 'You know as well as I do that the winters here are nothing like as bad as they are in the homelands of the Northmen.'

Alfred followed Aethelred's lead and took some food for himself although he barely tasted it as he chewed. 'Maybe not,' he conceded. 'But we cannot continue doing things as we've always done. It's getting us nowhere. Aye, most of the men here mocked Diuma's words, but not all. Those more willing to stand up to the Danes, like Ealdorman Aethelwulf, did not laugh. And don't forget Ubba's threat to us that day we met him on the beach. Wessex will not remain safe from the sea-wolves forever.'

Aethelred chewed his lip in thoughtful silence and, eventually, when the bread was finished and Alfred's cup was drained, the aetheling stood up and went out amongst the men feasting in the hall. They were happy to greet him, grasping his arm in enthusiastic drunken greetings, complimenting him on his fine clothes, his exquisite seax, and his proud captain, Wulfric. Alfred accepted the praise with good grace – he was somewhat inebriated himself after all – but gradually worked his way towards the table near the far corner of the hall.

'Lord Diuma.'

The thane looked up. His expression was lucid, suggesting he hadn't drunk as much as many of the other revellers, but his clear complexion and wispy beard betrayed his youth. Alfred felt an immediate affinity with Diuma, and not only because they were so close in age.

'My prince…!' The seated thane scrambled to stand up while at the same time bowing his head, and Alfred couldn't help laughing.

'Don't get up.' Alfred smiled, touching Diuma on the shoulder, voice raised so he could be heard over the shouts and laughter that filled the hall to the very rafters. 'I just wanted to apologise for the way my brother dismissed your suggestion. Taking the fight to the Danes might seem ridiculous to the old men of Wessex, but I thought it was a good idea, and so did a few others. I admire your courage in putting forward such a bold plan.'

Alfred had been worried the thane would be too angered by his earlier treatment to receive even praise with good grace, but Diuma's face lit up in a broad smile.

'Thank you, Prince Alfred,' the thane said. 'It means a lot to hear you say that.'

'Don't let Aethelred's words dissuade you from making such suggestions in future,' Alfred said. 'It's always good, I think, to have someone willing to go against the grain. To stick their neck out and voice unpopular opinions. I value such men, even if others don't.'

Diuma gazed up at him, as if trying to find some hidden meaning behind the aetheling's words. Everyone in the hall, or so it had seemed, had reacted to his earlier suggestion with, at best, laughter or, worse, outright mockery, as if such a young warrior could have no real clue of how war should be waged. Could Alfred merely be continuing that cruel theme?

'I'm serious,' the prince said, smiling and holding out his hand. They grasped wrists and Alfred nodded. 'The older men have done a good enough job, but they won't be around forever. Aethelred will need the counsel of younger warriors like you, even if he doesn't agree just now.'

Diuma thanked him again, almost awestruck to have been given this endorsement by the second most powerful nobleman in Wessex. 'Will you join me for a drink, my lord?' he asked, but Alfred shook his head with a wink.

'Not just now.' He winced as a sudden, sharp pain lanced through his stomach, but it passed quickly and his smile returned. 'I have another meeting to attend. You stay and enjoy yourself though. We'll speak again soon.'

They nodded farewell to one another and then Alfred headed for the main door. As he went, he nodded to one of the servants – a pretty young woman with a full figure, and bright, blue eyes – and, giggling, she followed the aetheling out into the night.

CHAPTER TEN

Ealhswith pushed open the door to the chamber at the rear of the royal palace in Wichamtun and stepped inside. Behind her came King Aethelred's wife, the Queen Consort Wulfthryth, a petite woman with hazel eyes and hair which she wore shorter than was the fashion. They stopped and smiled at one another as they saw their husbands standing before the windows with the shutters flung wide to let in the sunshine and crisp, winter air. A fire burned merrily in the centre of the room keeping the chill at bay. This chamber belonged to Aethelred and Wulfthryth's little sons, and the furnishings were even more exquisite than the other areas of the palace.

The youngest, Aethelwold, was a baby, having only been born that summer, so still required a lot of care and attention from a nursemaid. The firstborn son, Aethelhelm, had arrived four years before, in 865, and he was a bundle of energy and a constant source of pleasure and amusement for his parents.

Ealhswith was also very fond of the children, and it cheered her to see Alfred playing with his little nephew by the window. The pair had wooden horses and warriors which they were pretending to fight one another with, while the king was reading a bible story to the gurgling baby in his crib.

'Hail, my ladies,' Alfred said as the women came into the room, and Aethelhelm ran across to them, brandishing an invisible sword and threatening to deal with them if they, 'heathen brutes' that they were, came any closer.

'That's enough of that,' Wulfthryth scolded, sending her giggling son back to play with Alfred. 'There'll be no heathens in this house, brutes or otherwise.'

'Would you like to go outside to play for a while?' Aethelred said to his eldest child.

'Yes, Father,' Aethelhelm replied, eyes bright as he looked out at the cold but sunny morning. 'Can we go to the stream and catch fish?'

The king laughed. 'We can try. I doubt we'll catch anything though, not in this cold. Are you coming with us, Wulfthryth?'

The queen consort nodded happily. 'Of course, it'll be good to get some fresh air after the bad weather kept us indoors so much lately.' She turned to Alfred and Ealhswith. 'Would you two like to look after the baby? If he gets hungry just call for the maid, but he seems quite content for now.' She bent over the crib and touched little Aethelwold's cheek, making him reach out jerkily with his hands and kick his stubby legs beneath the blankets. Wulfthryth lifted the wooden rattle that he'd dropped and returned it to him. He grabbed it firmly, shook it about noisily for a few moments, then shoved it into his mouth and gnawed on it with his gums, staring fiercely at her.

'You be good,' Aethelred said to the baby with a smile then led Aethelhelm and his wife from the chamber. A few moments later they could be heard outside as the child ran ahead, calling for his mother and father to chase him, which they did with some gusto.

Alfred and Ealhswith listened, shaking their heads at the playful noises in the grounds.

'I don't know why, but your brother doesn't seem the type to act like that,' Ealhswith said, peering out of the window. She turned back to Alfred. 'Neither do you, to be honest. Too serious.'

Alfred's brow lifted. 'Serious? I suppose we are. I was supposed to be nowhere near inheriting the throne when I was born – I should have been a priest.' He shook his head and looked thoughtfully down at baby Aethelwold. 'Instead, I'm the heir-apparent, and I've spent recent months learning how to command armies against the Northmen.' His eyes seemed to glaze over as he thought about how his life was turning out. 'Instead of learning, and teaching, about God, I'm learning how to kill as many men as I possibly can. No wonder I'm serious.'

Ealhswith put her arm in his and drew him close. 'I'm sorry, my lord,' she said softly. 'I didn't mean to ruin your good humour.'

He met her gaze and forced a smile. 'No, it's all right. This is the fate God has given me and I must make the best of it, as Aethelred must. At least I don't have all the responsibilities he does as king.' He reached out and stroked the baby's downy hair.

'Do you like babies?' Ealhswith asked, changing the subject.

'I've never really thought about it,' Alfred replied. 'I like Aethelwold though.' He made a silly face and the baby stared back, wide-eyed, before jerking his arms and legs furiously again. 'And Aethelhelm,' the prince laughed. 'I like both of Aethelred's children, yes.'

They stood there for a time, simply watching the little one in his crib. It must have felt good for Alfred to celebrate life for a change, rather than fending off, or dealing, death.

'We should make some heirs of our own,' Ealhswith said, resting her head on his shoulder. She was quite a bit shorter than the prince and he looked down at her, apparently not exactly sure what she was saying.

'What, now?'

'Well, not in here, with the baby watching,' she laughed. 'But yes, why not?'

She could see Alfred becoming aroused, a common occurrence with the young man. He took in his wife's slim figure, smiling face, and freshly combed brown hair and nodded. He seemed to understand what she really meant now – Aethelred might be killed in battle the next time they were forced to stand against the Danes, and that would leave Alfred as king. It was a king's responsibility to provide heirs. Such bleak thoughts were hardly stimulating, but Alfred had never been one to refuse a tumble with her.

'All right,' he said, grinning. 'I suppose it is our *duty*.'

'Come on then,' she said, kissing him. 'Let's get that nurse-maid in here to look after Aethelwold. We must do as the West Saxon people demand, and give them a royal birth to celebrate!'

—

Alfred watched as Bishop Edwin walked into the church, shivering from the cold even within its thick stone walls. There was no firepit, but, despite the chill Alfred could see the same great sense of peace and calm he always felt within a house of God mirrored on the churchman's face. This was one of the few stone buildings in Wichamtun – most were built, like the town walls, from timber – and the bishop served King Aethelred, a man who did everything he could to celebrate and venerate God's power. The clergyman's sandaled feet slapped against the floor as he strode towards the altar, but he paused halfway there before coming to a stop beside the kneeling Alfred.

The prince imagined what the bishop was thinking as he looked at him. Alfred was a warrior, that much would be very clear from the clothing he wore and the breadth of his shoulders. He was also someone of wealth, for his tunic of green wool was of the finest quality and the seax at his waist was encrusted with precious stones and gilded with gold. A moment of panic was evident on Edwin's face as he surely wondered if this was some heathen outrider, come to lay waste to the town and strip the church of its treasures. His fears evaporated when Alfred blessed himself however, muttering the end of a prayer, and smiling up at the bishop.

'My lord, Prince Alfred!' said Edwin in a relieved tone 'I did not recognise you for a moment there. I also did not expect to find you here.'

Alfred stood up, nodding a greeting. 'Well met, Bishop Edwin,' he said, before asking almost sheepishly, 'may we talk somewhere discreet?'

'Of course,' replied the churchman, holding out a hand towards the rear of the church, to the east side of the building. 'We can talk in the chancel.' He led the way through an impressive double arch and gestured to a bench within the small anteroom. 'I'll leave the curtains open so no-one can come in without us seeing them.'

Alfred peered up at the woven, red drapes that could be used to close off the chancel from the main body of the church. 'That makes sense,' he agreed, sitting on the bench the bishop had indicated. The wood was cold even through his thick breeches and he pulled up his collar and blew on his hands in an attempt to warm up somewhat. He'd been at prayer for a while before the bishop arrived and a slight blue tinge showed just how numb his fingers had become.

Edwin watched the prince sympathetically and then said, 'Give me a moment, my lord.' He hurried from the chamber and disappeared, leaving Alfred shivering. He returned a short time later carrying two mugs. 'Here, this will warm you up,' he said, holding one out.

Alfred took it gladly, instantly feeling the heat emanating from the wooden receptacle. He sniffed, the strong aroma of warmed, spiced ale filling his nostrils and almost magically seeming to exorcise the chill from his body. 'Thank you, Bishop Edwin,' the prince said, sipping the drink with pleasure, his face lighting up as the ale went down and began its work.

'I wouldn't normally drink this early in the morning,' Edwin told him with a wink. 'But I think we can indulge ourselves this one time.' He took a sip of his own beverage, also savouring the slightly bitter taste. 'Now, lord prince. What can I do for you?'

Alfred looked at him then sighed. 'I've been getting pains,' he said in a low voice, as if worried someone might overhear his confession. 'Here.' He held his hand on his stomach.

The bishop's face did not betray any emotion. The man was used to hearing all sorts of unusual things from his flock. 'I see,' he said, bobbing his head gently. 'That must be concerning. Would you not be better seeking out a leech, however? I'm afraid I know little about curing physical ailments.' He smiled. 'I deal more with spiritual matters, my lord.'

'I believe this *is* a spiritual matter,' Alfred replied, forcing himself to meet Edwin's gaze although his jaw was set, almost as if he was about to engage in battle, or some other fearful task.

The bishop continued to nod. 'All right,' he said, putting both hands around his warm mug. 'Tell me about it, my lord. Do you fear some demon is tormenting you? Attacking your digestion?'

'Something like that, perhaps,' Alfred conceded, then he drew in a deep breath, steadying himself before forging ahead, his words coming out in a rush. 'I am being tortured because I... I regularly enjoy the company of women other than my wife, Bishop Edwin. I always have, and I cannot stop myself, although I know it's a terrible sin. Praying for forgiveness does not ease my burden, or my pain, and I am unsure what to do about it.'

The churchman took all this in, saying nothing for a time as he sorted the jumble of words in his head. 'Forgive me for stating the obvious,' he said eventually. 'But, my lord, it seems to me the obvious solution is to stop taking other women to bed.'

Alfred clasped his hands and looked up at the cross on the wall of the chancel. 'I know. But... I cannot...'

'Is it like how many men drink to excess every day?' the bishop asked curiously. 'That kind of compulsion? They know it will only lead to misery, but they continue to get drunk day after day regardless?'

'Yes!' Alfred replied almost excitedly, smiling at the bishop's apparent understanding. 'That's exactly what it's like. A compulsion.' His face fell suddenly and he looked down at the floor, hands still clasped although his fingers were moving nervously. 'I also enjoy drinking to excess most days. Another of my weaknesses, and another reason I find it hard to control my urges.'

The bishop nodded. 'The devil tempts us with many carnal delights, my lord. You, as a prince, and a man of means, have even more access to such temptations than most commoners. A beggar, unwashed and dressed in filthy rags, does not have beautiful women seeking his bed. Nor does he have the coin to buy ale every day.'

Alfred looked bemused by this line of thinking. 'Are you saying I should become a beggar?'

'No!' Edwin laughed. 'No, my lord, I'm not suggesting any such thing, I'm simply pointing out how you are tempted more than most men, so must show even greater restraint.' He reached out and patted Alfred's clasped hands reassuringly. 'It is only human to give in to temptation occasionally.'

'Occasionally.'

'Indeed. You are a young man, so your desire to...' The bishop paused, searching for the right words before saying, 'sow your seed in as many fields as possible, is only natural. With time, and age, that urge may lessen. In the meantime, you must pray, and remember you are a married man with duties and obligations to Lady Ealhswith.'

Arthur thought about that. 'What about the drinking?' he asked.

'Well, even I enjoy my warmed ale more than I should, especially in these cold winter months,' the bishop admitted with a grin. 'But eventually, after years of suffering terrible hangovers, even the biggest sot will begin to drink less. You must pray,' he repeated. 'Beg for God's help in your struggles. Who knows?' He leaned back and held up his palms. 'Your stomach pains may even be a result of your drinking habits. I've known many men with various ailments which have been completely cured when they gave up a life of drunkenness.'

Alfred's face seemed to light up at this suggestion. 'Then I will follow your advice, Bishop Edwin,' he promised. 'And limit my consumption of ale, mead and wine!'

The churchman smiled but cocked his head, almost like a dog, and said, 'That would be a good start, my lord. You must rein in your other appetites as well, though.'

The cheery expression faded from Alfred's face at that, but he muttered agreement with the bishop's exhortation and peered at Edwin earnestly. 'Have you heard of something like this before?' he asked. 'One's guilt making him physically ill, I mean?'

'Oh, yes,' the bishop said emphatically. 'Either guilt, or the devil's influence, who knows which? But aye, this kind of thing is very common.' He frowned. 'Have you not spoken with your own priest about this, my lord?'

Alfred shrugged guiltily. 'No, not really. I've been too embarrassed to mention it to Oswald. I see him often and...'

Edwin gave him a knowing look. 'You thought it would be easier to talk with me, since you don't really know me. That's understandable, but I would recommend talking with your own priest. He can give you regular advice on this problem when you return to your estate, or are off campaigning once spring returns. That is his job, after all, and I'm sure he's heard much worse confessions over the years.' He shuddered and looked away thoughtfully. 'Some of the things we hear would *turn* a man to drink...'

Alfred watched him, waiting for the bishop to expand on this enigmatic pronouncement, but Edwin merely smiled.

'God gives us strength though, does he not, lord prince? We must show ourselves worthy of his love and support, however, so you must strive to fight those vices of yours, all right?'

Alfred nodded heavily. 'I'll do my best, Bishop Edwin.'

'Splendid! You have a power in you, Prince Alfred. A God-given power. That is what drove you to seek me out – to seek out God's help.' He made the sign of the cross and followed Alfred's lead as the young man got to his feet. 'I believe you will show yourself to be a great man, as long as you do your best to follow Christ's teachings, and look to your priest for guidance when weakness threatens to overcome you.'

'Thank you,' Alfred said, reaching out to grasp the bishop's hand. 'Your advice has taken a weight from my shoulders and given me much to meditate on. I'll make sure a sizeable donation is made to your coffers on my behalf.'

Edwin held up a hand. 'That's very kind of you, my lord,' he said. 'But your brother, the king, makes sure we are well taken care of here. I would ask you to send your donation to the church within your own estate, or even put it towards building another church within Wessex.'

'As you say,' Alfred agreed. 'So it shall be.' He walked out of the chancel and bowed his head before the altar, where he also made the sign of the cross, then he turned and moved towards the doors at the western end of the church.

'Lord prince,' the bishop called as the morning sunlight framed Alfred within the archway.

'Yes?'

'In the name of Christ, keep the Danes from these lands, my lord. You and your brother are our only hope I fear.'

Alfred fancied the golden radiance coming through the doorway had formed a halo around him as he faced the bishop and laid a hand on the seax in his belt. 'We'll do our best,' he promised, and turned away to step out onto the bustling street outside with one last, parting request. 'Pray for us. We're going to need all the help we can get!'

CHAPTER ELEVEN

Ceodre, AD 870

Spring

'Good news, my lord!'

Alfred looked up from the book he was reading with his wife. Ealhswith was pregnant with their first child so had been spending even more time than usual enjoying the collection of books kept there in their own home, or at the church a short distance away. This particular tome included the Passion narratives from the four gospels and was a favourite of both Ealhswith and Alfred.

'Good news?' the aetheling said to Wulfric as the tall warrior strode past the firepit towards them. They were not at the table on the raised dais, instead choosing to sit on one of the lower benches usually occupied at night by the warriors, and Wulfric bowed low as he reached them.

'Aye, lord,' the warrior said, smiling broadly. 'I've just come from Wichamtun where word has reached your brother – Ivar the Detestable has gone!'

Alfred looked at his wife and they shared a hopeful glance. It had always been their dream to see the back of the Danish raiders, but now that Ealhswith was with child it seemed even more important. No parent wanted to bring their son or daughter into a world torn apart by war.

'Gone where?' the aetheling asked warily.

'North,' Wulfric said, towering over the seated lord and lady. 'To Strath-Clota.'

'Sit down, Wulfric,' Ealhswith ordered, grimacing and rubbing the back of her neck. 'You're far too big for us to be staring up at.' Her hand moved down, from neck to swelling belly, and she let out a long breath.

'No, don't sit,' Alfred said, patting his wife's hand and leaning over to kiss her on the cheek. 'We'll leave you to read, my lady. I'll take Wulfric to see the new minster and he can tell me all about the heathen warlord.'

'I want to know too,' Ealhswith protested, although half-heartedly.

'I'll tell you about it when I get back,' Alfred promised. 'You rest. Enjoy the book.'

She smiled at both him and Wulfric. 'Fine. I'll have the servants get some food ready for your return. Don't be too long, it's going to rain today, I can feel it.'

Alfred stood and lifted his thick, winter cloak from the chair beside him. The weather had been mild recently, but he'd learned to listen when his wife made predictions about it; if Ealhswith said it would rain, there would be rain.

He led Wulfric outside and together they walked towards the sounds of thumping, hammering and the cheery whistling that seemed to Alfred to be a critical component of every building site the aetheling had ever known, no matter where. Often it was accompanied by one workman who thought the world needed to hear his wonderful singing voice.

'Impressive,' Wulfric said as they neared the new minster, the overcast, grey skies doing little to diminish the sight of the sturdy edifice that was being constructed in the very centre of the settlement. Although it was far from the biggest church Alfred had ever seen, massive wooden pulleys and cranes were dotted about to help lift the stones for the walls into position, and timber scaffolding allowed the masons, carpenters and other workers to bring the whole thing together. The basic frame-work was already in place, and it was all progressing at a rapid pace.

'You're paying for all this, my lord?'

'I am,' Alfred said, gazing up as he pictured the final building in his mind's eye. 'Ceodre could do with a decent stone church. The people need a suitable place to worship God, and this,' he swept out his hand to encompass the partially constructed building, 'this will be it.'

Wulfric nodded. He was a Christian, but he was not as pious as Alfred and often voiced his opinion that money spent on churches would be better going towards strengthening town walls and providing better weapons for those of their people too poor to afford more than a fire-hardened spear or a crude one-piece maul cut from a branch.

Alfred looked at him, a small smile on his lips, wondering if his captain would voice those opinions just now.

He did not. Instead, Wulfric brought the subject of the conversation back to the one he'd started with in the great hall. 'King Ivar has gone north according to our reports,' he said, watching as a large block of stone was lifted into position by shouting workmen. 'Scouts from Northumbria followed his army as it passed through their territories without stopping to raid as they would normally do.'

The prince pursed his lips, then winced as one of the masons on the scaffolding dropped his hammer and cursed loudly as it clattered off the wooden spars and thumped onto the ground below.

'Saving his men for whatever fight they're heading to in the north,' Wulfric went on, oblivious to Alfred's irritation at the foul language used within his burgeoning monument to God's glory.

'The heathen scum have probably realised there's not much left of these lands to plunder. They've already stripped the other three kingdoms practically bare!'

'That's true, my lord,' Wulfric muttered gloomily. 'East Anglia, Mercia and Northumbria have been terribly weakened. Only our own lands have been mercifully left alone for the most part.'

Alfred beamed and pointed at the next stone that was being slowly lifted into place. 'And that is why building strong, stone churches is prudent, my friend,' he said forcefully. 'God deserves to be praised for keeping the Northmen at bay.'

Wulfric tipped his head and shrugged noncommittally. 'If you say so, my lord.'

Alfred shook his head. 'I sometimes wonder if you would be more suited to worshipping Þórr or Óðinn,' he told the ealdorman ruefully. 'But once this wonderful new minster is completed, Wulfric, we will have one more place to pray for your redemption.'

They stood for a time, continuing to watch as the workmen went about their business. Alfred's eyes gleamed as another stone was placed in position and he pictured the final edifice in his imagination. Then he looked down and saw the muddy streets and windswept, tattered thatch on the nearest roofs. The contrast was stark to what he'd been seeing in his head, but the smile soon returned to his face. 'There's that rain Ealhswith predicted. Come on, let's head back to the hall before it gets heavy.'

He threw up his fur-trimmed hood and hurried back along the road to the great timber hall that was his home while he was in Ceodre. Wulfric followed him and both were happy to get indoors as, sure enough, it started to pour, and thunder rumbled somewhere far in the distance.

'That'll be Þórr,' Alfred laughed, shaking the water from his cloak before he headed to the middle of the room and stopped before the firepit, warming his hands in the welcome heat. 'Angry that yet another Christian church is being built to further sweep away his influence on Britain. Ha, well, soon enough his name will be forgotten completely, eh, Wulfric?'

The ealdorman sat down at the bench Alfred had been sharing with Ealhswith. The lady was not in the hall any more, at least not in this main section, and the table was empty. A serving girl had already noted their arrival however, and was bringing over a trencher laden with cuts of roast meat, bread and cheese.

'I'm not so sure of that,' Wulfric said, nodding his thanks to the servant as she placed the food down and moved off to fetch them ale. 'After Ivar raids Strath-Clota he'll likely come back south and, eventually, I fear the bastards will overrun us completely.' He bit into a slice of beef and began chewing. 'There'll be no churches left then. The Danes will destroy them all, or perhaps use them as houses for their jarls.'

'By Christ's fingernails, man,' Alfred swore, throwing his cloak over a chair to dry out and sitting on the bench across from Wulfric. 'You're as gloomy as the weather. Have faith. Ivar is gone. We'll have a time of respite while he harries some other poor bastard's lands. Give thanks to God, and cheer up!'

In truth, the prince's optimism was infectious, and Wulfric was soon smiling as the two men ate, drank and conversed together, comfortable and cosy beside the blazing firepit while the storm broke outside.

A log was added to the firepit by another servant just as Ealhswith came back and joined them. The men greeted her warmly and Alfred hugged her as she took her seat beside them, but he noticed her mood was not as light as it had been earlier.

'What is it?' Alfred asked in surprise.

'Word came from Aethelred while you were out,' she told them with a portentous frown.

Alfred felt a sudden surge of fear and demanded, 'Is he alright?'

'Yes,' Ealhswith replied, taking his hand in hers and patting it reassuringly. 'He's fine. But the Danes have attacked Abbandune.'

Alfred stared at his wife for a long moment, wondering if he'd heard her correctly. Then he turned to Wulfric and said, accusingly, 'Didn't you just tell me the Danes had gone north, to Strath-Clota?'

'Ivar has,' Ealhswith broke in. 'And he's taken many of his men with him. But Halfdan remained in Mercia and—' she broke off, drawing in a long breath before letting it out with a sigh. 'His army has just taken Abbandune. He's calling himself king too now.'

The prince cursed loudly and most un-Christianly. 'So, they're now going to turn their attention on Wessex? Is this what our summer will consist of this year? Chasing the Northmen as they sail up and down the Tamyse in their cursed longships, raiding at will yet never standing still long enough for us to engage them in battle?' For just a moment he despaired of it all and wished he'd followed Wulfric's advice to spend the money for the new minster on extra fortifications in the north-ernmost towns of Wessex, like Abbandune. He reached inside his tunic, however, and drew out the cross he wore around his neck, squeezing it and silently begging God for strength to deal with the coming threat.

As always, his faith brought him relief and hardened his resolve. The momentary sensation of helplessness passed and, letting out his breath almost in a growl, he lifted his ale mug and drank deeply. Wulfric and Ealhswith did the same although neither spoke, sharing the aetheling's anguish at the unwelcome news.

'God will preserve us,' Alfred said firmly, placing his mug back on the table and looking at his captain. 'I'll need your leadership more than ever this year, Wulfric.'

'My sword is yours, lord,' the ealdorman replied, raising his mug in salute. 'If Ivar has taken many of their men away their great heathen army will not be as powerful as before. We can repel them. We *will* repel them.'

Alfred nodded, lips pursed thoughtfully, wondering where their enemies might strike after Abbandune. The problem was, the Danes' ships were so mobile thanks to their shallow keels that they could move with ease all across Wessex or even retreat back to Mercia or East Anglia. By Christ, they could even drag their ships across land, from one river to another! He looked at Ealhswith. 'What does my brother require from me, my love?'

'He asks that you take your fyrd north, to make sure the Danes don't get settled long enough to fortify the town.'

Alfred grunted. 'Indeed. That sounds like the obvious plan, and one I'm happy to follow. If we can defeat the pagan dogs before they start to make progress within our lands it might send them back to the north.'

'Aye,' Wulfric agreed. 'Maybe "King" Halfdan will decide it would be a better idea to follow his brother, Ivar, to Strath-Clota, or Ireland, than deal with us.'

'Begin preparations then, Wulfric,' the prince said as he stood up. 'No time to waste.'

Ealhswith also rose to her feet and Wulfric followed suit. 'I'll get your hearth-warriors ready to move, my lord,' promised the ealdorman. 'We can gather the fyrds of the towns we pass on the way to Abbandune. I would suggest we leave a decent garrison here in Ceodre, however, just in case Halfdan sends some of his ships around to the South Sea and comes at the town while we're away.'

Alfred nodded over his shoulder as he and his wife headed towards their chamber at the far end of the hall. 'Agreed. See to it, and I'll join you in a while to help.'

When they were behind the partition and alone they held each other in an embrace for a time before Ealhswith pulled away and pressed a hand to her tummy. 'Would you think me a fool if I told you I'd prayed we might bring our child up without the constant threat of war hanging over us?'

Alfred reached out and placed his own hand over Ealhswith's. 'Not at all,' he said. 'I prayed for the same thing.' He shook his head and looked down at her blossoming belly. 'Perhaps one day our prayers will be answered. We must continue to ask for God's mercy and succour. Until then,' he looked into his wife's eyes, and said grimly, 'I'll do what I can to kill every last one of the Danes who threaten us.'

Ealhswith took his hand and kissed it. There were tears in her eyes but she had been brought up to know her duty. 'Go then, my lord,' she told him. 'Go north and defend your people. I… we,' she patted her tummy gently, 'shall be waiting patiently for your return, so make sure you come back safely.'

'I will,' he vowed, leaning down to kiss her on the forehead. 'Even Satan himself could not stop me from seeing you holding our child, Ealhswith. Halfdan should be wary of pushing too far into Wessex, for our men won't rest until his sea-wolves are beaten. Aethelred will make sure of it, and I'll be at his side winning back every inch of ground the bastards try to steal!'

CHAPTER TWELVE

Halfdan watched his men at work and felt himself swelling with pride. These were hardy warriors that had chosen to follow him rather than going off to Strath-Clota with Ivar. Strong, capable, and willing to do the hard work he'd tasked them with. Right now they were loading the supplies they'd plundered from Abbandune into their ships. Food took up most of the available space in the shallow keels, for treasure was of little use when an army needed fed, and they would not be stopping here long.

Abbandune was merely a steppingstone that would lead the Danes deeper into Wessex. It was not a particularly large settlement but there had been enough entertainment for the army once they'd defeated the local militia. After a long and rather boring winter Halfdan saw his men like caged and starving dogs, desperate for their chance to run free, hunt, and rut with whatever bitches they came across.

So it had turned out when the pitifully unprepared West Saxon warband was smashed and the fleeing survivors taken care of, leaving Abbandune and the people within defenceless. Of course, some of those had, sensibly, fled the town and taken refuge in the hills but many were too stubborn to leave their homes. The Danes had quickly made them regret their foolish refusal to run. They were not always brutal conquerors, but Halfdan wanted this first, initial attack to send a powerful message to the people of Wessex.

His father might have died in Northumbria, but all the so-called noblemen of this island would suffer for what had happened to Ragnar.

Ubba appeared, grinning, apparently still half-drunk from the previous night's celebrations.

'Brother,' said the younger man, walking across and slapping Halfdan on the back. 'What great plans are swirling in your thought-cage now?' He held out an un-stoppered skin which, from the smell, Halfdan knew was filled with wine. 'Here. Have some. You are king here now that Ivar has left us. You should celebrate!'

'It's far too early in the day for that,' Halfdan said.

Ubba rolled his eyes. 'We are *vikingar*,' he protested. 'Not Christian monks. Here!' Again, he thrust out the wineskin then shook his head with a laugh when it was once again refused. 'Won't take a drink. Barely joined in with the men when they were enjoying themselves after we took Abbandune. You need to be careful, brother, or you'll lose their loyalty. A leader should celebrate with his warriors after a great victory, not sit aloof, like one of the Norns.'

Halfdan snorted at being compared to one of the female deities who controlled the fate of everyone. 'You call that a great victory? A few dozen farmers armed with little more than the tools they use to work the fields?' He did reach out and snatch the skin from Ubba's hand now, helping himself to a long draught and enjoying the warmth as the strong drink flowed through him. 'The men don't care whether their leaders join in with their debauchery – all they want from me are victories, and plunder.' He handed the wineskin back to his younger sibling, glaring at him. 'My desire is to win power and have my name ring out through the ages in the songs of the skalds. Raping women, or men, does not interest me. It sickens me.'

Ubba returned his stare and, despite the harsh words clearly being a criticism of Ubba's own behaviour, the smile did not leave his face. Instead, he said jovially, 'You are too tense, Halfdan. A good fuck would help you loosen up. Trust me.'

'Oh, I can see how loose you are, Ubba. Drunk in the middle of the morning! You haven't even combed your hair or your beard yet. You're a mess. *That* is something that will lose the respect of our men – a jarl should be well groomed and clear-eyed, little brother, not stinking of the terror-sweat from the last girl you forced into your bed.' Rape was a crime in the Northmen's homelands, but here in Wessex the raiders did as they pleased without fear of legal, or other, reprisals.

At last Ubba's smile faded and his jaw clenched. 'Ivar might have headed north,' he growled, 'and left you as king, but our warriors would be just as happy to follow me as you. I don't remember you complaining to him any time he ploughed the Mercian women, or drank himself into a stupor.'

Halfdan smiled and reached out to grip Ubba's upper arm in an almost conciliatory gesture. 'Ivar knew when to leave off the revelry, and when to take care of his duties. That's what makes him a fine leader. We should follow his example. Remember the old saying from the *Havamal*: "*Ölr ek varð, varð ofrölvi at ins fróða Fjalars; því er ölðr bazt, at aftr of heimtir hverr sitt geð gumi.*" Drunk was I then, I was over drunk in that crafty Jötun's court. But best is an ale feast when man is able to call back his wits at once.'

Ubba's frown lifted somewhat, and he even put the stopper back on his wineskin, as if his brother's words had finally made an impression on him. Everyone knew Halfdan spent as much time conversing with skalds and the wise-women known as *volur* as he did sharpening his weapons. As a result, he had learned much ancient lore and wisdom which he often shared with his friends.

'Go, brother.' Halfdan grinned. 'Wash your face and comb the lice from your beard, then come back and help me get our ships ready to move onto the next town along the Tamyse. There'll be plenty more opportunities to empty your balls and fill your belly with wine and mead before this summer is over, I promise you that.'

97

The younger jarl seemed happy that their brief argument was over. 'Maybe once we control Wessex you'll let yourself celebrate properly then,' he said.

'Count on it,' Halfdan laughed. He watched as his brother wandered off, not quite able to walk in a straight line. His smiled faded as he contemplated the coming months. Ivar had been able to look to Halfdan for support and advice. They'd worked well as a team for they were both fairly disciplined and had the drive to bring their ambitions to fruition.

Now, Ivar was gone and Halfdan had Ubba as his second-in-command. The youngest brother was a beast in battle, showing no fear and glorying in the brutality he meted out with sword and spear, but he did not share the tactical instincts of Halfdan and Ivar, and his unfettered enjoyment of carnal pleasures made him an erratic leader.

Part of Halfdan wished Ubba had travelled to Strath-Clota with Ivar, and he felt guilty at that thought for their father, Ragnar, had been devoted to his youngest son.

'How do I look now, *bretwalda*?'

Halfdan turned at the somewhat sarcastic honorific which meant 'war-leader' and saw Ubba, face ruddy from washing, hair and beard freshly combed. The wineskin was gone from his hand too, and, Halfdan had to admit, Ubba looked every part the proud *vikingr*. 'That's better,' he said approvingly. 'Like a young Þórr. Come, then, brother. We have work to do.'

'And thousands of Saxons to slaughter.'

'Aye,' Halfdan laughed. 'That too.'

CHAPTER THIRTEEN

The West Saxon fyrd that Alfred led snaked out behind them as Wulfric and the aetheling rode northwards to meet the Danes. They had planned to make for Abbandune but word had reached them that the raiders had taken what they wanted from that unfortunate town and moved on, their sleek longships making their way along the river towards the next settlement Halfdan coveted.

'How much farther?' Alfred asked, shading his eyes with a hand, for the sunshine was bright before them, making it difficult to see the old road.

Wulfric judged the time from the position of the sun and his own knowledge of the surrounding lands. Lands which he'd been soldiering in for most of his life. 'A couple of hours, I'd say, my lord. You still think we should make for Dorcaestre?'

'I do,' Alfred said, glancing over his shoulder to make sure the army was keeping up with them. 'It's only a few miles downriver from Abbandune and situated close to the Tamyse. I think it'll be too obvious a target for Halfdan to ignore.'

'Even with the new palisade wall?' Wulfric asked. Thanks to its proximity to the river Dorcaestre had seen its fortifications recently improved and expanded, as something of a deterrent to the very raiders who were now upon its borders.

'Aye, even with the new wall,' Alfred replied heavily. 'Such a wall, with its hastily constructed gatehouses, will not hold off the Northmen for long. Not if the reports are true about the size of Halfdan's army.' He sighed. 'I wouldn't blame the inhabitants if they abandoned the town, it'd be safer than trying to keep the bloody Danes outside until we got there. I've no idea what we'll do if we get there and Halfdan *has* taken the place and just shuts the gates on us.'

'He won't,' Wulfric predicted confidently. 'Not this early in the year. They'll want to move on and pick clean as many places as possible. Besides, the sea-wolves hate being besieged.'

Alfred was nodding, happy to trust his captain's greater experience and knowledge of the Danes particular style of warfare. 'They'll strike fast and hard, then move on, before we can force them into a pitched battle,' he agreed, smacking his fist into his palm. 'God grant us a chance to catch the bastards in the open this year, make them fight us, shieldwall to shieldwall, Aethelred's fyrd, and mine. The Christian hammer to Halfdan's heathen anvil.'

Spring had barely touched Wessex so far, but the occasional snowdrop or primrose was just enough to brighten the drab countryside and make the biting wind seem less bitter.

'Call a halt, Wulfric,' Alfred said as they were passing a field with twenty or so sheep in it. The animals watched, chewing the grass, as the prince slid down from his saddle and rummaged in his pack for something to eat. 'The men could do with a rest and we're making good time,' he said, finding some salted beef and tearing off a chunk with his teeth.

Soon the rest of the army — around four hundred men — had come to a stop behind them and were gladly sitting or lying down on the cold ground, happy to take the weight from their feet. Some had even started small fires, which drew their comrades like flies to an open honey pot. Alfred saw the smoke rising from the conflagrations and breathed in the familiar, homely smell. 'Grab a few of those twigs,' he said to a man near some trees beside the edge of the road, then he took out his flint and steel and set about kindling a flame.

Within moments the dried mushrooms he was using as tinder had caught the spark and he was blowing it into life with the chill northwesterly breeze helping. The man he'd tasked with fetching fuel quickly appeared with dry sticks of varying sizes, handing the smallest to the prince who took them gratefully. He made up the fire and then, when it was merrily blazing away, he glanced up at the twig-bearer.

'Lord Diuma,' he said, recognising the young thane who'd suggested attacking the Danes during winter at Aethelred's earlier feast and been rudely commanded to sit and be silent. 'I hadn't realised you were travelling with us. Come, sit by the fire and warm yourself.'

Wulfric was already there, holding his hands out to the flames, but he moved aside to let the newcomer sit on the grass with them. For a time the three men ate meat from their packs, content to fill their bellies and enjoy the heat, for it was a cold business riding to war before spring had fully bloomed. Eventually, Alfred said, to no-one in particular, 'Why do you think the Danes continue to plunder these lands?'

Wulfric eyed him, continuing to masticate his meat in near-silence, but Diuma was eager to give his opinion. 'They think us an easy target, my lord,' he said, swallowing his food and washing it down with a sip from his waterskin. 'Our fortifications are weak, and we have no real standing army to face them when they appear unexpectedly from their cursed ships.' He shook his head, gazing into the fire, a frown blemishing his otherwise unlined forehead. 'Having so much wealth stored in practically undefended minsters is too great a temptation, too big a prize, for the heathen Northmen to ignore.' He looked up somewhat anxiously then, perhaps fearful that Alfred would take Diuma's words as criticism of the royal family.

The prince nodded. 'You're right,' he admitted. 'We make it easy for the whoresons to take what they want. But we also pay them to leave our lands as soon as we get the chance.' He stood up, staring at the sheep in the nearby field. 'We give them meat, and grain, and horses, and silver, and whatever else they demand. It's no wonder their numbers swell every year with reinforcements from across the sea. They don't even need to face our armies in battle – kings like Edmund and Burgred pay them fortunes to *avoid* a fight!'

Wulfric rubbed his hands before the fire, looking up at his commander. 'There's only so much wealth left on this island,' he said grimly. 'The Danes have already stripped Francia which is why they've come over here. But they must have done the same in Mercia, East Anglia and Northumbria, so...'

'They've moved south, to attack us,' Diuma said.

'And north, to Strath-Clota and Ireland,' added Alfred.

'We can't let them ravage Wessex the way they've been doing in those other lands,' Wulfric muttered, getting to his feet and glancing at the warriors resting behind them. 'And some of our noblemen, like Bishop Deorlaf and Ealdorman Wulfhere, won't be happy if the king decides we must pay the Danes to leave our lands.'

'No,' Alfred agreed. 'They won't appreciate giving up their wealth. But with men like you two by my side,' he clapped Diuma on the back, smiling, 'we'll stop it ever coming to that.'

Diuma swelled with pleasure. He was only a relatively minor noble after all, with no lands of his own until the day his elderly father died, and Alfred's praise and familiarity was unexpected. 'My sword is yours, my lord,' he said to the prince. 'And your brother's.'

Alfred nodded and turned back to Wulfric, mouth open to ask his captain to get the fyrd moving again but Wulfric anticipated the order and had already kicked out their fire and was gesturing now for the men to be on their feet.

'Two hours,' Alfred shouted once he was back in the saddle and facing his army. 'Two more hours on the road, and then, God willing, we'll meet the Danes in battle. Are you ready?'

'Yes!'

Alfred frowned and shook his head in exaggerated disgust. 'I said, "Are you ready?"'

The cries of 'yes!' were much louder this time and the prince grinned. It felt good to be leading so many men in such a worthy cause.

'Good! Pray to God and his saints then, as we march to Dorcaestre. For victory, and an end to the heathen scum who would take our lands, and our women, and our wealth, for their own!'

There were many raucous shouts of agreement at his words, but it was noticeable that not all the army joined in. Those at the rear especially, did not seem so happy to be heading towards the infamously brutal Danes.

Alfred turned his horse about and started to move along the road again as the hundreds of warriors at his back ponderously followed suit. He noticed Diuma's angry, confused expression. 'What's wrong?' he asked the young thane.

Diuma looked awkwardly away, plainly surprised by the question and wishing he'd hid his emotions better.

'Spit it out, man,' Alfred encouraged. 'I like my officers to speak their mind and give advice when they think it's warranted.'

Diuma took a deep breath, then glanced over his shoulder at the men marching behind them. Many were chattering happily enough, some were quiet and thoughtful, but a large number of them wore black expressions and were obviously unhappy.

'My lord,' the thane said, almost apologetically. 'I just thought your words were more inspiring than some of our warriors appreciated. Dare I say it,' he fell silent, as if he did not wish to say more, but Alfred nodded for him to go on. 'Well, some of the ungrateful bastards look like they'd rather not be here! Don't they understand the importance of stopping the Northmen before they penetrate further into Wessex? It will be *their* lands,' he jerked a thumb backwards at the marching army, 'the pagan animals attack next, unless we defeat them.'

Wulfric looked amazed by the young man's outburst. 'Your father's lands are vast,' he said, head cocked on the side rather like a dog trying to understand something. 'Have you never spoken with the ceorls who work those lands?'

'No,' Diuma replied, and he appeared just as astonished as Wulfric now. 'Why would I?'

Alfred watched the exchange but remained silent as the two men continued.

'Well, those lands will be yours soon enough,' the older ealdorman said. 'Don't you think it would be a good idea to have some understanding of how they're farmed, and the thoughts and dreams of the people who keep things going there? The tanners, blacksmiths, farmers, shepherds, bakers…' He trailed off, shaking his head. 'A good leader has some knowledge of his people, don't you agree?'

Diuma simply shrugged. 'As long as they continue to work and do their jobs, that's good enough for me. We are all just smaller parts in a larger system after all, even you, my lord.'

Wulfric didn't reply, he merely stared at the thane for a moment, and then turned away, looking out at the fields they were passing.

'The men,' Alfred said into the awkward silence. 'Are not all happy to be here.'

'I understand that, lord,' Diuma said eagerly. 'I'd rather not be going into battle myself. I'd like to see my hair turn grey one day, rather than being run through by a Danish spear.' He smiled. 'But some of those warriors following you look sullen. Almost rebellious.'

Alfred turned to gaze at the column snaking through the countryside at their backs. Was Diuma really this dense? He eyed the young thane who was so obviously eager to impress the aetheling. He would, as Wulfric said, be a wealthy, powerful ealdorman one day and, in fact, was acting in that capacity just now, taking the place at the head of the fyrd of his father, Wealdmar, who was too infirm to travel himself so remained at home in Brycgstow. Alfred did not want to offend Diuma, but, at the same time, it would do the man good to hear the truth.

'Imagine you were a ceorl,' Alfred said, pointing at a young boy who was running with a dog and herding some sheep in a nearby field. 'Like that child's father.'

Diuma's lip curled as if such a life was inconceivable, but he nodded readily enough.

'You have a wife, and a few children, all needing to be fed during the winter when food is scarce and your meagre stocks have been running low. Now, imagine the terror they feel when their lord's soldiers come to requisition much of their food because the fyrd needs it. Imagine that pitiful store of meat and grain being taken from you and knowing that your family's survival has become almost impossible, thanks to the actions of your own lord.'

Diuma took this in, and Alfred knew his words had made an impression for the young thane seemed surprised.

'Then,' the prince forged on. 'Imagine those same soldiers who have essentially stolen your food, now telling you to get your cloak and go with them, for you are now part of the army. This army. And your wife and children will somehow have to fend for themselves until you return. If you return, and there's a good chance you will not, since you only have a sharpened stick as a spear, no helmet, no armour, and you'll be facing a thousand Danes with chainmail, axes, swords, shields, and the training to use them properly.'

Diuma's face had turned pale and his hand fidgeted with the pommel of his fine sword. He turned in the saddle and looked again at the 'warriors' trailing after them.

'What difference does it make to them whether Aethelred is their king, or Halfdan?' asked Alfred. 'Their life will not change. They will still have to wake at dawn every single day and tend to their duties, desperately hoping it'll be enough to feed their families once their lord has taken his share.'

Wulfric was watching Diuma too now, and the thane met his eyes. 'I see,' he said softly.

Alfred forced a smile. 'Good. You understand then, why many of those following us do not do so with a happy heart, or any enthusiasm or love for my brother, or me, or you, or Wulfric. They do it because they must, and that has to be enough for us.'

They rode on in silence towards Dorcaestre, wondering how many of their soldiers would return to their families once the fighting was over.

CHAPTER FOURTEEN

'We're too late.' Aethelred's jaw was clenched as he stared at the ruined gates of Dorcaestre. Thick, cloying smoke was still rising into the sky from the town within, from the buildings set ablaze by the Danes who, it seemed, had already departed. Alfred's army had met up with Aethelred's about five miles from the town, scouts leading one another to the meeting point and, although they'd wasted no time in marching to Dorcaestre together, the raiders were simply too well-drilled and had already moved on by the time the West Saxons had turned up.

The town seemed strangely quiet as Alfred rode after his brother and they passed through the smashed gatehouse. Here and there survivors cradled loved ones, crying bitter tears as they numbly watched king and prince ride by. Mostly the men and women of the town were moving to and fro, carrying water to put out the fires, or bandages to treat wounds, or wandering around shouting the names of missing family members.

No thanes or ealdormen came to meet them, which was a bad sign. Undoubtedly, Halfdan had either slaughtered or enslaved those brave enough to stand against them. For all Alfred's earlier talk of ceorls, they at least had one advantage over the noblemen: the Danes mostly left them alone once the battle was over. There was no point in killing the people who worked the land – without them the Danes would have nothing to plunder the next time they turned up. And the ceorls had nothing to steal, unlike the nobles. So the lowly workers were left in peace while the thanes and their families who hadn't managed to escape were robbed then killed or taken into slavery, assuming there was space on the longships.

'What's our next move?' Alfred asked, looking around in shock at the destruction. There was something indescribably terrible about the state of Dorcaestre. The way it had been picked clean but mostly left intact was disturbing to the young prince. It seemed more natural for raiders to attack a settlement, kill everyone within, then burn the entire place to the ground once they'd carried off anything of value.

Tears were in his eyes as he watched a little girl, face black with soot, run away from them into the shell of a house which looked like it had been set on fire and only recently extinguished.

'They've left the place standing,' he said. 'So they can come back and plunder it again next year. It's... evil.'

Aethelred glanced at him. 'This is what they do, brother,' he said. 'You must have known that.'

Alfred cuffed away the tears that spilled from his eyes. 'It's one thing to know it, another to see it for yourself. God have mercy on us all if this is what we have to look forward to in the coming months.'

Aethelred reached across and grasped his brother's wrist. 'Get a grip of yourself,' the king commanded. 'People are watching. It's never good for an army's leaders to give in to despair.'

Alfred flushed scarlet but, when Aethelred let go of him, he sat up straighter in the saddle and his expression changed from horror to anger. Not at the king, but at Halfdan and his despicable, murderous sea-wolves. 'We must stop them, Aethelred,' he growled through gritted teeth, breathing deeply of the smoke that swirled around them. 'We can't let another of our settlements go the way of this one.'

The king nodded slowly. 'Easier said than done, but we must do our best.'

'When the rest of our fyrds join us,' Alfred said. 'We will crush the raiders then. Ealdorman Aethelwulf will be here from

Berrocscire soon, and he'll take the fight to the bastards like they've never known before.'

'Lord king!'

There was a sudden shout from behind and the thudding of hooves, and the brothers turned to see Wulfric riding towards them, eyes burning like the embers in the ruined houses around them.

'What is it?' Aethelred demanded, loosening his sword in its scabbard.

'One of the Danish ships has foundered upstream. It's not far. Another ship must have stopped to help them. They're trying to get the damaged one back into the water but not having much luck.'

The king looked at Alfred and they both grinned. 'I'd rather we caught their whole damn army, but at least this is something. Do you want to deal with them?'

Alfred nodded eagerly, glad to have an opportunity to gain experience battling their enemies. 'Aye, brother, let me and Wulfric take care of them.'

'Go, then. But take care,' he added as Alfred and his captain kicked their mounts into a run towards the destroyed gates. 'Take plenty of men with you!'

Alfred waved a hand in recognition of the command but did not look back, his mind already focused completely on the task at hand. 'How many are there?' he asked Wulfric over their horses' pounding hooves and the yelps of the stunned locals scrambling out of their way.

'Looks like two of their larger ships,' the ealdorman called. 'The slower ones, built for trade rather than speed. I'd guess maybe thirty, forty crew.'

Alfred absorbed this, knowing such vessels could hold rather more than forty sea-wolves, but guessing Halfdan would not want to lose more of his warriors than necessary just to transport slaves and plunder back to their camps in the north. He would need as many men as possible to ravage Wessex, so Wulfric's seemingly low estimate of Danish numbers was most likely correct. It also meant some of the stolen wealth from Dorcaestre could be returned to its rightful owners, once the fighting was over.

'Diuma! Gather thirty of your men,' Alfred roared as they came back into sight of the thane and the rest of the troops that had marched there with the prince. 'Wulfric, bring our warriors from Ceodre. That should be more than enough to deal with the raiders, eh?'

There was uncertainty in Alfred's voice which told of his inexperience, but his captain nodded agreement. 'Aye, lord. Diuma's thirty, plus our own fifty. That's plenty.'

'Good, let's get moving then, before the bastards escape.' His eyes were shining and he made the sign of the cross as they started the journey along the banks of the Tamyse. He could see the sunlight rippling on the fast-flowing waters and, for some reason, the beauty of it filled his heart with joy. Perhaps it was merely the thrill, and the inevitable fear, of going into battle, but the river, and the burgeoning spring foliage that surrounded them, had never seemed so vibrant to the prince as it did then.

'Slow down, my lord. Remember the men aren't mounted.'

Alfred came back to himself with a start, glancing around and realising he was far out ahead of Wulfric and the rest of his warband, who were practically running to catch up. Foolish, but he was pleased to see his rashness was appreciated by his men. They were laughing by the time they caught up with him, amused by his eagerness to take the fight to their enemies and his courage. No man liked to be led into battle by a commander who hid behind the rear ranks of his army, and Alfred was clearly not such a leader.

Wulfric, however, did not look so pleased. He never said anything for it was not his place to reprimand the aetheling in front of the fyrd, but his dark look was enough to make Alfred feel like a child being scolded by his tutor.

'How far is it?' he asked, and Wulfric jerked his head upwards.

'Not far. Look.'

Alfred saw a man beside some bushes ahead, waving to them. Even at this distance he recognised the helmet the man wore, for it was of a distinctive design and superbly maintained, shining in the pale sunlight. He did not know the warrior's name, but he knew it was one of their own scouts, undoubtedly the very one who'd discovered the beached Danes.

'All right, are the two ships side by side, Wulfric?'

The ealdorman nodded. 'Yes, lord. One is fully out, on the riverbank being repaired. The other is, or at least was, halfway out, ready to be launched again.' He shrugged. 'There's a good chance the crew of that second ship will decide to leave when they see us coming, rather than helping their kinsmen in the holed vessel.'

'Let's hope not,' Alfred growled, then he leaned back in his saddle and found Diuma with his eyes. 'You take your men on ahead. Keep out of sight of the river and get on the other side of the Danes. We'll give you time to get there. When you see us attacking, you join us. All right?'

Diuma gave a thin smile, pleased to be given this important duty. 'Of course, my lord. You can count on me.'

'Good,' Alfred replied. 'God be with us.'

The thane led his men away, moving further from the riverbank as they went to make sure the tips of their spears weren't spotted by the Danes working beside the Tamyse. The sounds of hammering could be heard quite distinctly now and Alfred wondered what exactly the Danes were doing. Everyone knew they were master shipbuilders and carpenters but Alfred himself had very little knowledge of such things. He presumed the enemy sailors had cut down some tree or branch and were forming it into planks to repair their damaged hull. How that would be waterproof he could not imagine, unless the Danes had some pitch or other sealing substance with them.

It did not matter. The hammering told him that at least one ship and its crew were just ahead of them, and all Alfred wanted to do now was kill every last one of them and return their ill-gotten gains to Dorcaestre. Even that small victory would show him that God had not forsaken them, as so many of his subordinates whispered when they thought he was not listening.

He dismounted and Wulfric followed suit along with the handful of thanes who were on horseback. They all took their shields from their backs and made them ready along with their spears, and Alfred had them form quietly up into a line. When it was time to attack they would make a wall of interlocked shields, spears bristling, ready to turn the banks of the Tamyse red with heathen blood.

They waited, only the nervous shuffling of feet and the occasional retching or muffled coughing breaking the silence as the men prepared themselves for what might be their final moments alive. At last, Alfred looked at Wulfric and they bobbed their heads, agreeing that sufficient time had passed for Diuma's warband to take up a good position.

'Are we ready, lads?' The aetheling drew himself up to his full height and looked along the line. Anxious, frightened and excited faces gazed back at him. Men aged from around seventeen to fifty, all prepared for whatever wyrd would be theirs that day. The prince nodded, sharing his troops' trepidation. It was only natural to fear death.

'Let's move.' Alfred's voice was steady and powerful, surprising even himself for his guts were churning, but he put one foot ahead of the other and steadily they began to make their way towards the sounds of hammering.

'What a noise they're making,' one man muttered as they walked.

Wulfric growled in agreement, frowning as he looked at Alfred. He did not say anything but the confusion on his face only made the aetheling more anxious and Alfred gripped his spear firmly, his knuckles white on the dark wood. As they moved out from behind the line of bushes and crossed the shallow rise that had hidden the river from view until then, it became clear why the two shiploads of Danes seemed so loud.

There were actually three ships, and a lot more than thirty or forty sea-wolves had noticed the approach of Alfred's West Saxons and were running to form their own imposing shield-walls.

'God's blood,' Alfred gasped as he watched the Danes getting into formation, moving as their hersir's commanded, bearded faces staring out coldly at the West Saxons. He instantly regretted his words, not wishing to transfer any extra fear to his men, but what was supposed to be a fairly easy battle had suddenly become something he wasn't sure they could win. The numbers were even now, and the enemy were well versed in the ways of the shieldwall.

'Get into formation!' Wulfric bellowed, staring along the line which had become ragged as they moved. 'Lock your shield with the man next to you, unless you want a Danish spear in the face.'

Alfred could hear the clatter of the linden boards coming together as the men took in their captain's warning. He scanned the horizon and heaved a sigh of relief as he spotted Diuma's warband steadily trudging along the damp riverbank, spears levelled, shields held together. Even at this distance the anxiety could be seen on the warriors' faces and Alfred muttered first a curse at the folly of war, and then a prayer that God would grant his side the victory.

'Perhaps we should send a messenger to the king,' a thane just along the line from Alfred suggested. The prince recognised the voice, which sounded level and betrayed no fear.

'I fear it's too late for that, Lord Eadwig,' Alfred said. 'By the time someone reached the town and reinforcements were sent the battle would be over. We need to deal with these pagan rats ourselves.'

The thane nodded his helmeted head, a sneer curling his lip. He was a little smaller than the rest of the men but had a barrel chest and large arms which made him appear formidable. Exactly the type of soldier Alfred wanted beside him, and this seemed to be confirmed when Eadwig said, almost joyfully, 'Fair enough, my lord. Bring them on then, and let's show them the folly of raiding Wessex.'

'Aye,' someone else called, laughing louder than seemed necessary. 'Send them back to Mercia. They can plunder there as much as they like!'

There were more laughs and even some cheers at that, but they were half-hearted, and Alfred wished he'd had a skin of ale that morning to bolster his nerves, for his stomach was roiling and he wanted to vomit.

As they closed on the riverside, however, a strange icy calm came over him. The fear dissipated, replaced by a steely resolve and focus on the coming battle. His eyes took in the damaged ship, and another two which were stationary, drawn a little way up onto the beach. Frightened faces looked out at him from those ships – slaves. Their plight did not touch him at that moment as he focused again on the Northmen before his advancing formation, and then shouted, 'Archers!'

There were not many of his men carrying bows, but those who had them were positioned at the rear of the lumbering shieldwall and they raised them up now. There was a snapping of bowstrings and then the deadly black rain came down upon the Danes.

The iron-headed arrows thumped home in shields and many missed their targets completely, landing harmlessly in the soft grass, but some penetrated armour and injured or even killed some of the Danes.

'Again!' Alfred commanded. The enemy hersirs had ordered their men to charge, hoping to close the distance and make further missile attacks impossible, but Alfred had judged well and there was just enough time for another flurry of arrows to take out a few more unfortunate raiders.

And then the charging Danes slammed into the shields of the West Saxons and everything became a blur for Alfred. Men were gasping, screaming, roaring war-cries or prayers, and then it all seemed to become quieter, the shouting replaced by thumps and ringing metal and breathless grunts of exertion and terror.

Something smashed into Alfred's shield and he felt a terrific jolt of pain run through his arm and into his shoulder, but the wood held firm and he blindly thrust his spear ahead, feeling it scrape against something and then become stuck for just a moment. When he drew it back it was dripping red and he laughed as if he'd lost his mind, then thrust again and again.

Suddenly the Danish line faltered and their attacks lessened.

'Diuma!' Wulfric called to the prince. 'He must have hit them.'

Indeed, Alfred could see the enemy warriors in line ahead of him glancing over their shoulders, panicked expressions on their pale faces. 'Hit them again,' he screamed, the fatigue that was growing in his arms forgotten as he tried to spit another man on the end of his spear.

The fighting continued and, at last, Alfred felt like he couldn't hold his shield up any longer. He moved backwards into the second rank and then kept going, looking from one end of the battleline to the other. What he saw did not please him for the two sides were quite evenly matched, as he'd feared. Even with Diuma's force hitting the rear of the Danes it had not been enough to turn the tide. The way it was looking things would carry on until everyone was killed.

Despair washed over him, and he almost let the spear fall from his numbed fingers. So many of his men lay dead already, should he call the retreat?

'God, give me strength,' he muttered, glancing up as the sun was obscured and a light rain began to fall. Things would become even more treacherous now, as the combatants slipped and lost their footing on the sodden ground. As if it hadn't already been dangerous enough!

Wulfric, wiping blood from his face, stumbled back to join him, breathing heavily. The ealdorman looked even more tired than Alfred, although the aetheling suspected Wulfric had also likely killed double the number of Danes than he'd managed.

'How are we faring?'

Alfred shook his head. 'We're holding steady, but so are they. We're going to lose a *lot* of our men, even if we win, Wulfric. Is it worth it?'

They watched, both trying to see an opening in the Danish line that might be exploited but there was nothing.

'I'm going to call the retreat,' Alfred said eventually. 'The Danes can leave in their other two ships. At least we'll have whatever is left in the damaged one.'

'Not if they already transferred the booty to the other vessels,' Wulfric said.

The enemy hersirs must have been having a similar conversation at that very moment, for, just as Alfred opened his mouth to tell Wulfric to signal the retreat, there was a sudden lull in the fighting. The clatter of spear, sword and axe striking shield and bone appeared to lessen and, as the West Saxon commanders looked on in stunned relief, a large part of the Danish warband were running in the opposite direction.

'What's happening?' Alfred asked, more to himself than Wulfric, but his captain's face had lit up.

'The crew of the third ship have decided they don't want to die here. They're leaving.'

Alfred started running, back to his place at the forefront of the Saxon shieldwall, shouting, 'Forward! Forward! The bastards are routing!'

His words, and the clear thinning of enemy numbers, were enough to spur on the forces of Wessex and the tired men found a new burst of energy, driving ahead with a ferocity the outnumbered Danes could not match.

Wulfric had mounted his horse and the elevated position afforded him a better view of what was happening on the battlefield. 'The third ship has shoved off,' he shouted to Alfred, who only heard his captain's shout on the second attempt, so engrossed was he in trying to kill the enemy.

'Don't let the rest escape!' Alfred roared, teeth bared as he caught a Danish spear shaft and rolled his own around it before thrusting the tip into the attacker's cheek. It punched straight through the skin and out through the back of the enemy warrior's skull, dragging the weapon from Alfred's grip when the man collapsed onto the ground with it still embedded in his head. The prince drew his sword and somehow managed to bat aside another spear thrust before crouching low behind his shield. 'Don't let them escape!' he repeated. 'There's slaves and silver on those boats, we must retrieve them.'

The Danes knew they were beaten by this point, and they were all trying to reach the second, undamaged ship – even the crew from the holed vessel. It took a lot for a Dane to abandon his ship, but it was obvious there could only be one outcome to the battle now, and retreat was preferable to death.

'No mercy!' Wulfric shouted, kicking his horse into a canter past his own men. The captain's sword came down, cutting into the shoulder of a fleeing Northman, but the horse did not stop and neither did Wulfric, who raced along the line of retreating enemies, dealing out death to those foolish enough to keep their backs to him.

Soon almost all the Danes were dead and those who survived were doing their best to push their ship into the Tamyse. It was moving freely enough, as such ships were designed with flat keels so they could be moved even on land, but it was a slow process with slaves and booty on board weighing it down. Much too slow for an escape like this.

'Surround them!' Alfred ordered, coming at a walk beside his warband to encircle the longship and the twenty or so Danes who were standing beside it having given up trying to launch it again.

The two sides lined up against one another, and it was remarkable how the expressions on Alfred's men's faces differed from those of their trapped enemies. The West Saxons were gleeful, weapons held just as high as they had been at the start of the fighting, while the Danes looked frightened and drained of energy.

'Put down your weapons,' Alfred called, looking along the line of beaten sea-wolves. 'And I'll let you all live.'

'As slaves!' a massive warrior retorted furiously.

'Isn't that better than dying here?' Alfred asked, spreading his arms wide. 'In the mud?'

'Not for me,' the big Dane said, shaking his head and gesturing with his spear. 'None of us will live as your thralls, so... Come here, boy, and let me shove this up your arse.'

CHAPTER FIFTEEN

Alfred let out an exasperated breath and shared a look with Wulfric.

'This is how many of them behave,' the ealdorman told him. 'They believe their fate is predetermined, inescapable. Their day of death is set at birth and can't be changed no matter what, so there's no point fearing death.'

'And they engage in foolish acts of apparent bravery like that,' Alfred said, jerking his head at the huge Dane, who repeated his challenge and was ignored again. 'Will none of you drop your weapons?' the prince asked, scanning the enemy line. Three of the Northmen did crouch down and put their spears and shields on the ground and Diuma quickly gestured for them to come to him, which they did. They were searched for other, hidden weapons, then shoved roughly towards the rear of the West Saxon formation.

'Cowards!' the big Dane screamed at them.

'No – young men who see how foolish it is to give up years of life here for nothing,' Alfred replied bitterly. Then he turned and said over his shoulder, 'Archers.'

The Danes surrounding the boat lifted their shields and some of them charged towards Alfred, but the bowmen had already prepared for this outcome and had arrows nocked in their strings. They let fly and some of the missiles slammed home in Danish torsos, legs and even heads, while others ineffectually thundered into shields. Those enemy warriors lucky enough to survive the barrage of arrows gave final, screamed war cries, thrusting out with their weapons, desperately trying to kill as many West Saxons as possible, but, within moments, the battle was ended.

Alfred felt elation building within him as he looked down at the slaughtered sea-wolves, not even noticing the blood that covered his hands and face. His joy was tempered, however, when he turned and saw the number of dead within his own ranks. Bodies from both sides littered the beach and a sudden, crushing sadness filled the prince. He brought his gaze up, watching the third Danish ship being rowed away, upstream, its crew staring back at him.

'What a waste,' he muttered.

'My lord?' Wulfric asked, coming to stand beside him. The ealdorman was just as bloodstained as Alfred but there was no sign of sadness in his eyes. No great happiness at the victory either, just contentment at a job well done.

'Nothing,' Alfred replied, taking a deep breath and handing his spear to one of the nearby warriors. 'Strip the bodies of the Northmen,' he shouted. 'Take any valuables, then…' He thought about it. 'Push their damaged ship closer to the water, and pile their bodies inside. Search it first! Then we'll burn the whole lot.'

Diuma walked towards them, grinning widely, and with rather less blood on him than the other two commanders. Alfred had seen him fighting though, and knew the young thane deserved credit for both his bravery and his leadership.

'Well done, my lord,' he said, grasping Diuma's forearm and smiling broadly at him. 'You fought well, as did your men. I'll be sure to let the king know.'

Diuma's grin grew even wider. 'It was incredible, wasn't it, my lords?'

Wulfric snorted. 'Aye, it was a good victory,' he said.

'Oh, I'm sure you've fought in many bigger, more exciting battles, Wulfric,' said Diuma. 'That's the best one I've been part of though.'

Alfred released the thane's arm and clapped him on the back. 'You did well,' he reiterated. 'I'm glad you were with us. Now, we should get everything dealt with here and return to Dorcaestre. That was only a fraction of Halfdan's army, remember.'

Diuma's smile faded although only a little. 'Understood, my lord,' he said. 'I'll have my men help search the undamaged ship. We can take it to Dorcaestre as well if you like?'

Alfred pursed his lips. 'Aye, good idea. Let me check on the prisoners the Danes took first, though.' He turned to Wulfric, planning to ask his captain to oversee the clean-up operation, but there was no need. His command was anticipated and Wulfric, with a wave of salute, walked away, barking orders to any men he didn't feel were pulling their weight, literally.

'We'll have all the plunder taken from Dorcaestre put on the ship with you,' Alfred told Diuma. 'And you can return it all. What we take from the Danes I'll transport back to the king myself. He can give it out as he sees fit, but I'll make sure you're well rewarded.'

'Thank you, lord prince,' Diuma said, and it seemed like he'd grown in stature since the battle ended.

They boarded the ship which the Saxons had been trying to push into the water and Alfred went amongst the prisoners. There were men, women and children, all with their hands and feet tied, many with bruises, in tears, some stripped half-naked. A few even had iron slave collars already fastened around their necks. All looked at Alfred as if he was some kind of saint, sent down from Heaven by God to rescue them.

'My lord.' A woman reached out towards him. Her breasts were uncovered and dried blood caked her face. Alfred felt a pang as he recognised the woman. She was the wife of a thane and, until the Northmen had got hold of her, she'd been quite beautiful. He put out his left hand and took hold of hers, then he drew his seax and used it to gently cut the ropes binding her wrists.

'Where is your husband?' he asked, fearing the answer.

Tears filled her eyes and spilled down her cheeks, leaving tracks in the blood and soot. 'They killed him,' she said. 'He tried to stop them…'

'I understand,' Alfred told her, shouting to one of his warriors stripping a Danish corpse on the beach. 'Throw me his cloak.'

The man looked up in surprise, not quite understanding, but eventually he dragged the woollen cloak from the Dane and ran to hand it into the ship. Alfred took it and helped the lady cover herself as she sobbed and put an arm around a little girl who must surely be her daughter.

'My men will cut all your bonds,' the prince said, straightening up and addressing the rest of the prisoners. 'Then we'll take the ship back to Dorcaestre and you'll be set free along with any of your belongings that are on board. You're safe now, thanks be to God.'

He bowed his head, accepting the shouts of gratitude, and then he turned to Diuma.

'I'll see to it, lord,' the thane promised. 'And meet you back at the town.'

'Be gentle with them,' Alfred said. 'They've been through a lot this day.' He jumped back over the side of the longship and onto the muddy beach, heading for the damaged vessel whose need for repairs had allowed the West Saxons to win this victory in the first place. Wulfric was there, hands on his hips, watching as the last of the enemy's corpses were thrown into the hull like sacks of grain and he glanced around at Alfred's approach.

'The ship has been emptied, lord,' he said. 'The booty will be transferred to Diuma's ship.'

'And the weapons and valuables taken from the Danes' bodies? I want all that kept separate. That's Aethelred's, to be split as he sees fit.'

Wulfric smiled. 'Of course,' he said. 'I know how this works, Alfred.'

The aetheling allowed himself to mirror his captain's smile. 'Yes,' he said. 'Better than any of us.'

'That's the last of it, my lord,' a man shouted, handing a sack of plunder to one of his fellows on the riverside and then clambering out of the ship himself.

'Good, well done, lads,' Alfred shouted. He glanced over at Diuma, standing on board the other longship with its cargo of freed prisoners. 'Ready?' he called to the thane.

Diuma waved back. 'Ready, my lord!'

'Let's get you moving then.'

The warriors on the beach grabbed the ship and, teeth bared, put all their weight behind shoving the vessel into the Tamyse. Soon their efforts had the prow in the water and things became easier then.

'Nearly there, lads!' Alfred called, and he was there with them, feet slipping, arms and thighs straining, and then the weight was gone and he was splashing into the water as the longship moved away. The sail was not raised yet, and Diuma called for his men to use the oars to keep them on course in the middle of the water.

'See you in Dorcaestre, lord,' Diuma called as they floated away, waving to Alfred who grinned and pointed his men towards the final ship.

'Push it into the river, and set it alight.'

A fire had already been kindled nearby, and, again, Alfred thanked God for Wulfric. The captain certainly knew his business. Ironically, the holed ship seemed to have been repaired by the Danes for, when it was heaved into the Tamyse by the West Saxon warriors it bobbed quite well on the water, held in place by a pair of ropes fastened to thick trees. Had Alfred known that he might not have been so quick to order it destroyed but it was too late to worry about that now.

Branches were set ablaze and tossed across, into the keel. Some went out almost instantly, but others spread the flames to the clothes worn by the dead Danes, and then the ropes and sail caught light, and soon the entire hull with its coating of highly flammable tar was burning fiercely. Even in the daylight it was quite a sight, as the flames grew in intensity and embers were cast into the air, little glowing sparks that sizzled as they fell and hit the water.

'Cast if off,' Alfred ordered, holding up a hand to shield his face, for the heat was tremendous even at this distance. The ropes anchoring the burning ship in place were cut and the stench of woodsmoke and roasting flesh filled the air along with thick, black smoke as the vessel was carried away by the Tamyse.

'Won't it just get stuck at the next bend?' someone asked softly, but Alfred didn't care what happened to the ship now. It would burn long enough to deal with the corpses and, if it didn't just sink into the river, it would send a message to any other sea-wolves sailing this way.

Alfred and Wulfric went to their horses and mounted up as the fire that had been set on the grass was extinguished and then the victorious West Saxon army began the journey back to King Aethelred in Dorcaestre.

'It's been a long day,' Alfred said to his captain as they left the battlefield behind.

'Aye,' Wulfric agreed. 'It has, my lord. But this is just the beginning. I fear we'll have many more months of battles to look forward to, and not all of them will end so well for us...'

CHAPTER SIXTEEN

The church in Dorcaestre was not made from stone, just timber, yet it had survived the attack by the Northmen. Either the raiders had not known what it was, and it was admittedly a fairly small building, or, more likely, they simply didn't care enough to burn it down.

'Why not?' Alfred asked his priest, Oswald, as they stood within the church, having spent a good part of the last hour offering prayers to God. 'Don't the heathen scum despise Christ and the saints?'

Oswald pursed his lips, gazing at the bare altar. 'No, they worship many different gods and goddesses: Óðinn, Þórr, Frigg, Freyja, Frey, Loki, Baldur, Heimdall...' He trailed off, but Alfred felt like the priest could have continued listing names all day. 'The point is, the Danes don't mind who venerates what deity. It's a personal matter for them. They don't care if someone wants to follow Christ – in fact, a few of King Halfdan's *vikingar* may have already been baptised in our faith. Personally, I think most of the invaders are quite bemused by our belief in the One True God, rather than fearful of it.' He looked up and clasped his hands together. 'So, they allowed this church to remain standing.'

Alfred nodded thoughtfully. 'Still took all the treasures from it though.'

'Indeed,' Oswald agreed. 'Like I say, they don't fear our God, or care enough to try and disrupt our worshipping Him, but they won't miss any opportunity to steal gold or silver.'

'That's all they live for,' the aetheling muttered. 'Fighting, and fornicating, and wealth.'

Oswald threw him a wry look then stepped forward and ran a hand across the smooth, bare altar. 'We will rebuild, my lord,' he said with conviction. 'We'll bring Dorcaestre back to its former glory, and this church will be filled once more with treasures worthy of a house of God.'

'What's the point?' Alfred demanded, suddenly flaring into anger and coming to stand on the opposite side of the altar, facing the priest. 'The heathen bastards will just come back another day, and do it all again. We *cannot stop them*!' He winced and held a hand to his stomach as pain lanced through him but quickly faded.

Oswald watched him, a worried expression on his round face. 'You must have faith, Alfred,' he said levelly.

'Faith?' Alfred's mouth twisted as he practically shouted the word, making it sound like a curse. 'What if Halfdan, and Ivar, and Ubba, and all the rest of the pagan raiders, are right? What if their gods are the real ones, and Christ is...' He broke off, face pale as he realised what he was saying. Tears were in his eyes, and he went across to sit on a bench that was set against the northern wall. 'Forgive me,' he said. 'God, forgive me, but sometimes that's how it seems.'

Oswald came over to join him on the bench and Alfred half-expected the priest to put his arm around him consolingly. The prince might have welcomed it, for he could do with some comforting, but Oswald was not the type to act in such a familiar manner even though they'd known one another for years.

'I understand,' said the priest. 'And you are not the first man I've heard saying such things. It truly does seem like the Danes, Norse, whatever they are, have been sent here as some kind of punishment. But let us think about what you suggested: that Þórr and Óðinn are the 'true' gods, and that is why Halfdan's great heathen army is so powerful.'

Alfred contemplated the priest warily, wondering where this was going. 'All right,' he murmured.

'Are you going to surrender to them, then? Knowing they have divine assistance, while you would have none?'

The prince frowned. 'Of course not. My duty is to protect my people. My wife, and the child she carries.'

'But if there is no hope of ever defeating the Danes,' Oswald demanded. 'What would be the point in trying?'

Alfred stared at him in confusion. 'Are you saying we should just give in? Let Halfdan have Wessex?'

Oswald sighed. 'No, I'm asking what the point is in fighting if there is no hope of winning.'

'There is always hope,' Alfred replied. 'There has to be.'

'Then is it better to believe the Danes are stronger than us, and have the gods on their side? An unstoppable force, essentially. Or,' he reached out and tapped Alfred's sword hilt with his hand. 'Is it better to believe that they are a plague sent by Satan to test us, to punish us?'

The prince stood up and paced towards the empty altar, then back again towards the doors. 'One is futile,' he said. 'Hopeless. While the other...' He stopped pacing and looked down at Oswald who was smiling back.

'Exactly. You must have hope, and you must have faith, my lord. You, especially. If you, or your brother, give in to despair, what chance will your people have? Life is hard enough for the poor worker in the field without being told a plague of devils is coming to take everything he loves and there's nothing he can do about it. Besides, you are not alone. You have strong ealdormen like Aethelwulf, and Odda of Devon, to stand with you.'

Alfred nodded and gripped the handle of his sword while retaking his place on the bench next to the priest. 'You're right. And the fact this church still stands is a symbol of that *hope* that we must cling to. The Danes may not fear Christ enough to destroy His places of worship, but that is their weakness. They're too arrogant to believe our God is as strong as theirs, or that we, followers of Christ, can be a threat to them.'

'Then you must prove them wrong, my lord,' Oswald said encouragingly.

Alfred's eyes were shining now as the thoughts whirled within his head. 'It truly is a battle between good and evil,' he growled. 'How else could anyone see it? Halfdan's army do not create beauty, or improve the lands they take. They destroy, and rape, and bring nothing but misery to every town they visit. They are nothing but locusts!' He stood up, fists clenched, and his earlier despair had completely evaporated by now. 'But Halfdan is not Moses, my brother is not Pharoah, and Wessex is not Egypt.'

Oswald grinned at the rather crude analogy. 'Indeed,' he said.

'Thank you,' Alfred said bowing to the priest and crossing himself in the direction of the altar with its missing gold cross which had, unfortunately, not been amongst the plunder recovered from the two captured Danish ships. 'For opening my eyes, and restoring my sense of purpose.'

'That's the job of a priest,' Oswald said with a serene smile. 'I'm happy to have helped.'

'And I'm happy I brought you along as part of my retinue from Ceodre,' the prince said. 'Your wisdom will help guide me through this war, I'm certain of it.' With that, he strode from the little church, head held high, eyes shining with the glory of God and the righteous desire to see Halfdan's heathen army destroyed once and for all.

–

'Tell us a story, then, brother!'

Smoke was billowing from the chimney holes in the long hall's roof as great joints of pork and beef were roasted for the waiting army. As the warriors waited for the well-earned feast they downed copious amounts of mead, ale and wine, as if there was an endless supply. Which there might as well have been, for the army would move on from that town within the next few days, long before its stocks of food and drink were exhausted.

There might not be much left for the locals to survive on, but the laughing, singing men within the hall cared nothing for that.

'A story about what?' Halfdan asked, and even he was quite drunk, for their raiding had been hugely profitable since they'd sailed along the Tamyse into Wessex and barely faced any resistance. If ever there was a day when a man was allowed to get shit-faced, Halfdan thought, today was that day.

'The gods,' Ubba replied, grinning and raising his overflowing mug in the air. 'Your favourite subject.'

'That is true,' Halfdan admitted happily. 'And why not, when they've given us such easy victories so far?'

When the pagan horde left Dorcaestre they'd continued along the river, looking for more places to plunder. The people of Bensingtun had been shocked to find themselves facing hundreds of enemy warriors coming towards their town and, although they'd tried their best to offer some resistance to the Danes, it had been utterly futile. Just like in Dorcaestre, the defenders were slaughtered, and the victorious heathen army was led into the town by King Halfdan where the men were allowed to do whatever they wished to the inhabitants and their possessions.

The ealdorman of the West Saxon settlement, Wynnstan, had been found within this very hall, his hall, too frightened to take up arms against the invaders and stand beside his people in the shieldwall. Wynnstan should have made a good warrior too, being tall and broad, with piercing blue eyes, bristling sideburns and a long moustache. Yet he'd held up his hands as Halfdan and Ubba walked towards him, and begged them not to hurt him.

Ubba would gladly have ignored his pleas, and did strike him more than once with the shaft of his spear, knocking him to the ground with blood pouring from his freckled, bald, pate. Halfdan decided Wynnstan should be left alone though, for now at least, for he might be useful or, if not, provide some better entertainment than being beaten to death by Ubba.

'A story then!' the Danish king said with a smile, and Ubba cheered drunkenly as did the nearest men who'd heard Halfdan's pronouncement. Word quickly spread through the rest of the warriors gathered in the hall and everyone fell quiet, waiting to hear the tale. There were skalds and bards amongst the army of course – men who told stories, recited poetry, and sang songs. There were wise-women too, the famed, and feared, volur, who performed much the same functions as their male counterparts along with divination, spell-casting and other acts of magic.

Everyone knew Halfdan was as good a tale-teller as any of them.

'Do you all know the story of Þórr's wedding?' the king asked, standing up and coming down from the dais which supported his table. He looked around at the men, some of whom nodded, eyes glinting in the firelight, evidently pleased by the thought of this favourite old story. Others seemed confused, as if they'd never heard the tale before, or perhaps some variant of it that didn't fit what Halfdan had said.

'Tell us, lord,' one of the men sitting beside the firepit said, grinning. Those on the bench next to him called agreement, even thumping their mugs on the table, caring little for the ale that was spilled.

Halfdan eyed the warriors, recognising them as hailing from a small settlement on the coast of Jutland.

'Have you heard it before, Orvar?'

The man he'd addressed smiled, happy that the king knew his name. 'I have, lord,' he replied. 'But I've never heard you tell it, and it's a good tale.'

Halfdan nodded as the other revellers called agreement with Orvar's words, and he spread his hands wide before standing back up on the dais and lifting a ceramic cup filled with mead. 'Then fill your mugs, and listen,' he said grandly, tipping back the cup and swallowing its contents in one go. 'To the story of Þórr's wedding!'

He gave them a few moments to do as he'd commanded for he wanted his audience to be as quiet as possible while he spoke. The smoky atmosphere was not ideal for any storyteller, and he did not want to be interrupted any more than necessary.

'One morning,' he began, and was happy to see he had the men's full attention. 'One morning, Þórr woke from a deep sleep and realised his mighty war-hammer, Mjölnir, was not by his bed. It had been stolen.'

The warriors muttered and growled at this, for everyone was familiar with Mjölnir, and Þórr's bond with the magical weapon.

'Now, Þórr knew immediately who had taken his hammer: Thrym, King of the Giants. Thrym had been boasting for months that he wanted Mjölnir for himself and would take it one day from Þórr. The problem was, Thrym lived with the rest of the giants in Jotunheim, a lawless wilderness filled with inhabitants who were hostile to Þórr and the other gods. So, what could be done?'

Halfdan stepped down and walked amongst the warriors on benches, every face turned to him, ruddy from drink and the firepit's warmth.

'Attack the giants!' a warrior shouted, beard bristling.

'Aye, Mjölnir is too valuable to be left with the giants,' another agreed, and voices were raised indignantly at Thrym's audacity.

'True,' Halfdan shouted, bringing his listeners to order once more. 'Mjölnir was not a simple hammer. It could channel lightning and was a symbol of Þórr's power. Its theft was a terrible outrage that could not go unanswered. So, Þórr went to see Loki, the trickster, and asked him to visit Jotunheim, to see if there was any way Mjölnir could be recovered. Now, even Loki could not simply wander into the giants' homelands, but, with the help of Freyja, he was transformed into a great bird.' Halfdan raised his arms, like wings, and with a grin, pretended to fly towards his brother, Ubba, still seated at the high table.

'Loki flew to Jotunheim, straight to Thrym's mighty fortress of Utgard. And there he spoke with the giant, who freely admitted he'd stolen Þórr's hammer, buried it *eight miles* beneath the fortress, and would only return it if Freyja would marry him.'

The men, who'd been smiling as Halfdan pretended to be a bird, shouted in outrage at this. Although gods did sometimes marry giants, for Thrym to manipulate them, particularly beautiful Freyja, in such an underhand way was abhorrent.

A girl carrying drinks walked past and Halfdan lifted a mug of ale from it, bowing slightly to her and smiling, although she was a ceorl even among her own Saxon people. He sipped from it, easing his throat, and the girl bustled away, her load of drinks soon emptied by the thirsty Northmen.

'What else could Þórr do, but ask Freyja to marry Thrym? He had to get his hammer back, after all. Freyja would have none of it, though.' Halfdan affected a high-pitched, female voice as he went on, '"I'm not going to Jotunheim to be that idiot's bride," said Freyja. "If you want your hammer back, you'd better go to Utgard yourself and start digging."' His voice returned to its normal pitch as he said, sadly, 'All seemed lost.'

He took another sip of the ale, revelling in the warmth from the fire, and the drinks he'd imbibed, and felt like something close to a god himself. He turned to look at Ubba, and a rare rush of brotherly love filled him. Their father, Ragnar, had been a mighty king, but even he had not achieved what Halfdan had, and they were only just beginning that year's campaign.

'What did Þórr do?' Orvar asked, bringing Halfdan back to himself with a start.

'Well, he spoke with the other gods, asking their advice. Heimdall had an idea. "If someone stole Gjallarhorn," he said, showing Þórr his mighty horn, whose blast could be heard in all nine worlds. "I would do anything to get it back. Therefore, if Freyja will not go to Thrym, *you* must put on her dress, Þórr, and her veil, and pretend to be her. Go to Utgard yourself to marry him. That," avowed Heimdall, "is what I'd do."'

The men in the hall thought of this and found it hilarious. In their minds, Þórr, the Thunder God, was a tall, bearded warrior – the very pinnacle of manhood. The mental image of such a one putting on a dress and acting like a woman seemed ludicrous.

'I know,' Halfdan shouted, slapping a nearby man on the back and they laughed together. 'It sounds like a preposterous idea, and yet, that is what Þórr did. He borrowed Freyja's dress, and hid his face with her veil, then Loki shapeshifted into the form of a beautiful woman and together they travelled to Jotunheim where Thrym joyfully brought them into his fortress.'

Halfdan lifted a piece of roast pork from a trencher on one of the tables and chewed it thoughtfully, never standing still but stalking between the seated men, smiling as he ate. The *vikingar* watched him, thoroughly enjoying his tale if their expressions were anything to go by. When he finished the meat he licked his fingers, took a sip from his ale, belched loudly and then went on with the story.

'Thrym commanded his giants to arrange a wedding feast, and he sat at the high table with his bride-to-be, Þórr, and Loki. All was going well, with much meat and drink and singing and dancing and games and stories… And then Thrym realised Þórr had eaten a whole oxen, and drank three barrels of mead. Three!'

'That's nothing,' a massive, blond hersir shouted. 'I'm going to drink that tonight!'

'You'll try, Brynjar,' Halfdan called back. 'But you'll piss your pants again, long before you even finish the first barrel.'

Everyone roared with laughter at that, even Brynjar, who raised his ale mug and emptied it into his mouth, although most of it spilled out and down his yellow beard.

'Three barrels of mead,' the Danish king repeated in amazement. 'Understandably, Thrym was astonished, and suspicious, for he had never seen a woman eat and drink so much. But clever Loki shook his head and told the giant that

"Freyja" was so excited about marrying Thrym that she hadn't been able to eat or drink anything for days. Now, appetite restored, "she" was making up for lost time.' Halfdan shook his head. 'Thrym, perhaps not the cleverest of giants, believed Loki's lie, and so the feast continued.'

As if remembering he, too, was at a feast, Halfdan gestured to one of the men who was filling a mug with ale for himself. The man, already bleary eyed from drink, took a few moments to understand what the king meant, and then he grinned stupidly and stumbled over to give Halfdan the mug. 'There you go, my lord,' he slurred, then turned, tripping over his own feet and falling over, the jug smashing and spilling its foaming contents all over the straw. As is the tradition in such situations, the whole place erupted in cheering and laughter while the unfortunate warrior picked himself up, face flushing scarlet, and sat down on the nearest bench.

'My thanks,' Halfdan said, raising his mug to the embarrassed man which only brought more laughter. The king took a long pull and then, chuckling, looked into the dancing flames in the firepit and returned to his story. 'Thrym, King of the Jötnar, was so pleased that his bride-to-be was looking forward to their wedding that he asked for a kiss from "her".' He mimicked lifting a veil, puckering his lips as he did so. 'But, when Thrym saw Þórr's eyes, burning with hatred and fury, the giant became suspicious once more. Loki said to him, "No, my lord, she is looking forward so much to your wedding that she's not been able to sleep for days, and that's why her eyes have gone all funny."'

Halfdan put on an exaggerated female voice, and made the faces he was describing, and everyone in the hall was greatly enjoying the performance.

'Thrym once more believed Loki's lie, and, overjoyed at the coming union, called for Mjölnir to be brought out and placed in his betrothed's lap, that it might be used to bless the marriage. Soon enough, the magical weapon was carried forth and, as soon as it was given to Þórr, he threw off his dress and struck Thrym with Mjölnir until the King of the Jötnar was dead!' Flailing his arm about, wielding an invisible war-hammer, Halfdan cried, 'And then Þórr went on a murderous rampage, attacking the wedding guests until all were dead or had fled in terror!' He halted, eyes blazing, breathing heavily as if he had also been part of some epic battle, and upended the ale mug into his mouth. He'd worked his way around the entire hall during this final section of the tale and stepped back up onto the raised dais with the high table where his brother sat.

'What happened after that?' Ubba asked.

'After that?' Halfdan took his seat at the middle of the table and leaned back, smiling contentedly. 'After that, Þórr and Loki went home to Asgard with Mjölnir, and that was the end of the tale.'

The men cheered and thumped mugs on tables, chanting, 'Þórr! Þórr! Þórr!' The thunder god was generally the favourite amongst the warriors, along with one-eyed Óðinn. Stories about them always went down well, as Halfdan knew. He raised his arms above his head and waited for the chanting to subside.

'Eat and drink your fill, my friends,' he said, gazing out at them all with a serene smile. 'But try not to overdo it, eh? For we have many more Saxon settlements to conquer in the coming days, and I would have you all fit to fight at my side and share in the plunder we take!'

Predictably enough the place erupted once more and, although it was already late, the feast continued with renewed vigour, the bawdy singing and shouting filling the surrounding town and reminding the beaten locals, as if they needed reminding, that the Danes had finally come to take Wessex.

PART TWO

CHAPTER SEVENTEEN

Ceodre, AD 870

November

'Is she safe? Please, God, tell me she's safe!'

'My lord.' The midwife nodded her head reassuringly, although the bloodstains on her apron did nothing to alleviate Alfred's fears. He'd been in the field, patrolling with his warband when word came that his wife, Ealhswith, had gone into labour, and he'd ridden to Ceodre as fast as he could, leaving Wulfric in charge of the men. 'The lady is perfectly fine. Just tired. It was a long birth.'

Alfred practically burst into tears for, although he'd only been married for a short time, he'd already lost most of his family members and did not want to lose his wife before they could start a family of their own. 'What about my...'

'Daughter,' the midwife said, watching his face.

The prince knew she was looking to see if he was disappointed not to have been borne a son, but tears did come to his eyes now and he laughed joyfully. 'A daughter,' he said. 'My daughter. Is she—'

'She's fine, my lord.' The woman took his arm in a surprisingly familiar manner, but Alfred had always been good to his servants and the midwife must have known this. 'You can come in and see them, but please try to let them rest.'

Alfred nodded, and then he looked at the woman's face, realising he had absolutely no idea what to expect when he went into the birthing chamber. 'Are they… clean?' he asked, embarrassment making him blush.

'Yes.' The midwife smiled and opened the heavy door. 'We cleaned them up. The birth was hours ago now.'

Alfred nodded, swallowed, and followed her into the chamber, almost feeling like he was about to ride into battle.

Although it was deep into November and frost rimed the land outside the hall, the birthing room was warm, and smelled very strongly of… The aetheling was not sure what all the smells were – sweat, blood, woodsmoke, and God knew what else. Ealhswith was lying in a large bed, head propped up on a pillow, paler than he'd ever seen her before. She smiled though, when she saw him approaching, and she was not alone.

Their daughter was in her arms, sleeping.

Ealhswith saw her husband's face, and the happiness in his eyes, and she too smiled as he came over and kissed her on the forehead, pushing back a strand of hair and gazing down at her. He looked from her to the baby and felt overwhelmed for a moment, but the midwife placed a stool behind him and he sat down with a murmur of thanks. 'Are you well?' he asked.

His wife nodded. 'Yes,' she said. 'It was hard, Alfred. Very hard, and seemed to take a long time. But they took good care of me and…' She softly stroked the child's soft, downy hair. 'It was worth all the pain. *She* was worth it.'

'My lord. Lady.' The midwife was standing beside them again, but the other women in the room were walking out of the door. 'We'll leave you alone now. Would you like me to take the baby?'

Ealhswith shook her head. 'No, thank you. She's quite happy where she is.'

'As you wish, my lady. Just call if you need anything.'

The proud new mother smiled gratefully but was clearly exhausted and Alfred felt a stab of curiosity, wishing he'd been there earlier to get some idea of the ordeal his wife had gone through. He'd never seen a baby being born, but he knew it was not an easy thing and he felt guilty that he couldn't share, or in some way lessen, Ealhswith's pain.

The door closed behind them and, alone, they both simply stared at the new life they had created together. 'God be praised,' the aetheling whispered, reaching out to touch his daughter's tiny hand.

'What would you like to name her?' Ealhswith asked.

Alfred pursed his lips, never taking his eyes from the tiny girl. 'I'm not sure. Perhaps Osburh, after my mother? Unless you have anything—'

'Aethelflaed,' his wife said, so quickly that it was clear she'd been thinking about it long before Alfred had arrived.

'"Noble Beauty",' he said, giving the meaning of the name and nodding. 'Yes, I think that fits her perfectly. Baby Aethel-flaed, welcome to the world.'

'Would you like to hold her?'

Alfred hesitated. He had held his brother's children when they were just babies, but Aethelflaed was quite content resting in her mother's arms, and he didn't want to disturb her. He would have plenty of time to hold her in the coming days.

Unless the damned Danes attacked another settlement.

'How's the war going?' Ealhswith asked, as if reading his mind.

He waved his hand and sighed. 'Well, the Northmen have been quiet since winter came, but they still hold some of our towns.' He glanced over his shoulder at the door, as if fearful the nursemaids might be outside listening to their conversation. 'Aethelred hoped they would return to East Anglia once autumn came. Many of them have, thankfully, but some are still in our lands. At least winter should put a stop to their raiding for a while.'

'Are they as brutal as people say?'

'It's not so much that,' he told her gloomily. 'They just won't stand still long enough for us to bring them to battle. By the time we react, the Danes have moved on.' He shook his head, jaw clenched. 'Or they take one of our towns and fortify it, meaning we can't do anything without a siege, which we just don't have the resources for. I wish we could just catch them in the open, even once. I think our army would be a match for them, and it might bloody their nose badly enough that they'd leave our lands for good. Go find easier pickings.'

'Like Mercia.'

Alfred blanched. He'd momentarily forgotten where Ealhswith hailed from, and where her father was still an ealdorman. 'Sorry,' he said.

'It's fine,' she replied, absent-mindedly caressing their daughter's head. 'Now that we have Aethelflaed to protect I share your sentiments. It would be good if Halfdan would just leave us alone, even if that meant the heathen army returning to Mercia. If what you say is true, though, and the Danes are facing little resistance here in Wessex, well...'

'No,' Alfred murmured. 'They'll not be leaving any time soon.'

'Are we,' she glanced down at the baby, who took a deep breath but remained asleep, 'safe here?'

The prince nodded firmly. 'Aye. Ceodre is far enough away from the rivers the Danes use to move around.' He tipped his head on one side thoughtfully, wondering if those hated longships might sail all the way around the southern shore of the island and attack the eastern coast of Wessex. He knew the Danes had been around the Severn Sea thirty or so years ago when they'd joined forces with the locals and fought against Ecgberht, then King of Wessex. It was just as well, for, had the invaders been successful then they could have gained a foothold in the peninsula, allowing them to strike against Wessex from the east. The thought made his blood turn to ice, but he pushed it away. Thus far nothing of the sort had happened, and they had enough to worry about.

'Do they not travel by land very much?' Ealhswith asked.

'Yes, they can move fast by land as well,' he said. 'Especially with all the horses Edmund gave them when they first struck

East Anglia. They've taken more from other places since, of course so…' He sighed in disgust. 'The bastards are always one step ahead of us.'

They sat in silence for a time, the earlier happy mood somewhat tempered by thoughts of a gloomy future.

'What will we do?' Ealhswith asked eventually.

Alfred shrugged his broad shoulders. 'I don't know. Aethelred is king, and I don't envy him having to lead us through this. I imagine we'll end up paying the raiders off with silver and whatever else they demand. More horses probably!'

'They'll just come back.'

'Of course. It's a self-defeating circle,' he lamented. 'The Danes come because they know they can take plunder practically unimpeded, and eventually they'll be paid to leave. Why would they not return the following spring and do it all over again?'

'Well, then,' Ealhswith said. 'We must find a way to stop them.'

Alfred took her hand in hers and squeezed it, smiling indulgently at her. 'Easier said than done, my love,' he said.

'And yet,' she replied simply, 'it must be done. Aethelred, and you, as the aetheling, will come up with a way, where all other Saxon kings have failed.' He met her gaze, wondering at her words, but she smiled brightly. 'We've only been married for a short time, Alfred, but I know you. I know that, if anyone can find a way to stop the Danish raids, it will be you.'

He took that in, thinking that she was trying to make a joke which he was too dense to comprehend, but she was not. She truly believed in him, and her faith surprised him. She was an insightful and sharp young woman, and her opinion mattered a great deal to Alfred. It gave him confidence, and, at that moment, he knew he had to be worthy of her high opinion of his abilities. Could they stop the Danes without paying them off?

He remembered his discussion with the priest, Oswald, and the belief their talk had inspired within him, that they could indeed defeat the invaders. That earlier feeling of righteous purpose, and the joy it had engendered, refilled him and he leaned forward, kissing Ealhswith softly on the mouth. The stool he was sitting on creaked and suddenly Alfred found himself gazing down into the blue eyes of his newly awakened baby daughter. They looked at one another for a moment, and then Aethelflaed opened her mouth and began to cry.

'What's wrong?' he asked, startled by the strangely upsetting sound. 'Is she alright?'

Ealhswith laughed much harder than the prince thought necessary. 'Of course she is. She's just hungry, there's nothing to worry about, you silly man. Go on, fetch the wetnurse, and then, while Aethelflaed is being fed, you can read to me.'

He was already hurrying to the door, the baby's lusty cries somehow more fearsome than the screams of any attacking Dane.

–

'Are you enjoying being at home with us?' Ealhswith asked, popping a piece of buttered bread into her mouth and chewing slowly, with relish. She had regained her colour and looked like her usual self again after the baby's birth a month ago.

Alfred smiled at little Aethelflaed and touched her lightly on the nose. Her eyes widened but she did not laugh, she simply stared at the spot where his finger had been, and then up at his face. 'Of course,' he said. 'But Aethelred wants me back out patrolling with the fyrd as soon as possible, just as Wulfric is away doing just now. The Danes might have mostly returned to their base in East Anglia for winter, but some remain in Wessex and who knows what mischief they might get up to if they think we're not watching for them?'

His wife nodded but she was plainly saddened by the news. Although there were more than enough servants to make taking care of a newborn much less of a chore than it might be for a lady of lower social standing, she would surely have liked to see more of Alfred. He reached out and gave her hand a squeeze, sharing her feelings.

There was a knock on the door – they were in their private chamber, away from the bustle of the main hall – and the prince bade the visitor enter. His heart sank when he saw it was not one of the midwives, but a soldier.

'My lord,' the man said, bowing respectfully to both Alfred and Ealhswith. He barely seemed to register the baby and Alfred wasn't sure what to make of that. Little Aethelflaed was royalty after all, but what was proper etiquette for a common soldier upon meeting the king's cousin?

'Good morning,' Alfred said. 'I take it something has happened?'

'Yes, my lord,' the messenger replied. 'Good news.'

Alfred's face lit up for he'd been expecting to hear a report of something unpleasant, like another attack by the Danes, or even the death of some powerful West Saxon nobleman in the field. 'Really?' he asked, looking at Ealhswith and sharing a hopeful smile with her. 'Let's hear it then. Have the Northmen decided to leave our lands?'

'No, lord,' the messenger said, apparently oblivious to the humour in the prince's question. 'They – the Danes I mean – attacked Reading a few days ago, and took control.'

Alfred frowned. 'I thought you said you had good news. This is terrible! Reading is a royal vill.' He gingerly handed the baby to his wife and stood looking at the soldier, mind whirling. A vill was a royal estate, an administrative centre and, crucially, a place where the king's food rents were taken in and stored for the winter. To lose such a place was a devastating blow for Wessex, and an incredible boost for the raiders. Lack of food in the depths of winter, when there was little hunting and hardly a thing growing, was the main thing that traditionally kept warlords from campaigning at that time – now Halfdan's army would have a store of supplies ready at hand.

Alfred pictured in his mind the wealth of goods filling the storehouses in Reading at that moment: honey, loaves, ale, cows, geese, hens, cheeses, butter, salmon, eels, beef, and fodder for the animals, amongst other things.

Losing control of the town was a disaster.

'Yes, my lord, but Aethelwulf, Ealdorman of Berrocscire, met some of the raiders in battle a few days after that, and *defeated them!*'

Alfred could not help gaping at the messenger, so astonished was he. His open-mouthed stare soon turned to a lupine grin, however, as he realised this truly was good news.

'Who is Aethelwulf?' Ealhswith asked. 'I don't think I've met him.'

'No, you haven't yet,' Alfred confirmed. 'But Aethelwulf, well…' He trailed off and looked at her happily. 'Aethelwulf is Wessex's most experienced commander. He's won more battles than anyone in these lands. A true warrior.'

The messenger was nodding. 'He has the Danes penned up in Reading, my lord. King Aethelred is already on the way to join him.'

'Reading is a few days' march from here,' Alfred mused. 'With Ealdorman Aethelwulf's fyrd, and my brother's, that should be enough to deal with the enemy army. Would it be wise for me to join them, and leave Ceodre and the other lands in the east undefended?'

The messenger did not reply. It was not his place to offer counsel on such lofty matters, and Alfred wished Wulfric, or Aethelred, or one of his other advisors, were there at his side, for he could not make up his mind how to proceed. What if he took the fyrd away, and more of the Northmen landed their cursed longships on the southern coast? They could force their way north and end up taking Ceodre, along with Ealhswith and Aethelflaed… Maybe he should send word for Wulfric to return from his patrols so they could decide what to do together.

'You must go, and take this chance to crush the Danes.'

Alfred looked at Ealhswith in surprise. 'You think so?'

'Of course,' she said firmly. 'There are other fyrds to the south, in Dorcaestre and Polle for example, that can defend

146

Aethelred's lands if need be, and stop any possible advance from the coast up to here.'

Alfred grinned. He trusted his wife's judgement, and it was a relief to share the responsibility of how to proceed with her. 'You're right! I agree, this is the right thing to do. Thank you, my lady, for your advice.'

Now that it was settled, he was eager to reach his brother and the mighty ealdorman, Aethelwulf, who'd given them this opportunity to strike a truly tremendous blow against the Northmen. 'I'll muster the rest of the fyrd here in Ceodre, and send word for Wulfric to meet us on the road.' He kissed his wife and daughter farewell and then, face aglow, as if he'd seen a vision of Christ himself, he gestured to the messenger to go out into the hall. 'Rest, friend,' he told the man, following him out into the much smokier, noisier section of the great building. 'I'll see you're rewarded for your service today but, for now, I must get our troops ready to march.'

The messenger grinned. 'Thank you, my lord. I'll travel with you when you go, if that's all right.'

'Of course,' Alfred said. 'Now, I'd better get moving. The Danes won't hang around at Reading forever and I want to be there when Halfdan finally gets his arse kicked!'

CHAPTER EIGHTEEN

Capturing Reading was a clever move by the Danes and proved that Halfdan and his jarls had knowledge of the areas they were raiding. They hadn't just stumbled upon this town by sheer chance, they had targeted it, for Reading was located at the confluence of the Rivers Tamyse and Kennet. These natural defences had been supplemented, Alfred soon discovered, by the addition of an earthen rampart, providing Halfdan's army with a triangular stronghold boasting rivers on two sides and the rampart on the third.

'The bastards are clever,' Aethelred grumbled as he, Alfred and the Ealdorman of Berrocscire, Aethelwulf, sat on their horses gazing at the Viking earthwork. 'This was no random attack.'

'No,' Aethelwulf agreed, running a hand through his straw-coloured hair. 'They've sailed directly here on purpose. The rivers provide easy access for their ships, and there's plenty of places ripe for plunder nearby.'

'Like Abbandune Abbey,' Alfred said. 'And Wallingford isn't far away either.'

Aethelred muttered a quite un-Christian oath at that. Wallingford, like Reading, was a royal estate, and contained much wealth and many food supplies. Whoever controlled those towns immediately gained a great advantage.

The strange thing was, although Reading had fallen to the Danes, their army was not inside the walls. It was arrayed outside them, as if preparing for battle.

'This is not like them,' the king said, gazing at the host arrayed before them. 'From what we've heard, and from the evidence of past raids, the Danes don't usually like to meet in battle if it can be avoided. Why are they not hiding behind that rampart they've built?'

Aethelwulf turned to Aethelred and said, smiling, 'My men gave them quite a beating, lord. It looks like they want revenge for those we slaughtered.'

'Ah, indeed,' the king said cheerfully. 'We heard about your victory – another to add to your long list. Men still tell tales of that victory of yours against the Danes, what, ten years back? When you drove them from Wintanceaster against all odds. What happened this time?'

The ealdorman was too experienced to allow the king's praise to affect him, but he did offer a grim smile in response. 'I heard about their attack here in Reading,' he said. 'So I mustered my men and rode out to meet them. We had reports that two of their jarls were heading towards Englafeld.' He noticed Alfred's puzzled frown. 'It's just a small village, my lord.'

The aetheling nodded, ashamed that he wasn't familiar with the name, but he simply could not place it. He watched Aethelwulf as the ealdorman continued, somewhat in awe of the man who was a hero of great renown amongst the people of Wessex. Few commanders had defeated Danish raiders in the field, but Aethelwulf had managed it on several occasions. Alfred was glad to know they had him on their side. Neither he nor his brother had as much experience in battle, so the likes of Aethelwulf would be invaluable if they were to smash the great heathen army here.

'Anyway,' the ealdorman continued, oblivious to Alfred's scrutiny, 'we made our way to Englafeld and ambushed the two Danish jarls. Cut them off from the road so they couldn't sneak back here to their comrades in Reading without fighting us.'

'Jarls?' Aethelred asked. 'Who were they? Did you know them?' His voice had a hopeful tone in it, as if he hoped one of the most powerful warlords had been in that beaten warband.

'One of them we recognised,' Aethelwulf nodded. 'Once we got into it with them, and my men started to push them back, I met their leader myself. Sidroc.' He looked from the king to Alfred but neither showed any sign of recognition. 'A young man, apparently one of the most brutal of all the Danish jarls, or so I've heard.'

A crow shrieked overhead and Alfred glanced up at it, noticing a whole host of corvids had gathered in anticipation of the coming slaughter. 'Did he escape?' he asked the ealdorman.

'No,' Aethelwulf replied. 'I tore half his face off with my spear. He was trampled underfoot when he fell, screaming in the mud.'

The king laughed as if he'd heard a great joke. 'Good,' he grunted. 'I hope the bastard suffered.'

'When his men realised he'd been killed they lost heart,' Aethelwulf said. 'Turned and ran, with us hard on their heels cutting down those we could catch. We followed them, and they led us here.' He shivered and pulled up the collar on his cloak as an icy gust of wind whistled around them. It was a bitterly cold day, and the men's breath steamed as they spoke, but it seemed the Danes had become bored with standing around freezing.

'My lords,' someone shouted and, when Alfred followed the man's pointing finger, he noticed the enemy army was coming towards them.

'Form up!' Aethelwulf roared, nodding to Aethelred and riding off towards his own Berrocscire fyrd who were arrayed on the left of the Saxon line.

'But we haven't heard Mass yet,' the king called after him. 'We can't go into battle without praising God first!'

'No time, my lord!' Aethelwulf shouted. 'I don't think the Danes will wait! There'll be plenty of time afterwards to thank God for our victory.'

'Ready, brother?' Aethelred asked, and, although his voice was steady he looked visibly frightened, and shaken not to have prepared himself spiritually for what was to come.

Alfred felt the same fear, but he forced a smile. 'Aye. God is with us, Aethelred. We've been praying for this day – for the Danes to stop running and meet us in the field.' He spread his arms wide, palms up, looking around at the frost-rimed grass surrounding both armies. 'The day has come, lord king, when we do what the Mercians, Angles and Northumbrians could never do: Drive the Northmen from our lands!'

Aethelred's fear seemed to dissipate as he listened to his younger sibling's speech. By the time Alfred finished the king was nodding and the corners of his mouth were twitching. 'You're right,' he agreed vehemently. 'By Christ and his saints, you're right.'

The Danes were much closer already, a long line of round shields painted in various colours and with different designs on them including bears, wolves, birds and mythical creatures like dragons.

'Lock shields!' Aethelred cried.

Alfred kicked his heels into his mount's flanks and raced back to his own men from Ceodre and the lands between there and Reading.

By the Glory of God, what was about to happen there on the battlefield would set the course of events in Wessex for generations to come. Alfred jumped down from his saddle, feet thudding painfully onto the frozen ground, and grabbed his spear from Wulfric.

'Ready, lord?' the ealdorman asked.

'Aye, Wulfric. Let's show these heathen bastards that Aethel-wulf's warriors aren't the only Saxons they need to fear.'

CHAPTER NINETEEN

There was no great military strategy in King Aethelred's approach to the battle – his men formed into a long shield-wall a few ranks deep, red banner with the golden dragon of Wessex held high in the front row, and they walked forward to meet the Danes. Halfdan's forces were similarly arrayed although there were less of them than the West Saxons. Still, the Danes were generally better armed, with more swords and axes than their opponents, many of whom were equipped with nothing but pointed ash staves. The raiders' armour was overall of a better quality too, and more of them wore decent helmets.

In reality, the men of Wessex were mostly farmers or employed in some other menial task during their daily lives. The Danes on the other hand were professional soldiers whose entire belief system was based around the glory of fighting and dying well in battle. They loved to fight – *lived* to fight – and had great experience of it, given their exploits of the past few years, conquering so many towns to the north and east of Wessex.

Alfred was not afraid, however, as the armies closed on one another. The initial feeling of panic, of impending doom, had passed and he felt confident that they could defeat the sea-wolves. The Saxons outnumbered their enemy by quite a margin after all, and Ealdorman Aethelwulf's earlier victory at Englafeld proved that the raiders, professional soldiers or not, could be beaten just like any other men.

On top of that, although the Danes were renowned for their ferocity and the sheer brutality with which they raided settlements, they did not want to be engaged in open warfare.

Standing toe-to-toe with an enemy on the battlefield was simply not how the likes of Halfdan, Ivar the Detestable, or Ragnar Lodbrok liked to do things.

Alfred thought of all this as the faces of individual enemy warriors slowly came into focus and it filled him with confidence. Aethelwulf beating the Danish foraging parties so easily had enraged Halfdan and led him to this.

The enemy king wanted to make a point. Wanted to show the Saxons who they were dealing with.

Well, it would be a mistake Halfdan would not forget.

'Brace!' Alfred bellowed, raising his shield and levelling his spear. He wore a very fine sword, of course, but there was no better weapon in a shieldwall than a thick, ash spear with an iron tip. Spears might have been much cheaper to make than swords, and generally viewed as a ceorl's weapon, but anyone who'd ever been in a battle like this one knew their value. Swords, axes, seaxes, all were useful in various situations, but this first, initial clash of shieldwalls was the place for a spear.

Alfred was completely focused on the army marching towards him and all thoughts of why spears were so useful were suddenly driven from his mind as something smashed into his shield. He felt the impact travelling up his arm, but he did not hear it for the air was filled now with grunts and thumps and cracks and, more distractingly, screams. Screams of rage, pain, exertion, even delight, were suddenly all around Alfred but he was staring fixedly at the shields before him. Trying to see the faces behind them, bare and unarmoured, perfect targets for the deadly iron point of his spear.

It never crossed his mind that being in one of the rear ranks of the shieldwall would be much safer than here. He was a warrior, and, as he felt his weapon stabbing home into soft flesh he roared with the same battle-lust any Danish raider would have felt. Teeth gritted, he pulled the spear back, noted the blood on the tip, and immediately thrust it at another target. Again, it met its mark and destroyed the pale neck of the Dane who was unlucky enough to be on the receiving end.

'Kill the bastards!' he shouted, feeling more alive than he ever had before. The sensation was incredible and he suddenly understood why the raiders came across the sea looking for battle and plunder. Then he remembered what those raiders did to the people they conquered and his joy faded. Instead he felt only a cold, righteous fury as he continued to knock aside attacks with his shield and aim thrusts of his own at the heaving, churning mass of bodies before him.

Eventually, after what felt like hours, his battle-fever began to wane along with his strength. The shield was heavy and, although he was muscular, his arm was beginning to ache. The constant pressure of needing to hold it up had taken a toll, as had the relentless use of his spear. 'Forward rank, move back!' he shouted but it came out as a cracked, hoarse bellow and he was forced to repeat the command more than once before it was heard and repeated along the line.

With a gasp of relief he stepped back and the rows of spearmen behind him moved forward, continuing the fight. The Danes must have followed suit and there was a renewed burst of noise all along the line as fresh troops did their best to kill as many of their enemies as possible. Alfred's head felt stiflingly hot beneath his helmet and a trickle of sweat ran down his neck, but he knew it would be folly to remove it. He pushed his way through the ranks of his infantry and found his horse, held by a young boy whose eyes were wide with fear and nervous excitement.

'Thank you, lad,' the prince muttered, trying to smile but managing only a tired grimace. 'Help me up, eh?' Normally Alfred could jump onto his mount's back without assistance, even in armour, but his legs felt shaky and he was glad when, after some effort, he hauled himself upright in the saddle. He did not have his spear anymore although he couldn't remember where it had gone. Had he dropped it? Given it to someone? Had it become lodged in a Danish shield, or a torso? It didn't matter, he was away from the fighting for now and he kicked his horse into a walk, staring out across his men, trying to gain some sense of how the battle was going.

Aethelred had mirrored his movements, and the king was also on horseback, looking exhausted but excited as he scanned the battle lines.

'How goes it?' Alfred called as he rode up to his brother. 'Are we winning?'

'We are,' Aethelred replied, and he looked as amazed as he was pleased. 'We greatly outnumber them and are beginning to wrap around their flanks. Look at Aethelwulf's fyrd.'

From their slightly elevated vantage point they were able to see the West Saxon forces at that end of the shieldwall were pushing back the Danes there. 'It's the same at the other side,' the king said with a fierce smile. 'We have them this time!'

Alfred looked along the rows of men, numbed by the noise and the sight of so many bodies lying on the ground where they'd been trampled as the Saxons pushed their enemies back towards the newly built rampart outside Reading. 'There's Halfdan!' he shouted, and Aethelred saw the Danish king at the same moment, right in the centre of the shieldwall, hacking away with an axe, his shield a shredded, tattered mass of splinters. He was fighting like a demon but he and his army were slowly being forced backwards towards the town they'd only recently captured.

'At least we know this will be the end of him once we finish them off here and retake Reading,' crowed the king. 'Christ be praised, our prayers have been answered. This will be the end of *all* the Northmen at last!'

'We're winning, lads!' Alfred roared triumphantly. 'Get into the bastards. Show them what it means to face the men of Wessex!'

His words lifted the men nearest to him and, grinning savagely, those in the front ranks redoubled their efforts, thrusting and hacking with even greater ferocity, while those behind called for their chance to deal death to the enemy. Even the poorest armed of their men, the ceorls with their sharpened sticks and felt hats in place of proper helms, were eager to join the fight.

War cries grew to a crescendo, with the West Saxon fyrd shouting, 'Out! Out!' to the Danes, exhorting them to leave their lands, and 'Godemite!': God Almighty. For surely this was a stunning victory for Christianity over the pantheon of Danish deities led by Þórr and Óðinn.

A movement behind the dwindling Danish army caught Alfred's eye then and he straightened in the saddle, trying to get a better view of the gates of Reading which had been open during the whole battle. 'Oh, God,' he muttered, mouth dropping open in shock as he realised what the movement was. 'They have reinforcements,' he cried, panic flooding through him at the sight of dozens of spearmen suddenly charging out of the town like wolves towards the fighting, led by a warrior he'd never seen before. For one hopeful moment he'd thought they might be West Saxon soldiers, perhaps sent by Aethelred to get inside Reading and attack the Danish shieldwall from behind, but that was not the case.

These newcomers were Northmen, they were legion, and they were splitting into two sections, heading for the flanks of their shieldwall which had, until now, been just about ready to collapse.

'What do we do?' Aethelred demanded, eyes bulging as he took in the terrible sight unfolding before them.

Alfred had no idea. Like his brother this was his first real experience of something as momentous as this and now, no longer having the greater numbers, there seemed little they could do. He didn't even know where Wulfric was, or if the captain yet lived. 'We need to speak with Ealdorman Aethel-wulf,' he said, trying to hold his voice steady. 'He'll know what to do.'

'Can you see him anywhere?' Aethelred demanded, kicking his horse into a trot towards the left flank of their army.

Alfred followed him, straining his eyes to try and make out the experienced ealdorman amongst the maelstrom of battle. They neared the far end of the shieldwall before, at last, they saw Aethelwulf there, still in the front rank, fighting just as hard as Halfdan was further along on the Danish side of the line.

'There he is,' Alfred shouted in relief, glad to see the finest general the West Saxon army had was still alive and going strong. 'Aethelwulf! Come here! Aethelwulf!'

The king joined in with his brother, shouting the name of the ealdorman as loudly as they could although it seemed doomed to be lost amongst the sounds of combat. At last, though, Aethelwulf heard his name being called and turned to look back at them. His blond hair appeared to shine in the wan sunlight as he raised his shield in salute to Aethelred, and then a Danish axe came down on the ealdorman's skull.

Blood bloomed instantly, turning the golden hair crimson, and then Aethelwulf fell and the Dane who'd struck him was hammering down with his axe again and again.

Alfred couldn't see Aethelwulf now, for the press of bodies hid the fallen Saxon from view, but it was quite clear what was happening. Quite clear too that they could no longer look to the experienced ealdorman for advice. The one man who might have led them out of this hellish predicament was being bludgeoned to death as they watched.

'Oh, God,' the king gasped, and he was practically sobbing as he saw Aethelwulf's killer holding his bloodstained axe aloft in triumph. The man was a jarl, that much could be guessed from the iron helmet he wore and the mail vest that might have glittered had it not been covered in gore. The Dane noticed the king staring at him and shook his axe, bellowing a challenge, then started chopping at the shields in front of him, trying to cut his way towards Aethelred.

Alfred forced his gaze away from the terrible scene and another chill ran down his spine. In the few moments it had taken Aethelwulf to die, the flanks of the West Saxon army had collapsed. Already the dead ealdorman's troops were running from the battle and it was a similar story on the other flank, as the Danish reinforcements smashed into the exhausted warriors of Wessex. In the centre, the well-trained enemy line had quickly taken up the formation known as the *svinfylking*, or 'boar's snout'. Said by the Danes to be invented by Óðinn, this wedge-shaped formation smashed into the West Saxon shield-wall now, tearing through it like a hot seax through butter.

'Retreat!' Aethelred shouted, looking on in horror as what had seemed a certain victory turned into a rout. Alfred gaped at his brother's face and felt a pang at the shock and hurt he saw there. He knew what the king was thinking: God had forsaken them.

Again.

'Retreat!' The cry was taken up all along the West Saxon shieldwall now and, almost as one, like a dam bursting under the immense pressure of an unexpected flood, Aethelred's entire force began to run. They streamed past the king and his brother whose horses shied nervously, sensing the sudden change in mood from the renewed noise, although the cries were mostly from triumphant Northmen now.

'Ride, Alfred,' Aethelred called, nudging his horse closer to the aetheling's, for Alfred felt dazed and unable to react to what was happening. 'Ride!' Aethelred grasped the other horse's bridle and pulled on it as he urged his own mount into a walk, away from the cheering, grinning Danes. 'To the east, towards Whistley. We can ford the river there and regroup.'

Alfred nodded, pulling himself together and following his older brother's suggestion to head east, as some of their fleeing men were already doing. Many were aimlessly running to the west or south, though, and Alfred, knowing they would need those men if they were to have any chance of surviving future Danish onslaughts, kicked his horse into a canter.

He headed first for other mounted West Saxon thanes and ealdormen, exhorting them to lead their men east. 'To

Whistley,' he called to them. 'Stay together, and meet on the other side of the ford. It's our only chance!' Not all of the noblemen heard him, while others simply ignored him, caring little for any continuation of the fighting – instead, they rode off, following their men as they ran homewards.

'My lord!'

Alfred turned at the call, seeing Diuma riding towards him, long dark hair slick with sweat. 'I'm happy to see you alive,' the prince replied. 'You must help me guide our army east, to Whistley.'

'Done, lord,' the thane shouted. 'I'll do that. You start riding there yourself – we can't afford to lose you or the king, and the Danes don't look like they're going to let us escape easily.'

Alfred felt an enormous surge of gratitude towards the young warrior, whose loyalty seemed a rare positive on this day full of misery. His moment of pleasure was soon forgotten, however, as a volley of spears rained down around them, drawing screams from those Saxons unlucky enough to take the missiles in their backs as they attempted to flee.

'Go, Alfred,' Diuma shouted, nodding vigorously towards the east. 'Marshall our forces at Whistley. I'll make sure as many as possible meet us there!'

The prince looked from Diuma to the onrushing Danes, torn. As the enemy readied another volley of spears, and many of their reinforcements now also held bows and arrows, Alfred knew there was no point in him dying like Ealdorman Aethelwulf. He raised a hand in salute to Diuma and galloped hard in the direction of Aethelred, just as another hail of missiles came down behind him.

The battle might be over, but, turning in the saddle, he could see Halfdan and the new, unfamiliar Danish leader, urging their victorious forces to pursue him and his routed Saxons. If they could just reach the ford at Whistley they might be able to reform the army and hold back the enemy tide, but despair filled Alfred now for the inevitable was surely coming to pass.

Halfdan and the great heathen army had begun the conquest of Wessex and there seemed to be no way of stopping them.

CHAPTER TWENTY

'By the bones of Christ, the bastards won't stop!' Aethelred's captain, Sicgred, looked over his shoulder, face even redder than usual. 'I'm not sure we'll reach the ford, my lord. I think we might be better marshalling our forces here and making a stand.'

They were still a mile or so from Whistley and unbelievably, the Danes had followed them the whole way there, harrying them the entire time.

'Five miles,' Sicgred spat. 'Five miles with the sea-wolves at our backs, and still at least another mile to go.'

'What say you, Wulfric?' Alfred asked his own captain, who had mercifully survived the fighting. 'Should we make a stand?'

'No, my lord,' the ealdorman replied firmly, drawing a black look from Sicgred. 'Only some of their army have followed us, but still, they outnumber us even more than they did at Reading. Our only hope is to reach the ford and make a stand there, using the terrain to our benefit and hoping our scattered forces come to rejoin us.'

Aethelred looked from Sicgred to Wulfric. Sicgred was his captain, but the king had absolutely no desire to meet the Danes in another pitched battle, that much was obvious from his pained expression. 'I agree with Wulfric,' he said. 'We need to take whatever advantage we can get. And, if the enemy manage to come across the Loddon, we can make use of the forests near Whistley to escape further pursuit.'

'We should pick up the pace then,' Sicgred grumbled. 'The longer we take, the more men we lose.'

161

Alfred sighed. The captain was right – their pursuers were able to loose as many spears and arrows as they liked, for they could simply pick them up again as they advanced. Once the West Saxons let fly a missile, it was gone, until the Danes used it upon them once more. Same went for all the gear any Saxons died wearing. The corpse would be picked clean by the following army – expensive swords, byrnies, armour, helmets, silver coins – everything of value would be harvested. It all made the raiders stronger while severely weakening Aethelred's troops.

The brothers continued to ride in contemplative silence, lost in thought and even prayer for there seemed little else to do but hope God would come to their aid.

'Perhaps King Burgred will arrive from Mercia,' Alfred suggested, trying his best to raise everyone's spirits.

Wulfric and Sicgred were in agreement on this point at least, however, as both laughed in disgust at the aetheling's words.

'Burgred is little more than a vassal nowadays,' Sicgred spat. 'I'm sorry to say that, lord king,' he said to Aethelred. 'The man is your brother-in-law after all. But it's the truth. He's been beaten too many times by the Danes and there's no way he'll risk what little he has left – men, land, wealth – to march here and help us.'

Alfred felt irritated by the middle-aged captain's assessment of the situation. Sicgred was right, but the man's manner was so blunt it really grated on the aetheling's nerves.

'Can't blame him,' Wulfric said pragmatically. 'We're the last ones to fall to the Danes. There'll be no aid from Burgred, or King Oswald in East Anglia, or King Ecgberht in Northumbria, who are mere puppets of Halfdan's now. We're on our own, my lords, and we should plan our next move with that in mind.'

The mood was unsurprisingly gloomy but just then they saw the ford across the River Loddon and Alfred felt a wave of relief wash over him. 'We're not on our own,' he said, smiling at his companions. 'We still have God on our side.' He pointedly ignored Wulfric's brazen eye-roll and instead called to Bishop Edwin who was riding alongside them. 'Isn't that right, father?'

Even the clergyman didn't seem convinced by Alfred's pronouncement, but he nodded stoically. 'Of course, God is always with us, my lord. As long as we do not forsake him, he will not forsake us.'

'The men could do with reminding of that, though,' put in Alfred's priest, Oswald. He'd been brought along to provide extra spiritual support for the army and he spoke up now, a worried frown on his round face. 'I've ridden amongst them, my lords, and morale is lower than a serpent's belly.'

'Hardly a surprise,' Wulfric snorted. 'We've just had our arses handed to us, and the Danes are still harrying us.'

'Do we just give in, then, ealdorman?' Oswald asked caustically.

'Of course not!' Wulfric retorted, but the priest broke in again before he could say more.

'Then we need to restore their faith as quickly as possible, or face more desertions!'

That brought an awkward silence. It was obvious many of the West Saxon warriors, mostly the lower ranked ceorls, had melted away into the aether when the Danes broke through their shieldwall. Still, the commanders of the army had to pray those men would return soon, and not simply go back to their homes.

'How do we restore morale?' Aethelred asked, looking at both Oswald and Bishop Edwin.

'I think that is your job, lord king,' Edwin replied apologetically. 'The men will turn to you for leadership. You must make them believe they can survive this terrible defeat.'

'We should have celebrated Mass before the battle,' Aethelred muttered. 'Asked God for his blessing. Don't you think, Edwin?'

The bishop thought about that for a moment then shrugged. 'It might have helped,' he agreed.

Wulfric snorted. 'There was no time. Halfdan wasn't likely to stand and wait while we prayed.'

'One should always make time to praise God,' Edwin retorted. 'The pagans will be offering sacrifices to their vile gods as we speak. Perhaps the battle might have gone better if we had shown the same respect.' He stopped, perhaps realising his words could be seen as a rebuke, and nodded reassuringly. 'We can rectify our mistake before the next battle, lord king.'

Aethelred took a deep breath and sat up straighter on his horse, but Alfred could see his brother was lost. 'We're here at last,' the aetheling said loudly. 'Let's get in formation, eh, Aethelred?'

The king nodded, biting his top lip but visibly happy to have something to do. His horse splashed into the ford, which was deeper than usual thanks to the damp weather. 'Sicgred,' he called. 'You set up my hearth-warriors on the right, there. Have those who still have javelins, bows or slings in the front row. We need to keep the Danes as far away from us as possible. Wulfric? You do the same with Alfred's fyrd on the left there.'

The two captains instantly moved to follow their orders, marshalling the straggling forces into position, encouraging them to take heart, for the ford would provide them with protection from those who followed.

'Hurry, lads!' Aethelred called, positioning his horse right at the ford and smiling encouragingly to the beaten warriors as they moved past him. 'You fought bravely at Reading but now we must stand against the heathen filth again. Take heart! God is with us!'

Bishop Edwin was by his side, praying loudly and blessing the men as they went by. Alfred saw what his brother was doing and went to the far end of the ford with Oswald where they tried to perform the same function as the king.

'Look,' Alfred said to the priest as the last of their warriors filed past. The Danes who were following them had stopped, eyeing the newly formed line of Saxons on the opposite side of the river. To reach them the Danes would have to wade through the Loddon while missiles rained down upon them. 'Who is that, Oswald?'

The priest was more than double the prince's age and he squinted at the enemy troops. 'Who?' he said, and obviously couldn't see much more than a blur at this distance.

'The man leading them. I don't recognise him.'

'King Bagsecg,' a Saxon ceorl carrying an armful of damaged spears said as he limped past them. 'The bastards were shouting at us as they followed us from the battlefield. Telling us how another army had joined them from across the sea just a few weeks ago, led by King Bagsecg.' He jerked his head backwards. 'Him, my lord.'

Alfred nodded his thanks, but his mouth was a tight line as he took in this new information. 'Another army?' he muttered. 'Another king?'

'Saints preserve us,' Oswald said, making the sign of the cross. 'That's all we need.'

Alfred bowed his head and ran a hand across his eyes exhaustedly. 'This explains what happened at Reading. Halfdan and his army were outside the gates to lure us towards them. This new king was inside the town with his men, ready to strike once we were in position. The whole thing was a trick, and it worked because somehow – *somehow* – the bastards managed to sneak an army to Reading without us knowing.' He shook his head in amazement. 'How?'

'We can figure that out later, lord prince,' Oswald said. 'Look.'

A rider was coming towards them. Alone, as if he knew he had nothing to fear from the West Saxon warriors. And, as he came closer, Alfred understood why the man felt like that, and even wondered if they should be afraid of him, for he was an imposing individual, even for a Dane.

So tall his long legs almost seemed to touch the ground despite being on horseback, the newcomer had a dark beard and thick, long hair. He wore no armour, merely a thin shirt which showed his enormous arms and chest. He stopped just out of range of the Saxon bows, staring at Aethelred.

'You,' the Dane said, and raised one great arm to point at the King of Wessex. 'You will pay us, Aethelred, just as Aelle, and Burgred, and the other weak "lords" in these lands did. If not, our great army will slaughter every one of you, salt your fields, enslave your people, and rape your wives and daughters.'

'Come and—' Aethelred tried to shout a challenge at Bagsecg, but the Danish king ignored him and turned his horse, riding back towards his men. As the West Saxons watched in amazement, Bagsecg and the rest of the Danes who had harried them all the way there simply marched off, returning to the west.

'It's another trap,' Oswald mumbled. 'They'll double back and attack us when we're not expecting it.'

'I don't think so,' Aethelred said, riding towards them with Bishop Edwin. 'We all know the Danes don't like to fight unless they can choose the time and the place. They'd take heavy losses if they tried to cross the ford with us lined up ready for them.'

Alfred was nodding. 'And look,' he said, gesturing to the south. 'More of our men will come to join us every hour.' They all turned and saw the young thane, Diuma, cantering towards them, with dozens of soldiers riding or running at his back.

The men in the shieldwall on the far side of the ford were cheering and laughing in relief at this change in fortune, and Aethelred seemed rejuvenated too.

'Praise God,' called the king, looking up at the sky and clasping his hands in gratitude. 'We might have lost the battle but we're not dead yet.'

Alfred slapped the king on the back happily. 'Agreed, brother. Now we must reform the army and then...'

'And then,' Aethelred said, relief making him appear almost drunk. 'Then we can plan our next move. For now, we must fortify our position, have the wounded seen to, meat and drink served, and Bishop Edwin? You will say Mass, for we have much to thank God for this day.'

Alfred looked across the waters of the Loddon and saw Wulfric watching him. He did not need to hear what his captain was muttering, he could imagine his sarcastic response to the king's pious words and, for once, Alfred found himself in agreement.

They had survived, but there was little to thank God for.

A new army had come to bolster Halfdan's, and they would not leave Wessex until they were paid off or defeated.

'Come on, Oswald,' sighed the prince. 'Let's go and get a drink. I think we've earned it.'

CHAPTER TWENTY-ONE

'You went to Rome? When you were just a little boy?'

Alfred nodded, smiling, although the memory was bitter-sweet. He had indeed travelled all the way to Rome in his youth – sent by his father.

'I was only four that first time,' he said, brushing away the melancholy that often threatened to overwhelm him when he thought of those he'd lost.

'Four?' Oswald practically shouted, laughing in astonishment. 'Can you even remember it then?'

The two of them were enjoying mugs of ale together in the camp at Whistley. Scouts confirmed the Danes really had left them alone, so the army settled in to try and rest and regroup. Tents had been erected near the ford and dozens of campfires dotted the land as cold, weary soldiers attempted to keep warm despite the settling frost as night rolled in.

'Oh yes, I remember it quite well,' Alfred said. 'Would you like to hear about it?'

Oswald nodded his tonsured head emphatically. 'Very much,' he said, before smiling ruefully. 'It's not like we're going anywhere else for a while anyway.'

'All right,' the prince agreed, and cast his mind back across the two decades to when he'd been a small child.

–

Alfred was not sure how much of what he remembered was real, and how much he'd imagined over the years until it *felt* like it had really happened. He'd been a very small child when he went to Rome after all, and, to confuse things even more, there had been two separate trips – first, when he was four, then again when he was six and his father, King Aethelwulf, accompanied him. Events from both trips, and probably some things that never even happened, had blurred in Alfred's mind over the years so, although his memories felt real, Alfred could not be certain that they all were.

A journey from Wessex to Rome was no simple undertaking for, as well as the great distances involved, there were hostile pirates, Danes and Saracens that travellers had to avoid. Still, the young prince's father had thought it worthwhile to send him on the pilgrimage – Wessex and the other kingdoms were already being raided by the heathen Danes and sending one of the royal children to the most holy city in Christendom was seen as a sort of spiritual resistance to the invaders. Some thought it folly to send such a small child, but Alfred's oldest brothers were busy with other matters of statecraft and, since Alfred was the youngest, he was seen as the most expendable, although that was never openly admitted to anyone.

So, on both trips to Rome, Alfred was accompanied by an entourage of servants and guards. They travelled along the path known as the *via francigena*, staying in inns, hostels and monasteries that had sprung up along the route to serve the needs of pilgrims. The journey was truly eye-opening for the boy, who had rarely ever seen a stone building, other than the occasional modest church. Yet the cities of Europe which he passed through boasted all kinds of enormous structures, culminating in the astonishing Pantheon, mighty basilicas of St Peter and St Paul, and the even more incredible Colosseum. Alfred often wondered now that he was an adult, if his memories of those places were exaggerated, as it seemed impossible for something like the Colosseum to exist. Yet he knew it did, for he had seen it with his own eyes, and it was testament to the power and glory of God.

Alfred could recall the crowds, and the bright sunshine and stifling heat – more things he wasn't used to – as he gawped up at the circular, four-storey amphitheatre with its arcades framed in stone columns of the Doric, Ionic and Corinthian orders. When his party's guide had told them that 50,000 spectators would regularly fill the amphitheatre during the height of Rome's powers Alfred found himself completely incapable of imagining it. So many people, so much noise... It seemed like something from an old, fantastical tale of the heathen gods!

Everything in that great city had appeared larger than life, not only to little Alfred, but to the rest of his West Saxon companions. To people who had never known anything like it, the place was a marvel of wealth, architecture, sophistication and opulence.

They had stayed in the *Schola Saxonum*, which was a small quarter of the papal suburb boasting its own church, St Mary's. From that base Alfred and his adult protectors had explored the surrounding areas, which, to the impressionable child, had seemed to bring the stories of the bible to life. Thousands of Christian relics were there in the city, including the actual cross on which Jesus had been crucified. As well as that, the successor to St Peter himself lived in Rome: the Pope.

This was one memory which Alfred was particularly unsure about, for he had actually met two different popes on his visits – Leo IV the first time, and Benedict III during the second. His recollections of those holy men were hazy, yet he knew they had been magnificent, clad in their full papal vestments, and kind to him. Indeed, Leo had even sent a letter to Alfred's father, telling the king that he had 'decorated him, as a spiritual son, with the dignity of the belt and vestments of the consulate, as is customary with Roman consuls'. To be granted the ceremonial title of Roman consul by his new godfather was a great honour for young Alfred, and it created a spiritual bond with the Church that remained with him to this day.

Other memories that he felt more certain of were those of the second return trip from Rome. On the way back to

Wessex they'd travelled north, crossing the mighty Alps, and then stopped at the court of King Charles the Bald, in Francia. Alfred's mother, Osburh, had died just before that second pilgrimage got underway, and the boy had missed her terribly for their bond had been a close one. Yet, in Francia, Alfred's father took a new bride – the twelve-year-old daughter of Charles: Princess Judith.

Alfred could well recall his feelings of bemusement at what was happening. To lose his mother and gain a new step-mother who was not much older than him had been upsetting to say the least. The boy was not kind to Judith on that trip from Francia to Wessex, and, looking back now, Alfred felt guilty about that, for she had been a child herself and probably terrified by the whole situation.

When they finally made it home, Athelwulf's own son, Alfred's brother Aethelbald, had seized the throne of Wessex during the king's long visit to Rome. That had meant months and years of turmoil, culminating in Aethelbald marrying Judith himself once the old king died in AD 858.

Going from the magnificent, holy splendour of Rome to the infighting and grasping, naked ambition of his own family back in rainy Wessex had been a shock. It had also made Alfred aware at a young age of the fragility of power. When Aethelbald himself died, Judith, still only seventeen, returned to her father in Francia. Alfred hoped she had found happiness after her strange time with the West Saxons.

–

His story came to an end at that point and Alfred and Oswald sat in contemplative silence for a time, sipping their drinks and enjoying the warmth from the crackling fire that was blazing merrily before them. The men were noisy around them, chattering loudly and even singing bawdy songs – it seemed the earlier defeat, as terrible as it had been, was forgotten, for that night at least. That was a good sign, Alfred thought. As was the number of fires around them that seemed to grow with every passing hour, as more and more of their routed army trickled in to rejoin them.

It was amazing what camaraderie, warm food, and a few mugs of ale could do for a man's morale.

'What have you two been talking about?'

Aethelred came out of his tent behind them and stretched his arms up to the sky. From the slightly dazed expression on his face Alfred could tell he'd been sleeping. Fair enough – if anyone deserved a rest from everything that had happened that day it was the king.

'Rome,' he replied, filling another mug and holding it out as his brother came across to join them. 'And our mother.' A stool had already been set up by the ceorls who'd erected the tents for the army's commanders and Aethelred sat down, rubbing his eyes and rolling his head to ease his tense neck muscles.

'Ah, I miss her,' said the king. 'She was a kind woman.' He sipped his ale and his eyes were sparkling over the rim of the mug as he said, 'You probably don't remember her much, but you were always her favourite.'

Oswald laughed and so did Alfred, and Wulfric came over into the light of the fire. The huge ealdorman looked as fresh as he had in the morning. The blood and sweat had been washed from his face and his steely blue eyes were as alert as ever.

'Join us,' Aethelred said to him, and Wulfric sat down, the camp stool groaning under his bulk.

'I'll do that, my lord,' the captain said to Alfred, filling his own mug and swallowing a long draught with the obligatory sigh and wiping of lips at the end of it. 'Your mother was indeed a fine lady,' he said, looking at the brothers. 'She served me meat and drink herself at a feast in Wichamtun once. She served all the thanes and ealdorman in the hall that night. I thought it admirable that the king's wife should treat her guests so well.'

'You want me to fetch you some roast pork, Wulfric?' Aethelred asked with a smile, and the ealdorman laughed.

'Well, I *am* hungry, lord king,' he admitted.

'You sit there then,' Aethelred said, rising and gesturing for the big man to remain where he was, but a ceorl was already walking towards them carrying a trencher laden with meat and soon the men were all chewing happily.

'Your brother was just telling me that he'd been to Rome,' Oswald said to Aethelred. 'It must have been an incredible experience.'

'Twice,' Alfred said, wiping juice from his chin as he chewed a piece of pork.

'He was off seeing the world while the rest of us stayed at home looking after things,' Aethelred said, but his tone was light and Alfred was glad to see him more relaxed now. The loss at Reading had been a hammer blow, but they had to dust themselves down and move on. The Danes would still need to be dealt with, one way or another, and talk inevitably turned to that as Sicgred joined them. He did not look anything like as fresh as Wulfric, having made no attempt to clean himself up, and his forty-plus years seemed to weigh heavy on him as he took a drink from a ceorl with a grunt of thanks.

'How is the mood amongst the men?' Alfred asked him as he collapsed onto a stool and yawned mightily.

'Better than might have been expected, lord,' Sicgred replied. 'I've warned them not to drink too much tonight though, and I'll be patrolling to make sure they all get to sleep soon. We need to be ready for battle come the dawn.'

Aethelred frowned. 'Really? You think the Danes will come after us so fast?'

Sicgred shrugged. He looked like he might fall asleep right there. 'If not tomorrow, the day after, or the day after that. It won't be long anyway. We should be prepared. Send out scouts, watch their movements and take advantage of the terrain if we can.'

'An early night for us all then,' the king said. 'You get some sleep though, Sicgred. You look like you need it. I'll check on the men later – I've just woken up so I'm fresh.'

His captain nodded and swallowed his ale before taking his leave.

'It's early yet, lads,' Aethelred said at last. 'Drink up, make the most of the few hours we have left before it'll be time to bed down! Wulfric, I know you like to sing, so let's hear it.'

More soldiers came to join them around the fire, drinking and singing along with Wulfric who, although an enthusiastic vocalist, was not particularly tuneful. It didn't matter – the warriors just needed to celebrate surviving their defeat at Reading and drunken singing was always a good way to do that.

'Diuma!' Alfred spotted the thane singing amongst the small crowd that had gathered around their fire and waved him over. They grinned at one another, both quite inebriated, and grasped arms in the familiar warriors' greeting. Then the prince raised his hands and called for silence. It took quite some time to be heard and understood amongst the revellers but, at last, he was surrounded by a sea of expectant faces, all wondering what he wanted to say.

He looked about and spotted a couple of small barrels, then, gingerly for he knew himself he was not really sober enough to be climbing on things, he pulled himself onto one and stood up. 'Catch me if I fall off, right, lads?' he said, only half joking. The men laughed but he was happy to see Wulfric was right in front of him.

'What are you doing up there?' Aethelred called. 'You'll break your neck, and then who'll be aetheling?'

'I'll do it,' someone from amongst the crowd shouted, drawing laughs and cheers.

'I just wanted to quickly thank Lord Diuma,' Alfred shouted, nodding his head towards the young thane who looked up at him in surprise, face turning red under the sudden scrutiny of so many of his peers. 'I know many of you, perhaps all of you, fought well today, despite our defeat. And there will be an accounting for that, once everything is settled with the Danes.'

He waited for the boos to die down before continuing. 'But Lord Diuma performed a great service for us today, marshalling our retreating forces and directing them here that we might reform our army.'

There were scattered cheers although some of the men eyed Diuma jealously, irritated that the young man was being singled out by the prince for such praise. 'Here.' Alfred said, removing his own seax from its sheath. 'It's a blade forged by the famous smith, Osbeorn of Ryssebroc. It has served me well, but I gift it to you, Diuma, in thanks for your service to the people of Wessex, and your king, Aethelred.'

The warriors could all see that the seax was of the highest quality and worth a great deal. One side of the blade was inscribed with the runic alphabet in gold and silver, and the other bore the smith's name. It was truly a magnificent gift.

Speechless, Diuma bowed his head to Alfred and then to the king who'd moved closer to watch his brother's speech. Alfred undid the weapon's sheath from his belt and handed them both down to the thane who took them with glittering eyes.

'My lord, I... Thank you. I merely did my duty.'

'And you did it well,' Aethelred said solemnly. 'May God bless you.'

Diuma held up the blade, examining its exquisite workmanship, and Alfred jumped down beside him.

'Well,' he shouted. 'What are you all standing there gaping at? Let's have another song!'

Someone, undoubtedly one of Diuma's own kinsmen or at least someone from his fyrd, took up a chant of 'Diuma! Diuma! Diuma!' and it was repeated, with Alfred, Wulfric, and even the king joining in before it finally faded out and was replaced with a song about drinking.

'My lord, I don't know what to say,' the young thane murmured, staring at Alfred as if he was some kind of saint. 'I'll never forget this night, and the honour you've bestowed upon me.'

'You deserve it, lad,' Wulfric said, clapping Diuma on the arm and making him swell with pride even more.

Alfred smiled. 'Aye, you do deserve it, my friend. Without your aid today many of these men would have kept running south, until they were home. You've given us a chance to stand against the Danes if – when! – they come looking to finish what they started at Reading.' He smiled and jerked his head towards the fire. 'Go, Diuma. Drink and be merry. And enjoy the seax!'

The thane laughed and, still offering his profuse thanks, wandered off to celebrate with his friends and kinsmen.

Alfred watched him go and then called farewell to the men before he turned to head for his own tent, ready to grab a few hours' sleep, if that was possible with all the singing and shouting going on around him. He prayed that the sentries they'd posted around the camp were alert for if the enemy managed to sneak up on them unseen there would be absolute carnage.

'That was nicely done, my lord.'

Alfred looked up, startled, recognising his captain's voice. Sure enough Wulfric was walking alongside him having somehow managed to get within touching distance without Alfred noticing.

'God's blood, man, I wish you'd not sneak about like that. A man your size should make more noise.'

Wulfric grinned but ignored the comment. 'That was clever work with Diuma,' he said. 'A good lord wins loyalty by, among other things, giving expensive gifts.'

'I'm glad you approve,' Alfred replied with a sardonic smile. 'I sense an element of cynicism in your tone though, Wulfric. Well, I can tell you there was nothing premeditated about what I did. Diuma performed a great service for all of us today, and I'm happy to think of him as a friend. It's men like Diuma who are the future of Wessex. We need to appreciate them as much as we do the old guard.'

The ealdorman accepted that. 'Either way, rewarding your loyal followers will only engender further loyalty. It was good to see. You're becoming a fine commander, Alfred.'

For some reason Wulfric's praise brought a lump to the aetheling's throat and he was glad to reach his tent and bid the captain good night. As he drifted off to sleep, the sound of laughter and song ringing all across the camp and beyond, Alfred thought wistfully of his dead mother, father and brothers. And then he thought of his wife, Ealhswith, and their baby, Aethelflaed, and the feelings of sadness changed to resolve.

Halfdan and this terrifying new king, Bagsecg, could not be allowed to reach his family in Ceodre.

CHAPTER TWENTY-TWO

Scouts went out from the West Saxon camp the next morning, some looking for the remainder of the army which had been scattered after the battle, others riding to Reading to see what the Danes were up to.

Halfdan and Bagsecg did not seem to be doing anything much, the scouts reported. The bodies of the soldiers of Wessex had been stripped of their armour and valuables and left to rot where they'd fallen. This had been expected of course, but it still upset Aethelred and his men. Not only had they lost all those warriors, with their expensive gear, food and whatever other wealth they'd carried, but the dead would not receive a Christian burial. Many West Saxons believed that without the proper funeral rites the fallen would be excluded from Heaven, or even be doomed to haunt the earth as one of the undead.

There was nothing to be done about any of that however, so the king allowed the men another day to rest in camp, giving stragglers more time to rejoin them. The wounded were tended to, and riders sent further afield to command more of the West Saxon fyrd to muster at a place a few miles west of Reading.

The Danes might not be coming to Whistley to continue their assault on Aethelred's forces, but neither would they be going away any time soon. The army of Wessex had to be ready for the next battle.

Alfred went amongst the men during the day, watching them training – Wulfric and Sigred made sure every spare moment was put to good use. It was very obvious who were the *hearthweru*, the hearth-warriors, and who were the members of the general fyrd. Not only did the professional soldiers of the *hearthweru* have vastly superior arms and armour, but they were far more skilled in the use of their weapons.

The sight of farmers trying to throw spears and javelins was a depressing one for the aetheling in many ways. He sighed as yet another spear fell short of its target and the thane leading that particular group of soldiers roared at the unfortunate thrower to pick it up and try again.

'It's sad,' Alfred said to Wulfric as they watched. 'These men want nothing more than to grow their crops and raise their families. That we have to call on them to make up our numbers is a terrible thing.'

'That's how the world works,' Wulfric replied levelly.

'There should be a better way,' Alfred protested. 'The Danes are more like our *hearthweru*. They all have proper chainmail, fine swords and axes, shields, helmets, and they are well versed in the ways of war. They *know how to fight*, and they believe their gods will reward them if they are killed in battle. Us?' He grimaced as another spear was thrown wide of its target, and another. 'We are forced to rely on these men. Good men,' he added quickly. 'But not true warriors.'

Wulfric shrugged his great shoulders. 'We have enough professional soldiers to deal with the Danes, my lord. Those levies will be invaluable simply for their numbers, not their skill or equipment. It is up to us to use what resources we have to defeat our enemies.'

Alfred glanced at him, wondering if his comment was a rebuke aimed at himself or Aethelred, but Wulfric's face was blank.

It was a relief when dawn came the following morning and the army quickly broke camp. They were marching west not long after dawn, Alfred right at the front beside his brother.

–

'What next then?' The newcomer to the great heathen army, King Bagsecg, strode into Halfdan's hall in Reading with half a dozen of his men and sat down at the high table.

Halfdan was already seated there, and it irritated him that Bagsecg assumed his place was right there next to him. Although, in truth, Bagsecg had brought a lot of men with him, and they had been the difference in the fight with the West Saxons. Still, this enormous, dark-haired warrior had, as far as Halfdan knew, no royal blood – he was simply a mighty warrior who'd gathered would-be *vikingar* to his banner and decided to call himself a king. His father was no great hero like Ragnar Lodbrok, his brothers were not revered – feared – like Halfdan's sibling, Ivar the Detestable. His own men gathered within the hall glared at the newcomers the way a dog would eye another encroaching on its territory and Halfdan knew that kind of rivalry could mean trouble brewing over time.

Still, Bagsecg and his army would be invaluable in the coming months as the Danes took what they wanted from Wessex. Halfdan forced himself to smile in welcome and poured Bagsecg a horn of mead himself, which the big man snatched from him and downed with gusto.

'Eh?' Bagsecg belched. 'What next for us, now that we've sent the Saxon sheep running away, and plundered their corpses? I want more, Halfdan. I didn't sail here just to sit around eating and drinking mead.'

'You'll not be wanting any more of that then?' Halfdan asked, reaching out as if to take the horn from Bagsecg's hand.

'I'm happy to drink today,' the big man replied with a laugh. 'But not forever. I was told there was much silver to be had in Wessex.'

Halfdan nodded amiably and refilled the other king's horn before swallowing some himself. 'There is,' he agreed. 'Silver, slaves, horses… Whatever you want. But it's winter, and we've got all the food and supplies we need right here in Reading. I would suggest we settle in here, grow fat eating the Saxons' own winter supplies they kindly provided for us, and then begin to raid anew when spring comes around.'

His own men, veterans of three, four, even five years campaigning in Britain, murmured agreement with their king's plan. 'Winter's no time to be fighting,' Ubba said. He was seated on Halfdan's other side and he was even less impressed than his brother by the way Bagsecg had assumed the same status as theirs within the heathen army. 'Not unless the men are bored, or an easy target is available. You'll learn that yourself, Bagsecg, when you've been here as long as the rest of us.'

That, of course, drew outraged muttering from the newcomers but their king was not easily offended by such jibes. 'Ubba,' he retorted. 'You've barely seen twenty-five summers, yet you talk as if you've spent decades raiding. We,' he stood up, sweeping out his heavily muscled arm to encompass his warriors. 'Know all about war. We came here from Francia because that country has been bled dry by us. You have grown soft, fighting the weaklings here in these lands.'

Halfdan placed a hand on Ubba's wrist, warning his brother not to react to the barb. 'What do you suggest, then?' he asked Bagsecg.

'I suggest we take advantage of the defeat we have just inflicted on the Saxon king. We attack the nearest large settlements, before Aethelred can persuade his army of farmers to regroup.'

'And then?' Ubba spat, glaring murderously at the giant king who seemed to have arrived with intentions of supplanting his family as leaders of the Danish army.

'And then,' Bagsecg grinned. 'We return here to drink and fuck and fight amongst ourselves, Jarl Ubba, while the Saxon army sits outside the walls, as impotent as a drunk in a whore-house!'

His men cheered, and Halfdan was dismayed to see even his own warriors joining in enthusiastically. It was easy to see how the charismatic Bagsecg had ended up as a king.

'Agreed!' Halfdan laughed, looking warningly down at Ubba as he got to his feet and cheered along with the rest of the warriors in the hall. There was no point in trying to go against Bagsecg in this – the man had tapped into the feelings of the army and to deny the plan he'd laid out would merely turn people against Halfdan. So, he would go along with it.

'What are you doing?' Ubba hissed, jumping to his feet and glaring into his brother's eyes. 'We cannot let him believe he's in charge here. He will think us weak.'

'I know that,' Halfdan replied. 'But, let's be honest, another raid is what the men want. And besides, maybe Bagsecg is right: we have grown lazy. No-one has really stood up to us in Mercia, Northumbria or East Anglia. Maybe things have been too easy for us. It's time to show Aethelred and his whelp of a brother what happens when you decide to stand against us.'

Ubba looked unconvinced.

'Cheer up,' Halfdan said as the celebrations went on around them. 'I thought you liked to raid.'

A small, grim smile did begin to appear on Ubba's face then. 'Aye, fair enough, I do,' he conceded. 'But I'll be watching that big bastard Bagsecg. If he thinks he can just wander in here and take over our army he can think again. These men are ours.'

'Onwards, then!' Halfdan roared, turning and clattering his mead horn against Bagsecg's as the other threw an arm around him, hugging him in the way all drunken men are wont to do. 'To the next Saxon settlement in the west. To Ascesdune!'

CHAPTER TWENTY-THREE

Aethelred's scouts had noted the preparations within Reading and taken word to the king. It seemed the Danes were not about to rest on their laurels and would soon be leaving their stolen fortress to march on another poorly defended town in Wessex.

'Where do you think they'll go?' Aethelred had asked as he'd broken his fast that morning with his advisors.

There had been various opinions, with some suggesting the sea-wolves would use their longships to continue east along the Tamyse, perhaps even going as far as Windlesora. Their confidence would be high after their victory at Reading, and they'd hope to take as much plunder as possible while the beaten Saxons licked their wounds. Others, such as Wulfric, feared Halfdan and his new ally Bagsecg would push deeper west, occupying as much territory as they could. There was talk of splitting the army into two halves, with one remaining in the east while the other went west. It was hardly the ideal plan but there seemed little else to do until they had a better idea of the Danes' intentions.

Then another scout rode into camp and passed on news he'd heard from one of the Saxon hunters who lived in Reading. The hunter had been allowed to leave the town to forage and the scout had approached him. The hunter said that the Danes were going to attack the settlements around Ascesdune and everyone in Reading knew about it for the Northmen made little attempt to hide their plans and had, in fact, been boasting about it.

'It could be a trick,' Alfred had warned. 'That hunter could have been sent out by Halfdan to spread a lie. So we will ride to Ascesdune while the raiders sail their boats down to the river and attack a different town.'

'I don't believe so, my lord,' the scout had replied, respectfully but firmly. 'The hunter was not lying. He hates the Danes as much as any of us – more, since he's been forced to watch the bastards take control of his home and abuse his kinsmen.'

'Oh, I'm sure that's true,' the aetheling admitted. 'But it doesn't mean we aren't being tricked by King Halfdan. From what we know of him, Halfdan is not quite as direct as Ivar, Ubba, or even their father Ragnar. Halfdan is more cunning.'

There had been much more discussion, but the majority of Aethelred's ealdormen and thanes thought the hunter's intelligence was worth trusting.

'All right,' the king had said, finishing the last of the bread he was eating. 'We march west, to Ascesdune, and hope to meet the enemy there. Let's move!'

So the army went west, towards the Berrocscire downland. Ascesdune was not a specific town or settlement, it was the name for a general area. There could still be a number of places the Danes might target first, but it was somewhere to start. It was also a good place to meet up with any other West Saxon fyrds that hadn't joined the main army already.

Thankfully it was dry, for there was nothing worse than an army trudging through mud, the supply wagons constantly becoming bogged down, making even short journeys longer and harder than they should be. It was dry but bitterly cold, with an icy wind that buffeted them from what felt like all directions other than behind, which might have at least made their progress faster.

Their route took them close to the River Tamyse in places but they never saw any longships. On one hand Alfred was pleased by that, for he did not want the Danes to know their movements, but on the other, if they'd seen the enemy sailing west it might have confirmed Halfdan and Bagsecg's plans.

On January 8th, a mere four days after the battle at Reading, King Aethelred's West Saxon army reached Ascesdune. Now their enemy's intentions were clear for, as they crossed the Tamyse at Muleforda a number of Danish ships were sighted. The vessels were practically empty and quickly headed upriver as soon as their crews spotted Aethelred's host approaching.

'Have they all come here?' Alfred wondered, watching the last of the ships disappear around a bend in the river.

'Some by the river, some on horseback or foot,' Wulfric replied, pointing at the land around them which was soft here and showed the impressions of many shoes and hooves. 'We're in for another mighty battle, my lord, you can be sure of that.'

Scouts were sent out and it wasn't long before they returned with news: the Danes were ahead, but they knew the West Saxon army was coming and had positioned themselves on the high ground.

'Ah, damn them,' Sicgred cursed. 'They've already got the advantage then. It's no fun trying to run uphill wearing battle-gear while javelins rain down on you.'

'We have our shields,' Aethelred replied and there appeared to be a steely resolve in him that Alfred had not seen in his brother before. The days since Reading had played on the king's mind but it seemed the prayer and reflection he'd undertaken in that time had helped him come to terms with the defeat and prepared him for what was to come next. 'How are they set up?' he asked the scouts.

The outriders gave their reports and Alfred and the other leaders drew a mental image of the place where the Danes had positioned themselves.

'The main thing is, my lords,' one of the scouts said, 'the Danes have split into two separate forces. I saw Halfdan and Bagsecg in the centre of the westernmost group.'

'The other looks to be commanded by their earls,' another scout reported. 'I thought I also saw Ubba, but I'm not sure. They all look much the same to be honest, with their helmets and beards and stuff.'

Alfred couldn't help but smile at that, looking around at the ealdormen and thanes that formed Aethelred's council; most of them also fitted the scout's description of the enemy warriors.

'Then we must do the same,' Aethelred said decisively. 'We'll form two armies, one led by me, the other by you, brother.'

'Are you sure about this?' Sicgred asked softly, not wanting the other men to hear him questioning the king's plan. 'They outnumber us. Splitting into two will make each half more vulnerable if this is another of their tricks.'

Aethelred shook his head, mind made up. 'I don't think this is a trick. We've caught up with them and surprised them, and they've done the natural thing by making for the higher ground. Our scouts would have noticed if Halfdan had sent troops to hide elsewhere. Wouldn't you?'

The outriders looked at one another warily, knowing they would be blamed if they had indeed missed a large body of Danes concealed somewhere, ready to ambush the Saxons when battle commenced.

'We'd have noticed, lord,' one of the scouts eventually replied. He was a middle-aged man with a battle-scarred face and a competent air about him. Alfred recognised him as one of fallen Ealdorman Aethelwulf's soldiers. A native of this area. 'There's no-one hiding around here, they're all on top of the rise.'

'It's settled then,' the king said. 'Let's move, before they get a chance to dig themselves in even deeper than they already have. Alfred, remember our mistake at Reading: we must celebrate Mass before battle commences. All right?'

Alfred nodded immediately. If ever there was a good time to pray, it was before one was about to meet a man like Bagsecg in a fight. 'Agreed, lord king,' he said, and the commanders all grasped forearms for a final time before Aethelred rode off.

It was no easy matter splitting the army into two, with most of the men being poorly trained levies, but Sicgred and Wulfric knew their jobs and, at last, the king was leading his half of the men eastwards, along the churned track. They would line up facing the Danish kings' force, while Alfred would follow and face off against the rest of the sea-wolves.

Again, there were no convoluted tactics from Aethelred. It would be a typical battle, beginning with the opposing sides softening their enemy from a distance by using javelins and bows or slings, although the latter two were quite rare amongst both the Danes and the West Saxons. After that, the shieldwalls would come together and the warriors would use spear, sword, axe, hammer and whatever else they had to hack the opposing army into bloody submission. It would not be clever, or pretty, and would mostly come down to numbers, terrain and even a bit of God-given luck, but there was nothing else for it, Alfred thought.

The days of the mighty Roman legions building fantastic engines of war — ballistae, catapults, onagers throwing enormous rocks... Those days were gone. Battles nowadays didn't even use cavalry, for horses could not be relied on to charge at a bristling wall of spears. Any time it had been tried it had ended in disaster.

There was something incredibly stupid about all this, Alfred mused as he and Wulfric took their section of the army and organised them into a line. There had to be a better, more efficient way to wage war. No matter which side won today, hundreds of lives would be needlessly thrown away, valuable weapons and armour damaged beyond repair. And, on a spiritual level, good Christians would do horrific things, leaving a black stain on their memories if not their very souls.

There was nothing else for it though. The great heathen army had to be beaten, and Alfred would seek God's assistance to help achieve that lofty goal.

'Oswald!'

The priest came to him, riding across and dismounting quite nimbly.

'Will you say Mass for us, brother? Quickly, before the Danes attack?'

Oswald nodded. 'Of course, my lord.' He gestured to the young man, a ceorl, who travelled with him to help with situations like this. The lad immediately set about erecting a folding table which was stowed on a cart he himself pulled. On the table he placed a bible, a cup which he filled with wine, some bread and a cross. It was not the most impressive altar in Christendom but it would suffice. The priest positioned himself behind this altar and raised his arms to heaven. He prayed softly, consecrating the bread and wine then, addressing God the Father, Oswald began the Mass. He petitioned God for victory in the coming battle, and then, mindful of the need for haste, the warriors gathered around said, 'Amen,' and the priest lifted the bread. He tore off a small piece and ate it with his eyes shut, head bowed, then he swallowed a sip of the wine and made the sign of the cross.

Alfred came forward at Oswald's nod, and he too celebrated the Eucharist. Then he went back to his place at the front and centre of the shieldwall as the other high-ranking members of his army took the bread and wine. And then, with quite unusual alacrity, the priest sang a hymn praising God, the 'guardian of the heavenly kingdom', while the warriors all joined in. It was quite a spectacle seeing, and hearing such a thing just before a titanic battle was about to take place, and Alfred felt the hairs rising on the back of his neck as the final word – 'allmectig', meaning 'Almighty' – rang out across the frosty downs.

The aetheling breathed the icy air, allowing the moment to pass, and then he turned first left and then right, gazing all along his line of eager warriors. Shields were held up, locked against one another, and javelins were prepared for throwing. Alfred walked out in front of the army, looking across to the west, wondering if Aethelred had also finished celebrating Mass and would be ready to mount the attack soon.

To his surprise a large tent had been set up with the banner of Wessex – a golden dragon on a red background – fluttering in the breeze outside. The king's section of the army was arrayed in a line similar to Alfred's men, and they fidgeted as they waited for their commander to come out from his tent and lead them.

'Are you ready to die, Aethelred?'

Alfred turned and looked up the slope as he heard the words called down. They were heavily accented but understood easily enough by the aetheling and the rest of the West Saxon troops who watched as King Bagsecg strode confidently out from the Danish ranks. Even at this distance his great size was impressive, and Alfred was not surprised Halfdan had allowed this newcomer to the heathen army to be its spokesman. He could already hear the men behind him muttering in trepidation at the prospect of facing such a man in battle.

'No!' the aetheling shouted back with venom. 'King Aethelred is not ready to die, Bagsecg. He's celebrating Mass. We'll be ready to slaughter every last one of you soon enough though. Just go back to your sty for now, and grunt like the pig you are!'

His words brought cheers and laughter from the West Saxons but, when the mirth faded, Bagsecg called back in a steady voice, 'Mass? Is that some kind of prayer to your weak Christ? I would say that's a good idea, boy. You're going to need all the help you can get today, but even praying will not be enough to save you now.' He was dressed in more than the thin shirt he'd worn after the pursuit from Reading, and, if anything he seemed even more imposing, clad in a mail shirt with dark trousers and leather bracers to protect his forearms. He drew his sword and held it in the air, spreading his arms rather as Oswald had done before celebrating Mass. 'We will finish what we started at Reading,' he bellowed, voice seeming to echo all across the downs. 'Every one of you will die here, and then your lands and your families will be ours to despoil, as will your bodies. Oh, we had fun with the corpses of your fallen after that last battle!' With that he laughed and walked back to rejoin his army, which had remained ominously silent as the two opposing noblemen traded threats.

'Did you hear that?' Alfred demanded furiously, turning to face his army and calling loudly so even the nearest troops in Aethelred's division might hear his words. 'If the Danes win Wessex will be theirs. Your wives and children will become their slaves, suffering terrible indignities and agonies. Do you want that for them?'

There were murmurs at that, but Alfred practically screamed, 'Do you want that for your families? Rape? Enslavement? Torture? Murder?'

'No!' came the reply, much louder this time.

'I can't hear you!' Alfred roared, and it seemed like the entire West Saxon army cried out in response now.

'No!'

'Then make sure we beat the bastards,' shouted the prince.

'My lord!'

He looked along the shieldwall, hearing the alarm in the voice which sought his attention. He spotted Wulfric, and turned at his captain's nod, cursing as he realised what was happening.

'They're coming!' he called unnecessarily, hurrying back to stand beside Wulfric in the forefront of the shieldwall. The ealdorman handed him his helmet and he quickly buckled it in place before accepting his shield, spear and a javelin.

'What's the king doing?' Wulfric asked in clipped tones. 'We need him to attack with us.'

'I'm sure he will soon enough,' Alfred replied and now his guts were churning with fear for the sight of the Danish host was enough to give even the bravest man pause. 'We can't stand here waiting on him however, so...' He raised his javelin in the air and shouted, 'Advance!'

CHAPTER TWENTY-FOUR

Alfred's short speech, along with a goodly amount of mead and ale, had rekindled the men's fury against the oncoming invaders. They followed him towards the slope eagerly, teeth bared, striking the shafts of their weapons against shields in time with their steps.

At the very front of the line, Alfred could see both sections of the Danish horde were coming down to meet them. Bagsecg and Halfdan led the group furthest away and they were almost indistinguishable at this distance. Directly facing his half of the army were the Danes who were led by their jarls.

'There's that whoreson Ubba,' Wulfric said. 'Right in the very centre of their line.'

'A hundred shillings to the man who kills Ubba!' Alfred called out, pointing towards the Northman who, with his distinctive blue-and-white shield, was easy enough to spot. The words were out of his mouth before he had time to think about them and he cursed himself, realising all those around him would aim their javelins at the jarl, reducing the efficacy of that first attack.

Still, if one of those missiles managed to take out Ubba it could prove decisive at the very outset of the battle, so he made no attempt to rescind the bounty he'd placed on the jarl's head. He might not have much experience in battle but he knew from his tutors, and from hearing the likes of Wulfric's tales, that the Danes could quickly lose their thirst for battle if their leaders were killed.

That was one weakness the Northmen had: no loyalty to one another. They did not all come from the same geographical area, they were not bound by bonds of blood or even friendship in most cases. They simply joined together as a result of their shared desire for easy plunder, and gravitated towards the strongest leaders, such as Ragnar Lodbrok, Halfdan, Ubba and Bagsecg, because those men were the likeliest to bring glory and wealth to aspiring *vikingar*.

'Loose!' Wulfric commanded, and the word was repeated along the line by the other ealdormen and thanes.

The javelins soared up, into the air, and came down into the heaving mass of Danes who were just about to launch their own weapons. There was a terrific noise, like the heaviest hail storm imaginable, as the Saxon weapons struck shields, helmets, armour, flesh and bone. Alfred could see that the javelins had taken a heavy toll on the enemy ranks and, as the screams and war-cries of the Danes filled the air he bellowed, 'Charge!'

Up the slope the West Saxon warriors ran, legs powering across the grass, somehow maintaining the advance despite the frost on the ground.

'Shields up!'

The Danes now threw their own missile weapons and Alfred continued to trot forward as he crouched low behind his shield, praying that God would watch over him. Within moments they had covered the distance between the opposing factions and the prince thrust his spear forward, into the chest of a huge Northman who was so consumed by battle-rage that he'd let his shield drop.

Alfred's entire world became enclosed in that tiny pocket of space and time as he thrust, parried, ducked, cursed, and screamed oaths that Oswald or Bishop Edwin might have blushed to hear. Bagsecg's threats filled his mind, as did the thoughts of the good Christian soldiers whose bodies had been defiled and denied the proper burial rites after Reading. He would suffer the same fate should his army fail here, and that thought drove him on. He lost count of the bearded, hate-filled foes that came before him, only to fall on the end of his spear, or that of one of his comrades'.

The fight became almost a transcendental experience for Alfred, who felt like he was filled with God's Holy Spirit as his body moved in an effortless dance. His blows landed, his shield deflected enemy attacks, and he felt as light as a feather, mind utterly focused.

It was a shock when a Northman's shield boss smashed into his face, sending him sprawling backwards, mouth suddenly filling with blood. Brought back to reality in that sudden, painful moment, he felt an immediate sense of terror as the men behind him supported him, but then shoved him forward again, back into the melee. The Dane who'd hit him with the shield was snarling and Alfred only just managed to dodge the point of his spear. Screaming, the West Saxon prince kicked out, his foot connecting ineffectually with the enemy shield.

Another blow struck his own shield and, with a sense of rising panic, Alfred tried to make his mind calm once more, to re-enter the earlier state of serenity in slaughter. His limbs ached with exhaustion now, though, and his senses were overwhelmed with the sounds and sights before him. It was all he could do to parry more of his opponents' attacks while prodding with his spear at any unprotected spot he could see on their bodies. He spat and realised with some relief that his nose had stopped bleeding; it had caked around his philtrum, mouth and chin however, and soon became yet another unpleasant distraction.

To his right, a warrior screamed as a Dane's axe practically cleaved his arm from his shoulder. Blood sprayed from the wound, covering that side of Alfred's cheek. The axeman pushed forward, right into the hole left by the incapacitated West Saxon, and began hacking at anyone in his path.

Alfred had no idea what he should do. His spear was much too long to turn and stab the Dane, and doing so would leave himself exposed to the enemy warriors in the shieldwall in front. 'Kill him!' he cried in desperation. 'Kill him!'

He raised his shield and felt the point of a spear crunch into the linden boards before being roughly jerked back, and he aimed a thrust of his own, feeling the iron tip grating against a mail shirt before sliding into flesh. He pulled it free and quickly glanced to the side. The enemy axeman was gone. Where, Alfred had no idea, but he must be dead now, trampled beneath West Saxon feet. He allowed himself a quick glance downwards and realised there were lots of bodies lying there, stamped on and ground into the blood-drenched grass.

Something hit him on the crest of his helmet and his eyes turned back to the front. His ears rang and his knees felt like they would give way. The Dane who'd struck his head was raising his arm for another strike, and it was all Alfred could do to slump down and hide behind his shield, riding the blows until the dizziness passed.

'Where the hell is the king?' a thane to the left of him shouted, and Alfred forced himself upright once more.

Another Dane lunged at him, axe raised high for a killing strike, but the Saxon prince slammed the pointed boss of his shield into the man's face and the weight of the blow shattered the enemy's eye socket. A spear thrust from some other warrior of Wessex finished the unfortunate *vikingr* off and then Alfred, arms suddenly beginning to shake from exhaustion, pushed his way back through the ranks of his own men.

When he at last had a clear view of the ground at the bottom of the slope he was shocked to realise Aethelred's contingent of troops had not joined the battle. 'The bloody fool is still hearing Mass?' he whispered to himself, dismayed.

'My lord!'

Alfred spun around, seeing Diuma, covered in blood from a long cut that ran almost the full length of his face.

'My lord prince,' the thane gasped, coming to join him at the rear of their army. 'What's your brother doing? By St Alban's cock, we need his men! Halfdan and Bagsecg's forces are destroying our left flank while the king's fyrd just stand over there watching!'

Despite the circumstances Alfred felt a surge of annoyance at Diuma's disrespectful tone and criticism of Aethelred, but as he glared at the young man his anger dissipated. Or at least transferred, from Diuma to Aethelred.

'We're losing this,' Wulfric shouted, barging through the thinning ranks of West Saxons. 'Is this some clever plan you and the king hatched? Why is he not joining us?'

Alfred's head spun and he felt like puking. He reached up to his helmet and felt a dent in it. He could not remember that happening.

'It's no plan of mine,' he replied, steadying himself and taking deep breaths. He could see the entire left flank of his army was beset by the enemy who were now beginning to loop around and, soon enough, would encircle them completely. It was obvious what would happen then. 'What should we do, Wulfric?' he asked, suddenly feeling like a child again, and terrified that all his men would die because of his lack of leadership.

'We need the king's army, my lord. Send a messenger to ask him to join us!'

'This is insane,' Diuma breathed, wincing as he saw Bagsecg launching himself into the air, towering over the West Saxons on that collapsing left flank, before slamming his great axe down into the collarbone of some poor levy who had nothing more than a thin tunic as protection. 'Why is the king not helping?'

'I think you should retreat, Alfred,' Wulfric advised. 'Diuma's right, this is madness. That flank has already caved in at some points. It'll be gone completely in a few moments and then our men will break and run. It'll be a bloodbath. You need to go now, my lord. Save yourself. You've fought like a demon this day; you're a hero, by God. But we'll need you no matter what happens next.'

For just a moment Alfred was relieved to be given permission to save his own skin, but anger quickly replaced that relief. Anger that his men were being slaughtered while he stood there doing nothing, and anger that his brother, the king, was in his tent praying for a victory that might have been theirs had Aethelred actually joined the battle.

'If we run,' he replied through gritted teeth. 'Wessex belongs to Halfdan and Bagsecg.' He shook his head and repositioned his shield on his left arm, making sure it was comfortable. 'I'll fight on.'

He looked at Diuma who appeared on the verge of tears, so enraged was he by the king's refusal to join them. 'God go with us, lord,' said the thane, wiping blood from his chin as it rolled down the long scar on his face. 'May He guide our spears as we die heroically here on this blasted hillside!'

Alfred nodded and shoved back into the rear rank of his West Saxons – mostly terrified, poorly trained, pitifully armed levies – calling encouragement to them as he slowly worked his way towards that collapsing left flank and the giant Bagsecg, who must already have killed a dozen men of Wessex himself.

Behind them, Wulfric's voice suddenly boomed out. 'Don't lose heart just yet. Look!'

Alfred, Diuma, and all the levies in the rear ranks turned at the unmistakeable excitement in the ealdorman's voice and instantly their faces lit up.

'Look!' Wulfric repeated, much louder now, pointing down the slope to the left of their position. 'The king! The king is coming at last!'

–

Bishop Edwin came out of the tent and watched King Aethelred lead his army in a charge up the slope to join the battle. Alfred's priest, Oswald, joined him and they stood in silence, praying that God would be on the side of the West Saxons.

There were other non-combatants around them, priests as well as the ceorls and servants – young and old men – who helped carry the fyrd's equipment, cook meals, repair gear, take messages, and a multitude of other logistical tasks. Some were busy, perhaps fearing to look up at the fighting, knowing their lot would be a bad one should the Danes win. Others stood like the clergymen, watching as events unfolded.

'It doesn't seem to be going well,' the bishop noted, alarm in his otherwise rich voice.

'No wonder, my lord,' Oswald replied testily. 'Prince Alfred has been engaging the enemy on his own while you gave Mass for the king! What took so long?'

Edwin frowned at him but the priest's words, although harsh, were clearly justified. It didn't take a military genius to see that. 'The king felt he didn't praise God enough before the battle at Reading,' came the reply. 'He insisted we do things properly today. "I will not forsake divine service for that of men", were his words to me.'

'Well, let's hope he didn't leave it too late. Alfred's soldiers have fought well, but their flank was just about to collapse. Even from here I can see that devil, Bagsecg, scything down our troops as if they were but ripe wheat.'

Bishop Edwin made the sign of the cross and they fell silent, breath steaming in the frigid air but neither noticing how cold they were.

Eventually, Oswald, squinting as he tried to make out what was happening, murmured, 'I don't think the Danes have real-ised Aethelred's army are charging towards them.'

'God, let that be the case,' Edwin breathed, and his tone betrayed his disbelief. How could Halfdan and his captains fail to notice hundreds of men coming towards them?

'They're not making any noise,' Oswald finally noticed. 'The king's men, I mean. No war cries. No screamed threats, like warriors running into battle usually make. They're completely silent. Was this planned all along?' he wondered, glancing at the bishop who made no reply. 'A clever trap, like the one the Danes sprang on us at Reading?'

Oswald had been around the West Saxon commanders throughout the past few days but he'd heard no talk of anything like this. It was possible the king had discussed it with his brother and, to be fair, the whole thing did seem to have caught the enemy unawares yet… The priest stared up the hill, trying to pick out Alfred amongst the seething mass of men. It had not looked like some grand plan when the Danes were obliterating the left flank of the West Saxon army, and Oswald had noticed Alfred and Wulfric staring down at Aethelred's tent. True, they had been mere stick figures, dots in the distance, but they'd obviously been looking for the king.

'By the blood of Christ.' Bishop Edwin blessed himself again and he turned to Oswald with a hopeful smile tugging at the corners of his mouth. 'The tide is turning.'

They were joined by the other clergymen who travelled with the army and all of them looked on in wonder for, almost to a man, they'd thought the Northmen were winning this battle, just as they'd done at Reading.

'Pray with me, my brothers,' Edwin said passionately, clasping his hands and falling to his knees on the damp, icy grass.

The others followed his lead and Oswald felt a surge of… hope? Relief? No, he felt slightly ashamed to admit it, but he knew that even though what he was feeling was a mixture of many emotions, it was mainly righteous joy. The division of Danes led by the kings, Halfdan and Bagsecg, had now been beset by Aethelred's fresh troops and it had caused absolute mayhem amongst the enemy ranks.

Screams of fear and pain drifted eerily across the downs, while more and more Saxon voices could be heard raised in triumph. Already Danes were streaming uphill, towards the rise, their staggering, fleeing outlines framed against the horizon. And then came what Oswald sensed immediately would be the decisive blow.

'Christ be praised!' A young priest with clearer eyesight than the rest of them suddenly clambered to his feet and raised his arms in the air. His eyes were shining as he looked back at the other men of God and laughed in disbelief. 'The sea-wolves' king has fallen. I saw him go down, and he's not come back up!'

'Which king?' Oswald demanded, gazing up at the carnage swirling halfway up the low rise.

'The big one,' replied the young priest. 'Bagsecg. Look! They're running!'

He was right. Whether Bagsecg had been killed or merely injured, the Danes caught between Alfred and Aethelred's hammer and anvil had lost their stomach for the fight. Heavy spears had been thrown down and the entire central section of the army – the one commanded by the enemy kings – was routing, following their other fleeing comrades up, towards the slope and escape.

'I can see the aetheling,' Oswald laughed, pointing at a helmeted figure who was hacking at the back of a retreating Dane before moving on to chase after another. 'Kill them all, my lord!' he practically screamed, forgetting where he was and whose company he was in as the lust for blood washed over him.

He was not the only priest cheering on the victorious warriors of Wessex. Even Bishop Edwin's eyes were glittering and his hands were balled into fists which moved as if he was amongst the army and plunging a weapon into the back of a departing foe.

Part of Oswald had always wanted to be a soldier, rather than a priest. In the end, his desire to serve God as a man of peace had won out, but he could not help feeling a pang of jealousy as he recognised another warrior savagely hacking the life from a screaming Northman.

'Is that...?'

Oswald nodded at Edwin's unfinished question. 'Aye, it is,' he confirmed. 'Heahmund, Bishop of Sherborne.'

Awed, the men of God watched their brother in Christ as he ran after terrified Northmen, thrusting his sword into exposed

199

backs, hacking down into skulls and shoulders, and, when any tried to fight him off, he responded with such skill and ferocity that the encounters were always short lived.

Oswald did not know what to think as he looked on. A bishop should be a man of peace – the monks at Lindisfarne had not even thought to fight back when those very first raiders had come in their longships to rape and pillage the monastery in the mist. They, like Edwin, Oswald and the others who stood beside them at that moment, had chosen to live a life without violence.

Yet, a part of Oswald felt envious of Bishop Heahmund as he rampaged about the battlefield dispatching Danes. It was inspiring, seeing one of their own amongst the warriors of Wessex although, in truth, it was no fairy-tale they were watching. Not something from a glorious saga. The ground was hilly, uneven, strewn with corpses, and made slippery with frost, mud and blood, and Heahmund, like those he pursued so mercilessly, fell over a number of times, arms and legs flailing ludicrously.

So, thought Oswald, *this is what victory looks like*.

Better this than the alternative.

'Are you all ready?' Bishop Edwin called once the outcome of the battle was certain. He turned to the ceorls and servants who were also waiting for the conflict to come to an end. 'Ready, men?'

There were nods and murmurs of assent from all, and then the bishop led them up the slope. The warriors had done their job, and continued to do so, pursuing the routed enemy back to the east, slaughtering as many as possible. Now the men of God had an equally important task, attending to the souls of the dying West Saxons and guiding them towards their place in Heaven, while the ceorls would look to assist the wounded and, of course, loot the enemy corpses.

Each man in the army had a part to play and, with victory, that part could be completed with something approaching joy, rather than the despair they'd all felt after Reading.

Oswald was grinning from ear to ear as he strode up the slope. He could still see the West Saxon soldiers hunting down the Danes who were heading for the ford at the Tamyse from the looks of it, probably hoping to make it back to Reading where they could regroup and lick their wounds. They had done it. Here, at Ascesdune, Aethelred and Alfred, with God's help, had defeated the heathen horde. This was surely a victory men would talk of for generations to come!

Oswald's joy soon faded, however, as he reached the battlefield and saw up close the dead men littering the field and, perhaps even worse, the injured.

'God give us all strength,' the priest whispered, feeling a sudden urge to retch as he approached a sobbing man, a boy really, whose hand had been severed at the wrist. 'Please, God, give *me* strength,' he begged; and then he set about trying to ease the suffering of the dying warriors as ceorls drew their blades across the throats of injured Danes and stripped the bodies of valuables.

CHAPTER TWENTY-FIVE

The Danes fled to Reading, harried much of the way by Aethelred and Alfred's men who were drunk on their victory at Ascesdune and determined to take vengeance for those kinsmen who'd died at Reading.

Neither of the commanders took part in the pursuit. Aethelred insisted on praying, again, with Bishop Edwin and many of his thanes. God had blessed them with victory, so it was only right He should be thanked. Alfred was happy to hear Mass for he was utterly exhausted after the battle, having given his all and personally cut down many Danes. He felt great joy at the West Saxon triumph, but more tired than he'd ever been before.

Praying was exactly what both brothers needed.

When Mass was finished Alfred and Aethelred, grinning like naughty children, embraced.

'What a day this is,' the king said, eyes shining. 'Our first major victory over Halfdan and his men. Bagsecg, the big bastard, dead!' He stepped back, looking at Alfred with something approaching awe. 'I've heard some of the men saying it was *you*, brother, who killed Bagsecg. Is it true?'

Alfred frowned. He genuinely could not remember if he'd faced off against the enormous Danish king. Surely such a confrontation would burn in his memory like fire? Bagsecg was... memorable, if nothing else. 'Did I?' Alfred asked.

Aethelred laughed. 'So the men are saying.' He leaned in close and whispered, 'I'd take the credit. Killing a great warrior like Bagsecg will only do your reputation good.'

Alfred nodded, searching his brother's face for any hidden meaning. He knew very well that many of their men, ealdormen and ceorls alike, still spoke of the sudden illness that had struck him down during his wedding to Ealhswith. It was still seen as a weakness and, if the world believed he'd dispatched the massive Dane, it would go some way to restoring his standing. Alfred could see only happiness and pride in his brother's expression, and he nodded.

'We'll see if anyone else claims the kill,' he said. 'I honestly don't remember much about individual Danes I engaged. Maybe I did manage to take down Bagsecg, but I'd not steal the credit if some other man deserves it.'

Aethelred nodded. 'Well said. Whoever killed him did us a great service anyway. His loss was devastating to the enemy.'

Alfred saw Wulfric approaching. He'd planned to ask his brother why he'd taken so long to join the battle but decided that question could wait until later. All that mattered right now was the victory.

'Left it a bit late, my lord,' Wulfric said, apparently not feeling as tactful as Alfred. 'We,' he nodded at the prince, 'were almost overrun by those bastards!'

'You weren't though, were you, ealdorman?' Aethelred retorted somewhat testily. 'My charge brought us victory. I'd have thought you'd be happy.'

Wulfric opened his mouth as if to continue berating the king but Alfred grasped his arm and squeezed it. Aethelred was right: they had won. They could dissect the battle later, when passions were not running so high, and the rest of the army wasn't watching. He could already see a number of thanes, including Diuma, watching them with keen interest.

'Go and get a drink,' Alfred commanded Wulfric. 'We'll talk in a bit. Let's get the battlefield cleared and the dead dealt with first, eh?'

His captain huffed in annoyance and even threw the king a black look, but at last he muttered, 'My lords,' and stalked off towards a ceorl who was supervising the ale rations on the back of a wagon. An army could not march on bread alone, after all, and ale was always welcome both before and after a fight.

'The cheek of the man,' Aethelred growled, watching as Wulfric took a cup and then wandered back up the hill, shouting at the troops and ceorls and making sure they worked efficiently to strip the fallen Danes of their goods. 'And don't you start.' This was directed at Sicgred who had just appeared, absolutely caked in dry blood although apparently from those he'd struck down rather than any serious injuries of his own.

'Start what?' the king's captain asked, looking at Alfred in confusion.

'Nothing,' the prince replied and changed the subject by praising Sicgred's bravery.

Eventually the sun began to sink beneath the horizon and camp was set up. Those warriors who'd pursued the beaten Danes filtered back to join Aethelred and the rest of the army and, by the time it was dark, tents were up, fires lit, bellies filled, and plentiful amounts of ale downed.

It was a quite different camp to the one that followed the defeat at Reading.

Wulfric did not continue his earlier criticism of the king, much to Alfred's relief. Aethelred was a fair man, but he seemed to fully believe that his extended Mass had won them the victory over the Danes, and he would not hear a word said against it. The Danes were surely a punishment sent from God, so wasn't praying for His favour the best way to win against them?

Alfred thought it was an interesting question to ponder, but he could speak to Oswald or Bishop Edwin about it another day.

'Have you decided where we go from here?' he asked his brother as they sat by the fire trying to keep warm. Wulfric, Sicgred, Diuma and the warrior-bishop, Heahmund, were all there, as were many other West Saxon noblemen. All had given their counsel in the aftermath of the battle, with many suggesting they try to re-take Reading now that the Danes were weakened, and others advising the army should be allowed to return home to their families. The latter argument had angered Sicgred in particular, but Alfred knew they could not force their untrained warriors from simply sneaking off. And why should they not? Their families needed them, and they'd done their part in beating Halfdan's forces, so had they not earned a rest? Besides, supplies would soon run low and a hungry army was more trouble than it was worth, or so the prince had been told.

Aethelred gazed into the fire for a long time but, at last, he looked from Alfred to Sicgred and then all around at the men watching him. 'We keep the core of the army together,' he said. 'Those who are badly injured may return home, but the rest of us will march to Reading and see what we find there.'

This brought enthusiastic nods and murmurs of agreement from the other noblemen.

Even Wulfric seemed happy. At last, they'd beaten the Danes in battle.

Now the army of Wessex, led by King Aethelred, had the upper hand and future victories would be sure to follow this momentous day at Ascesdune.

—

Winter struck hard in the following weeks, with snow making travel treacherous so, when the Danes locked themselves away in Reading, it seemed like they might remain there, at least until spring, and the army of Wessex gradually disbanded.

The raiders eventually marched out again, however, rampaging across the land and forcing the West Saxon army to come together as best it could once more. This proved predictably difficult, for men living outside the towns directly under threat had no desire to come and fight the Northmen again. With no real way to force those unwilling levies to join them in time, Aethelred, Alfred, and their thanes and ealdormen with whatever forces they could muster met Halfdan in battle, this time at a place called Baseng.

Halfdan's army had been badly depleted at Ascesdune, which had been fought just two weeks before, but it was the Danes who were victorious at Baseng. Again, both sides lost many of their warriors and again they both retreated to try and regroup.

Even the Danes did not wish to fight during February of 871 for it was cold enough to chill even the hardiest of *vikingar*, so an uneasy peace came into effect for a time. Halfdan's men continued to forage, which essentially meant stealing food and goods from the settlements nearest to their encampments, while West Saxon militia tried to fend them off. It was bloody and violent, but on a much smaller scale than the battles at Reading, Ascesdune and Baseng.

Alfred knew his brother would not want to sit idly waiting for spring to bring the Danes out of their holes once again and so it came as no surprise when a messenger arrived at Ceodre, summoning the prince to a Witan at Swinbeorg.

Alfred had no great desire to ride for almost three days, but he knew he could not avoid it. A Witan was a meeting of all the king's closest, most trusted advisors – the wealthiest and most powerful noblemen of Wessex. They would gather and Aethelred would seek their advice on whatever matters he put before them, and Alfred could imagine most of the council's time would be taken up in discussing how to remove the great heathen army from their lands.

Alfred had to go, even if the land was frozen solid and the wind blew as if it would strip the very flesh from a traveller's bones.

The night before he left he enjoyed a feast with his hearth-warriors, including Wulfric and the priest, Oswald. Ealhswith was there, of course, but baby Aethelflaed grew more alert to the world around her every time Alfred returned from a battle and she was put to bed early that night with her nursemaid. The mead hall was no place for such a small child, with its noise, cooking smoke and drunken revelry that could, on occasion, even flare into violence.

'Do you think the Danes will ever be beaten?' Ealhswith asked as they sat eating cuts of roast meat. Although it was bitterly cold outside and every so often a gust of wind would shake the rafters, the fire blazed merrily in the hearth and the walls kept out most of the draughts, so the feast was cosy enough.

Alfred looked at Wulfric who remained silent. Ealhswith's question had been asked many times in recent months and with every passing day it seemed like the eventual answer would be 'no'. Still, the prince had no desire to spend his final night before leaving for the Witan in gloomy conversation over their enemies. 'Yes,' he replied firmly. 'One day.'

His wife accepted the answer and sipped her wine slowly. Alfred watched her, smiling, then instinctively reached out and squeezed her hand. She laid her head on his shoulder and, at that moment, the prince wished they could remain there, in that great hall on this evening, forever.

He'd already downed a few cups of ale, one or two of mead, and some wine. His vow to abstain from the stuff was easier to maintain when he was on campaign with the army for he never wanted his men to think him a sot, unable to think clearly when their lives were all at risk from Halfdan's raiders. Here at his home in Ceodre, however, he'd found himself slowly slipping back into his old ways, drinking from early in the morning until late in the night. He also ate far more while at home, simply because there was so much more available.

Life as a soldier was, paradoxically, healthier for Alfred than spending time safely tucked away in his hall. The thought amused him but then he remembered the terror of battle, and the good men of Wessex who'd lain dead on the ground even after a victory, and...

A sudden, terrible pain struck him, as if someone had just stabbed a seax into his guts and he gasped, doubling over so fast he almost struck his head on the table.

'What's wrong?' Ealhswith asked fearfully.

Alfred felt like he was dying. *Wished* he would, for the pain in the left side of his belly was excruciating. Sweat broke out on his face and he gritted his teeth to keep from crying out, and then, thank God, the pain faded and he sat up straight again. He did not turn to see if Wulfric was watching him – he already knew his captain would be, for his weakness had been noticed by almost everyone within the hall. Warriors and servants alike stared at him anxiously and he forced himself to laugh.

'I think the roast duck disagrees with me,' he called, mustering a jovial tone. 'My wife warned me not to eat it, but I always enjoy duck!' His comment did bring uncertain laughter from some of the men and he got to his feet a little shakily. The pain was gone, but the effects still lingered both in his body and mind, and he was terrified it would strike again as he walked as calmly as possible outside, past the door guards, and into the light of the freezing moon.

The cesspit was a short distance away from the hall and he passed a couple of swaying warriors relieving themselves. The wind whipped the streams of urine this way and that but both men were too drunk to notice – they barely even noticed their prince walking past them.

There was a fence around the cesspit and it was just high enough to hide Alfred from view as he sat down on the wooden bench and tried to empty his bowels. Sometimes, when these pains struck, that could help. Not this time.

'Damn it, I don't even need a shit,' he muttered, pulling his trousers back up and tucking himself in before hurrying back to the hall. His teeth were chattering and his legs were numb from being bared, but the freezing air had at least cleared his head a little and he felt somewhat better for the time outside. Before going into the hall again he stopped at the doors, took a few long, deep breaths, and just spent a moment praying that the pain would not return that night.

Was this, like the Danish raids, a punishment from God? Alfred felt sure it was. As Halfdan's hordes had been sent to

punish the people of Wessex for not living by His command-
ments, Alfred's stomach pains were divine retribution for his life
of debauchery.

And yet, the prince had known men who lived far more
sinful lives than he did. Why were they not struck down
by some affliction? Alfred rarely even lay with other women
nowadays, as he and Ealhswith were trying to bring more royal
children into the world, as was their Christian duty. As a result,
Alfred's carnal needs were well catered for whenever he was
at home with his wife and, although women did follow the
army performing various duties from cooking to prostitution,
the prince had hardly availed himself of their services recently.
So what was God punishing him for?

Eating too much rich food during winter, while so many
ceorls were struggling to fill their own bellies and those of their
children? Drinking too much ale? Again, Alfred thought of the
times when he'd been away with the fyrd in the past year and
noted that his pains had generally been less severe.

It made sense: when he was behaving slothfully or giving
into his carnal vices he was going against the Holy Bible's
teachings. All he had to do was live as chaste a life when he
was at home as he did on campaign.

His mouth felt dry, and a sudden gust of wind blew down
the back of his cloak, making him shiver uncontrollably. Just
then, another inebriated warrior opened the door of the hall
and stumbled out, and Alfred headed inside, revelling in the heat
from the firepit. He walked quickly, pushing past the crowded,
laughing men, grinning at any who looked at him. Soon he
was back in his seat at the high table, between Ealhswith and
Wulfric, both of whom enquired after his health.

'I'm fine,' he replied, and it seemed to be true. The pain
had completely disappeared. He reached out and lifted his cup,
quickly swallowing the wine inside while promising himself,
and God, that he'd not drink too much more that night.

The three sat quietly for a time, just watching the men in the
hall. Loyal and true men, who would be travelling with Alfred

to the Witan the following morning. Some were flyting – taking turns to insult one another with crude rhymes – while others were telling stories, singing songs, playing dice or *hnefatafl*, arm-wrestling, or merely chatting animatedly with one another.

Alfred wondered what Halfdan's hall was like at that very moment. Similar to this, undoubtedly, for the Danes came from much the same traditions as the Saxons, but they were not Christians. No, Halfdan's men would be fighting one another, drunk beyond comprehension, and probably raping the servant girls who were unlucky enough to have been forced into service when the Northmen took control of Reading. It was disgusting, and Alfred felt a cold rage replace the earlier pain in the pit of his stomach.

Reaching out, he lifted his cup, which had been refilled although he hadn't noticed when or by whom, and downed most of the contents in one long swallow, feeling the wine warming his mouth, throat and eventually spreading its glowing tendrils all through his body and spirit.

Now was not the time to think of Danes. Tomorrow he would be gone, again, and he meant to make the most of his time here, warm and—

'My lord,' Wulfric's commanding voice broke into Alfred's thoughts and the prince felt a sinking feeling as he turned to peer at the older man. There was more than drinking and singing on Wulfric's mind, judging by his serious expression.

'Yes?' Alfred replied, trying to keep the irritation from his voice. Probably unsuccessfully, but Wulfric was never one to care about annoying someone anyway, even an aetheling. Being irritated with Wulfric was about as productive as it would be with baby Aethelflaed. Or a rock.

'We,' the ealdorman nodded towards Ealhswith, surprising Alfred, who frowned as Wulfric continued. 'We believe you should speak with your brother at the Witan.'

'That's why we're going,' Alfred replied incredulously. 'What do you mean? Spit it out, man, it's not like you to be vague!'

'You need to speak to Aethelred,' Ealhswith broke in, and there was as much strength in her tone as Wulfric's. 'About the line of succession.'

'What about it?'

'Well, your brothers have...' Ealhswith trailed off, looking uncomfortable, before forging on. 'They have a terrible habit of dying young, my love.'

Alfred gazed at her for a few heartbeats, then he swallowed and bowed his head. 'They do,' he admitted sadly. It was something he tried not to think about but, in truth, he had never believed he would be the heir apparent to Wessex's throne. It was not an honour he'd ever sought or coveted, but there it was.

'Aethelred is only in his thirties,' he said firmly. 'And in far better health than I.'

'Perhaps,' Wulfric conceded. 'But with the number of battles we'll need to fight this coming spring, anyone could be killed.'

'It would be prudent to make sure everyone in Wessex knows who should be crowned king if Aethelred falls,' Ealhswith said gently. 'His sons are growing older, and many would support Aethelhelm – his eldest's – claim to the throne, despite his youth.'

Alfred felt tears welling in his eyes and became angry rather than giving in to the sorrow that threatened to overwhelm him. If Aethelred died that would be all his brothers gone, and he was barely into his twenties!

'Lady Ealhswith is right, my lord,' Wulfric said gently. 'It would do us no favours if some ealdorman, Wulfhere for example, or Diuma's father, Wealdmar, decided they had a better claim to the throne than you, or little Aethelhelm. It could start a civil war, to go along with the war we already face with the great heathen army.'

Alfred listened to them, and he knew they were right. There would always be powerful men looking to take advantage of the death of a king. It made perfect sense to make sure Alfred's path to the throne was set down in law.

The Witan at Swinbeorg was the ideal place to do so.

He swallowed again, feeling a sudden thickness in his throat. Reaching out for his cup, he took another sip of wine, nodding at his captain and wife's proposal, then he drew in a deep, steadying breath. As he opened his mouth to tell them he agreed with them, the pain from earlier struck once more, sudden agony searing through his guts like a red-hot spearpoint.

'Not again,' Ealhswith gasped, taking his hand and squeezing it reassuringly, although she looked frightened herself. 'Can we do anything to help, my love?'

Wulfric was not looking at the prince, he was glaring at the men who'd once again turned to watch as Alfred suffered. As they saw the ealdorman looking at them they averted their gaze, but it was no use. Everyone there knew that Alfred, despite his bravery and heroics on the battlefield, was weak, and likely to die of his mystery illness long before the king.

'I'm going to bed,' Alfred growled, trying not to squeal as he used the table as leverage to help him stand up. 'I'll see you in the morning, Wulfric. I'll be fine then, I'm sure.'

The ealdorman stood up himself, and tilted his head to the side in silent assent as Alfred walked unsteadily to his bedchamber at the far end of the great hall, Ealhswith grasping his arm and smiling at the men they passed on their way as if nothing was wrong.

CHAPTER TWENTY-SIX

The ride to Swinbeorg was not pleasant. Alfred's pains had subsided the day after the feast but the weather was freezing and his hands and face were numb from the wind driving against them. It was not a time for travel, he thought, cursing Halfdan's Danes for upsetting the natural order of things in Wessex. Winter was a time for resting within one's hall, not riding to far-off Witans while your fingers and toes felt like they might turn black from frostbite.

'Nearly there, my lord,' Wulfric said cheerily, and, as usual, the captain's hardiness was a source of both inspiration and irritation. Even the cold didn't seem to bother Wulfric.

'Did you have Norse parents?' Alfred asked him somewhat waspishly. 'Anyone would think you'd been raised amongst the Northmen, in the icy wastes. Are you not even a little bit cold?'

Wulfric grinned, breath steaming in the wan sunshine. 'Of course I am,' he said. 'I just don't show it. The men need an example to follow.'

As usual, Alfred wondered if that was a dig at him, and his weakness. The prince was bundled up in heavy furs and looked quite miserable after all. He knew Wulfric's words were not intended as an insult though, the ealdorman just held himself to a higher standard than everyone else. Even royalty.

'There's the trail up to Swinbeorg,' one of Alfred's other hearth-warriors called, pointing off to the left where a frosty brown path bisected the green grass. 'But look, someone else approaches.' There was a note of alarm in the man's voice and everyone in Alfred's party gripped spears or sword hilts warily.

'Well met, my lord!' The distant voice had a clear West Saxon accent and the men relaxed.

'It's Diuma,' Alfred said, happy to see the young thane and the men he commanded in his elderly father's absence.

The two parties closed on one another, and the bright-eyed thane smiled respectfully at the prince. 'My rear-guard spotted you coming,' he said. 'So, I thought we'd wait and accompany you to the Witan.' He stopped, ran a hand through his dark hair, and then said, more hesitantly, 'If you don't mind, that is?'

'Not at all,' replied Alfred jovially. 'Glad to have you with us, my friend.'

Diuma's face lit up and the combined groups continued onwards, up the trail towards the meeting point King Aethelred had called them to.

'It's bloody freezing,' Diuma noted, to murmurs of agreement from all in earshot. 'And my suggestion to attack the Danes in winter doesn't seem quite so laughable now, eh, Lord Wulfric?'

Alfred's captain frowned at him. 'Eh?' he grunted.

'I'm sure you were one of the men who laughed when I suggested we attack the Danes—'

'No, I wasn't,' Wulfric broke in, and his dour expression made it seem like he had *never* laughed, at anything in his life.

Alfred did snort with mirth though, at Diuma's amazed look. 'He's right,' the aetheling said. 'Wulfric is much too disciplined to behave so disrespectfully to a thane during the king's council. He didn't laugh at you.'

Diuma was obviously still upset at the mocking sniggers and catcalls he'd faced all that time ago. 'My apologies then,' he muttered, nodding at Wulfric. 'But here we are – travelling in this icy weather, freezing our bollocks off. And we've fought a few battles as well this winter. So...' He trailed off and gazed around at the frozen, frigid fields surrounding them. '*We* could have attacked *them*, and probably beaten the bastards, for they'd not have been expecting it.'

Alfred nodded. 'Perhaps something to think about in the future,' he conceded, but said no more for he did not want to criticise his brother's tactics. Still, if they wanted to ever truly defeat the Danes new ways of doing things would be necessary and Diuma was someone he wanted on his side in the coming years.

If they survived that long.

An older nobleman went by on a powerful, white horse, accompanied by a dozen warriors, and Diuma scowled in his direction. 'Now, *he* was definitely one of those who laughed at me that night in the hall.'

Alfred nodded. 'Bishop Deorlaf,' he said. 'A man who does not like change.'

'And a man who doesn't like to lose his wealth,' Wulfric growled. 'He'll be here to remind the king, and everyone else, that paying off the Danes is not the way to win the war. He'd rather throw away men's lives than give up his hoarded silver.'

They made their way up the slope in thoughtful silence, until they at last came to the summit, where a number of tents were already set up by those attendees who lived closer than Alfred or Diuma. Their men set about making camp themselves with the grandest tents reserved for the nobles, or the clergymen like the priest Oswald, who travelled everywhere with Alfred these days. Over the next couple of days more men came to join the Witan and, eventually, even Ealdorman Odda from far-off Devon arrived to much fanfare, and business could truly begin.

Alfred had spent many hours chatting with his brother while they waited for everyone to turn up and it was pleasant for they barely mentioned the Danes or any other lofty matters. Their conversation was mostly about their wives and children, the harsh weather and their shared childhood. It was nice just to be siblings for a time, rather than the men the people of Wessex were looking to for protection against Halfdan's heathen scourge.

When Odda, a tall, plump man with red hair and a bushy beard, had settled in, however, it was time for the Witan to come together properly and Alfred was forced to once more play the part of the aetheling, while King Aethelred called the meeting to order.

'My lord,' Odda called out, before any other business could be broached. 'Is it necessary to have these Witans outdoors, in the middle of nowhere, at this time of year?'

A few of the other noblemen laughed and cheered at this. They were indeed outside, on the top of a hillock, and the icy wind was enough to make even Wulfric draw his cloak up around his neck.

'Could we not meet in one of our great halls? Alfred's hall at Ceodre is a fine place for a feast, and not too far from my own lands.'

Aethelred was frowning, unhappy at this disruption, and Sicgred who was at his side, stood up as if to berate Odda for his words, but Alfred beat him to it.

'This is how my family has always done it, Odda,' called the prince, getting to his feet and walking towards the Ealdorman of Devon. As he moved he looked around at the other powerful, wealthy men gathered there, drawing their attention to him as he spoke. 'Aye, it's cold, and damp, but we have our traditions and, when your king summons you,' he paused and turned to gesture back towards his brother. 'You go where he asks.'

'Exactly right, my lord,' Sicgred shouted, glaring at Odda, who seemed somewhat mortified now that so many people were eyeing him accusingly.

'Now,' Alfred said, casting his gaze across the men who sat in a large semi-circle around him and Aethelred. 'Can we get this Witan over with? It's bloody freezing.'

Odda, along with everyone else, laughed loudly at that, glad that the atmosphere had been lifted, and Alfred stepped quickly back to the chair that was sitting to the right of the king's. Aethelred nodded gratefully to him and called the meeting to order.

As expected, the Witan's discussions centred around the West Saxon strategy for dealing with the Danes, every man there knowing Halfdan would strike without mercy come the spring, if not before. Over the next three days they talked of taxes, of food supplies, weapon and armour manufacture, ship construction, fortifications, training the various fyrds, and many other topics. There was mostly agreement, for, as Alfred had already pointed out, tradition was strong with the noblemen of Wessex. Not many of them would call for a change to the old ways, especially when doing so would bring anger and derision, as Diuma had found out not so long before.

'Well,' Aethelred said smiling in satisfaction on the afternoon of the third day. 'I think our business is concluded, gentlemen.' The main points had already been summed up and all that remained now was to get roaring drunk together before travelling homewards. Everyone was looking forward to that, especially as the weather had remained damp and cold for the whole duration of the Witan.

Alfred glanced at Wulfric, who nodded encouragingly, and the aetheling took a long breath, steeling himself for what he knew he had to do. 'My lords,' he said loudly, standing and offering a shallow bow to his brother. 'I would speak before we call an end to the meeting.'

There was some grumbling at this. The ealdormen and thanes were fed up with the Witan now, it was just too cold and uncomfortable. Alfred forged on, however, before he lost his nerve.

'My lord,' he said directly to Aethelred. 'My king.'

His brother frowned. It was clear to everyone gathered there that something unexpected, yet hugely significant, was about to happen.

'As we both know all too well, our house has not fared well over recent years.' He stepped out in front of the gathering, speaking clearly so there could be no misunderstanding of his words. 'Our mother and father are dead. Our brothers are dead.' He shook his head sorrowfully. 'I never thought I would be anywhere near to inheriting the throne of Wessex, and I know you never really thought you would end up as king when we were growing up, Aethelred. Fate has not been kind to our family.'

The king nodded somewhat warily. 'That's true, brother. And the Danes are not helping. That is why we must all pray to God for salvation.'

There were murmurs of agreement and Alfred nodded vigorously. 'We must! And yet...' He paused and looked up to the sky, as if seeking guidance from God. 'We must also do what we can here on Earth to make sure Wessex does not fall into civil war, no matter what.'

Aethelred was not the only one frowning now. Sicgred's forehead was so furrowed Alfred thought his ceorls might plant turnips in the ealdorman's brow.

'What do you mean, brother?' Aethelred asked. 'Get to the point.'

'I think,' said Alfred, 'that we must make it clear, in law, what should happen if you, or I, should die, my lord.'

There was a stunned silence. By rights, if he was to die, the king's oldest son should take the crown. That was how Aethelred had ended up with it after all. And Aethelred had not just one, but two young sons. What was Alfred suggesting?

'You know I love your boys, Aethelhelm, and Aethelwold,' said the prince earnestly. 'But they are children. If something should happen to you, Aethelred – God forbid – your sons are far too young to lead the forces of Wessex.'

He paused again, allowing his words to sink in. The Witan knew he was right, and they also knew there was every chance the king would fall in the battles that would certainly take place with Halfdan's forces in the coming months. Indeed, some of the ealdormen were *hoping* Aethelred would fall, so that they might press their own claim to rule Wessex.

Aethelred was still staring at him with an unreadable expression. 'What are you saying, exactly?' he asked softly.

'I'm saying,' Alfred replied, glancing at Wulfric who again nodded encouragingly. 'That the Witan must agree that I will be king if you should fall within the next ten years. And, furthermore, that, as the last of our male siblings, the line of succession will then move on *through my children*.'

CHAPTER TWENTY-SEVEN

There was a stunned silence at that. Alfred, and *Alfred's children*, would take the throne, rather than Aethelred's own issue? Sicgred looked incensed, as might be expected from the king's most loyal supporter and captain, but Aethelred himself appeared more thoughtful than angered or even shocked.

'What's your reasoning for this, my lord?' Ealdorman Odda asked. He was one of the wealthier, and thus more powerful, of all the West Saxon nobles, but his lands in Devon were too far in the east for him to stake a claim for the crown himself. As such, he would be a valuable ally for whoever did eventually take the throne, and Alfred knew that, so he made certain his tone was respectful, almost deferential, as he addressed the man.

'The crown has, until now, passed down through my brothers. From Aethelstan who was King of Kent under my father, Aethelwulf's overlordship, to Aethelbald, Aethelbert, and now Aethelred – all have been Kings of Wessex. As the last of that line, it should be me who succeeds Aethelred if anything, God forbid, should happen to him.'

Many members of the council nodded at this reasoning, and Odda said, 'Indeed, that would make more sense than Aethelred's six-year-old son becoming king and relying on a regent to oversee things until he came of age. Now, with Halfdan's heathen plague upon us, we need a proper king, not a child.'

There was a chorus of agreement at that, but Aethelred, visibly flustered now, broke in. 'This is all very well, but why should *your* children then become next in line, brother? You don't even have a son yet, and might never have one.'

'In that case,' Alfred said, 'your eldest son, Aethelhelm would succeed me.'

There was silence as the Witan took all this in. So many similar names to think about, and children not even born yet!

'But it would not be right for me to become king, and then, if I should fall, for the line of succession to move back to Aethelred's side if I father a son before then.'

Again, there was a lull as everyone digested Alfred's argument.

'My lord,' Odda said directly to Aethelred. 'You are king. What say you about this?'

Alfred watched his brother's face as conflicting emotions played across it. Distrust, disappointment, sadness, anger, fear. And yet, when the king spoke it was from the head rather than the heart.

'As you say, Alfred, if I should be killed in battle it would save any civil unrest if the crown passed directly to you. That security is what Wessex needs at this time, more than ever.' He drew in a long breath, then let it out. 'And I agree that, should you have a son, the crown may pass on to them, rather than my own sons.'

Murmurs then from the members of the Witan, surprised that Aethelred gave in to Alfred's demands so readily.

'If you do not have sons, however, we must agree that on your death my eldest boy will take the crown. Yes?'

'Of course,' Alfred replied steadily and the brothers eyed one another in silence.

'Let the Witan record this agreement then, with God as our Witness,' Aethelred finally said. 'And then, Bishop Edwin will say Mass for us, and after that we shall seal the agreement with a toast.'

No-one made any jocular remarks about getting home to their warm hall, or their desire to drink themselves into a stupor. It did not seem appropriate following such a momentous Witan.

Afterwards, when everything had been formalised, written down and witnessed, Mass was celebrated and, since it was late afternoon by that point, there was no suggestion of anyone travelling home. With no need to remain clear-headed now that the important business had been attended to, the atmosphere was relaxed as the men drank together. A cloudy sky meant that there was no frost as night fell, making it seem just a little warmer than the previous nights in Swinbeorg.

The men were hopeful, and looking forward to the coming spring, at least as much as could be expected with the Danish army still camped at Reading. Food was prepared by the servants, fires lit, and barrels of ale broached for one last feast before the Witan disbanded.

'Happy, my lord?'

Alfred looked up to see Wulfric smiling down at him after making sure their men had posted sentries and set a watch on the perimeter of the camp. 'I am,' the aetheling replied. 'Sit with me, my friend.'

The ealdorman gladly sat on an empty camp chair next to him. He already had a horn of mead in his hand although he sipped from it only occasionally, for he liked to remain alert when in the field, even if there was no chance of an enemy force sneaking up on them there.

'I must admit, Aethelred surprised me,' said Alfred quietly. The camp was noisy that night with raucous singing and drunken laughter filling the air so there was little chance of them being overheard, but, even so, Wulfric was forced to lean in close to hear what his lord was saying.

'Surprised?' the captain asked. 'Why?'

'He gave in to my demands without any argument.'

Wulfric grunted. 'Well, he wants what's best for Wessex. Passing it to you makes sense, and means the kingdom remains in your – his – family.'

Alfred nodded slowly, watching as a couple of men arm-wrestled nearby, teeth gritted and showing white in the flickering light from campfires. 'But the children,' he said.

'Alfred,' Wulfric said, also lowering his voice warily. 'Think about it. If Aethelred dies you will become king. It's only natural that you would want your own children to succeed you – where would that leave your brother's infant sons who some might think had a better claim to the throne?'

Shocked, Alfred turned to him. 'I'd never harm those boys,' he hissed. 'They're my nephews. My blood. And they're good little lads!'

Wulfric shrugged. 'I know you wouldn't hurt them, my lord. But someone else might, thinking they'd be doing you a favour. Which they would be, if this agreement hadn't been finalised here today. Aethelred made the only choice he could that would see his family safe if you become king.'

They sat in gloomy silence after that, drinking and listening to the babble all around them. Alfred could see that Wulfric was right about everything and it depressed him. Men and women all throughout history had killed even their own family members in order to seize wealth and power. Indeed, his own older brother, Aethelbald, had tried to wrest the crown from their father, causing much disruption within Wessex. Alfred had been very young at the time but he knew how deeply the scars had run in his family after that.

He got up and went to speak with Aethelred, who was in his own grand tent a short distance away, conversing with Bishop Edwin. The clergyman left when he saw the prince's grim expression, leaving the king and his heir-apparent alone, but for the two guards positioned outside.

'Brother,' said Alfred coming to stand before Aethelred. 'You must know, I would never, *will* never harm a hair on your sons' heads. If you die before me, I swear by Christ and all the saints to protect them both, and your wife, Lady Wulfthryth.' He shook his head. 'I never...'

Aethelred watched him struggle for the right words, but at last he took pity and stepped forward, grasping Alfred by the wrist and drawing him into an embrace. 'I know,' he said. 'But this is the way of things and we must make the most of it. Besides, you might very well die before me, and then none of this will matter.' He laughed humourlessly.

'That'll be the talk of the camp anyway,' Alfred agreed, turning to look out through the tent's open entrance flaps at the warriors gathered all around them. 'Ever since I collapsed at my own wedding, people have been expecting me to fall down dead at any moment.' He placed a hand on his stomach, recalling the most recent attack just a few days before, back in Ceodre. 'Sometimes I wish I *would* just die; the pain is almost unbearable.' He sighed and made the sign of the cross. 'It always goes away eventually though, praise God.'

'Is it truly so bad?' Aethelred asked, concern etching deep furrows in his forehead. 'I had no idea. Can a leech not help?'

Alfred snorted. 'I've spoken to many. The latest one was a fellow who read some "cure" that had been written down by a monk or the like, and insisted it would work. He went out and found a dung beetle, and its ball of dung, then threw it over his shoulder saying, "*Remedium facio ad ventris dolorem.*"' The aetheling blew out a heavy breath and glanced at Aethelred. 'Apparently doing all that meant the leech could cure my bad stomach simply by placing his hands on it. Needless to say, it didn't work! Nothing has, and I've tried "cures" from as far away as Jerusalem.'

The king shook his head disgustedly. 'You do wonder where the healers get their ideas from at times.'

'All I can do,' said Alfred, 'is pray that the pain never gets too bad, or at least never persists for too long. Or kills me...'

'How is it now?' Aethelred asked, stepping outside and leading the way back towards Alfred's tent with its crackling fire and Wulfric sitting gazing into the flames.

'It's been fine since the day we travelled here from Ceodre,' the prince replied, stepping nimbly over a bundle of rope that some thralls were using to secure empty barrels onto a cart. Again, he realised how much better he felt, physically, when he was on campaign or employed in some other important work.

They stopped at the edge of the camp, away from the light of the fires, and gazed up at the night sky. Despite the noise of the men it was surprisingly peaceful there and neither said a word for a long time. At last, Aethelred turned and faced his brother and Alfred felt a moment of anxiety for he was sure the king was going to upbraid him for what had happened at the Witan. Instead, Aethelred said earnestly, 'I am proud of you, little brother.'

Alfred took that in, wondering if he'd heard right. 'You are?' he said eventually.

'I am. Mother and Father would be too.'

A lump formed in Alfred's throat and he averted his eyes for fear tears might spring from them.

'Before you married Ealhswith I thought you would never fulfil your potential,' the king went on, oblivious to his brother's discomfort. 'But you've become the man I always hoped you would, accepting your responsibilities and learning how to command the fyrd with skill and confidence. The men love and respect you, and the tales the scops tell of you will eventually surpass even those about Ealdorman Mucel.'

'Thank you,' Alfred replied, pitching his voice low for fear it would break. 'You've taught me well. And wedding me to Ealhswith was an inspired move on your part. She's been perfect for me.'

'I knew she would be,' Aethelred grinned, before he became serious again. 'But you must take credit yourself. You have a drive and a confidence in you, Alfred, that I envy.' He held up a hand, forestalling his brother's protestations. 'You do,' he insisted. 'That's one reason why I agreed to your demands about the succession. If you are to become king after me, I believe you will go on to do great things. Greater than I could manage.'

Alfred's brows came together now, and he felt a wave of fear run across him. 'Why are you telling me all this?' he asked. 'Are you dying or something?'

The king's reaction was not at all what he expected, as Aethelred burst out laughing, long, loud and unrestrained. It was almost insulting.

'No, you fool! I'm as strong as an ox. I just wanted to let you know how proud I am of you. Is that all right? Can a big brother not compliment his siblings when they've done well?'

Alfred grinned in relief, then felt the breath knocked out of him as Aethelred grabbed him in a bear hug for a moment, then the pressure was gone and the king was wandering away, back towards the flickering campfires. 'Come on,' he called over his shoulder. 'That's enough praise for one night. Let's get a drink.'

Alfred hurried after him, wondering if his brother had already had a skinful, but he felt almost as if he was walking on air. It meant everything to know Aethelred was proud of him, and he wished their parents could have been there to see the men they'd grown into.

'Lord king,' Wulfric said, getting to his feet respectfully as Aethelred and Alfred came into the circle of light cast by their fire. There were half a dozen other thanes and ealdormen there, including Diuma, and they followed Wulfric's lead. When they were seated again, and all who wanted food or drink had been served by ceorls with trenchers of food and jugs of ale, mead or wine, Aethelred raised his cup high in the air.

'To a prosperous spring, and a fruitful summer,' he said, smiling. 'And may God bring us victory over the Northmen!'

It had been a productive Witan, thought Alfred, greatly relieved to know his beloved big brother was not angry with him. Most of the men at the gathering probably thought Alfred could hardly wait to take the throne for himself, but, as he met Aethelred's gaze they smiled at one another, just as they'd done since they were children. Wessex was stronger with the two of them around, Alfred knew. He truly hoped things would continue as they were for many years to come, even if that meant he would never be king.

Especially if it meant he would never be king!

CHAPTER TWENTY-EIGHT

Meretun, AD 871

March 22nd

Two months after the battle at Baseng, as spring finally seemed to be blooming in Wessex, the Danes moved out in force once more, forsaking the safety of Reading's walls. They moved southeast, sailing their longships down the River Kennet or riding along its banks, attacking settlements along the way until they came at last to a tiny village known as Meretun.

Here, Aethelred and Alfred's forces managed to halt the Danish advance and yet another battle was fought. Again, as at Ashdown, each side split into two but this was a more evenly matched encounter than the previous confrontation.

It was a sunny day and, before the fighting started, Alfred had looked out at the field ahead. It was just beginning to show some signs of colour, as bluebells, violets, white anemones and yellow cowslips pushed their way through the green grass, reaching their petals outwards to the warmth and light of the spring sunshine. The air was crisp and cool and, on such a beautiful day, the prince truly felt God's presence in every breath.

Until he took in the sight of the hordes of Northmen approaching the West Saxon army, colourful heathen banners rippling behind them like serpents' tails.

It had only got worse from there, as the shieldwalls smashed into one another and men began dying. Again. It was almost a routine now. Alfred could feel himself becoming desensitised to the screams of his own brave West Saxon warriors, never mind those of the hated enemy. Considering the prince had literally no experience of leading his men into a pitched battle just a year ago, he'd now been involved in so many such clashes that he no longer felt the same levels of fear or dread as he thrust and parried and did his best to slaughter Halfdan's followers.

This time the sides were more evenly matched, with neither shieldwall giving way, and hundreds of men died on both sides before the sun began its slow descent beneath the horizon.

Alfred had started the battle at the front of his column, as had Aethelred, and Wulfric, and Sicgred, and Diuma, and all the rest of the West Saxon captains and commanders. As the day progressed, however, they were forced to give in to fatigue and move to the rear ranks in order to rest exhausted muscles or seek assistance from the healers for wounds inflicted by Danish spears and axes.

There were no surprise flanking manoeuvres or other clever tactics in this battle. Meretun would not be remembered for anything like that – this was simply two armies coming together and hacking and slashing until the other was defeated.

Alfred climbed on top of a wagon carrying food supplies and gazed out at the ranks of fighters arrayed before him. The sun was so low by now that it was difficult to get a true measure of how things were going but he knew Aethelred and Halfdan would soon call their forces back, for it was pure folly to try and wage a battle such as this in the dark of night.

'My lord.'

Alfred glanced down and saw a young boy holding out a cup of ale. He took it with a word of thanks and was grateful as the liquid lubricated his parched mouth and throat. It felt like he'd been there in Meretun, fighting, for a week. He wondered how older men managed it. Even in his early twenties, in the prime of his life, these battles left him utterly drained.

He smiled wryly then as he saw Bishop Heahmund, pushing his way back through the West Saxon rows of men, coming to join Alfred for a well-earned rest. The man was a veritable marvel! In, at least, his late forties or early fifties, the bishop fought with a savagery to match even one of the fabled Danish berserkers. He wore a helmet with a golden crest, which meant he was easily able to be picked out amongst the combatants. Many lesser men would shy away from such attention, not wanting to draw danger to themselves, but not Heahmund. He revelled in dispatching enemy soldiers for they were no more than heathen scum intent on destroying good Christians.

Alfred knew an army needed men like Bishop Heahmund. Men who could inspire bravery and lead by example. The prince hoped and prayed that he could be such a figurehead one day.

'Lad,' he called down to the young ceorl who was serving out cups of ale. 'Get one for the bishop. He's going to need it after the number of Northmen he's sent to Valhöll this day!'

The servant was already filling a cup and Alfred, smiling, for he felt sure God was with them that day and victory would be theirs come sundown, turned to watch Heahmund.

The bishop's helmet with its golden cross glinted in what was left of the light but, as Alfred watched him approach, he was utterly astonished to see the entire top section of the helm crumple. The warrior bishop fell and did not move again as the men around continued to push forward, oblivious.

Alfred stared in shock, wondering what had just happened. He replayed the scene in his head as he jumped down from the cart and sprinted, as fast as possible given the weight of armour he had about him, to the fallen clergyman.

The prince reached the fallen bishop, lying face down on the grass. There would be no helping him, Alfred could tell, for the back of Heahmund's skull had been shattered completely, killing him instantly. There was a heavy lump of iron lying on the ground and Alfred recognised it as the top of a hammer. He looked up at the warriors in the rear ranks of the shieldwall, but whoever the broken weapon had belonged to had moved away without even knowing what he'd done.

The head of the hammer must have snapped off, either in combat, or perhaps by being battered against the owner's own shield as he joined in with the incessant, discordant noise that marked every battlefield. The heavy metal lump had snapped off and flown through the air with such force that it killed the bishop as he pushed his way through the ranks to safety.

Alfred shook his head in despair. For such a fierce, skilled and honourable warrior as Heahmund to be killed in a freak accident... It was devastating.

Some of the warriors nearby had noticed the dead bishop and Alfred's dismay now, and word was beginning to spread through the ranks. Tears were in the aetheling's eyes as he got to his feet and drew his sword, striding towards the back rows of the army and shoving between them.

'Avenge him,' he shouted, glaring at the men. 'Make these heathen bastards pay for the death of a good Christian! Do you hear me?' He gazed directly at one warrior who had his head bowed and looked like the fight had left him after the long battle. 'Do you hear me?' Alfred demanded. 'Are you going to let Halfdan and his scum kill us all? Are you?'

The warrior, shocked to be addressed by his prince, stood up straight, towering over Alfred, and his eyes blazed as the battle lust was rekindled.

'No, my lord!' the soldier shouted, gripping his spear tighter, nostrils flaring.

'Are you?' Alfred demanded of another man who immediately responded much as the first warrior had done.

'For God and Wessex!' one of the troops cried, and Alfred seized the chance to begin a chant. Soon, everyone around him had joined in and, 'For God and Wessex!' filled the air, moving out towards the front row of the army. Alfred followed its progress until he too was standing in the foremost rank of the shieldwall. Someone had given him a spear for he'd left his back at the ale cart and, filled with righteous fury, he attacked the Danes before him.

'For God and Wessex!'

The sudden surge of battle fever that had spread throughout the entire West Saxon army gave them enough momentum to push the Northmen back. Thrusting, stabbing, slashing, Alfred, Aethelred and the rest of the shieldwall killed dozens of the enemy in that short period alone but it was growing dark now, the sun slipping beneath the horizon, leaving only a thin sliver of light in the western sky.

Some of the combatants, following shouted commands from their leaders, broke off from the fighting and began to move back, preparing to give up the battle for the time being. A few, lost in the fever that slaughter sometimes brings on in men, continued to hack at their opponents, discarding spears in favour of swords or axes. As the shieldwalls moved further apart those few murderous souls could be seen in the dusk, weapons clashing and thudding, grunts and bellows filling the silence left by their departed comrades.

Alfred was one of the warriors who had not realised everyone around him was retreating. His spear had snapped at some point and he'd drawn his sword to trade blows with a stocky Dane whose blond hair was streaked with blood. Both their shields were in tatters and offered little protection, but, when his enemy slipped on a patch of mud, Alfred slammed the iron boss into the man's face. Even through the metal he could feel the crunch of bone and cartilage, and when the Dane fell down Alfred's blade hacked into his skull with a terrific crack. The aetheling screamed something unintelligible and looked at the withdrawn line of enemy soldiers, baring his teeth in triumph. He would have raised his arms high in challenge but his sword was stuck in the dead man's head and he was forced to hold the body down while levering the blade free.

'Aye, retreat you fucking dogs!' he screamed. 'Run back to hide under your mothers' skirts, before we kill you all.'

Behind him, the men of Wessex laughed and cheered. No man wanted to put his own life on the line for a commander who hid in the rear ranks, and Alfred was proving himself as brave, or perhaps foolhardy, as any of their number. They loved it.

A carrion crow, sleek and shiny, landed near the prince and he grinned at it, wondering what it would feel like to stroke its smooth feathers. 'Eat well, my friend,' he laughed, nodding towards the Dane he'd just dispatched. 'Fill your belly with his flesh!'

He turned to walk back to his own shieldwall, looking across at a handful of other men who were still struggling with enemy warriors. Surprised, he realised one of them was his brother. Aethelred was with Sicgred and three of his other hearth-warriors, and they were getting the best of a similar number of Danes. One of the enemies fell as Alfred watched, cut down by Sicgred's sword.

Now, with the advantage of numbers, Aethelred's little band pushed forward and another Dane went down, screaming, before a boot in the face from the King of Wessex silenced him.

The army roared in delight and bellowed encouragement to Aethelred, who raised his sword and shook it defiantly at Halfdan's troops.

Alfred was laughing and giving loud thanks to God, but the shouts died in his throat as he noticed a single arrow soaring through the air. It seemed to move across the sky in slow motion, and Alfred fancied he could even make out the wood-grain of the shaft and the details of the grey, goose-feather vanes, before the missile began its inevitable descent. It was a strangely beautiful sight, calm and serene after a day of savagery and blood. Somehow the arrow gained terrific speed then, moving in a blur, before it hammered straight into the king.

'No,' Alfred gasped, staring in horror as his brother collapsed like a sack of grain dropped from a wagon. 'Please, God, no! Not him too.'

CHAPTER TWENTY-NINE

Sicgred and the others quickly took care of the remaining enemy warriors, with the last deciding there was no point in dying that day and running away, back to the safety of Halfdan's shieldwall. They were cheering, the Danes, for they recognised Aethelred and knew his death would be a terrible blow to the people of Wessex.

'How could they have even hit him from there?' Alfred was shouting as he ran towards Sicgred and his fallen brother. 'Surely they're out of range!'

'A freak shot,' Sicgred grunted, reaching down and, along with two of his men, lifting Aethelred up and striding back towards the rest of the West Saxon army. 'Come on, my lord, before they try to hit you too.'

Alfred was staring at the jeering Danes, half hoping one or two of them would rush him, but common sense overtook his battle rage, and he hurried after the others, praying that Aethelred's wound would not be a serious one. The Danes' bows were not particularly powerful and, as Alfred had noted, they'd been almost out of range. Some rogue gust of wind, some unusual air current, must have pushed the arrow further than normal but, given that, surely most of the power had already left it by the time it struck Aethelred's armour. It had been a one-in-a-million shot, just like the one that had killed Bishop Heahmund.

'How is he?'

Sicgred looked up as Alfred approached. They were both squinting for darkness was upon them almost completely now and it was difficult to make anything out.

'Can't say,' the king's captain replied.

'God above,' Aethelred grunted, and Alfred could clearly see the whites of his brother's eyes for they were wide with pain and shock. 'Get it out of me!'

'We can't, lord,' Sicgred said. 'Not here. The Danes might come at us again.' He looked back to Alfred. 'We should get away from this place, my lord. Set up a camp back there, on top of that rise so we can keep an eye out for the enemy. Once we've done that, and got some lamps lit, the leech can help the king.'

Alfred glanced back over his shoulder. Halfdan's army was also moving away. They appeared to have no inclination to continue the fight in the dark, and why would they? For all they knew, the King of Wessex was mortally wounded. They could afford to retreat and see to their wounded. Tomorrow might bring them an easy victory since, without their king, the West Saxon army would lose heart.

'Agreed,' said Alfred, looking around for Wulfric. He felt a momentary sense of panic when he could not see the ealdorman anywhere and feared Wulfric might also have been killed in the fighting. Eventually, however, his captain came from amongst the nearby ranks and the aetheling sighed in relief.

'Let's move back then!' Wulfric bellowed, having just caught the end of Alfred and Sicgred's hurried conversation. 'To the ridge, there.' He was pointing and there was just enough light left for everyone to make out the nearby hillock against the horizon. 'Hurry up, come on!'

Soon the entire army was in position and a camp was being set up. Exhausted men were tasked with digging defensive ditches around the ridge, sentries were set, and scouts sent out to make sure no Danish raiders sneaked up on the army of Wessex. Fires were lit, tents raised, and food and drink passed out amongst the grateful troops. There was no way to tell which side had come off the best in the day's fighting, but the tired men were just happy to be alive and safe, even if it might only be for one more night.

The best of the leeches were summoned and they worked on the king by the light of oil lamps and beeswax candles, although the faint aroma they gave off could not mask the sweet stench of sweat within the tent.

'The arrow did not penetrate the flesh all that deeply,' one leech muttered as he examined Aethelred's injury. 'Above the heart, mercifully.'

'Then he'll be all right?' Alfred demanded.

The leech – a small man with nimble fingers, ideally suited to this kind of work – shrugged, squinting at the king's body. 'He should be,' he said at last, to an audible gasp of relief from the king. 'But it's going to hurt removing this.'

Aethelred groaned, but he'd been given a lot of mead to drink and was quite inebriated. 'Get on with it then,' he said. 'Yank it out!'

Alfred opened his mouth in alarm, he knew what kind of damage that would do, but, of course, so did the leeches.

'Patience, lord,' said the small one. 'You have them?' he asked, turning to one of his colleagues.

The other leech, a tall man who was forced to stoop to work on the king, nodded and produced two feathers. 'Here they are,' he said. 'Brace yourself, lord king.'

Sicgred was at the king's head and he placed a piece of wood in Aethelred's mouth as the small leech took the feathers and began to work. It took four burly warriors to hold down the king's limbs as he thrashed and bit down on the stick, roaring in agony while the leech pushed the hollow tips of the quills into his flesh, probing until they covered the two barbed points of the arrow head. At last, he had the quills in place and, sucking in a deep breath, he slowly drew the arrow out of the king's body, doing surprisingly little damage to the flesh although there was a lot of blood.

The second leech said, 'Don't let him go just yet,' to the four warriors holding Aethelred down on the table, and then, without warning, pressed a red-hot poker he'd taken from the campfire outside onto the king's bleeding wound. There was a sizzling sound, and the smell of roasting meat filled the tent as the patient roared once more, practically biting through the wood that Sicgred was holding in his mouth.

Alfred watched in horrified fascination, tears in his eyes at the pain his brother was going through.

The leeches cleaned the wound and bandaged it up while Sicgred removed the stick from Aethelred's mouth and held a cup of mead out to him in its place. The king, sweating profusely and breathing heavily, gulped down the drink with a noise somewhere between choking and sobbing.

'Christ above,' he cried. 'That was the worst pain I've ever felt.'

'It's over now, my lord,' said the leech, showing Aethelred the arrow. 'You can keep this as a memento of the day. Show it to your grandchildren when they want to know what happened at the Battle of Meretun.'

Alfred patted his brother on the arm, smiled reassuringly, and then followed the little leech out of the tent where he stopped him and asked in a quiet voice, 'Will he survive that?'

'It's not the worst wound I've ever seen,' replied the man brightly. 'As long as he lets it heal he should be fine.'

A wave of relief washed over Alfred. 'Thank you,' he said to the leech, who nodded and hurried away to see to other casualties of the battle. Alfred's head was spinning from all that had happened that day, and the inevitable tiredness that set in once the battle fever wore off. He felt like he might collapse right there outside Aethelred's tent, but Wulfric appeared out of the darkness and led him to one of the fires.

Seated, with a cup of mead, and the warmth of the blaze chasing the chill from the night, Alfred felt the stress and fear fading from him until, at last, his head slumped and he fell fast asleep.

CHAPTER THIRTY

The Danes were gone when Alfred woke the next morning. Although the battle had no clear victor, Halfdan must have decided he'd lost enough men and marched off somewhere to lick his wounds; back to their stolen fortress at Reading probably. Which was good news for the West Saxon army, for they'd suffered terrible casualties as well.

The prince visited Aethelred in his tent and was pleased to see him sitting up on a chair, features drawn but with some of his usual colour returned to them.

'You're looking well,' said Alfred, nodding down at the king's hand. 'I assume whatever's in there is helping.'

'Just ale,' his brother laughed, wincing at a sudden stab of pain and saluting him with the cup. 'Although I've already had a fair bit of mead this morning.'

'Well, if it helps ease the pain,' said Alfred, growing serious. 'The leech tells me you'll recover well enough, so take things easy for now. Sicgred and Wulfric, along with young Diuma and the rest, will make sure the bodies are cleared from the battlefield. Oswald and Edwin will give our own fallen a proper Christian burial.'

'Burn the Danes,' Aethelred muttered. 'I don't want their festering corpses lying here in our beautiful countryside.'

Alfred nodded. A servant brought him a drink and he sat with his brother for a long time, watching as the camp went about its business. They shared tales of what they'd seen during the fighting the day before, boasted of great feats, laughed at

237

Bishop Heahmund's insane bravery, and mourned his tragic death, along with all their slaughtered people.

Perhaps it was the ale, or perhaps the fact both of them had survived yet another battle with the rampaging Northmen, but Alfred found himself feeling strangely content that spring morning as he sat with his brother. Happy, even. He'd always been close to Aethelred and it truly gladdened his heart to see him on the mend.

'I see you did keep it after all,' he said, pointing into the tent. The arrow that had skewered the king was lying beside Aethelred's bedroll, cleaned of the blood and gore that had been on it the night before.

'Aye,' the king nodded. He made as if to look around at the missile but grimaced in pain and changed his mind. 'A nice keepsake. The arrow that almost killed me. A reminder of my own mortality, and to thank God for allowing me to live. Bishop Edwin is quite taken with it – I suspect he might have it placed in Canterbury when I do die, as if it was some saint's relic!'

They laughed at that. Halfdan had done his best to kill them, but here they were, still fighting and sending the great heathen army fleeing the field of battle. The idea that either one of them might become a saint any time soon was ludicrous.

'You praised me, at the Witan, brother. Remember?'

Aethelred nodded weakly. 'I do. It was deserved.'

'Well, it's my turn now,' Alfred said seriously. 'You've been a good king thus far, and the people love you, but Wessex still needs you, d'you hear me? So you do as the leeches say, and make sure you rest until you're fully healed, all right?'

Despite the discomfort his injury was causing, Aethelred grinned at his brother's commanding tone. 'Is that an order?'

'Aye, it is!' Alfred replied without smiling. 'I mean it, Aethelred. You came close to dying here, and we still have much work to do together, so you take care. I don't want to lose you.'

They eyed one another for a time and it seemed like their roles had been reversed, with Alfred becoming the older, more senior of the pair.

'I'll be careful,' Aethelred promised at last and they grasped one another's wrists before the king said gruffly, 'Now refill those cups, damn it! I can feel the pain returning.'

As the day wore on the brothers talked, joked, reminisced, and became more and more inebriated with every passing hour, but scouts returned in the afternoon with news that the Danes had indeed travelled northeast, back to Reading. It seemed the rest of Wessex would find respite from Halfdan and his sea-wolves for now.

A couple of days later, Alfred rode south with Wulfric and the men of their fyrd, back to Ceodre. Aethelred was not able to ride horseback, but he was placed as comfortably as possible on a wagon and escorted to his own home in Wichamtun, to rest and recuperate and hopefully be fully healed in time for the next attack by the Danes. The other thanes and ealdormen also took their fyrds and returned to their homes around Wessex.

Spring was upon them, and much work needed to be done. Alfred knew that 871 would be a hard year, for the farms would still need to be tended, grain harvested, meat hunted, fortifications built or mended, along with all the other tasks that had to be taken care of every year. The difference this year was that many of the labourers had been killed fighting the Danes.

Same work, but a greatly reduced workforce. And the Danes were still in Wessex.

There was nothing to do but carry on as best they could, and hope to eventually give King Halfdan's army such a severe beating that they'd go elsewhere for their plunder. The victory at Ashdown, and the stalemate at Meretun, proved the levies and hearth-warriors of Wessex could be a match for the professional soldiers that formed most of their enemy's army. That was more than the men of Mercia, Northumbria or East Anglia could say.

It might not be very Christian of Alfred, but he prayed Halfdan would decide it was too dangerous here in the south and sail away to one of those neighbouring kingdoms again. Or Francia.

Anywhere but Wessex.

Perhaps God heard Alfred's prayers, as the Northmen mostly remained in Reading for the next few weeks. Occasionally small bands would ride out from the town and raid nearby settlements, and the nearest Saxon ealdorman would lead the fyrd out to chase them off, but the main army stayed behind its walls. Alfred did not know what was happening within Reading but he presumed the ceorls would be allowed to work as usual. Halfdan didn't want to kill everyone in Wessex after all, what would be the point in that? His men would need fed in the coming months so he would, surely, allow the farmers to tend their fields and beasts, bakers to make their wares, brewers to fill the ale barrels and so on.

Ceodre's workers busied themselves with their usual business too, working extra hard to make up for their reduced numbers. Thankfully the weather was mild that April and, as it moved into May, Alfred was feeling quite content with how things were going in his lands. Easter approached, and he spoke with the priest, Oswald, regularly.

'The new church is coming along well now, my lord,' Oswald said to him as they strolled along the main road on Maundy Thursday, which was the Thursday before Easter Sunday.

'It is,' Alfred agreed, beaming with pleasure at the stone structure which dominated the town now. Construction had been halted during the battles with the Danes, as men and resources were diverted towards the war effort, but the builders had been hard at work during April and the building was almost completed now. 'It should be finished not long after Easter,' said the prince hopefully.

'That would be good,' Oswald said, 'if we moved from the old, wooden building, into this one. A wonderful symbol of new life for us all here in Ceodre.'

They moved to the side of the road as a wagon drawn by a pair of oxen rumbled past, taking freshly butchered meat to

Alfred's hall for the coming feasts. They walked on, passing into the new church and drawing up their cloaks, for it was cool inside the thick stone walls. The windows were covered with boards to protect them while construction continued so little light, or heat, came in.

'You know,' said Alfred, gazing around at the stone columns and herringbone patterned masonry in the walls. 'I'll allow the people to take a couple of days off to properly celebrate Easter, but I think it would be better to let them have even longer. Don't you think?'

Oswald pursed his lips and thought about that. 'As long as they came to Mass, and spent a goodly proportion of their time in prayer, that would be a good idea. If they were simply to spend their time feasting, with the usual fighting and fornicating that follows such events, well, that would not be a suitable way to thank God for spring.'

Alfred grunted, watching the priest from the corner of his eye. Were the priest's words aimed at him? He had been spending a bit of time recently drinking more than he should and had, on occasion, woken some mornings in the company of women other than his wife. Ealhswith knew about this for such things could not be kept secret in a place like Ceodre, and she told Alfred off for his dalliances. She had not fallen pregnant again, despite Alfred doing his best and staying completely faithful to her for months but...

As he knew, too much drink while in a town with a steady supply of eager, willing young women, was a temptation he simply could not resist. He felt a twinge in his guts then, a foreshadowing of the old, familiar pain which had struck regularly over recent weeks. God punishing him for his weakness. And it would surely become worse in the coming days, for there would be much feasting to celebrate Easter. Alfred knew he should not eat and drink so much, but he also knew that he would be unable to stop himself when the ceorls began serving him meat and ale in abundance.

It was a source of great conflict within him, but he did not mention it to Oswald, fearing the priest's disapproving, almost mocking, glance when he saw Alfred calling for refill after refill in the hall later that day. Living life to excess was something young noblemen were *supposed* to do, Alfred thought. And he had a lot of troubles and anxieties to deal with, not least the ever-present threat of Danish raids.

'I very much enjoyed Palm Sunday,' Oswald said, breaking Alfred out of his reverie.

'Oh, I did too,' said the prince, nodding his head firmly.

'The procession all through the town, monks and lay-people alike, re-enacting Christ's arrival in Jerusalem,' went on the priest, describing the scene that had taken place a few days earlier. 'And the palm-branches held aloft before the offering hymn. It was a very moving service.'

Alfred smiled and patted Oswald on the back. 'Next year, the procession will end up here.' He held his hands aloft and spun around in a circle, drinking in the sight of the glorious church he had commissioned.

'Indeed,' said the priest with a grin. 'Now, I must take my leave, my lord. The service of Tenebrae is later tonight, and I must prepare for it.'

They parted, and Alfred remained in the new church for a time. Workmen continued to hammer and shout to one another but the prince ignored it, letting the holiness of the building fill him with peace. It might not, officially, be a church yet, but it didn't matter.

When he left, belly rumbling to remind him he hadn't eaten in hours, night was already drawing in and he hurried back to the hall to meet Ealhswith and baby Aethelflaed. Then, dressed in suitably warm attire, they made their way to the old, wooden church in the corner of the town.

Maundy Thursday was a day when monks would wash the feet of the poor and distribute clothing and even money to those in most need. Alfred himself had given out alms that morning, to families who'd suffered the worst during winter. It was a good tradition, he thought, and a fine way to help those townsfolk who'd fallen on hard times.

Now, as it approached midnight, Oswald would celebrate Tenebrae here in the church, the first of three such services before Easter Sunday itself.

Tenebrae was always at night, hence its name, which meant 'darkness' in Latin. Alfred always found it a powerful experience and he bowed his head now as Oswald and a handful of monks led the congregation in hymns and readings from the bible. It was a very cold night, and Ealhswith had been unsure of bringing Aethelflaed along with them, but she was a good baby and, although still awake, silently gazed up at her parents from the arms of the wet-nurse.

Alfred smiled down at her and the girl made a cheerful noise and kicked her stubby legs within the thick blankets she was swaddled in, drawing a gentle word of 'hush' from the wet-nurse who glanced at the prince. Her look made him feel guilty for not treating the service with the solemnity it deserved and that too made him smile, for how could a servant girl rebuke an aetheling of Wessex?

The candles flickered as a gust of wind blew outside, coming through the many gaps in the wooden walls. Alfred watched the shadows dance and looked forward to moving into the wonderful new stone church. There were no gaps or cracks in those walls.

Ealhswith held his arm and pressed against him for warmth; she felt the cold much worse than he did and he squeezed her tightly, doing his best to impart some of his body heat. It really was quite chilly considering it was only a few days before Easter but Alfred did not mind being there at midnight. A service like this always reminded him of his childhood for his parents observed such occasions fastidiously and he intended to bestow similar pleasant memories on his own children, even if he only had baby Aethelflaed at that moment and she was too young to ever remember this night.

He smiled at the child again, but her eyes were wandering as she gazed up at the ceiling beams as if they were the most fascinating things in all Christendom. Perhaps she was wondering why it was already darker within the building than it had been for, as the service had gone on, candles had been steadily extinguished.

To start with, there had been twelve large candles burning on a stand at the front of the church. Six had been put out during the service at matins that morning, one after each psalm. Five of the remaining six had been extinguished tonight, again after each of the psalms, leaving only one still flickering at the top of the iron stand. Now, that small point of illumination was the only source of light in the entire church.

Everyone knew this service, and the congregation knelt now.

This was the part of Tenebrae which Alfred always found most interesting. He met his wife's gaze and, from the glint in her eyes, he could tell that she had been looking forward to this with the same expectation as he was.

Oswald looked out at them, face dim in the meagre light, and quoted Jesus's words on the cross, his voice filled with anguish: 'My God, my God, why have you forsaken me?' As he finished speaking the remaining candle was extinguished and there was a loud thump that reverberated around the room.

The church was engulfed in total, utter darkness, so black that Alfred almost felt like a monstrous beast had somehow swallowed him whole. It was unnerving and, even though he'd known it was coming, there was something terribly shocking about being there, surrounded by dozens of other people, yet not being able to catch even the merest glimpse of them. It felt like death.

Suddenly, from the back of the church came a pair of clear, children's voices, calling out to God. They were quickly followed by another pair on the left side of the darkened building, then another pair on the right. The atmosphere was intense, and Alfred took Ealhswith's hand in his, seeking reassurance. It was not the same kind of fear one felt facing marauding Danes on the battlefield, but it was just as real for the prince, for Tenebrae symbolised something that terrified him: the light of Christ being extinguished from the world as he was crucified by the Romans on Golgotha.

Even baby Aethelflaed must have felt the power of the moment, making not so much as a whimper in the oppressive gloom. Perhaps she'd fallen asleep, thought Alfred. Perhaps they were *all* asleep, or dead. He thought of Christ's suffering as he slowly, painfully, expired on the cross, alone. He thought too of Bishop Heahmund, and Ealdormen Leofdaeg and Aethel-wulf, and all the other good West Saxons who'd fallen in battle recently. Tears streamed down his face, and he could hear more people, both men and women, sobbing quietly all around the church.

A few moments later a handful of candles were relit or perhaps simply uncovered around the room and the people filed outside in silence, guided by the dim light. Aethelflaed started to cry as they left the building and made their way along the road to Alfred's great hall.

–

When Alfred was in bed next to Ealhswith and they were holding onto one another beneath the blankets, he relived the Tenebrae service in his mind, but the pain of loss had slowly started to pass as he looked forward to Easter. Yes, Christ had died on this day, for it was now Good Friday, but He would be reborn on Sunday.

The thought gave Alfred hope. Christ's enemies had beaten Him bloody and hung Him from the cross for all to see, yet God's love had overcome even death.

As the prince drifted off to sleep he saw similarities between Christ's experience and the one Wessex was going through just now, with Halfdan's great heathen army being analogous to the

Romans. God would help Wessex, he was sure of it – Alfred and Aethelred, warriors of Christ against the pagan invaders.

Yet, at the final, conscious moment between waking and sleep, Alfred pictured Oswald in the church as that final candle was extinguished, and heard the priest's anguished cry in his head once more: 'My God, My God, why have you forsaken me?'

CHAPTER THIRTY-ONE

'He's dead! The king is dead!'

Alfred came awake with a start, sucking in a deep breath, eyes wide in fright before he realised he'd been dreaming. Already the nightmare was receding, fading from his memory, leaving only jumbled images and a deep feeling of unease.

And then the shout came again from somewhere outside, muffled by the thick walls of the hall but quite intelligible.

'The king is dead!'

'What's happening?' Ealhswith was rubbing sleep from her eyes, just as confused as her husband.

'I don't know,' Alfred replied, swinging his legs out of the bed and standing up. 'Something to do with last night's Tenebrae service?' To his tired mind it seemed logical that the townsfolk would be shouting about Christ's death as symbolised by the previous night's ceremony. It was Good Friday after all, the day Christ had been crucified.

There was a sudden rapping on the heavy wooden door that separated the royal chamber from the main hall and Alfred took out his seax from where it lay beside the bed. The ferocity of the knocking told him it was no meek serving girl outside.

'Who's that?' he demanded. 'We're not even dressed in here!'

'It's me, my lord,' came Wulfric's powerful baritone.

Alfred waited for his captain to elaborate on the reason for this unexpected, and not entirely welcome, visit, but nothing more was said, and the prince opened the door, frowning heavily.

'Your brother is dead, my lord,' Wulfric told him, and dipped his head as he delivered the terrible message. 'I'm sorry. He died at his home in Wichamtun.'

Ealhswith gasped behind him, but Alfred could only stare at Wulfric while trying to gather his thoughts. 'But... How?' was all he managed to say, although even that trailed off as he watched his captain, ealdorman and friend, drop to one knee before him, head bowed.

'You are now the king,' Wulfric said, although he did not raise his eyes from the floor. 'Hail, King Alfred of Wessex.'

Nothing more was said for a time, and the shouts and cries outside could be heard, clearly coming closer as, undoubtedly, the people of Ceodre would want to see their new king. And then Alfred muttered, 'Thank you, Wulfric. Give me some time alone with Ealhswith, please. Let me gather my thoughts.'

The captain looked up then and there was pity in his eyes. Many men might have been overjoyed at their sudden elevation to the throne, but the brothers were – had been – close. Wulfric must have known this news felt like a bolt of lightning striking Alfred from a clear sky.

'Was it...?' Alfred trailed off as Wulfric got to his feet, nodding as he guessed what the question would be.

'Aye, my lord. It was the Northman's arrow that killed him. Apparently the wound had never healed properly and eventually became infected.'

Alfred heaved a shuddering sigh. They'd all hoped Aethelred's injury would be a relatively minor one, especially after the leeches had seemed to deal with it effectively. Even the most innocuous wound taken on a battlefield could prove fatal, though, Alfred knew that. Even at his young age he had seen too many of his own men killed in such a way, a shallow cut turning to a festering, pus-filled sore that spread fever throughout the unfortunate patient's body.

Wulfric rested a hand on his arm and they locked eyes for a heartbeat before the captain bowed respectfully. Then he looked at Ealhswith, as if wondering if she would take care of Alfred. She nodded, and Wulfric went away to make sure no-one disturbed the new king and his wife until they were ready.

Alfred softly closed the door and walked back to the bed. Ealhswith was already out of it and she came to him now, hugging him as he began to sob and buried his head in her shoulder.

'There, there,' she whispered. 'We'll get through this, together. You, me and Aethelflaed.'

'They're all dead,' he mumbled into her linen night-gown. 'My parents. My brothers. They're all gone now. Only Aethelswith and I are left...'

His legs began to give way and they sat down on the edge of the bed, still clinging onto one another as if they were on the last floating section of a ship torn apart by rocks.

Alfred didn't speak again for a long time, just held Ealhswith as he wept. At last, he drew in a long breath and sat back, wiping away the tears with the backs of his hands. He looked at his wife and forced a smile. 'It seems,' he said, 'that you are married to a king, my lady.'

Ealhswith laughed and hugged him again. Her eyes were wet with tears too for she had liked Aethelred and felt sorry for his family's loss. Not just Alfred, but Aethelred's consort, Wulf-thryth, and their two little sons, Aethelhelm and Aethelwold.

There was a great clamour outside now, the thick timber walls doing little to muffle the sound.

'You had better get ready,' Ealhswith said after a time. 'Your people are waiting to see you.' Her voice was strong and reas-suring and it brought Alfred a welcome sense of calm.

'You're right,' he said, reluctantly letting go of her and heading towards the chest which held his best clothes. 'Will you come with me?'

His voice was almost childlike and Ealhswith smiled brightly. 'Of course. I'll always be here when you need me, Alfred.'

They dressed together and then, tears dried, went out, hand in hand, to greet the people of Ceodre.

The journey to Aethelred's home in Wichamtun was a sombre one, despite the warm weather and blooming flowers that spring had brought in the wake of one of the hardest winters anyone in Wessex could remember. Alfred travelled with Ealhswith but they left baby Aethelflaed in Ceodre, fearing their party might be attacked by Halfdan who would surely know of King Aethelred's death by now. The little girl already had a good bond with her nursemaid, Godgifu, and would be quite content while her parents were away. Indeed, Ealhswith had complained more than once to her husband that she would miss Aethelflaed more than the child would miss her.

Talking about their beloved little girl made the days pass somewhat more pleasantly for the new king and his wife, but Alfred's thoughts often turned to his dead brothers and then a melancholy would come over him. That was to be expected, however, especially now as they honoured the *moneth's mynde* – the 'month's mind' – that marked a month of prayer for the soul of the departed.

They saw no sign of the Danes on the road, thankfully, although even that made Alfred worry. What if they'd marched on Ceodre? He knew that was highly unlikely, of course, for Halfdan's forces had been badly depleted after all the battles in recent months which was why they'd been squirreled away in Reading for weeks. One could never predict what the Danes would do next, however, and he'd made sure the men he'd left in charge of Ceodre would have mounted units patrolling the area for any signs of enemy activity.

They arrived in Wichamtun three days after leaving Ceodre, even travelling during Easter Sunday, although Oswald celebrated Mass when they stopped to rest. If it hadn't been such a sad occasion Alfred would have enjoyed the journey, but he was glad when they reached their destination.

'My lord.' Sicgred was waiting to greet them when they came to Aethelred's royal palace, which was a hall very much like Alfred's in Ceodre although even bigger. 'I am sorry for your loss.'

Alfred gripped Sicgred by the arm and they embraced as warriors. 'Your loss too,' he said. 'I know you were great friends with my brother. I trust you will serve me as well as you served him.'

Sicgred seemed a little taken aback by the question, as if he thought asking for fealty before Aethelred was even in the ground was impolite or perhaps insulting to the dead man's memory. He hesitated for a long moment, looked at Ealhswith and Wulfric, and then he nodded firmly, rather to Alfred's relief.

'Of course, my lord,' he said, apparently happy to follow the new king but unable to address him as such before the coronation ceremony. 'Come, I'll take you to your brother.'

Wulfric did not follow and neither did Diuma or any of the other thanes and ealdormen who'd arrived in Wichamtun to pay their respects to the fallen ruler. Only Ealhswith accompanied Alfred as he was taken into the church which was situated just a short distance from the great hall.

There were guards outside the stone building to make sure nothing happened to the king's body as it awaited the funerary rites. Alfred took in the size of the building and felt a momentary surge of pride as he realised his own new church in Ceodre was grander than this one, but guilt quickly dampened his pleasure. God did not reward men simply for building big structures in His name, and besides, this church was Alfred's as well now. So was much of Aethelred's estates and wealth, although some of it would naturally pass to Aethelred's wife and sons.

Alfred's mind spun with all these thoughts and more as he walked into the church, shivering as he passed out of the warm sunshine into the cool interior. Ealhswith pressed against him as they walked and he drew her in tighter, glad of her strength for there, lying before the altar, was Aethelred's body.

Alfred had not expected to cry again when he saw his brother. He had not cried when his father had died, or any of his other brothers. Only his mother's passing had upset him so badly that he'd sobbed for many days afterwards, but he'd been very close to her, and only a child then. Now he was a man, a warrior, a king, by God!

And yet, as he looked down on Aethelred's pale, still features, thoughts of their last meeting came to him; outside his brother's tent at Meretun, where they'd shared drinks and laughed together for hours, reminiscing and making bold plans for the future of Wessex together. Alfred could not stop the tears from forming in his eyes and he grabbed onto Ealhswith, his heart breaking not just for Aethelred but for everything and everyone that had been lost with the coming of the Danes.

They remained like that for a long time, as Alfred purged himself of his sorrow, or at least tried to, for he knew he could not continue like this. Wessex needed him to be strong now, and the people already thought him weak thanks to his stomach ailment. He could not afford to break down weeping like a child in front of anyone other than Ealhswith.

She held him like that until, at last, he drew a deep, shuddering sigh and straightened once more to his full height. He wiped his cheeks and nose and then grasped his brother's cold hand and said, 'Go to God, Aethelred, and to mother.'

They might have stood like that all day, but at last Ealhswith said, 'Come, my love. It's time to go.'

Alfred gave one final choking sob and then they walked back outside to join Sicgred, feeling as if they'd stepped into another world. Where the church had been cool and quiet thanks to the thick, stone walls and heavy door, out here in the town it was sunny and noisy as the people went about their usual business.

Life went on, as it always did, as it always would.

Even when a king died.

CHAPTER THIRTY-TWO

Halfdan sat with a horn of mead, sipping it slowly as he listened to one of his men, a skald, tell the story of Loki turning himself into a mare so he could mate with a stallion he liked the look of. It was a well-known tale, with Loki becoming pregnant and giving birth to an eight-legged horse which became Þórr's steed, Sleipnir, but there were slightly different versions of it and Halfdan found himself bored with this one. The skald was not particularly good, although, the king had to admit most of the other Danes around him seemed to be enjoying his story. Men who did not have the learning Halfdan had, or the wit.

He threw back the last of his mead and, sighing, stood up.

'Going for a piss, brother?' Ubba asked, staring up at him. 'I'll come with you, I could do with one myself, although I don't really want to miss the rest of the skald's tale.'

Halfdan smiled wryly. 'I'm not going for a piss, Ubba, so you wait and enjoy the story. I'm just going out for a walk, I think this chair is beginning to grow around my legs, I've been sitting in it for so long.'

Ubba laughed and waved his own horn in salute, mead spilling from it onto the empty trenchers the table was stacked with. 'Don't get lost then,' he said. 'Or killed. I'd have to become king in your place if that happened!'

He winked at Halfdan, who merely raised his eyebrows in response for he was never sure what to make of Ubba's jests. If it was a jest...

The king wandered out of the hall, into the bright sunshine which made him feel even more irritable. This was a day for sailing, or raiding, not sitting around eating, getting drunk, and listening to bland stories told by unimaginative skalds! Those were all honourable pursuits but a sunny, spring afternoon like this deserved better.

He looked around the bustling town which he'd been the lord of for months now. Reading. A town the people of Wessex called a 'royal vill'. Rich with stored food and silver taken in taxes, not to mention plenty of people the Danes had shipped off as slaves over the winter months. Yes, Reading was exactly the kind of town Halfdan would like to be attacking right now, somewhere outside these sturdy walls which might be ideal for keeping attackers out, but which had now become like a prison for those within.

An old woman appeared beside him as if from out of nowhere, and tapped him on the shoulder with the iron wand she carried.

Halfdan, startled for he'd been completely lost in his thoughts, turned and cursed at the woman. 'Sigrun! By Óðinn's cock, would you stop doing that?'

'What?' she asked, and her tone was innocent but her smile playful, almost mocking.

Halfdan shook his head ruefully, amazed that she was able to catch him unawares when she always wore a heavy necklace of beads around her neck which rattled whenever she moved. Still, she was a volva, a Norse wise-woman or seeress, and everyone knew they could do magic. He laughed and waved his hand at her as he started to walk again, no clear destination in mind.

Sigrun followed him, and sure enough her necklace clattered as she wandered after him. 'You were lost in thought, Halfdan,' she said, foregoing any honorific such as 'king' or 'lord' that everyone else used when addressing him. 'What's wrong?'

'Wrong?' He shook his head and looked at her from the corner of his eye. She seemed old to him but he knew she was no more than fifty. He wondered if she seemed older because she was so wise. Certainly, she dressed like a younger woman, with her hair tied up in a bun, a fine linen tunic which trailed on the ground behind her and was fastened with a silver brooch, and over it all a short red cloak of bright red. The wand she carried marked her as one of the volur and it was made from iron with a small basket at the top, the whole thing engraved with protective runes; Halfdan thought it would be a formidable weapon if required, although Sigrun also carried a seax as well, which she sometimes used in her rituals.

'You should be happy,' the volva told him as they passed the market in the centre of town. Even with the place occupied by Danes, trade went on as usual with sellers hawking their wares, dogs barking, children running between the stalls, and over it all hung the smell of food cooking. 'You are the king, the leader of a great army, and you have stolen this place, Reading, from the men of Wessex. So why do you not *look* happy?'

Halfdan shook his head, gazing about at the locals who watched fearfully as they passed. 'This is no way for a king to live,' he said. 'Trapped within walls, with people who despise us even more than they fear us.'

'Then leave,' Sigrun said simply.

'And go where?' Halfdan demanded. 'Back to Mercia? East Anglia? With our tails between our legs like beaten dogs?' He shook his head. 'That would not look good for me. My reputation would suffer. No. I came here with Ubba and our warriors to take what we could from Wessex, and I cannot leave until we have completed that mission.'

Sigrun nodded. She knew – everyone close to the king knew – that the most recent battles with the West Saxon army had badly depleted Halfdan's numbers. And, on top of that, some of the jarls had taken their men and simply sailed away to find their fortune with another king, in some other land. They did not like being stuck within Reading either. And, when the Danes sent out groups of raiders to the nearby settlements to steal food, slaves and goods, they were quickly engaged by mounted cavalry units which the Saxons used to patrol the area.

'Morale is bad,' Halfdan muttered. 'And I am feeling it just as much as any of my men. Worse, for it is my failures that have brought us to this point.'

Sigrun looked at him in surprise. 'Self-pity, Halfdan? I never thought you susceptible to such a thing.'

He snorted mirthlessly, stepping aside as a baker's apprentice chased after a skinny, filthy child who'd stolen a loaf of bread. 'Not self-pity,' he said, sounding as if he wanted to persuade himself more than her. 'Just disappointment that our advance has been halted.'

'You sent word did you not? Messengers, asking for more of our people to come from across the sea to join us?'

Halfdan nodded, reaching out to take a piece of cooked trout from one of the stalls. The fishmonger opened his mouth to demand payment for his wares, then realised who the tall, bearded warrior was and turned away meekly. Halfdan offered the food to Sigrun but she shook her head and they walked on, the king chewing as they went.

'I did,' he said in reply to her question. 'I sent word home, and with Jarl Magnus when he took his Norse warriors back to Kaupang, and with the others when they left to sail for Francia a month ago.'

Sigrun let out a long breath. 'I'm surprised,' she said. 'That no-one came to join us. These lands are indeed ripe for plucking, if only we could replace the men we lost during the winter.'

'Exactly,' Halfdan practically shouted, flakes of trout spilling from his mouth or catching in his beard. 'The Saxons lost plenty of their soldiers too, and they have no way of calling on reinforcements since the rulers of the neighbouring kingdoms are in thrall to us.' He cursed and threw the remainder of the fish to an emaciated dog that had been trailing them for that very reason. 'What should I do, Sigrun? You are a volva. What do you see in the future for me? Can you not work your *seidr* magic and bring my army good fortune?'

They stopped walking, looking at each another, one tall and muscular if a touch portly after months of feasting, the other small and slight.

'I can use my magic to see your future, Halfdan,' Sigrun said. 'It is no easy thing, though. It requires preparation, and a sacrifice.' She looked up and, although it was still daytime, proclaimed, 'The moon is right, however, or at least it will be tonight, which will make any ritual more powerful. But the gods often demand a price from those seeking their favour, you know this.'

'I do,' Halfdan admitted. With his great knowledge of the lore of his homeland he had a better understanding than most of how magic and the gods worked. He shrugged. 'Like any transaction, there is always a price to be paid.'

Sigrun raised an eyebrow. 'Really?' she demanded. 'What about the trout you stole? You did not give the merchant a single coin for that.'

Halfdan shook his head. 'That fish was paid for by the blood of my men, who fell taking control of this town. That grants me the right to take anything I want from this place and its people.'

Sigrun smiled, but Halfdan did not think it a very pleasing expression. 'Very well, my lord. I shall perform my magic this very night.'

'Thank you,' said the king, nodding graciously. 'I'll see you tonight, then.' He turned to walk back to the hall, but the volva called him back.

'Not so fast, Halfdan,' she growled, nodding towards a pen which was filled with squawking chickens. 'I'll need a sacrifice, and I'm not carrying it all the way back. You can do it.'

Laughing, the big Dane stroked his beard, amused by the way she casually ordered him around, as if she were the leader of the army rather than he. 'Fine,' he cried. 'Let's choose a bird. Pick the biggest you can find, I'm strong enough to carry it back to the hall.'

'Oh, I intend to,' she replied, striding towards the penned-up animals. 'I know how broad your shoulders are. Let's just hope

257

they are strong enough to bear the weight of whatever fee the gods demand of you this night, though.'

That statement, rather predictably, wiped the smile from Halfdan's face, but he comforted himself with the knowledge that the volur and others of their ilk always liked to make their work seem darker and more dangerous than it really was.

Or so he hoped.

—

The most important of Halfdan's jarls, hersir, and anyone else big or scary enough to force their way into Reading's great hall that night watched in excited anticipation as the volva, Sigrun, finished her preparations for the ritual. The temperature had dropped but the firepit was well ablaze, casting flickering, dancing shadows around the sturdy walls and supporting beams, and making even friendly faces seem sinister.

Halfdan gripped his mead horn and occasionally sipped from it, but he did not want to be drunk for this. It was always an event when one of the volur performed a ceremony. Something to look forward to, breaking up the monotony of nights spent cooped up indoors with the same men and women. Like a skald's tale or song, Sigrun's ritual would be entertaining, and it would have the added spice of perhaps being dangerous, for who knew how the gods would react to the magic called forth by the volva? The divine denizens of Asgard were well known for their fickle, mischievous and often violent nature.

A space had been cleared at the far end of the hall, allowing Sigrun to sit in her special seat which was made from finely carved wood and engraved with runes. Around her was a circle of young women, all dressed in white robes which gave them an ethereal, ghostly look. Some of them were quite lovely but no man, even Ubba, would try to touch them, for they were protected by the volva's magic. Sigrun herself wore her red cloak with the hood up, delicate blue gloves, and her iron wand gripped in her right hand.

As she turned to look at him, Halfdan took a deep, steadying breath, and walked towards her. Everyone fell silent as he approached, moving between the circle of women, and stood before the volva, holding out a gold arm ring and brooch with red gemstones that glittered in the firelight. Payment for her services.

She took them and they disappeared somewhere within the folds of her robe. 'What would you ask of me?' she said to the king.

'I would ask you to read the future, Sigrun.' Although he was used to addressing his warriors even in the heat of the most terrifying of battles, his voice sounded tremulous and he cursed himself for it. 'Also,' he went on, trying to steady himself as he met her gaze and noticed her strangely dilated pupils. 'To ask the gods to bring us favour in the coming months.'

Sigrun nodded and it was a clearly dismissive gesture which Halfdan followed without question, returning to his seat at the high table beside Ubba. The brothers shared an expectant look and eyed the volva as if they were outside watching a hawk hovering over its unsuspecting prey. Halfdan shivered at the thought, wondering if he was to be the gods' prey in this display of *seidr* magic.

Perhaps this wasn't such a good idea after all.

He forced himself to put aside his misgivings; his men were being entertained and only a coward turned his back on a chance to watch one of the volur at work on his behalf.

In her seat, Sigrun raised her wand high in the air then brought it down and placed it across her lap, closing her eyes as she did so. The girls around her began to sing. There were eight of them, and half were positioned at the cardinal points, north, east, south and west. Those four led the singing with the others joining in a short time later.

Their song was strange, and Halfdan tried to make out what the words were to it, but it was like trying to catch fish in a torn net. In the end, he gave up and simply allowed the sound to wash over him. Their voices were high and clear and perfectly in tune with one another, and the king wondered if a man heard something like this song when he was struck down on the battlefield and discovered whether he had earned himself a place in Valhöll beside Óðinn or not.

With a jolt, Halfdan realised he had almost fallen into a trance – the heat from the fire, along with the small amount of mead he'd downed, and the melodious singing, had all combined to make him drowsy. He understood this was how the volva communed with the gods and goddesses – her body might remain seated in the hall, but her spirit would travel to Asgard. He remembered Sigrun's brown eyes when he'd handed her the gifts too, suspecting the enlarged pupils were evidence of some potion she'd imbibed before the ceremony began.

He blinked, amazed to find he'd once again fallen into a strange kind of stupor and wondered if Sigrun or one of her young helpers had perhaps sprinkled a magical dust or powder into the firepit, making everyone within the hall susceptible to the magic. He could not be sure, but the sensation was not at all unpleasant. Forcing his eyes away from Sigrun, who remained motionless upon her seat, Halfdan looked around at the mighty warriors sharing the hall with him that night. They looked suitably awed, enraptured almost, by the singers and still, red-cloaked volva, which made the king smile. His men were not as subdued as this very often.

The singing slowly trailed off until only one girl's voice remained, high and sweet yet somehow foreboding. Then her voice also faded and everyone watched Sigrun. This was the most important moment: the gods would only commune with the volva if they had been impressed with the girls' music and it wouldn't be the first time Halfdan had seen the ritual fail for this very reason. Nerves taut with anticipation, the king gazed at Sigrun who remained still, eyes shut, as if she were sleeping, or dead.

And then she opened her mouth and called out in a voice deeper than the young singers' but no less powerful, 'Óðinn,

All-Father, the lord Halfdan, King, asks you to bring our great army success in the coming months. Make our sword-arms strong, our resolve as hard as iron, and our ships as deadly as the dragons on their prows.'

Halfdan nodded and many of the warriors within the hall muttered agreement with Sigrun's prayer to the one-eyed god of wisdom who ruled in Asgard.

A log suddenly cracked and spat in the firepit making some start in alarm before they laughed self-consciously, ashamed to have shown even momentary fear over such an innocuous sound. Even Ubba took a deep breath, having almost drawn his seax when the crack reverberated around the room. Halfdan noticed that Sigrun did not flinch or make any kind of movement at all. It seemed her spirit truly was travelling in some other realm that only the volur could gain access to.

'Halfdan, king!' The volva's voice echoed around the room and her eyes opened although they stared at the wall, unseeing, as if she were blind or perhaps looking at something in another, hidden realm. 'Come to me!'

He took a moment to steady himself then stood up and walked forward. He did not kneel to her for he was a king and bowed to no man or woman in all Midgard. 'I am here,' he said, relieved to hear his voice was strong and did not waver.

'You wish to know the future,' she said in a strange voice, almost masculine, as if Óðinn One-Eyed had taken control of her vocal cords and spoke to Halfdan through her. 'And seek my favour.'

'I do.'

'I will tell you,' said the voice. 'The brothers have faced you, now one lies dead. Hard times for men of Wessex, age of axes, age of swords, shields split, wind age, wolf age, until their world falls into ruin.'

Halfdan's brow furrowed. He recognised some of these words for they came from an old prophecy, but they were slightly different – modified, as if to fit the present situation the Danes found themselves in.

The volur continued, everyone in the hall entranced by the strange speech. 'A ship sails from the east, men are coming across the sea, and Loki is steering. Stone cliffs tumble, and troll witches stumble, men tread the road to Hel as the sky splits apart and the great summer army marches on.'

There was much concerned muttering then for the prophecy was dark and foreboding although, as always seemed to be the way of these things, it was impossible to say what exactly Sigrun was foretelling. The volva's words were vague and could be interpreted various ways but, as Halfdan absorbed them, trying to make sense of them, the doors were suddenly thrown wide and the guards stepped into the hall.

'What are you doing?' the king demanded, rising from his seat in anger, amazed that his men would disturb this ceremony.

'My lord,' one of the guards called. He was a huge man with a fiery red beard which seemed to blaze in the light from the firepit. 'Lord,' the man repeated, but before he could say another word another red-bearded warrior shoved past him, striding into the great hall and peering at the faces staring back at him.

'What's this?' the man demanded and Halfdan recognised his accent. He was one of the Norse, and from the great weight of gold arm rings and other finery he wore about his person it was clear he was a warrior of some repute.

A king, even.

'Is this the welcome you offer visitors, Halfdan?' the fellow asked, smiling and walking through the ranks of seated men towards the high table.

'I offer no welcome until I know who it is I am speaking with,' Halfdan retorted, wondering how this interruption would affect the volva's ritual. Sigrun, as if reading his mind, called out then, still in that strange masculine voice that seemed like it could not come from such a slight woman.

'I told you. A ship sailed from the east, steered by Loki.' She pointed at the newcomer who looked back at her with amazement. 'He has come, and victory will be ours.'

The Danes filling the hall grinned for that was a prophecy that was unambiguous and easy to understand. 'Victory,' they said to one another, laughing and raising mugs and horns of mead in salute to Sigrun's promise.

'Who are you?' Halfdan asked again of the tall, well-dressed warrior.

'As she says,' replied the man who continued to eye the volva with a confused look on his face. 'I have sailed here from the east to join you. We came up the Tamyse this morning, to help you plunder these lands.' He tore his eyes away from Sigrun and looked at Halfdan, smiling and puffing out his chest with pride. 'I am Guthrum, king, and I have brought many ships and many warriors, with even more coming behind me.'

'A great summer army,' Ubba murmured. 'Just as the volva prophesied.'

Halfdan felt a wave of joy and relief wash over him and he turned to look at Sigrun. It seemed she had come out of her trance and was no longer travelling with the gods in Asgard. She was slumped forward on her seat and two of the young, white-robed girls were supporting her, as if the magic had drained all her energy.

A momentary flash of wariness flickered in Halfdan's mind at the idea of sharing leadership of the army again, as he'd been forced to do before Bagsecg had been killed, but it quickly passed. This is exactly what he'd been praying for! What he'd paid the volva to petition the gods for!

Reinforcements had come from the east to bolster his army and now they could finally leave Reading and push out into Wessex again.

'Brothers and sisters!' he cried grabbing his mead horn and holding it aloft. 'King Guthrum and his warriors have come to join us, praise Óðinn! Already we have killed the Saxon king, Aethelred, and now we have the means to destroy his successor, Alfred, and all the rest of the weak fools in Wessex.'

'Just as our brother, Ivar, did in the other pitiful kingdoms on this island,' Ubba added, standing with his own cup lifted high. 'Now we will finish what he started, and make Wessex our own.'

There were deafening cheers, and mead, ale and wine flew everywhere as the gathered warriors saluted with their own cups and mugs before bringing them down on the benches and hammering out a ragged rhythm. 'Death to Alfred!' they chanted with each thump. 'Death to Wessex!'

'Our axes and swords shall split their shields,' Halfdan laughed. 'Their wealth shall be ours. Their horses. Their lands. Their gold. Their women!' The rest of his words were lost in the babble of cheering and laughter and he gave up, turning once more to Guthrum and holding out his own mead horn to the newly arrived king. 'Here, friend, drink with us and be welcome.'

The hall was already filled to bursting but now even more men pushed inside, strangers who'd sailed there with Guthrum. They were welcomed with open arms and opened barrels of ale and Halfdan truly felt blessed by the gods. Ubba had mentioned their brother, Ivar, who everyone knew as Ivar the Detestable, and there was their father Ragnar Lodbrok as well – both mighty kings who'd forged great reputations and would probably be remembered in legend for many generations to come. Now, with this great summer army at his back, Halfdan could go one step further and carve his name in runes that would shine out for eternity.

He thought then of Sigrun and her maidens and turned to make his way through the crowd to check on the volva, but they were gone. The space her seat had occupied was filled now with rowdy men and Halfdan guessed the women had taken Sigrun off to recover her strength in a quieter place. His thoughts of the volva were quickly forgotten however, as Ubba threw an arm around his shoulders and Guthrum stood before them laughing and guzzling ale like a man dying of thirst.

Their days penned up within Reading's walls were at an end and glory awaited. Halfdan had not felt so happy in a long time.

But then he remembered the rest of Sigrun's strange, rambling prophecy and what she had said about who was steering the ships that were coming to join them from the east: Loki. The trickster god, who delighted in causing mischief and trouble. Halfdan looked again at Guthrum and wondered exactly what sort of man this new king would turn out to be.

After that it did not matter how much mead Halfdan drank; for the rest of the night he could not banish the sense of unease and foreboding that had suddenly settled across his shoulders like the flea-infested pelt of a mangy wolf.

CHAPTER THIRTY-THREE

'By Christ, look at them all!' Alfred, newly crowned King of
Wessex, stared at the multitude of longships before them and
felt a tidal wave of despair threaten to drown him. 'Where have
they all come from?'

He did not ask *why* they had come for it was obvious word
of Wessex's weakened state after the winter's battles would have
passed around the various kings of the Northmen. Wulfric gave
him the answer to *where* they'd come from.

'The majority are Danes and Norse, of course, but they've
travelled here from Francia, mostly,' said the ealdorman and, as
usual, his voice betrayed no emotion despite the fresh hordes of
enemies they would need to fight soon enough. 'They've been
raiding over there for a long time now, but the Franks have
finally begun to push them back. On top of that, they've bled
that country dry, so it seems Wessex has proved too tempting a
target to ignore.'

'That bastard Halfdan,' Alfred spat. 'He's sent messengers out,
begging for help because he knew we had the beating of him.
Knew he'd be stuck in Reading until their blasted Ragnarok
unless more sea-wolves came to reinforce his depleted army.'

Wulfric was nodding. 'Our spies in Reading have told us
three new kings came to join Halfdan.'

'Three?' Alfred asked. This was information which must
have only reached Wulfric that morning.

'Guthrum is the most powerful of them,' the ealdorman
said. 'He commands the most men – perhaps as many as two
thousand.'

Alfred's face might have turned pale but he'd already guessed the numbers at Halfdan's disposal after watching the myriad longships passing along the Avon that morning. 'And the other two?' he said, trying to keep the dejection from his voice, for there were others of his advisors standing with them, including Diuma and Sicgred.

'Oscetel and Anwend,' Wulfric replied. 'We don't know much about them, but our spies and scouts suggest they've brought hundreds, possibly even a thousand men each with them.'

Diuma cried out at that. 'So we're facing Halfdan and Ubba's original heathen army *and* another four thousand fresh Northmen? My God, what have we done to deserve this? What are our priests, our bishops doing? Why haven't our prayers worked?'

'Get a hold of yourself,' Sicgred hissed, giving Diuma a dark look. 'You're a thane, not some farmer watching his cattle being driven off by raiders.'

Diuma's eyes blazed in anger at that and he began arguing with the older man who'd taken on even more duties now that his former lord, Aethelred, was dead. Some of the other nobles arrayed around Alfred joined in, a few taking Diuma's side and asking why God was punishing them, while the others did not try to answer that but instead called for courage and faith.

Alfred thought it was very difficult to retain his faith in God as he watched the dozens of ships sail past, bedecked with freshly painted shields and the menacing animal or monster heads on their prows. It truly did seem like the Endtimes in Wessex, as foretold in the Book of Revelation and in Matthew 24: 7–9.

"*For nation shall rise against nation, and realm against realm, and there shall be famine, and pestilence, and earthquakes in divers places. All these are but the beginning of sorrows.*"

'My lord?' Wulfric asked as he heard the young king murmuring to himself.

'A verse from the bible,' said Alfred. With that he turned away from the river and the ships and walked off, leaving his advisors to their bickering.

Wulfric followed, as he always did unless specifically ordered otherwise. 'What would you have us do, lord?' the ealdorman asked as his long stride easily narrowed the distance between them.

'What would you suggest?'

'We only have two choices, it seems to me,' Wulfric said.

'Fight them,' Alfred nodded grimly. 'Or pay them to leave our lands.'

'Aye,' his captain replied levelly.

'The Danes expect us to pay them,' the king noted, turning onto the street that led to the nearest church. 'That's why these new kings have come. They think we'll give them a fortune in silver to leave Wessex. Well, Wulfric, they're in for a surprise.'

'We'll fight them?' the ealdorman asked, his tone neutral, betraying no judgement of the king's plan one way or another.

'We will fight,' Alfred confirmed. 'And I will pray now that God and his saints will not forsake us.' He stopped as they came to the small, wooden church and gripped Wulfric by the upper arm. 'Tell the ealdormen and thanes to gather their fyrds,' he said, then smiled grimly. 'It's a stroke of good fortune that we were all gathered together for my brother's funeral, eh? At least some good has come of that dark day. Well, we'll meet the Danes in the field, and show these newcomers what happens to those who sail here without an invitation.'

—

Alfred's coronation had been a sombre, funereal affair, rather than the celebration it might have been. With Aethelred's death, and the swelling of Halfdan's army, there had been no time for the grand ceremony the Witan expected. Instead of days of feasting, Alfred was hastily anointed by Bishop Edwin just a day after Aethelred's funeral and burial in Winburnan, and then sworn in before the ealdormen and thanes. After that, the news had come in of the longships sailing up the Tamyse and the Avon, and Wessex began to prepare yet again for war.

'I'm sick of these bastards,' Diuma said as they rode at the head of the fyrd towards Wilton just one month after Alfred took the throne. 'We should have had time to properly mourn your brother's death, not to mention give you a real coronation ceremony.'

Wulfric gave the young thane a sideways glance which Alfred noticed but did not remark upon. He knew exactly what his captain was thinking: of all the bad things Halfdan's army had done to the West Saxon people over the past few months, disturbing a couple of ceremonies did not seem that important. Certainly, the ceorls, peasants, farmers, labourers and all the other poor people at the bottom of the social ladder would think their swollen bellies a far worse consequence of the war than King Alfred not being allowed time to feast in celebration of taking the crown.

Still, Alfred appreciated Diuma's righteous anger on his behalf, and didn't have the heart to argue with him. He desperately needed such loyalty and wished more of his subjects were like Diuma, in that respect at least.

'We're outnumbered,' Wulfric said as they came at last to Wilton and saw the Danes lined up, already prepared for battle.

'Again,' Sicgred agreed sourly. 'But we'll still kick their arses, eh, lads?'

There were some half-hearted grunts of agreement but Alfred could feel his army's reticence. Their lack of confidence hung over them like a grey cloud, one that had begun to form months ago and coalesced into something even murkier as they travelled here. Well, it was his job to rally them, and make them believe they had a chance of winning under his command. He had worked with Wulfric to prepare a speech on the road, using the ealdorman's experience to come up with something short but powerful, which he'd memorised.

It was time now to deliver those rousing words.

'Shit, they're attacking already!'

Alfred cursed, seeing the great line of Danes coming slowly towards them. There were to be none of the usual pre-battle rituals it seemed: no priests or volur praying or casting spells of victory; no insults between rival lords; no single combat as opposing champions faced off against one another; and no inspirational speeches from the new King of Wessex.

'Get ready!' Alfred shouted. 'Get your men ready, by God. Shields up, hold the line, and remember you are fighting for your lands, your wealth, your children and your very lives against this scum who think they can just sail here and take whatever they like from us while we stand meekly by.' It was only a small part of what he'd wanted to say to the men, but there was simply no time.

'Shields!' Diuma screeched as he, along with the rest of Alfred's commanders, raced to join their own sections of the great fyrd which, after so many battles and losses, was not quite so great anymore. 'It's time to do our duty, and send this heathen filth back to suck on Óðinn's cock!'

'That's a new one,' Alfred said, even managing to raise a smile at the thane's insult, but Wulfric's stony expression never changed.

'Nah, his father used to say things like that all the time,' said the ealdorman, then almost deafened Alfred as he roared, 'Shieldwall! Do not leave the line unless you are told to do so by your commander! Hold the fucking line!'

All along that line the men who'd been given command by way of noble birth or outstanding skill in previous battles were exhorting their charges to raise their shields, if they had one, for the Danes had already launched a volley of throwing spears. Not even the dark cloud of depression that Alfred imagined following his army could hold those missiles at bay, and they lanced down from the sky. Shields did their jobs, but not all of the warriors were lucky enough to carry one. Those too poor to afford the protection of stout linden boards were at the mercy of luck, and quite a few found themselves struck down, removed from the fight before they'd even had a chance to strike a blow.

Alfred and Wulfric ordered their own men to use whatever missiles they had, be it throwing spears, arrows, slingshot or simple rocks, but already Halfdan's hated face could be made out at the very forefront of the approaching enemy shieldwall. The Danes had struck with unexpected speed, and were now almost upon the shocked West Saxons.

Panic filled Alfred at that moment. The line of Danes stretched as far as the eye could see in both directions and was many deep. The bearded warriors that made up Halfdan's army carried better gear than Alfred's ceorls, and the newly arrived reinforcements who'd sailed to Reading in recent days were fresh and eager to fight, unlike the downtrodden levies of Wessex.

It was unfair. And there was not a damn thing the young king could do about it, for praying seemed to have had little effect thus far.

Halfdan's grinning face came rushing towards him, and the younger brother, Ubba, was at the enemy king's side, malevolence emanating from him as if he was some dark star that had been cast down to earth by Óðinn or one of the other pagan war-gods.

The terror that was making Alfred's limbs feel as if they were filled with ice-cold pins and needles all of a sudden changed, morphing into something new and shockingly welcome: rage.

'Brace!' Wulfric commanded and the two sides came together in a cacophony of screams, shouts, thumps, and the horrible metallic screeching of iron spearheads scraping along helmets or armour.

The West Saxon king heard little of it; the world seemed to become almost silent for him as he bared his teeth and thrust the point of his spear again and again, trying to slaughter the Danes who sought to push him back and steal his birthright from him. More than one unfortunate enemy soldier lost his life in those crazed moments, as Alfred wielded his weapon with the skill of a grizzled veteran. He grunted as a wide-eyed Dane lifted his shield and the king's spearpoint hammered into it with such force that it stuck deep in the wood. The weight was too much for the warrior to bear on his wrist and down the shield dropped. Without stopping to draw breath, Alfred pulled out his sword and took advantage of his opponent's defenceless left side, hacking down into the man's shoulder. Even the finely crafted chainmail vest which the Dane wore could not stop such a blow and he collapsed, screaming, before some other Saxon spear snaked out and shattered the side of his skull.

Alfred's right arm continued to move, up and down, backwards and forwards, and somehow his shield kept the enemy blades from his body as he chopped down Dane after Dane. At some point Wulfric commanded the front line of the shieldwall to move backwards, to let fresh men face their foes. Alfred had to be dragged back by his captain, for he was so lost in battle-fury that he did not understand what was happening at first.

'Rest, my lord!' Wulfric shouted as he forcibly led his king back through the massed ranks of their fyrd. 'You've fought like a rabid wolf this morning, but you must rest now. We all must.'

The pair made it to the rear of the army and turned to look back at the battle. Someone handed Alfred a cup of water and he drank it without noticing what it even was. Now that the lust for enemy blood had worn off somewhat he realised that his right bicep was sore, and his shield-arm ached terribly. He glanced at it, seeing no wound, and sucked in a deep, relieved breath. Somehow, he'd survived intact, despite fighting with little regard for his own safety.

'By Christ, I think we're actually winning.'

There was a note of disbelief in Wulfric's voice and Alfred was not surprised. He too did not really believe, deep down, that they could defeat Halfdan's newly reinforced army. One great heathen army combined with this new summer army –

how could the depleted forces of Wessex hope to prevail? Yet, as he gazed out at the scene before them he was astonished to see the ranks of the Danes had thinned out much more than those of his West Saxons.

'We are!' laughed the king.

'This is the difference,' Wulfric said. 'When men fight for mere plunder, against an army defending their own lands; their own people.' He jerked his chin upwards, towards the combatants. 'This is what can happen.'

'Better weapons, armour, even greater numbers,' Alfred agreed. 'None of it matters if one side is as desperate for victory as we are.' He finished the water in his cup and dropped it, taking out his sword once more. 'Come on. I'm rested enough. Let's finish this while we have the chance.'

Wulfric hesitated – he was older than Alfred after all, and even more tired – but then he looked again at the battling armies and smiled menacingly as he hurried after the king.

'We're pushing them back!' Alfred called as they shoved through the ranks once more. 'Don't give them any chance to rest, lads, keep going!' He reached the front line again and Wulfric commanded the second row to move forward. Alfred took the spear from the man behind him and once again settled into a steady rhythm of thrusting and raising his shield. He could not see Halfdan or any of the other enemy kings, but the expressions of the Danes facing him were markedly different to when the battle had commenced. They looked nervous, and many cast glances back over their shoulders, as if expecting the retreat to be called any moment. As if *hoping* for the retreat to be called.

The West Saxon shieldwall, in contrast, was filled with confidence. They knew they had been moving forward, winning ground with every Dane they slaughtered, and, like Alfred, their sense of injustice had combined with hate to lend strength to their blows.

They were winning, and it felt good for the two sides had met on level ground. The poorly trained levies of Wessex were not only holding their own, but they were also killing two or three of the enemy for every one of their own that fell. It was a stunning achievement, and Alfred had never been prouder of his people.

The Mercians had not been able to face off against the Northmen like this, and neither had the East Anglians, or the Northumbrians. Only Alfred's ferocious wolves of Wessex had balls big enough. The young king laughed as he felt the tip of his spear slip through layers of mail and scrape past bone as he dispatched yet another grimacing warrior. 'Push them back!' he roared, voice cracking as he drew back his spear, tugging until it ripped free of the torn flesh and chainmail that sought to snag its leaf-shaped iron blade.

As if his command had been repeated and heard all along the line, there was a sudden surge forward and then cheers went up as the entire line of Danes disintegrated. The enemy warriors were jogging backwards, indeed many of them were actually running, and Alfred watched, elated. He'd not been on the winning side against Halfdan's forces since Meretun, two months and many miles ago, and it felt incredible to be winning his first battle as King of Wessex.

They'd done it! They'd stood up to the Danes and, despite being outnumbered, sent the heathen rats running for their lives.

Wulfric's enraged shouting eventually filtered through his celebrating mind, the alarm in his captain's words bringing the king back to reality with a start.

'Hold the line! Hold the fucking line, you stupid bastards!'

Alfred's battle-fever instantly evaporated as he watched his men giving up the formation that had got them into this position, racing forward in a ragged, uneven line to hack at the fleeing Danes.

'We need to get them back into line,' Wulfric said, turning to Alfred, eyes blazing. 'My lord, we need to form them up again.'

In Alfred's mind he replayed that day outside Reading when something much like this had happened. Back then, it had been a clever ruse by Halfdan, to trick the army of Wessex into chasing after them. This did not feel like that, but Alfred trusted Wulfric's judgement and did not question the older man as he hurried after his warriors, screaming at them to come back into formation.

Perhaps if the tables were turned, and it was the Danes doing the pursuing, Halfdan and his commanders could have called their men back, for they were well trained and war was their profession. The vast majority of the West Saxon fyrd were not full-time soldiers though, and they had the training and discipline of farmers, bakers, carpenters, smiths… The commands of their thanes, ealdormen, and even king, went unheeded as the sight of the retreating enemy proved too tempting. Why should they stop attacking now, when the Danes were running away? To the untrained levy seeking battle fame and glory the order was nonsensical, and as a result it went unheeded.

Alfred looked on in despair, fearing what might happen next.

Wulfric groaned as, section by section, the fleeing warriors found their courage once more and turned to face the chasing West Saxons. The relatively disciplined hack and thrust of the shieldwall gave way to one-on-one fights, and that suited the Danes completely. Not only were Halfdan's forces still greater in number, but the one thing that had been keeping Alfred's men safe – the protective shields of the men in the line next to them – was gone.

The vicious wrath of the Danes was given free rein now, and the farmers who had been so full of confidence moments before were now being hacked to pieces by the better armed and more skilled enemy warriors.

'Come back!' Alfred bellowed. 'Come back.'

But it was too late. He stared at Wulfric, devastated, knowing victory had just been snatched from them. They had this one, final chance to smash Halfdan's army, and it was gone.

'What are we going to do?' Wulfric asked, staring dully, exhaustedly, as the men of Wessex were systematically routed.

Alfred felt like weeping as he heard his captain's beaten tone. He had never before heard Wulfric sound like that and it made the defeat even harder to bear.

'What else can we do?' the king replied dejectedly. 'We've tried fighting and lost. There's only one thing left to get rid of them.'

'Silver.'

Alfred nodded, and now tears of sorrow, rage and shame blurred his vision as he saw King Halfdan in the distance, arms aloft in triumph after cutting down a West Saxon hearth-warrior. 'Aye, Wulfric,' he sighed. 'We'll have to pay them to leave us alone.'

He looked up at the pale grey clouds overhead knowing things would never be the same again in Wessex, and wondering once more why God had so cruelly forsaken them.

Perhaps the heathen gods were more powerful after all.

CHAPTER THIRTY-FOUR

Halfdan's head was aching but he sipped merely water from a skin one of his women had filled earlier that morning. His brother also had a hangover from celebrating their great victory over King Alfred's army, but Ubba had simply started drinking ale again and, as a result, was almost as boisterous and joyous as he'd been the night before when the Danes had feasted.

The new kings who had brought the reinforcements from across the sea – Oscetel, Anwend and Guthrum – enjoyed the festivities along with their triumphant men, supping mead and singing long into the night, but Halfdan was pleased to see all three of his fellow war-leaders bright-eyed and alert. They had combed their hair and beards, washed their faces, polished arm-rings and other jewellery, and cleaned any blood or gore from their clothing. They were there that day to speak with the beaten King of Wessex, and Halfdan had hoped the other kings would show Alfred that the various peoples he called 'Danes' were not the filthy savages told of in tales by the folk of these lands.

'Will you calm down?' Halfdan barked, snapping his fingers in front of Ubba's maniacally grinning face. 'I want this enemy king to see us as equals, not cavorting fools. If you can't stand still and act like a grown man you can go back into the town and sit with the children.'

His rebuke, in front of the newcomers, had the desired effect, and Ubba's silly grin was instantly replaced with a sullen frown. He opened his mouth, perhaps to offer some insult of his own, but then he glanced at the other kings and thought better of it.

Halfdan nodded. Ubba might appear somewhat moon-touched at times, but he knew not to challenge his older brother while three possible rivals to their position looked on.

So, they stood conversing, four kings and their closest advisors or jarls, just outside Reading. It was fine and sunny, and Halfdan was proud of the men stood with him awaiting the arrival of the beaten enemy delegation. He watched the three newly arrived kings as they spoke, appraising them surreptitiously.

Anwend was the smallest of them, but sturdily built. Ubba had drunkenly suggested the stocky king was descended from the dwarves, and thankfully the comment had been taken in good humour by Anwend.

Oscetel was the most unremarkable of the three – of average height and build with a neat, dark beard. He seemed clever and competent but, like Anwend, lacked the charisma the truly great leaders usually displayed, either on the battlefield or in general conversation.

Guthrum, however, now he was the type of man Halfdan expected warriors to flock to, and, indeed, Guthrum had brought more men than either of the other two kings. Perhaps fifteen hundred troops had sailed to Wessex with the Norse king who, with his bushy red beard, broad shoulders and powerful voice, stood out even amongst a host of similar men. Even if he had not had so many men at his command, Guthrum would undoubtedly be the biggest threat to Halfdan's overall leadership of the combined armies.

With fewer than a thousand of his own warriors remaining, Halfdan had less than Guthrum, but more than Anwend or Oscetel, and it had been agreed that, since Halfdan was a son of Ragnar Lodbrok, knew these lands, and had experience winning battles here, he should remain as the overall commander. He understood, though, that his position would be under constant scrutiny.

'Here they come,' said Ubba, catching sight of a mounted scout in the distance, waving his arm.

'Here comes the silver!' Anwend shouted, eyes sparkling, a wide grin just visible beneath his great beard. The others, including Halfdan, laughed and cheered in response.

Soon enough, the West Saxon party came into sight, moving slowly despite the fact the men at the front were on horseback. It quickly became apparent why the group was taking so long to reach them, as several wagons appeared, hauled by lumbering oxen. The wagons were piled high, and clearly heavy and, although their cargo was covered with tarpaulins, the Danes whistled and looked happily at one another as they imagined the riches that would soon be theirs.

'This is going to weaken Alfred much more than just financially,' Guthrum said, staring at the man who led the wagons towards them. 'To raise so much wealth he must have forced his ealdormen and bishops to pay an extra tax. Those people will not forget it.'

'Perhaps not,' Halfdan said, nodding thoughtfully. 'But the armies of Wessex have given us much more trouble than any of the other kingdoms in this island. We took East Anglia, Northumbria and Mercia without much trouble.' He stared at the straight-backed young king who rode proudly towards them, despite the occasion, and felt grudging admiration for him. 'By contrast, this Alfred, and his fyrd, have fought us almost to a standstill. Indeed, they might have defeated us if you three hadn't arrived in time to reinforce us.'

'What are you saying?' Oscetel demanded, seemingly irritated by Halfdan's praise of the King of Wessex. 'You sound afraid of him.'

'Not afraid,' Halfdan growled, giving Oscetel a withering glance. 'I'm simply suggesting we don't underestimate him.'

Oscetel opened his mouth as if to argue the point but Guthrum broke in, his loud voice projecting over everyone else. 'It matters little,' he boomed. 'They're paying us to leave Wessex, aren't they? We take the silver and go raid one of the other kingdoms you spoke of, Halfdan.'

'And then, when Wessex has rebuilt some of its wealth,' Ubba put in, 'we can come back and kill more of them until they pay us to go away again. And again.' He snorted, lip curling as Alfred dismounted a short distance away. 'He's another idiot, like Edmund or Burgred. They never realise that by paying us off, it maintains the cycle.'

'He has no other choice,' Halfdan said, and even he realised it sounded as if he was defending Alfred, but he didn't care. Of all the other enemies they'd faced here on this fertile island, the West Saxons deserved the most respect. Still, he didn't want the other kings to think he was going soft, so he grinned at them. 'But yes, Ubba is right. We will return here soon enough and bleed Alfred's lands, and his coffers, dry again!'

Alfred was walking towards them, eyeing each without a hint of fear. Halfdan had heard the stories about this young king, apparently such a nervous wreck that even the stress of his own wedding feast had made him violently ill. The rumours of Alfred's debilitating stomach pains were common knowledge, even amongst the Danes. Yet, as the newly crowned ruler of Wessex came to stand before them Halfdan could see no sign of weakness. Alfred was a little taller than most of his kinsmen, with the athletic build of a true warrior, and his brown eyes were as piercing as Halfdan's infamous brother, Ivar's. Despite his youth, Alfred was an impressive figure, as was the much taller, broader ealdorman at his side.

'You must be Wulfric,' Oscetel demanded, before anyone even offered a greeting to Alfred. 'You killed my friend in that last battle. I did my best to reach you, to take that big head from your shoulders, but I couldn't push my way through the ranks.'

The massive West Saxon stared at Oscetel for a long, uncomfortable moment, and then said, 'It's just as well you didn't reach me, or you'd not be sitting there today.'

Guthrum grabbed Oscetel's arm as the other king tried to move forward, face flushing scarlet. 'Go back to the tent,' commanded Guthrum coldly. 'We're not here to compare cock sizes! You too Anwend, and you Jarl Ubba. Me and Halfdan will parley with the Saxons.'

For a moment the other Danes looked like they would argue with Guthrum but, eventually, Anwend and Oscetel nodded ungraciously and strode back to the tent which had been erected just outside the town in case it rained during this meeting. At a look from Halfdan, Ubba also retreated.

Halfdan felt greatly irritated by the way Guthrum ordered the other Northmen around, but he decided it might be for the best, and there was no way to go against his fellow king now without them appearing divided and even weak.

'Hail, King Alfred,' he said, making sure to keep any hint of sarcasm or humour from his voice. 'We finally meet without the sounds of men dying all around us.' He bowed his head and even thought of offering his wrist to Alfred, but they were not there as equals. Halfdan and Guthrum were the victors, and Alfred could not be allowed to forget that. Still, there were rules of hospitality that applied even to enemies. 'Would you like a drink, my lords?' he asked. 'Mead? Ale? Wine?'

Alfred shook his head somewhat sullenly. 'No, I would rather keep my wits about me.'

'Very wise,' Halfdan smiled approvingly. '*Er-a svá gótt sem gótt kveða öl alda sona, því at færa veit, er fleira drekkr síns til geðs gumi.*'

The King of Wessex digested that, struggling with Halfdan's language and accent, but then he was visibly taken aback once his mind translated the words. *Ale is not so good as they say for the sons of men, For the more they drink, the less can they think and keep a watch o'er their wits.*

'A passage from the *Havamal*,' Halfdan told him.

'Apparently Halfdan loves the *Havamal*,' Guthrum laughed, as if he thought such learning was a waste of time. Alfred's eyes betrayed a newfound level of respect for the warlord however and Halfdan was pleased to let the West Saxons know that he, at least, was not a simple savage.

Then Alfred's gaze moved to Guthrum. The Saxon tried his best to keep his face neutral, to give away as little of his thoughts as possible, but he could not help his lips curling ever so slightly as he eyed his enemies. Disdain? Hatred? Whatever it was, it did not last for long and Alfred drew in a long breath.

'I want you to leave my lands,' he said coldly.

The Danes chuckled and Halfdan raised his eyebrows, pursing his lips in an exaggerated display of surprise. 'As simple as that?' he asked.

'As simple as that, Halfdan,' Alfred replied.

'But where would we go?' Guthrum asked lightly. 'Reading has become like a second home to Halfdan and his men, and I can see why. I've only been here for a short time, but I would hate to leave it. The people are so... friendly.'

Again came the laughter which Halfdan could see irritated the enemy king although he tried not to show it.

'Reading must be bled dry by now,' Alfred grated, staring balefully at Guthrum before looking again at Halfdan. 'I know the food supplies were almost exhausted even before your...' his lip curled and he swept a withering glance towards the tent containing Ubba and the two other kings, '...*reinforcements*, arrived. Wessex has nothing more to offer you. It's time you moved on.'

Halfdan spread his hands. 'But like King Guthrum asked: where will we go?'

Alfred shook his head irritably. 'I care little, as long as it's out of Wessex. Go back to whatever frozen, Godforsaken wasteland you were shat out of. Or, if you do not wish to go home to find your thralls bedding your ugly wives, what about Mercia? Lundenwic is pleasant at this time of year. Plenty of grain, and it's near to the port so there's always cargo ships pirates like you can rob. Go there.'

'Pirates?' Guthrum demanded in mock outrage, stroking his fiery orange beard. 'We are *vikingar*, not pirates, whelp.'

'From what I understand of your tongue,' Alfred retorted. 'Both words mean much the same thing.'

'Lundenwic?' Halfdan interjected. 'That belongs to your brother-in-law, Burgred. Would you be so quick to send us to raid his lands?'

Alfred shrugged, a gesture that made him seem even younger than he was, almost like a petulant child. 'King Burgred might be married to my sister, but he ignored my requests for men to fight you. I feel no loyalty to him. I want you gone from Wessex and if that means you go to Mercia, so be it.'

Halfdan looked from Guthrum, back to his brother and fellow kings in the tent who were close enough to hear what was being said. All were nodding. Lundenwic was as good a place to sail to as anywhere else, and Burgred would certainly offer little resistance.

'All right, my lord,' he said to Alfred. 'Perhaps we will go home, or perhaps we will go to Mercia. I assume you've brought something to make leaving worth our while?'

'Gold and silver,' the king said, gesturing behind him. 'You can keep the oxen as well.'

'How much?' Guthrum asked.

'It should be at least as much as your brother-in-law, Burgred, paid us to leave Snotengaham,' Halfdan said, reminding Alfred that he had been there when that payment was made, beside his brother Ivar. He knew how much, exactly, was paid by the Mercian king.

Alfred glanced at Wulfric and Halfdan guessed, from the uncertain look that passed between them, that neither of the men knew how much Burgred had paid the Danes. The King of Mercia had kept it a secret. Halfdan smiled. Intelligence like this was always good to know. The fact that the Mercian army had not marched south to assist Wessex against Halfdan's raiders had been much remarked on by the Danes, and, with this new little piece of information, it was made even clearer that relations between Mercia and Wessex were not as close as they might be. No wonder Alfred was happy for the great summer army to sail away to Lundenwic.

'Seven thousand pounds,' Alfred growled. 'Some gold, mostly silver.'

Halfdan turned to his fellow noblemen. Guthrum remained stony faced, but, in the tent Oscetel, Anwend, and particularly Ubba, were grinning as if Freyja herself had agreed to spend the night with them. Idiots! There would be no chance of squeezing more from the beaten West Saxons when it was so obvious that the payment was larger than any of the Danes expected. Halfdan had thought Alfred would come with, at most, five thousand pounds of silver, so this was a pleasant surprise.

'I can see that is acceptable.' Alfred ground out the words as if each one cost him another thousand pounds. 'You will swear on your own heathen gods to leave Wessex and never return? If you take our silver and do not hold to your oath we will have no choice but to—'

Halfdan held up a hand, smiling and bowing his head ever so slightly to the side. 'We know how this works, my lord. We will take the payment and leave your lands immediately.'

'Is Reading a ruin?' Wulfric demanded.

Halfdan shook his head. There was something disconcerting about the tall ealdorman. Alfred was younger and, although he tried to hide his feelings, it was clear he was angry and nervous. Wulfric, on the other hand, seemed utterly in control of himself. There was an undercurrent of rage in his tone and expression, but the man's discipline was as hard as any steel blade. An extremely dangerous man to have as an enemy, Halfdan thought.

'No, your town is just as it was when Halfdan took control,' Guthrum replied. 'Well, nearly. Your women are going to miss having real men around to hump every night, though.'

The withering look Wulfric bestowed on him was as eloquent as any spoken retort, and Halfdan shook his head as he addressed Alfred again.

'Reading is fine, my lord. We do not destroy towns that are valuable to us. The place has continued to operate as usual, although most of the stored food and wealth has been, ah… used up.'

Again, Wulfric's disdainful stare was worse than any insult might have been and Halfdan couldn't help giving a short laugh. Who was in charge here? Was he the victor, or was the taciturn Saxon ealdorman? 'Do you want to go in and take a look, my lord?' he asked Wulfric testily. 'Go on, feel free. I'm sure a man of your obvious strength will have no trouble.'

Alfred's captain merely gazed at him in silence and Halfdan mentally kicked himself for losing his composure. 'Seven thousand pounds of gold and silver will be enough,' he said. 'May Óðinn strike me down if I do not leave your lands, never to return.'

Alfred nodded and looked at Guthrum who repeated Halfdan's vow to leave Wessex.

'Good. It's settled then. Come Wulfric, we'll leave them to make their preparations for their onward journey. God help whoever's lands they turn up in next.'

'You know, Alfred,' Halfdan called as the West Saxons turned to walk back to the protective ranks of their own waiting warriors. 'We are not so different. You, I, or even our two peoples. That is why we have left Reading standing; we are not animals, just men who want a share of what everyone else has.'

Alfred stopped and turned back, frowning. 'Each man is master of his fate,' he said. 'And what you say may have some small grain of truth to it. But we *are* different, Halfdan. You, and your people – be they Dane, Norse, whatever – are pagan. You worship false gods. Until the day you renounce those gods, and are baptised in the Christian faith, we shall always be different.'

Halfdan nodded grimly, angered by the pious king's words. 'That is true,' he said. 'Yet where is your God now, as you deliver us your seven thousand pounds of silver in desperate hope that we will leave you alone?' He raised his hands in the air and looked up at the sky. 'Will your God strike me down? Ha!' He laughed, and so did his men behind him. 'Your God is weak, Alfred. Weak! And my people shall never bend the knee to you, or Him!'

Alfred gazed back, waiting for the mocking laughter to die away, and then he said simply, 'We'll see,' and strode away to join his waiting guards.

The Danes watched him go, grinning. Halfdan felt happier than he had in quite some time, for everything was going his way now. From being trapped in Reading with the food supplies running low and an army half the size it had been when they first took that town, to here! He had thousands of pounds to share out amongst his rejuvenated army, three powerful new kings as allies, and an open river leading to Lundenwic which the Mercian king, Burgred, could not hope to defend against them. It seemed the gods were smiling on Halfdan.

'Well, lads,' Halfdan said, spreading his arms and addressing Ubba and the other kings as they came forward to stand around him. 'Let's get the thralls to bring that silver into Reading, where we can share it out between us and our men.'

'And then,' Guthrum roared over the thunderous laughter. 'Let's give thanks to Óðinn and Þórr, and get drunker than any man in Midgard has ever been before!'

Halfdan's cheers were as loud as any other's but, before he began the walk back to Reading, he saw Alfred mount his horse gracefully and then, to Halfdan's astonishment, the West Saxon king made the sign of the cross, as if thanking his weak God for something. The Dane shook his head. What did Alfred possibly have to be thankful for, other than the fact the Northmen were leaving him in peace for a time?

Truly, Alfred's trust in this Christian God of his seemed unbreakable. Being deeply spiritual himself, Halfdan admired his foe's faith but firmly believed that following such a weak religion would eventually lead to Alfred's downfall. That was not his problem, however and, with wagons full of West

Saxon silver, Halfdan and Guthrum, along with the rest of their heathen horde, journeyed east in the coming days, to Lundenwic.

PART THREE

CHAPTER THIRTY-FIVE

Wintanceaster, AD 875

For four years, Wessex enjoyed relative peace. Alfred's payment to Halfdan and Guthrum had been successful in keeping the Northmen's forces away. It had allowed the people to rebuild shattered towns and homes, and the wealthy to regain some of the money they'd lost thanks to the invasion. Food supplies were nearly back to the levels they had been a decade before, with storehouses holding enough to feed even the poorest of Alfred's subjects. Fields were full of grain in the summers, and sheep, cattle and poultry were in plentiful supply after they'd been slaughtered to near extinction during the war. Horses, many of which had been killed or taken away by Halfdan's sea-wolves, were being bred and trained, and many new trees had been planted to make up for the ones torn down for the rebuilding efforts.

Alfred had even started work on a navy of sorts, ordering a number of ships to be built that might offer some kind of protection for the waters in and around Wessex. He also had plans to strengthen the defences of his settlements, and hoped to improve education within his lands now that they were not constantly being harried by raiders.

To Alfred's surprise, the scars on the land itself had also quickly healed, with battle sites at the likes of Reading and Ascesdune seeing growth of fresh new grass and foliage to replace the mud, blood and corpse-strewn fields that had been left after the fighting there.

It seemed like God's healing power had spread all through Wessex with the passing of Halfdan and Guthrum's rampaging hordes, and all was well in the world again.

Not all the West Saxons were happy with how things had turned out, however.

'The bishop is comparing you to Judas, my lord. He's telling everyone that you've betrayed the Church, and betrayed God Himself. He suggests that many religious houses have been robbed both by the Danes and by you, their king...'

Alfred cursed under his breath. He wondered if this was God testing him again. The great summer army might have moved on to once again renew their grip on Mercia and Northumbria, but it seemed the clergymen of Wessex had still not forgiven their king for the tax he'd demanded from them in order to pay off their enemies.

He sighed heavily and looked at Oswald. 'You're a priest,' he said. 'Do you think I'm like Judas Iscariot?'

Oswald shook his head. 'No, my lord. However,' he went on, Alfred's smile fading as he did so. 'I can understand why some of the bishops are angry.'

'Oh?'

The priest did not seem to notice Alfred's low tone or the raised eyebrow, and he continued with his line of reasoning. He had been serving Alfred for years now; perhaps he did recognise the signs of the king's rising irritation and ignored it. That was what made him valuable to the young ruler after all – like Wulfric, he was honest and spoke his mind when asked to. 'To the likes of Bishop Deorlaf, it seems as though you took advantage of the situation with the Danes back in 871, to make yourself wealthier at the Church's expense.'

'And how is that?'

Again, Oswald was either oblivious to Alfred's threatening tone, or wilfully ignoring it. 'Well,' he said. 'You demanded so much silver from Bishop Deorlaf even though you knew, he says, that he could not afford to pay it. So, you paid his share of the tax, and took some of his land in return.'

'So?' Alfred demanded. 'A fair exchange surely. Or does Bishop Deorlaf think he should not have been made to pay his share to get rid of the Danes? Everyone, Oswald, *everyone* of means paid an amount relative to their standing and their personal wealth.'

'Yes, but you, and your brother Aethelred before you, had been trying to buy those lands from the bishop for a while before we were forced to pay off Halfdan.'

Alfred shook his head, as if confused. 'Again, so what? Bishop Deorlaf was required to pay his share of the *gafol* and he didn't have it. I paid it for him in return for certain land I wanted. Why would I pay his share and receive something I did *not* want in return? If you went to the ale-seller, Oswald, and paid him your pennies for a jug of ale, and instead he gave you water, would that make sense?' The king smacked his hands on the arms of his chair and stood up, smiling as if he had just made a great legal argument. 'You see what I'm saying? This is the very basis of an economy, Oswald! And Deorlaf should be wary of calling me "Judas". Wulfric does not like it when people insult me.'

Oswald blinked, as if wondering if he was understanding Alfred properly. The grim glare he received from the king confirmed the threat was very real and the priest nodded, the hint of a smile tugging at the edges of his mouth. He did not like Bishop Deorlaf any more than Alfred did.

'Ah, speaking of Wulfric,' said Alfred, waving his hand at the door as it was thrown open and the tall figure of the ealdorman came striding into the room. 'There he is. And, from the grim look on his face, he also brings bad tidings.'

'Danes, my lord,' Wulfric said without preamble. 'Sighted off the southern coast at Tweoxneam. Our new fleet have been watching them but haven't engaged them yet.'

'Ah, God's blood, not again,' the king muttered, sinking back into his chair at this unwelcome news. When Halfdan and his fellow kings had stuck to their word and left Wessex alone for the past few years it had been easy to believe they would never return. Burgred's Mercia, along with Northumbria and East Anglia had not fared so well in the intervening years, but that was not Alfred's concern. Danish longships being seen at Tweoxneam *was* his concern, however, for it might mean the start of another series of raids by the sea-wolves, or even another war. True, he had commissioned several ships to patrol the Wessex coastline and provide early warning of more enemy raids, which they'd now done, but were Alfred's sailors ready to attack the Danes, expert seamen, on their own 'whale road'?

'How many longships?' he demanded.

'Only seven,' Wulfric replied.

'"Only",' Alfred murmured sourly, adding up the numbers in his head. Even if the enemy ships were of the smaller type, that could mean twenty-five men in each one: 175 Danes. Not quite another great heathen army but still enough to cause a lot of trouble. 'Well, it's been a while since I fought Halfdan and his lackeys,' he said, getting to his feet and striding towards Wulfric. 'Let's ride to Tweoxneam and make sure these pirates don't set up a forward camp for a larger fleet.' He grinned, suddenly excited and happy to be getting away from the petty politics Bishop Deorlaf and his peers seemed to thrive on. 'Maybe we'll see for ourselves how well our new ships compare to those of the Danes!'

–

'You're not suggesting we actually sail the ships ourselves,' Wulfric asked as they rode towards Tweoxneam. 'Are you?'

Alfred almost burst out laughing at the trepidation in his captain's tone. It was a fine summer day, the grass was green, and it was as if Wessex had healed itself after the troubles it had seen just a few years before. The king ran a hand through his shoulder-length hair and smiled. 'Do you not like the sea?' he asked.

Wulfric eyed him sidelong and snorted, 'I don't mind the sea, I just don't like trying to fight on it!'

Alfred did laugh then, long and loud, for this journey had made him feel more alive than he had for a while. The prospect of a battle was not as frightening as it perhaps should have been, and the beautiful sunshine illuminating his green and pleasant lands stirred his blood far more than overseeing building projects or dealing with old ealdormen who looked down on him simply because he was young. 'Don't worry, my friend,' he said to Wulfric, voice clear and melodious as the sea air filled his lungs. 'I agree, it would be better to fight these Danes on land than from the deck of a ship. Our fleet can just continue to patrol the coastline for signs of more enemy vessels.'

They had brought Alfred's hearth-warriors, and gathered some of the local fyrds as they passed through towns on their way from Wintanceaster to Tweoxneam, so, in total, they were accompanied by almost two hundred and fifty hardy troops. Most had seen action during the war with Halfdan's armies, while others were young, brave men looking to gain experience and glory fighting this despised enemy. Although it was not certain whether the seven ships sighted around the southern shores of Wessex had been sent by Halfdan, Guthrum, or even some new, unknown king of the Northmen, it hardly mattered. They were sea-wolves, and they should not be near West Saxon lands.

'I'd like to scout ahead when we reach the town,' Wulfric said. 'We're not far now, and I want some idea of how the land lies. See if we can take advantage of the terrain.'

Alfred nodded. 'Of course. But I think we should try something other than simply setting up our shieldwall and meeting theirs like we always do.'

Wulfric frowned, for he was used to waging war a certain way and did not really like change, but he did not question the king. Alfred knew his older, more veteran thanes and ealdormen thought his ideas strange and even subversive so, in these first, early years of his kingship he'd not been too drastic in changing how things were run. But, as he'd said more than once to Wulfric, 'Look where the old ways have got us.' And it was true – Northumbria, Mercia and East Anglia had not modified the way they governed their lands and now they were, essentially, no more, consumed by Ivar, Halfdan, Guthrum and the rest of the Danes. Wessex had come perilously close to suffering the same fate, and might well do in the coming months and years, but Alfred hoped his plans would secure a lasting foundation for his West Saxons. These pirates on Tweoxneam's coast would provide an opportunity to try something different, and hopefully show Wulfric and the rest that change was not always something to be resisted.

They reached the coastal town early on the third day, having covered the fifty or so miles in good time, and then Alfred amazed his captain, and the fyrd, by telling them to settle in.

'Are we not engaging the enemy today?' Wulfric asked as he and Alfred went ahead to scout the land. 'Why wait, and possibly allow them time to bring in even more reinforcements?'

They reached a low hillock and dropped to their bellies, edging forward cautiously so the Danes on the beach would not notice them. There were indeed seven ships pulled up on the sand, and, counting the sailors, Alfred thought his earlier estimate of 175 was very close to being accurate. They clearly thought they were safe for only a few guards sat watching the land around them, and none were very alert. Most of the ships' crewmen were sitting around fires, roasting meat – no doubt from livestock stolen from nearby farms – and telling stories. Some worked on their war-gear, cleaning and polishing swords, repairing worn shields, and buffing mail vests in barrels of sand.

'They look at home,' Alfred growled, angered by the sight before them. Hadn't he paid the Danes a literal fortune to stay out of Wessex? Yet here they were, on Alfred's beach, eating his pork and beef and lounging around as if they hadn't a care in the world. 'You're right, Wulfric, we should attack soon.'

They finished scouting the terrain, not being particularly careful about remaining out of sight of the watching Danes, who would likely just think them curious, frightened locals, and then returned to the waiting fyrd.

Much to Wulfric's surprise, Alfred did not immediately command the men to prepare for battle. Instead, they continued to wait, until the sun sank into the sea and night fell.

'We will attack in the dark,' the king said to Wulfric and the other commanders, who stared at him as if he was mad.

'That will lead to confusion in our ranks as much as theirs,' a middle-aged thane protested. 'That's why it's rarely done.'

Alfred shook his head. 'They are all gathered around their ships in that small section of beach,' he said confidently. 'They probably know we're here, for they likely have scouts just as we do. But they will not be expecting us to attack by night.'

His enthusiasm was infectious although some of his men remained unconvinced and went out to their warriors with expressions almost as black as the sky, muttering about how mad this plan was. At least it was a simple plan, Alfred thought, ignoring their angry whispers.

'Wulfric, we need to take out as many of the enemy watchmen as we can, so our fyrd can move in close enough for the missiles to be effective.'

'I'll go,' volunteered the ealdorman, predictably.

'Good,' Alfred grinned. 'I'll come with you.'

'What?' Wulfric gaped at him. 'You can't come. You're the king, by God! What if we're caught? It would leave the fyrd leaderless to lose us both.'

'Then we'd better not get caught.'

The captain continued to protest but Alfred merely smiled and made ready to move. They used soot to dull the blades of their seaxes, and their faces, and then they slipped into the darkness, moving towards the beach.

The Danes made no attempts to disguise their presence on the beach, singing and shouting as if they were enjoying a feast.

Which they probably were, Alfred thought, angrily imagining the sheep and ale the raiders would have taken from the poor farmers of Tweoxneam, killing any who tried to stop them in the process. 'Bastards,' he muttered, imagination beginning to run away with itself as he pictured that terrible scene in his head and the terrifying return of Halfdan's full army. 'Let's go,' the king hissed, leading the way.

Wulfric slipped past him, taking point, for he was by far the more experienced of the pair at this kind of work. Indeed, Alfred had never undertaken a mission such as this, so he allowed his captain to take the lead, forcing himself to remain calm and not let his roiling emotions overtake him.

Suddenly, Wulfric paused, lifting his right hand with its blackened seax, and pointing the blade ahead. A man stood there, little more than a dark shape on the horizon, and, as they watched, he started to walk slowly away from them. Alfred did not need his captain to tell him the Dane was patrolling the perimeter of the raiders' camp.

Turning to look at him, Wulfric held up his palm, silently telling Alfred to remain where he was, and then the ealdorman slipped away, alone, following the wandering guard. The sand made it harder to move than hard ground, but it was also perfect for masking one's footsteps and Wulfric was able to creep right up behind the Dane before he was detected. The dim light from the nearby campfires offered just enough illumination for Alfred to see the guard spin around in confusion, before Wulfric's seax came up and plunged through his jaw and on into the brain. It was a strike designed to kill instantly, and silently, and, sure enough, the guard collapsed against Wulfric who dropped the body onto the sand.

Alfred stared, amazed at his friend's lethal efficiency, but they could not afford to stop just yet, for another guard was walking towards them, and he noticed Wulfric now for he said something – a greeting.

Immediately, the king moved further away from the beach, just enough to remain in the deepest shadows, and then he hurried forward. His swishing footsteps were masked by the raucous shouts at the raiders' camp and he was able to move around the second guard who Wulfric had tried to reply to in his own tongue.

Whatever the ealdorman had said, it seemed the guard became instantly suspicious, for he drew his sword and, since this blade had not been blackened with soot, it glinted in the dim light. Alfred had only heard Wulfric give the most basic of greetings to the guard, but the king guessed that he'd been expecting to hear a different voice, a different accent, whatever. Something had alarmed him, and it was only a matter of time before the clashing of blades alerted anyone nearby to their presence.

Alfred offered a silent prayer of thanks to God for the sand which masked his movements and allowed him to come up behind the guard, who was now urgently demanding to know who Wulfric was, and where Torvo – presumably the first guard – had gone.

Alfred's arm snaked out, seax blade hammering into the Dane's back. It slipped through the man's leather body armour and, such was the force of the king's thrust that almost the entire blade went in. The guard gasped in sudden shock and tried to turn, to face this new threat, but, as he spun, Wulfric slammed the pommel of his seax into his skull. He collapsed, and Alfred stabbed him again until the man lay still, face pressed into the soft sand.

'God in Heaven,' the king gasped, blood pounding in his veins. 'That was close.' He stared at the dead guard, trying to calm himself once more. This was far from being the first man he'd ever killed, but this was completely different to the red mist that came down over one during a battle.

'Come on,' Wulfric growled. 'We'll clear any more of 'em, then get back to the fyrd and begin the attack.'

Alfred dragged his eyes away from the corpse in the sand and looked up, scanning the beach. They could still hear the raiders, singing a drunken song now, cheering every so often as if there was some other 'entertainment' going on. The king did not allow his imagination to fill in the blanks this time, instead nodding to Wulfric. 'You go on and make sure there's no more guards patrolling this section of the beach. Then head back to the army. I'll join you there.'

Wulfric frowned, the scant light casting his craggy features in deep shadows. 'Where are you going?'

Alfred shook his head. 'Wulfric, will you stop questioning my orders?' His words were harsh but he tempered them by making his tone light, for, although he did want his captain to do as he asked him to, he also appreciated Wulfric was the best ally he could ever hope for.

The ealdorman's gaze remained fixed on Alfred for a moment longer, and then he gave a shallow bow which, had it not been so dark, might have been interpreted by the king as somewhat sardonic. 'As you command, my lord,' he said, and then, 'Please be careful,' as he moved away into the gloom, alone.

Alfred watched him go, suddenly wishing he was going with him, but then he steeled himself, undid his hair which he'd tied behind his head in a ponytail, and took the long, blue tunic from the dead Dane. Throwing it around his own shoulders, he strode with far more confidence than he really felt towards the singing raiders.

It was a ridiculous thing to do, wandering straight into the enemy encampment, but Alfred was hoping no-one there would recognise him. In the dark, with his beard and long hair concealing most of his face, and a genuine Northman's cape hiding his own West Saxon clothes, surely none of the sailors would know him. A sudden thrill of fear ran through him as the possibility of Halfdan or Guthrum being part of this group and seeing through his pitiful 'disguise' presented itself to his churning imagination – Alfred knew all too well what the Danes did to the enemy kings they captured.

The heat from the fires reached him as he came closer to the happy sailors, singing, chatting and gaming. All had food or drink in hand, and all seemed blissfully content with their lot. Alfred actually felt a tiny pang of sorrow, for these were just men like any other, enjoying one another's company on a pleasant evening by the sea, and soon enough he would order the attack that condemned them all to death.

Yet, as he walked by them, doing his best to keep his face in the shadows, he noted there were no women. If this was merely a group of travellers looking for land to settle upon, they would have their families with them. These were no farmers searching for fields to plant, though – they were warriors. Pirates. *Vikingar.*

He had hoped to gain some insight into their full purpose by walking amongst them. To find out, perhaps, if they were the vanguard for a bigger invasion force. Instead, he discovered nothing for all he could hear was singing, and his courage – or stupidity – did not stretch to persuade him to mingle with the groups of gamers. *Hnefatafl* might require a level of concentration, but there were less than two-hundred raiders here, and the sudden appearance of an unrecognised face at the side of their game would surely spark suspicion.

So, walking on the outskirts of the camp, Alfred headed towards the furthest longship, seeking the deeper darkness where the light of the fires did not quite reach. From there he would hurry north and rejoin his men. As he passed that final, beached vessel, he examined it, impressed by the shields which adorned the sides. They were well maintained, of sturdy wood, and painted imaginatively in what appeared to be vibrant colours although it was hard to tell in the meagre light. The rudder, and oars, had runes burned into them, probably to protect the vessel from storms. Most strikingly, attached to the prow was a large copper weathervane decorated with the figure of some great, mythical beast. It had a row of holes with ribbons attached, which would flutter and stream out behind when the ship was coursing through the sea. Alfred marvelled at the image of it that his mind conjured, struck, as always, by the contrast between the Northmen's art and their savagery during raids.

Soon enough he was past the line of ships, and began to walk faster, the hairs on the back of his neck prickling as he feared someone would realise he was an interloper and come after him to plunge their spear into his back.

'Hey!'

He slowed instinctively at the sudden shout, but continued to walk without turning, praying that the man was calling on someone else.

'Hey!'

The call came again, accompanied by the soft thumps of feet running in the sand. Those sounds were not going in the other direction, Alfred could tell. They were coming for him.

He placed a hand on his sheathed seax and drew it out just a little, ready to defend himself from whoever this was, and then, remembering the earlier fear of a spear taking him in the back, he half turned to face his pursuer.

An enormous, bearded Dane, face almost entirely obscured in shadow, thundered across the beach towards him. He wasn't even moving that fast, but his size and lumbering gait seemed to make the ground shake and Alfred stared, wondering how he could defeat someone so massive. The Dane said something to him, but the words were spoken quickly, were heavily accented, and somewhat slurred.

The King of Wessex stood completely still, brain working feverishly to decipher the man's garbled speech, trying to pick out even a single word that would explain why he was running after Alfred.

In the end, no words were needed. As the giant reached him, he thrust out his right hand, and barked, 'Drykkr!'

Alfred stared at him, but he understood this single word well enough, and he looked down at what the giant was holding before grinning in relief. He reached out and took the ale-skin from the Dane, who repeated the Norse word for 'drink', while bobbing his head and returning Alfred's smile, white teeth visible even in the gloom.

'Skaal!' Alfred practically shouted in reply, and the enormous Dane grinned, raised a hand in farewell, and then turned to stride back through the sand to rejoin his friends singing around the nearest campfire.

The king grasped the ale-skin as if it were a holy relic and started moving again, making his way past the last of the beached ships and into the deeper darkness. At this point he felt safe enough to run, and this he did, still grinning and looking forward to the moment this night's work would be over and he could drain the contents of the skin. He doubted the ale would be of good quality, but it was a gift and deserved to be savoured, even if it might taste like cat's piss.

'My lord!'

He heard the low call coming from his left and his smile grew even wider as he recognised Wulfric's bass voice.

'Where have you been?' the ealdorman demanded, sounding more like Alfred's father than his captain. 'What the hell is that you're carrying? An ale-skin? Where—'

'Come on,' the king laughed. 'I'll explain afterwards. First, we have a beach full of Danes to wash away.'

CHAPTER THIRTY-SIX

It was a strange and eerie sight, Alfred thought, as he watched his fyrd's throwing spears sail into the air in what seemed to be a single, dark mass in the night sky. As they neared the Northmen's fires the iron blades almost seemed to catch ablaze, reflecting red and orange as they dropped like falling stars and tore into the flesh of the singing Danes.

Screams of pain mingled with shouts of alarm, but already Alfred's men were releasing a second volley. There were thumps as these too thundered down into the sand, the ships and, of course, the enemy troops.

Wulfric, eyes shining, looked at Alfred who nodded.

'For the glory of God! Charge!'

The Danes who hadn't been killed or badly injured by the deadly missiles were doing their best to form some sort of defence. Their leaders tried to marshal them, commanding them to fetch their shields, which looked so impressive on the sides of their ships but were entirely useless hanging there.

The West Saxon fyrd ran across the beach, the softer sand hindering their charge at first, before it gave way to the damper stuff, allowing them to move more quickly. They bellowed war-cries, calling for God to aid them, chanting Alfred's name, or simply, 'Wessex! Wessex!' as they lowered their spears and hammered into the barely formed enemy line.

The Danes who stood against them were poorly armed, for, like their shields, they had left their spears behind on their ships, thinking there would be no use for the unwieldy lengths of wood. Their seaxs and swords were no match whatsoever for the shields and spears of Alfred's warriors, and the pitiful line was smashed apart in mere moments.

'Kill them all!' Wulfric shouted. 'But hold your formation!'

They advanced in a single, impenetrable wall, closing in on the campfires. Many of the Danes attacked them with terrible ferocity, realising how desperate their position was, but, in small groups as they were, they had no hope of breaking through the West Saxon line and were quickly killed.

Wulfric continued to shout commands, although there was really no need. The fyrd had held their discipline, and the battle was as good as won. Alfred looked around, wondering if he was missing something. Was this another trap, like the one Halfdan had sprung on them outside Reading? Would hundreds more Northmen suddenly appear, screaming, from behind them? The king looked back, towards Tweoxneam, but no charging horde was coming. Victory surely belonged to the men of Wessex.

The Danes knew it too. Some of them, too brave or stupid to flee, continued to hammer at the wave of West Saxon shields forcing them back, but now a few had decided they wanted to live to fight another day. One man, golden rings glittering on his arms to mark him as a hersir or even a jarl, was roaring at those who had lost the stomach for the battle but he was not exhorting them to continue the attack. Instead, he was directing them towards one particular ship – the one nearest the sea. A few of them had already started to push it into the water and the dragon-head on its prow was bobbing up and down as the waves rolled beneath it.

'Keep advancing,' Wulfric ordered. 'Don't let them escape!'

The shieldwall had been forced to split into smaller sections now, to pass by the campfires which continued to blaze merrily away. Some of the Danes took advantage of this to attack one of the separate groups, even managing to kill a dozen or so of Alfred's men and break through the line. They realised their mistake once the fires were passed, though, and the shieldwall reformed, leaving the Danes trapped on the wrong side, away from their comrades.

Alfred gazed at the sailors that were trying to escape. Their longship was heavily laden, for it was designed to hold around twenty-five men and at least ten more than that had jumped on board, leaving another handful to strain at the rear, trying to push it that final, short distance over the sand until the water would successfully claim it and they could sail off.

As he watched, the king saw an enormous Northman, towering over his companions in the hull of the ship. Their eyes met, and Alfred remembered the ale he'd been gifted by the friendly giant.

'Let them go!' he shouted, running ahead of the advancing shieldwall and spreading his arms, using them to gesture as if he was pushing his fyrd backwards, away from the ship. 'Let them go!' he repeated. 'Deal with the bastards behind us!'

Wulfric opened his mouth, surprise on his face, but he thought twice of questioning Alfred's orders this time. 'Turn and face the town!' he shouted, his powerful voice carrying further than the king's.

The men did as they were told, word travelling quickly along the line, until the entire bristling wall of shields and spears was facing the other way. At the point where the remaining Danes continued to fight desperately to break through once more the West Saxon warriors flowed around them, coming at them like a pair of pincers pressing together.

Alfred nodded in satisfaction as his spearmen did their bloody work, then glanced back at the ship which had finally made it into the water. Oars had been deployed, and someone was beating out a rhythm for them to follow, each powerful stroke taking them away from the shore. The giant remained in the stern, and they stared at one another until at last the man raised one hand as if in farewell – perhaps thanking the king for allowing him to escape with his life – and the ship disappeared into the night.

Cheers and whoops of triumph erupted then, as the fyrd knew the battle was finished, and they had won it with considerable ease.

'It's over,' Wulfric said, removing his helmet and wiping sweat from his forehead. Even he managed a tired grin as he came to stand beside Alfred. 'Congratulations, my lord. Your plan worked. It looks like we've hardly taken any casualties, while we almost completely destroyed their entire force.' He paused, then jerked his chin towards the sea, and the now departed ship. 'Apart from them. Why did you let them go?'

Alfred laughed and threw his arm around Wulfric's shoulder, squeezing him in a heartfelt, joyful hug. 'A good Christian king knows when to show mercy,' he said, glorying in the sight of the celebrating, victorious army, his red banner with its proud golden dragon flying above them. 'Besides, those survivors will take word to their kings – be that Halfdan, Guthrum, or whoever – and tell them the men of Wessex are prepared for their raids. Perhaps they'll think twice about returning here again, so soon after we paid them to leave.'

Wulfric grunted. He was unconvinced, but just as happy as the king to win the battle. 'Maybe,' he said. 'But I wouldn't count on it.'

'Oh, I won't,' Alfred replied grimly. 'When we get back to Wintanceaster, I have some ideas about defending our lands properly. For now, though? Let's just get a drink, Wulfric, and celebrate sending those sea-wolves back along the damn whale road with their tails between their legs!'

CHAPTER THIRTY-SEVEN

Wintanceaster, AD 876

Although the Danes were easily seen off by Alfred at Tweoxneam, when Halfdan, Guthrum and the other kings first led their great summer army out of Wessex in AD 871 they did not simply head back to their homelands. Instead, they went once more to Lundenwic, a town and trading port which belonged to King Burgred of Mercia at that time. They wintered there, causing much trouble, until Burgred was forced to make yet another payment to get them to leave. Halfdan was happy to move on again, for his puppet king in Northumbria, Ecgberht I, had been cast out during the Danes' absence from those lands, and Halfdan went north to remind the people, and the new king, Ricsige, of his supremacy.

The Northmen set up camp in Torksey, a town with clear, easy access to Northumbria, Mercia and East Anglia. It was actually located within Burgred's kingdom, despite the fact he had paid the raiders to leave his lands and, when Burgred paid them *again* to leave his kingdom, Halfdan did the opposite. Realising how desperately weak Burgred's position was, the Danes sent men to build a fortress near Snotengaham. It was too much for the Mercian king, and he fled to Rome with his wife, Aethelswith. So, Alfred's final remaining sibling passed out of his life forever.

Another puppet king, Ceolwulf, was given the vacant Mercian throne by the Danes, while Halfdan took his men to retake control of Northumbria, and Guthrum led another army to once more assert the Danes' dominance over East Anglia.

'It's been a time of great peace here in Wessex these past five years,' Ealhswith noted one morning as she and Alfred were in the library organising the king's growing collection of books. 'God has truly been good to us.'

Alfred put down the codex he was holding, a lavishly illustrated biblical tome with gold lettering which he'd been keen to add to his archives. He looked at his wife, and she shrugged.

'Well, it's true,' she said, almost defensively. 'I know the other kingdoms haven't fared so well, including my own homelands…' She trailed off and Alfred knew she was thinking of her father, Ealdorman Mucel. Word had come the previous year that he'd died suddenly, but there had been so much fighting going on in Northumbria that Ealhswith was unable to attend his funeral. That had greatly upset her, although she had tried to hide it, just as she did now despite the tears in her eyes. She sighed, and smiled as Alfred came over and drew her into an embrace. 'The Danes have ravaged so much of the neighbouring lands,' she said. 'And it's a shame for the people living there. But Wessex has been spared, and for that, at least, we must be thankful.'

Alfred hugged her tightly, and kissed the top of her head. He'd been happy to marry her, but even he had not expected their relationship to blossom as it had during their eight years together. The birth of Aethelflaed had given them a deep bond, and in the past two years they'd been blessed with first a son, Edward, and then another baby girl, Aethelgifu. Alfred counted himself fortunate to have a family he loved so much, knowing many kings never enjoyed such a close bond with their spouse or children. Indeed, if he had been forced to spend that last half-decade on campaign, battling the Danes all across Wessex and hardly ever seeing Ealhswith or their children, the family dynamic would have been quite different.

'You're right,' he agreed, leaning down to brush her lips with his before returning to the task of sorting books. 'We must thank God for our many blessings. Although…' He placed the gold-lettered codex on a shelf next to similar documents and lifted the next book in the piles cluttering the table.

'Although?' Ealhswith prompted as Alfred seemed to have become lost in thought, leafing carefully through the volume in his hand, which looked at least a hundred years old, being terribly dusty and fragile.

'The years have given Halfdan and Guthrum time to take almost complete control over the other three kingdoms.'

'They've also given us time to rebuild our army, strengthen our fortifications, rebuild our wealth. Here.' She handed him a small, slim book with an almost illegible title scrawled on the front, undoubtedly by some aged monk. 'This belongs on that shelf beside you.'

Alfred took it and put it on top of the larger volume with gold letters. 'True, Wessex has been able to flourish again since the heathen army took our silver and sailed west. But...' He let out a long sigh and walked across to look out through the door at the sunlit courtyard of his palace. 'I fear it'll not be enough. The Danes will come again, one day, and they'll be stronger than ever, with as many resources, as many supplies, as they'll need to...' He trailed off, unwilling to speak his fears out loud in case it brought them somehow closer to reality.

'You're not the man you were back then,' Ealhswith said confidently, coming to stand in the doorway beside him and squeezing his hand. 'You were new to the throne, and unused to command. Now, you're more of a man than a boy.' As she said this she squeezed his backside, making him jump, and they laughed together until the priest, Oswald, walked by, and they stifled their laughter like naughty children.

'That's true,' Alfred conceded, breathing in the fresh air, the fragrance of wildflowers mingling with the lavender water Ealhswith had washed in that morning. 'And I've ensured that our borders are being carefully watched for signs of enemy raiders.'

'Even the waters around Wessex are better patrolled now, thanks to the extra ships you've had built,' Ealhswith noted.

'True. That's how we knew about the ships heading to Tweoxnam last year, and had time to march there to attack them.'

'So, you've done everything you can to prepare for any more invading forces, my love. It's time to stop worrying about it so much.'

Her tone left no room for argument, and they went back into the little library and set to cataloguing and arranging the books once more. They worked in companionable silence as servants and other members of the royal household walked past in the courtyard outside, and the sound of birdsong filled the air as blue tits gathered in the nearby woods. Youthful voices, high and melodious, grew louder until Aethelflaed and two other little girls burst into the courtyard, breathing hard. The little princess, five years old now, peered into the library, face red from running. She was grinning, as were the other two children, daughters of royal clerks.

'The boys are chasing us,' gasped the princess, just as the sound of slightly lower pitched voices and feet slapping grew in volume.

'Quick! Run!' Aethelflaed screamed, making Alfred wince before the girls all sprinted away to the far end of the courtyard and out another door. Aethelflaed was at least a couple of years younger than her companions yet, even so, was obviously the leader. Four boys raced after them, calling and laughing, almost falling over their own feet as they sought to catch up with the disappearing girls.

'Don't you hurt my daughter!' Ealhswith scolded as they ran past. 'Or you'll have me to deal with.'

'Hurt Aethelflaed?' one boy called back. 'She's more likely to hurt us!'

And then they were gone, laughing and hooting in sheer youthful delight.

'Not a care in the world,' Ealhswith said to her husband once calm had returned to the library. 'You should be more like them. Don't dwell on the future so much.'

'Maybe you're right,' Alfred said eventually. Ealhswith's words had reassured him as they always did, and, here in their library, with his treasured books, it did seem as if this golden age would never end for them. He was no fool, however, and he knew hard times would come again at some point, but like Ealhswith said, he must stop worrying about what *might* happen and just enjoy what they had at that moment. 'We should have Oswald celebrate a special Mass tomorrow, to let us thank God properly. And then we'll have a feast, for there's no place on earth more like Heaven for a man than in a hall filled with song, surrounded by his family and his hearth-warriors.'

'Excellent idea,' Ealhswith chuckled. 'I suppose I'd better go and set about preparing it all then, eh?'

'Thank you,' Alfred said, grasping her by the waist and kissing her as she headed towards the door. 'For everything. I couldn't ask for a better wife. You keep my household running smoothly, and take care of our children, as well as always being ready to listen to me.'

Ealhswith smiled, flashing her white teeth at him as she walked across the courtyard. 'You're right,' she called playfully. 'I am a good wife. Now get on with sorting out those books – they won't do it by themselves.'

He laughed and turned away, staring at the slim tome in his hand, wondering what Wulfric would think of this task he'd given himself. The lifelong soldier would no doubt shake his head and grumble at the king performing such a menial task, but Alfred realised at that moment that he could not remember ever feeling more content. Happy! Everything was right in Wessex, and that was all most people expected from their king.

Alfred prayed there would be many more years of this peace to come, and the Danes would bother them no more.

CHAPTER THIRTY-EIGHT

Alfred's prayers that Wessex would enjoy years of peace were not heard by God. Before he had even finished sorting out the shelves of his library word came that the Danes had struck yet again, this time at Werham, in the south. It was no mere handful of ships that had landed either – the messengers claimed it was a full-on invasion force, and the army of Wessex was forced into the field once more.

Alfred and Wulfric looked now at the massive fortifications newly built around Werham, and the king cursed loudly and in a most un-Christian manner.

Diuma was there, the young thane having brought his father's fyrd from their lands in Brycgstow, and he shook his head as he took in the sight before them. 'Again, my lord, the Danes have taken control of a town ideally positioned for their purposes.' He pointed at the glistening waters of the River Pydel to their left, then swung his arm across to the south where a second river, the Frome, could be seen snaking through the land. 'Those two rivers protect each side of Werham, but they come together on the eastern side, so, effectively this side is the only way we could get into the town. And, looking at this new earthen rampart the heathen scum have thrown up, I don't see how we can possibly retake the place without a long siege.'

'It's Reading all over again,' Alfred growled, scanning the terrain before them and recognising the truth of Diuma's assessment. He watched as a bearded warrior appeared on top of the rampart, made a rude and universally understood gesture towards the West Saxon commanders, and then pulled down his green trousers and emptied his bladder in their direction. The man was shouting unintelligible insults at them the entire time and was very drunk for he apparently fell back down the side of the fortification, disappearing from sight and bringing some small measure of amusement to Alfred's watching army. Moments later the man's head reappeared, and then his hand, again making an obscene sign, before he was gone for good.

'Like children,' Wulfric muttered, waiting to see if the inebriated Dane would make another appearance. 'They truly are like silly little boys. Why haven't you already killed them all, Diuma, and saved us the trouble?'

The thane laughed and Alfred was happy to see the two men were finally becoming comfortable with one another. Humour was always welcome, even in times of dire threat like this. Perhaps especially in times like this.

'I would have, but I thought you'd want the chance to show us all how it should be done, my lord,' Diuma replied, still smiling. 'And where the rest of us are going wrong.'

'Who leads them?' Alfred asked as Wulfric almost managed a chuckle. 'Is it Halfdan again?'

Diuma had reached Werham days before Alfred's fyrd had made it there, and he'd managed to gather some intelligence on the occupying enemy force. 'No, lord,' he said, shaking his head. 'We've not seen him. It's one of the other dogs who joined Halfdan a few years ago: Guthrum.'

Alfred took that in, partly glad that he didn't have to deal with Halfdan this time, but also somewhat anxious for he well remembered the day when he'd paid the Danes to leave Wessex in 871, and Guthrum had seemed a formidable, shrewd king even during that short meeting. Alfred did not look forward to crossing swords with the man. The fact that he'd somehow managed to lead an army here without Alfred even hearing about it was evidence enough of Guthrum's leadership qualities.

And, worryingly, the Danes had come here to Werham *by land*. They'd marched here from Grantebrycge as Alfred had eventually discovered, moving so fast that the West Saxons had been unable to offer any real resistance, and those thanes who did attempt to fight were quickly defeated. All this was worrying enough, but it left one truly terrifying question unanswered: where were the Northmen's longboats?

Alfred knew very well that Guthrum commanded a huge fleet, and the fact those vessels with their crewmen – which must number in the thousands – were not here, seemed more than a little strange. Were they at that very moment coming to join Guthrum here at Werham, swelling his numbers so enormously that Alfred could not hope to stand against them? Or were they attacking some other port in Wessex?

'Whatever the bastards are up to,' he said out loud as more of his advisors came to join them. 'We must deal with Guthrum as quickly as possible, before the rest of his men turn up.'

There was a dejected silence for Wulfric, Diuma and the rest of the West Saxon lords knew very well how foolish it would be to attack Werham, especially with its freshly constructed earthen rampart. Even if Alfred's army somehow made it inside and defeated the Danes, it would come at a horrific cost, and the young king already knew he was not particularly popular amongst many of his nobles.

He looked around, utterly dejected by the view of the countryside around them, for the Danes had ravaged it before locking themselves safely within Werham. Nearby farms had been picked clean, their occupants raped, murdered or taken into slavery. Settlements were nothing but smoking ruins where once they had been thriving hubs of life and production.

It was clear Guthrum wanted to show Alfred what would happen if the Danes were not dealt with, one way or another. But there was only one way the king of Wessex could resolve this quickly, before the enemy fleet appeared.

'We're going to have to pay them to leave again,' he said, grinding out the words in a harsh tone, for he feared his voice might crack with emotion.

Diuma stared at him, and the young thane's look of shock told Alfred all he needed to know about how this course of action would be viewed by the wealthy nobles of Wessex. Diuma had made his admiration for Alfred clear since the day they'd first met, and had supported him as aetheling, and then king. But the thought of handing over yet more wealth to the Danes was clearly appalling.

'I'm not sure my father, Ealdorman Wealdmar, will like that,' the young thane said, almost apologetically.

'What more can we do?' Alfred demanded, using his anger to override the feelings of impotence and sadness that were building inside him.

'We can fight them!' A red-faced, bald man of around sixty winters pushed past Diuma, enraged. 'You haven't even tried to assault the town. You're far too quick to throw away our wealth, Alfred. Haven't you learned anything from what's happened to King Burgred?'

There were around a dozen nobles there, ealdormen and thanes who'd brought their fyrds to join up with Alfred. More than half muttered agreement with the red-faced man.

'Burgred?' the king demanded. 'What's Burgred got to do with anything, Bishop Deorlaf? The facts are: the Danes are dug into Werham, and even if we had double the numbers we have, we could still not take the town. All the bastards have to do is wait for us to approach their rampart and launch arrows, rocks, and whatever else at us. Are you willing to lead the charge, my lord?' Alfred glared at the bishop until the man looked away, entirely unwilling to commit himself to an obvious death sentence. 'No. Anyone else? No, me neither! And the longer we remain here, the more chance Guthrum's reinforcements will arrive, and then what?'

Bishop Deorlaf wore a rich, fur-edged, purple tunic known as a dalmatic, a gold ring set with an amethyst that must have cost more than most men's war-gear, and a mitre which was simply a small cap. He glared at the king but had no reply to give him.

Wulfhere, ealdorman of Wiltunshire, did speak up, but he too avoided the question of the Danes possibly being reinforced, instead focusing on the financial aspect of dealing with Guthrum. 'You are the king,' he said to Alfred, speaking calmly, but firmly. 'It is your responsibility to come up with a way to protect Wessex. To find strategies that can keep the sea-wolves from our doors. You have failed to do it, my lord, and now we find ourselves once more being extorted, after slowly rebuilding our wealth over the past four years.'

Alfred felt rage boiling up within him as he looked at his mutinous nobles, but he forced himself to speak coolly. 'What would you have done in my position, Wulfhere? The Danes are like a plague of locusts, moving from one place to another, destroying everything in their path. Wessex is the only kingdom left – Northumbria, Mercia, East Anglia are all gone, swallowed up by Halfdan and his brothers, and now Guthrum.'

Wulfric nodded. 'The king is right,' he said. 'The Danes have taken all the food from the nearby farms, and burned what they couldn't carry, leaving nothing for us. They're well stocked with provisions and prepared for a long siege. The best we can do is pay Guthrum to leave Werham, and then do what we can to rebuild our defences.'

'Before the rats return!' Bishop Deorlaf cried in exasperation. 'For that is what they do! We pay them off, they leave for a while, then they come back, and on it goes.'

'What else can we do?' Alfred roared, losing his temper now. He moved to stand in front of the bishop, not even noticing that his hand had gripped the hilt of his sword. 'Advise me, Deorlaf, with your infinite wisdom. Tell me what we should do!' He glared at the clergyman who fell back a pace, alarmed by the king's sudden loss of temper.

There was a long, uncomfortable moment of silence as they eyed one another, and then Wulfhere said in his irritatingly calm voice, 'As the bishop says, Alfred, it is your responsibility to protect Wessex. You are the king, not us.'

Alfred looked at him and, if anything, found Wulfhere's cool demeanour even more infuriating than Bishop Deorlaf's petulance. 'Aye,' he muttered through gritted teeth. 'I am the king. And I say we will pay Guthrum to leave Werham. I'll not throw away the lives of our people in a futile assault on that great rampart, simply to protect your wealth.'

No-one spoke for a long time, and most of the men drifted away, realising continued protestations would only enrage Alfred further. None there wanted to directly challenge the king's authority, at least not right then, and not so publicly. Alfred guessed some of them had turned against him after the confrontation, and his decision not to fight, but there was little he could do about it, at least until Guthrum was dealt with.

'Diuma,' he said.

The thane was not one of the ones who'd wandered away. 'Lord king?' he replied.

'Would you go and parley with the Danes on my behalf? Find out if Guthrum will accept payment to leave our lands?'

'Aye, my lord.'

Alfred nodded, glad that at least one of his commanders could follow his orders without questioning them. 'Thank you,' he said. 'Make yourself ready, then. And let's get the vermin cleared from Werham.'

–

Alfred was a little surprised by Guthrum's willingness to nego-tiate. When Diuma returned from talking to the enemy king he said Guthrum happily accepted the offer of payment and promised to leave as soon as the silver was delivered.

It made Alfred question his decision not to fight.

'Maybe they don't have a fleet on the way to support them,' he said to Wulfric as they stood outside the king's tent waiting for the word to go out across Wessex that the ealdormen and thanes should send a portion of their wealth to Werham as fast as possible. 'Maybe his position isn't as strong as we thought.'

Wulfric let out a long, thoughtful breath and rubbed his eyes. 'Do we take that chance? Storm their rampart?' He shook his head uncertainly. 'Even if they have less numbers than reported, we would still lose a lot of men, my lord. And the Danes might start slaughtering the people of Werham.'

'To the likes of Bishop Deorlaf,' Alfred muttered, watching as his soldiers went about the business of setting up camp. 'This is a simple question of what's more important: people, or money. He would gladly throw a hundred, a thousand, men's lives away in order to protect his hoarded silver. Thankfully not all men of God are as greedy as Bishop Deorlaf.' He suspected he was being somewhat unfair to the wealthy clergyman, but, at its core, this was the question facing Wessex at that moment. It was never quite as simple or as black and white as 'lives versus money', for there were other factors at play, such as what message Alfred would send to the Danes if he paid them again to leave his lands.

'Undoubtedly it's an admission of weakness,' he said quietly, trying to order his thoughts as he spoke. 'And we do know where that led Burgred. But...' He trailed off, staring at the distant earthwork the Danes had erected, eyes slowly moving to the River Pydel which flowed past the camp on the left. 'I have a terrible premonition of dozens of longships sailing along there and an enormous horde of Northmen attacking us, Wulfric.'

The captain turned and looked at the river himself. 'That's the danger,' he agreed. 'We would not be able to withstand such an attack.' He turned back to fix the king with that familiar steely gaze and spoke more candidly than he would in front of the other nobles. 'The question is, though, what do we do when we pay Guthrum and he leaves? We can't go on like this. You have my support, and many of the other powerful men of Wessex will follow your lead, but with every payment we give to the Danes, and every defeat they inflict on us on the field of battle...' He shook his head in exasperation, voice growing harsh. 'Bishop Deorlaf and Ealdorman Wulfhere are not the only ones questioning your right to the throne, Alfred.

Some are suggesting your brother's eldest son, Aethelhelm, is old enough to be king now that he's seen eleven winters. Of course, there's plenty of powerful noblemen who'd offer to guide him until he comes of age fully.'

'Aethelred's son...' Alfred took that in, feeling a pang of guilt for he'd had very little to do with his brother's children in recent years. He hadn't been much of an uncle to Aethelhelm or Aethelwold, he realised.

They stood in silence for a long time, desperately hoping for a solution to this perpetual problem of Danish raiders. Heavy grey clouds scudded across the sky threatening to dump rain upon them, and a sudden, cold gust made both men huddle deeper into their cloaks.

'You're right,' the king said. 'And, honestly, who can blame those who question my ability to rule? It's common knowledge that I often take to my sick-bed, and no man wants to follow a leader who's plagued by such weakness.'

'Is that why you walked amongst the Danes on the beach at Tweoxneam? To prove your courage? Your willingness to walk straight into the lion's den?'

Alfred didn't answer immediately. He had often asked himself that question over the past year. He recalled those longships now, with their intricately carved dragon and serpent prows flickering in the light from the enemy campfires, and the terror as the giant Dane chased after him with the aleskin. At last, he shrugged noncommittally. 'Maybe,' he admitted. 'At the time I just felt like it would be useful to get close, to see and hear what they were doing. But perhaps your suggestion is near to the truth.' He laughed. 'It worked though, eh? Everyone thinks I'm afraid of nothing now.' His smile faded, replaced by a palpable sense of melancholy. 'If only that were true.' He straightened, gathering himself once more so that his men would not notice his poor humour. 'We're the last ones remaining, Wulfric. I'm the last independent king – all the others are puppets of the Danes. Perhaps if we had all stood together as one against the invaders we might have defeated them. Formed one, great kingdom of Angles and Saxons.'

Wulfric smiled, clearly taken by this idea of Alfred's, which he had occasionally mentioned before. 'The four kingdoms together could have easily beaten back that first great heathen army in 865 if we were united. But getting all the different peoples to work together would have been impossible. There was simply no mechanism, no system in place, to do it successfully.'

'Of course,' Alfred agreed. 'And now it's too late. We must somehow look to secure our own borders so, to answer your earlier question about what we do next, Wulfric, I suggest we look at reforming our entire system here in Wessex.'

'In what way?' The ealdorman was interested, but plainly sceptical.

'Well, for one, we look at how our fyrd is set up.' He swept his arm out, gesturing at the soldiers in the camp. 'You know these men will not remain here for very long. They cannot! They will need to return to work their farms and so on, and then what? We have no army. The Danes know this.'

Wulfric gazed at him curiously but said nothing.

'So, what we need to do,' Alfred went on, voice rising as his enthusiasm and excitement for his vision grew. 'Is split our overall fyrd into two parts. One half will come on campaign when needed, while the other remains at home to continue working as normal. And then, after a certain time, the half on campaign will return home, and swap places with those who remained.' His eyes were shining and his smile had returned. He'd almost forgotten where they were and how perilous their position was as he cast his mind ahead into the imagined future. 'What do you think?' he demanded. 'Could it work?'

Wulfric chuckled, glad to see his king filled with hope again. 'I don't see why not,' he said. 'But it will take some time to put into place.'

'Ha!' Alfred cheered so loudly that the men working nearby turned to look at him, wondering if he'd gone mad. 'Time?'

he repeated, grasping Wulfric by the upper arms. 'We will have time, once we pay Guthrum to leave. And the moment he's gone, we'll begin these reforms.' He gazed out at the camp, shoulders back, chest pushed out as if ready to go into battle. 'By Christ's bones, this is just the beginning, Wulfric! I have other ideas. Ideas about building new fortifications – *useful* fortifications, that the Danes won't be able to simply knock over and walk right past. And a better system of communication. And...' He shook his head, still grinning like little Aethelflaed when he'd gifted her a new doll. 'What say you, old friend?'

Wulfric hooked his thumbs into his sword belt and stared thoughtfully into the middle distance. It seemed like he was taking pleasure in making Alfred wait for his opinion, but he finally gave a small smile and a shallow nod. 'I think, my lord,' he said, 'that you might have been better spending money on these things before, rather than building stone churches. But, now that you've come to this decision, you have my full backing. I think your ideas sound wonderful. Overdue, even. If you can pull it off, Wessex will be able to stand against any invaders for decades to come.'

Alfred listened, irritated at first by his captain's criticism – that church in Ceodre had been worth every silver penny it had cost! – but then laughing in relief as Wulfric praised his plans, admittedly in his own downbeat way. It was enough.

'Excellent!' he shouted, slapping Wulfric on the back to the continuing amazement of the men nearby. Alfred turned to look at them now, grinning. 'Right lads,' he called. 'Let's get this camp set up and settle in. Might as well make ourselves at home while we wait for the silver to arrive so we can pay that Danish whoreson, Guthrum, to bugger off. Where's the barrels of ale?'

A tall, young warrior who was helping a comrade set up a tent across from Alfred pointed shyly at a wagon just a few paces away. 'I think that's it, my lord,' he said.

'Good. Come on, get that tent up before the rain starts, and then join us for a drink. Remember this moment, lads. This is a new dawn for Wessex!'

It was quite plain the men had no idea what he meant, but it hardly mattered. An offer of an ale with the king himself was something to be grasped with both hands, and they all cheered and got back to work with renewed vigour, hammering wooden pins into tent poles and lashing down the linen coverings that made the large tents both waterproof and comfortable to live in for more than just a night or two.

By the time night fell, Alfred was leading the entire fyrd in drunken victory songs.

He wondered what the Danes holed up within Werham must have made of it all. No doubt they would be confused, and possibly a little worried by the strange behaviour of the West Saxons.

Good, thought Alfred. *You* should *be worried, Guthrum. This is the last time you'll ever steal a wagonload of silver from me, by God!*

CHAPTER THIRTY-NINE

Guthrum was as impressive as Alfred remembered him from their previous meeting when, just like now, he'd been handing over silver to the Danes. As before, a table had been set up outside the town, Werham now instead of Reading, and the kings came together there to finalise the treaty that would see the invaders leave Wessex. Guthrum was now in his mid-thirties and his red beard was as fierce as the warriors he commanded. His green eyes were clear and showed a keen intelligence, while his wide grin seemed genuinely affectionate as Alfred approached.

'We meet again, my lord,' the Dane said happily. 'It is good to see you. You are quite famous among my people now. They tell stories about you killing Bagsecg, and walking in disguise on a beach filled with *vikingar*. Are the tales true, I wonder? Would you be so brave?'

Alfred grunted and took a stool opposite him without answering. The last time they'd met he had been younger and new to the throne, lacking in confidence and perhaps even afraid the Danes might attack him if he let down his guard and sat with them. This time, he was determined to show them a different side; to let Guthrum know he was no pushover, despite the fact he'd chosen not to fight the sea-wolves here. 'It is *not* good to see you,' he retorted, reaching out and helping himself to a cup of he knew not what. Wulfric and ten of his hearth-warriors were ranged close behind him, giving him confidence that, should the Danes try to attack him, it would not be a one-sided fight. 'I must admit, I've no idea how you managed to march here overland, without it coming to my attention in time to stop you. You must have covered near two hundred miles with great speed.'

Guthrum's grin grew even wider. "'*Afhvarf mikið er til ills vinar, þótt á brautu búi, en til góðs vinar liggja gagnvegir, þótt hann sé firr farinn*,'" he said, reciting part of a verse from the Northmen's collection of inspirational proverbs known as the *Havamal*. "'Crooked and far is the road to a foe, but wide and straight is the road to a friend though far away he fare.'"

'We are not friends,' Alfred said icily. 'And I recall your compatriot, King Halfdan, was well known for quoting the *Havamal*. You've stolen the idea from him?'

'I have,' Guthrum laughed, not embarrassed at all. 'Some thought Halfdan pretentious, but I found his little verses quite amusing, so I learned a few myself. They are very clever – those old philosophers of my people were wise in ways that are sadly lost to the world these days.'

Alfred had also been taken by those verses recited by Halfdan at their past meetings, and had gone to the trouble of adding a copy of the *Havamal* to his own treasured library in the intervening years, translated so that the West Saxon king could understand it. He amazed Guthrum now by quoting, "'*Ganga skal, skal-a gestr vera ey í einum stað; ljúfr verðr leiðr, ef lengi sitr annars fletjum á*. A guest should depart, not stay in one place. The welcome becomes unwelcome if he sits too long in another's house.'"

'Ha!' The Dane erupted in a great fit of laughter, spitting out a mouthful of mead as he turned to his own bodyguards. 'Did you hear that? The Saxon king is no fool, for he too has studied the *Havamal*.'

'Let's dispense with the needless chatter,' Alfred growled, not sharing his counterpart's good humour. Instead, he took a sip from the cup he'd lifted, which turned out to contain mead. It was a strong brew, burning the West Saxon king's throat all the way down and seeming to light a fire in his belly. He regretted drinking it then, momentarily terrified his guts would react and send him running to empty his bowels or become incapacitated with pains. He pushed those fears aside and spoke on, wishing to bring a swift end to the meeting. 'I've brought you what silver we could gather,' he said, trying not to cough as the cold air hit the back of his burning throat.

'How much?' The disarming smile did not waver, but Guthrum's eyes narrowed shrewdly as they took in the laden wagon behind the West Saxon hearth-warriors.

'Four thousand pounds.'

Now the smile disappeared, replaced by a frown. Guthrum tugged at his beard thoughtfully. 'That's much less than last time, Alfred,' he noted. 'I remember it was seven thousand then.'

Alfred nodded, eyes locked on the enemy king's. 'It is. But you have a smaller army. Less followers to pay.' He leaned back on the stool and spread his arms wide. 'Besides, it was all I could gather in this short space of time. I want you gone *now*, Guthrum. I don't have time to sit and wait for more wealth to trickle in from my ealdormen. Anyway, those same ealdormen are furious that I've decided to pay you off. They'd rather we attacked you.'

Guthrum's good humour returned then, and he laughed along with his guards. 'No doubt that's true,' he said. 'But it would be incredibly foolish, as you must have recognised, my lord, or you would not be here.'

'I will not waste the lives of my people,' Alfred said. 'If you can be bribed to leave. Can you?'

Guthrum made a show of thinking about it, but it was obvious he would take the money. At last he slammed his hand on the table and shouted, 'Ja! I will take your silver. Bring it into the town and, once it's been evenly distributed among my men, we will leave Wessex.'

'By tomorrow,' Alfred growled.

'All right,' Guthrum agreed, and he was visibly pleased with the deal.

And why would he not be? Alfred wondered. The Danes really did not like to fight battles they might lose. They wanted easy plunder, and time to enjoy the things that plunder would bring.

'Swear it,' Alfred said, and he watched Guthrum's confidence fade as he finished, 'swear it on your own holiest relic: the ring of Þórr.'

The enemy warriors muttered amongst themselves at this unusual demand, for Alfred knew the Danes had sworn oaths in the past, but the likes of Burgred, and King Edmund of East Anglia had asked them to swear on the Christian bible. Making a heathen take a vow over a book he did not believe in was utterly futile, as had been proved time and again.

Alfred would not make the same mistake.

'I know you have the ring,' he said, staring at Guthrum's arm. It was right there, the heavy gold armlet which must have been worth a fortune. 'Swear on it, lord king, that you and your army of sea-wolves will leave Werham and leave Wessex, and not return for at least five years.'

Filling his cup to the very top, Guthrum downed it, then refilled it again in thoughtful silence, as if agonising over this decision. Alfred watched in satisfaction. The Danes might not honour a vow to Christ, but they were spiritual in their own way, and placed great stock in worshipping the likes of Óðinn, Freyja and Þórr.

'Fine,' the red-bearded king agreed at last, working the gold ring down his arm and staring at Alfred as he angrily swore his oath to lead his men from West Saxon lands.

'And now, we shall exchange hostages,' Alfred said, again surprising the Danes. Guthrum shrugged however, agreeing to the trade readily enough, with the understanding that both sets of hostages be of equally high status.

As it came to midday, clouds obscured the sun and it grew cold again, prompting Alfred to stand and pronounce the meeting at an end. 'Don't forget your oath,' he warned. 'Be gone from here tomorrow.'

Guthrum nodded contentedly, green eyes only a little glazed despite the mead he'd consumed. 'I gave you my oath, didn't I? We will be gone, you can be sure of it.'

Alfred nodded. 'I'll return to my camp then. Our hostages have already been chosen. Bring yours here within the hour and the exchange will be made. You have my word we'll treat your men with respect as long as our treaty holds. I trust you will do the same.'

'Oh, yes,' Guthrum grinned. 'Yes, indeed. Farewell, Alfred. It was nice seeing you again. I look forward to trading verses from the *Havamal* with you again another time.' He paused, and then added with a laugh, 'Not for another five years though, eh?'

'At least,' Alfred retorted, and, with that, the kings parted, and the deal was done.

—

The Danes held true to their word, marching, or riding out of Werham that very night. Alfred and his army watched them from a distance, moving with the speed and efficiency expected of truly professional soldiers. It was as impressive as ever, Alfred thought, knowing his own levies would never be able to work in such a controlled manner – they simply did not have the training for it.

He was glad they did not have to fight Guthrum's sea-wolves – paying them off had been the right thing to do.

It took a while for the enemy force to disappear into the darkness and Wulfric estimated their numbers at close to four hundred, although it was difficult to count accurately in the gloom. What was certain, though, was that trying to defeat that number of Danes even in open battle would be a difficult task for Alfred's hastily gathered army, and attempting to take Werham by force with four hundred Northmen within would have been utterly futile.

'Come on,' the king said when the last of Guthrum's soldiers had cleared the town. 'Wulfric, we'll take my hearth-warriors into the town and see what damage the bastards have done.'

'I'm coming too!' Bishop Deorlaf said, and some of the other noblemen also demanded to join them, but Alfred shook his head.

'There's no point in us all going,' he said firmly. 'The Danes have left the town so there's unlikely to be any danger. There's still a chance the sneaky rats might return though, and attack us, so...' He looked at Diuma and the other fyrd commanders. 'Bishop Deorlaf can accompany me into Werham. The rest of you remain here, and remain alert. Deorlaf, and you too Wulfric, let's go.'

'Yes, lord,' his captain replied, issuing his orders and riding after Alfred towards the open gates of Werham with Deorlaf, who grumbled all the way, only falling silent when they passed the great earthen rampart Guthrum had erected. There were fires within the town which offered enough light for the riders to see where they were going, but, until they got closer it was impossible to say what the fires were. Bodies of the West Saxon fyrd who'd tried to defend the town, probably. Tossed onto pyres and set alight by Guthrum's people to keep the streets free of rotting corpses, without the proper Christian rites. It was an affront to God, Alfred brooded as they cantered through the unmanned gates and past the ruined buildings within.

The streets were eerily empty, with only a few frightened souls peering out from their homes, although the snaps and cracks of burning timber, sobs of despair, and the smoke and ash which filled the night air meant there was nothing peaceful about the scene. Most of the town seemed to be in decent condition though, and Alfred wondered at that. Guthrum's warriors could certainly be destructive when it suited them, but here, as in Reading, it seemed like the Danes had left the people and the buildings alone unless someone tried to get in their way.

They could see the piles of bodies burning now, and smell them too, the meaty-smoke wafting across the riders as they passed, making them cover their mouths and noses with hands or sleeves. Alfred made the sign of the cross absentmindedly and muttered a prayer for the souls of those who'd lost their lives attempting to stem the tide of Danes as it surged over the ill-prepared town.

Still, it could have been worse. Alfred guessed there had been some advance warning of the enemy approaching – some shepherd out in the surrounding fields had perhaps spotted the army and come to warn the people of Werham. Some of them must have fled, carrying what they could, so, when Guthrum turned up many of the town's inhabitants were gone, and safe from the physical, sexual and psychological violence they might otherwise have been subjected to. Well, those folk would return now that the danger had passed, and the town could go about the task of rebuilding itself.

Again, Alfred congratulated himself on making the Danes leave so peacefully but, as they came to the centre of town they saw more bodies, and these had not been set alight.

'For God's sake,' Wulfric muttered. 'Why has no-one given those men a proper burial? The Danes are gone!'

'Perhaps they were killed by the Danes as they were leaving,' Alfred suggested, and then he broke off as sudden understanding hit him.

Bishop Deorlaf practically fell off the back of his horse and then he sprinted towards the bodies, crying out in despair, before finally falling to his knees and staring in horror at the unmoving form of a young man. Pale, almost marble-white skin showed clearly the enormous cut that had opened his throat and ended his life.

It was Deorlaf's son, Cadfan.

'This is your fault!' the bishop shrieked, turning his despairing gaze on the king. 'I told you we should have fought the Northmen!' His eyes scanned the rest of the corpses, discarded like rubbish in the middle of town, each one with their throats brutally cut open.

'The hostages,' Wulfric said, and even he was visibly shaken by what the Danes had done. 'Guthrum swore an oath, on his own god's sacred arm-ring, yet he's done this?'

Alfred was too dumbfounded to speak. His mind was whirling and, when he dismounted he felt that old, familiar stabbing sensation in his guts and it was all he could do to remain standing without crying out in pain. Tears filled his eyes and he held onto his mount's reins for support as Deorlaf continued to sob and scream at him, blaming Alfred for this terrible tragedy.

The king just stood there, too stunned to take control of the situation, feeling as if the world was crashing down about his ears.

'You!' Wulfric said, pointing at a dull-eyed man sitting in the shadows with his back against the wall of what looked like a carpenter's workshop. 'Did you see what happened here?'

The man did not hear him, or at least did not react, and Wulfric strode across to him. It was clear the fellow had suffered some trauma for he had a huge, purple bruise on his forehead and did not move or look up even when the big ealdorman was standing directly over him. Wulfric leaned down and placed a hand on his shoulder, which finally elicited a reaction.

'What?' the man asked in a hoarse, emotionless voice.

'Are you unwell? Do you need aid?' Wulfric asked in a gentle tone, or at least as gentle as he could manage.

'No.'

'Did you see what happened here?'

Tears filled the man's light blue eyes and he seemed to gaze right through Wulfric at the bodies strewn across the ground. 'Aye,' he whispered. 'The Danes…' He trailed off, gave one loud sob, and then went on in a furious tone. 'The Danes came into my workshop looking for rope to tie up the hostages.'

Alfred looked at the bodies and saw that all of them had their hands and feet bound with sturdy rope.

'My wife tried to get them to pay for the rope,' the carpenter went on. 'I told her to be quiet, but she kept on, demanding the bastards hand over some of the silver they'd stolen from our people, so they killed her. Just like that, as if she was nothing. When I tried to stop them, one of them smashed me in the face with his axe, knocked me down here. He hit me so hard that I couldn't move, but… I could see and hear what they did to those hostages.'

The king did not really want to hear any more of the man's tale. It was quite obvious what had happened to the hostages, but the carpenter went on, as if reliving those terrible moments.

'Their king, Guthrum, told his men to bind the hostages. Any of them who protested got the same as me: smacked in the mouth or worse, and forced onto their knees. They tied their hands and feet, and then Guthrum stood in front of them all like one of our priests celebrating Mass and said, 'Odin, All-Father, accept the blood of these men as my sacrifice to you. May their deaths bring us good fortune, and victory!''

Bishop Deorlaf sobbed and Alfred felt bile rise in his throat at the scene the carpenter had witnessed. He did not have to imagine how it had played out, for the man went on.

'They did it one by one,' he said. 'Starting on the left. The first hostage had his throat cut, slowly, as he begged them not to.' The carpenter shuddered and drew his arms into his chest, as if protecting himself from the horrific memories. 'The sounds as he died…' he murmured.

'I don't think we need to hear any more,' Alfred said, but Bishop Deorlaf pushed himself to his feet and came to stand in front of the king, pointing up into his face.

'No! You *will* hear more, Alfred,' he screeched. 'This is all your fault, and you should hear how every one of those hostages was slaughtered. Their deaths are on you, so the least you can do is stand and listen to what happened!'

Alfred met Wulfric's eyes and he knew his captain would remove Deorlaf if he asked him to. In truth, though, he feared the bishop's accusation was true, and the guilt of it weighed the king down. A beam collapsed in a burning house close-by but, strangely, no-one gathered there seemed to notice. It was as if that small space with the bodies was all that mattered now – their own private corner of Hell.

'Fine,' Alfred said, breathing heavily. He looked at the carpenter and nodded. 'Go on.'

'One by one,' the man murmured, still staring straight ahead without focusing on anything in particular. 'They went along the line, cutting. Some of the hostages begged for their lives, some struggled, some shit themselves, some prayed to God…' He snorted, as if praying was ridiculous, which, Alfred had to admit, it had been for those poor wretches. 'Some of them, braver than I could have been, remained quiet, or cursed Guthrum, but he just laughed.'

Wulfric came to stand beside Alfred and together they examined the bodies. Blood was everywhere and it was not hard to imagine the terror the unfortunate victims had felt as their throats were slowly carved open, the Danes laughing at their fear and desperation. The king felt shaky, like he might collapse, and he grasped Wulfric's arm, using the bigger man's strength to prop himself up. It would not do to show weakness at a time like this. Compassion, perhaps. Vengeful rage, yes. But not weakness.

Now that the carpenter had started his tale it seemed he could not rest until he finished, so on he went, describing the tears and screams of the dying until, at last, it was Wulfric who told him to stop. There was horrified silence for a time, until the carpenter stumbled dizzily into his workshop and fell to sobbing again as he found his dead wife.

'Well,' Bishop Deorlaf shouted, pushing himself back to his feet and wiping tears and snot from his face as he stumbled over to his wide-eyed horse. 'If the Danes think it's acceptable to murder their hostages, we can do the same to theirs.' He made an attempt to haul himself up into the saddle but he was not strong enough and fell back onto the ground. He tried again and just managed it this time, sitting atop the horse and dragging in great deep breaths as if he might expire at any moment himself. He stared at Alfred, challenging him to argue with him, but the king said nothing and the bishop galloped back through the town towards the gates, purple tunic whipping wildly, his guards thundering along behind him.

'You want me to stop him?' Wulfric asked. 'The mood he's in, he will kill those hostages we took. With his own seax too, I'd wager. It won't be pretty.'

'Pretty?' Alfred asked dully, still staring at the sightless eyes of the slaughtered men in the road. 'Nothing about this is *pretty*. Let him go, and do whatever he must.'

Wulfric nodded, accepting his orders without comment. 'What are we going to do about this then?'

'Bury them,' the king replied. 'Properly. Like the good Christians they were. And then?' He tore his gaze from the dead men and stared at Wulfric. 'If Guthrum was not held by his oath to protect the lives of these hostages, we can't assume he'll follow his other promise.'

'To leave Wessex.'

'Aye,' Alfred nodded, gripping the hilt of his sword. 'Wherever the Danes have marched off to, I fear there's more mischief to come from them. You may not be a very spiritual person, Wulfric, but I would ask you to pray for us and for Wessex, for, despite taking our silver Guthrum may not be finished with us yet.'

Outside the town distant screams could be heard, but no-one commented on it. They knew they would return to a bloody camp, strewn with the hacked-up bodies of a dozen unarmed, defenceless Danes.

'The siege of Werham is over,' Alfred gasped, clutching his stomach as the pain flared once more. 'But we must find out where Guthrum's going, and thwart whatever plan he's set in motion before our lands are lost forever. Come, Wulfric, we must ride!'

CHAPTER FORTY

With Werham once more in the hands of its own people, Alfred led a detachment of his men in pursuit of the Danes. Rather than travelling north, or east, and leaving Wessex as Guthrum had sworn he would, they went west, even deeper into West Saxon lands. And again, as at Reading and Werham, the Northmen attacked and took control of a town – Exanceaster this time – where they dug in and could not be got at by Alfred's riders.

'What is Guthrum doing?' Wulfric wondered as they stood outside the besieged town with an overwhelming feeling of déjà vu. 'He's just repeated his tactics at Werham, but he must know we have no more silver to pay him off this time.'

'So, he has no intention of leaving,' Alfred replied bleakly. 'We feared he was waiting for his fleet to reinforce his numbers back at Werham, but, for whatever reason, it never arrived. I'd wager the fleet is on its way now, and we will soon be overrun by a plague of Northmen to rival anything in the bible.'

They stood there, utterly dejected, minds racing as they tried to come up with a solution to this problem but knowing it was impossible. Guthrum's army was inside Exanceaster, a town fully stocked up for winter with provisions, and, again, Alfred's army would be left scrabbling around the countryside for food which simply wasn't there.

The young king turned and looked at the warriors they'd brought with them in that mad dash from Werham. Not many, and certainly not enough to storm Exanceaster. 'Do you think the rest of the army will come to join us from Werham?' he asked fretfully.

Wulfric's face betrayed his feelings, but it didn't matter for he did not attempt to fool Alfred with platitudes or soothing words. Instead, he muttered, 'No. Some, those most loyal to you, might. But even they may see this as a step too far, and slink back to their own lands to look after themselves for the winter.'

Alfred sighed. 'I can't really blame them. This is… It's a living hell, Wulfric.' His eyes were red-rimmed, his cheeks hollow, at the sight of the West Saxon corpses Guthrum's men had tossed out of Exanceaster to rot. Innocent men and women whose only crime was to try and defend their town against the horde of pagans who'd turned up without warning and…

'It *is* draining, my lord,' Wulfric said. 'But we can't allow ourselves to become disheartened.'

'Can we not? Why?'

'Because you are king,' Wulfric retorted, and there was a hint of annoyance in his tone. 'You, and I, must remain strong until either the Danes are pushed back again, or—'

'Or we are dead,' Alfred finished for him. He was tempted to simply broach a cask of ale and drink until he passed out, and he might have done it if he didn't fear the inevitable stomach pains that tended to follow such sessions.

'What are your orders?' the ealdorman asked, his calm demeanour as reassuring as always.

Wulfric truly was the rock Alfred had been able to build his kingdom upon. He had to trust that they could, somehow, prevail even when everything seemed lost. He turned to Wulfric, standing erect, much taller and broader than Alfred, and laughed. 'My orders? Ah, my faithful captain, always here to guide me and kick my arse when I start to get maudlin.'

A hint of a smile touched Wulfric's mouth but he said nothing. Simply waited.

'Have the men set up camp,' ordered the king. 'We do as we did at Werham, contain Guthrum within the town, and pray that enough of my ealdormen bring their fyrds to join us. If they do, we attack the town. If they do not?' He shrugged, but felt in better humour thanks to Wulfric's steadying presence. 'We'll cross that bridge when we reach it. For now, I will hear Mass, and beg God to bring us salvation.'

'Very good, my lord,' Wulfric nodded. 'Stay optimistic. Exanceaster is only one small part of Wessex – the rest of it, and all the people in it, are yours. Many will rally to your banner, and together we'll slaughter Guthrum and his vermin.' He bowed and then turned and stalked away, already barking out orders to the warriors lounging around.

–

Many of the soldiers who'd been at Werham did come to Exanceaster, and others who had not made it there did now cover the miles to swell Alfred's gathered forces. Wulfric's counsel that the king remain optimistic was easy enough to follow over the next few days, as the West Saxons tightened the siege of Exanceaster, and the prayers of the Christians seemed to be finding favour with God. Even Bishop Deorlaf brought his fyrd, for he wanted revenge on Guthrum for murdering his son, as did the other noblemen who'd seen their loved ones handed over to the Danes as hostages and then brutally slain.

There was enough food and drink to go around for a while, and, since Alfred knew Guthrum had only four hundred men behind the walls, he planned to lead an assault on the town just as soon as his numbers exceeded the Danes'. A great battering ram had already been constructed, along with ladders to scale the walls. It would be a bloody, brutal conflict, but the men of Wessex were looking forward to taking out years of pent-up rage and hatred on this enemy who would simply not leave them in peace.

The sense of positivity flowed down from Alfred throughout the entire army, and the camp here at Exanceaster was a very different one to what it had been at Werham. Bishop Deorlaf brooded, but the rank and file, the ceorls and hearth-warriors, sang hymns and battle songs, practised with weapon and shield, and, at the end of each day, they played games and told tales around their campfires.

Of course, envoys were sent to speak with Guthrum, to demand he leave the town and march out of Wessex as he'd sworn to do. It was worrying when the enemy king would not speak with those emissaries, and, when they were cut down by a hail of spears thrown from the walls of Exanceaster it merely added to the West Saxons' sense of injustice.

'When will you order the attack?' It was Bishop Deorlaf, storming into Alfred's tent without being announced on the thirteenth day of the siege.

The king frowned at the guards who'd let the clergyman pass, but commanded them to return outside to their posts when he realised they could hardly have stopped the bishop by force.

'We've been here for too long already,' Deorlaf ranted, face redder than ever. His eyes were bloodshot but whether from grief or drink it was hard to say. Probably both. 'The heathen scum only number four hundred or so, and we've already got more than that. Another forty men came in today from Twyford. Are you going to sit here forever? How many men do you need to take one town, by God?'

Alfred felt his own anger rising as he stared at the powerful nobleman, but he forced himself to remain calm. The bishop was a good ally to have, and he had lost his son in a most brutal fashion after all.

'I feel it prudent to wait another day or two,' he said, meeting Deorlaf's angry gaze. 'There's no point in attacking the town only to be beaten back for lack of numbers. Guthrum will have rubble piled up behind the gates so, even when we smash through them, it will be a struggle to push forward into the streets beyond. And he will have the walls well defended, so the more men we can muster to climb the ladders the better.'

The bishop glared at him, chewing his lip in consternation. There was almost a madness in his expression, as if finding his son's mutilated corpse had broken something within his mind. He was not completely reckless however, and listened to Alfred's reasoning before growling, 'I fear you will wait too long, Alfred, hoping for a numerical advantage that will never be ours. What if this is all the men who are coming? It's the middle of winter, far from home for your ealdormen in the north and west. Should they decide it's their duty to come, by the time they reach us it could be too late.' He pointed a wrinkled, shaking finger at Alfred. 'It was you who suggested we had to pay the Danes to leave Werham,' he reminded the king. 'Because you feared a great fleet would turn up and kill us all. Well, surely that's still the case?'

Alfred took a deep breath then turned away and rubbed his eyes which were stinging from lack of sleep and the smoke that hung perpetually over the camp from the cooking fires. He had actually been napping when the bishop had so rudely awoken him, although it was an unplanned nap, for he'd been praying before exhaustion claimed him. 'You make a fair point,' he conceded. 'I wish to God we had some idea where those damn longships are hiding.'

'Halfdan is far in the north,' Deorlaf noted. 'Fighting the wild men of Strath-Clota. It's more than likely the ships have gone with him, or perhaps even further west, to support their kinsmen who raid and call themselves kings in Ireland nowadays. Or maybe they've returned to plunder Francia again.'

Any of those scenarios were possible and Alfred comforted himself by believing one or all were true. 'Fine,' he said. 'We'll wait one more day and hope our numbers grow by at least another twenty or thirty or so. The day after tomorrow,' he punched his palm and smiled grimly. 'We will retake Exanceaster.'

Deorlaf nodded and his eyes burned with a fervour Alfred had never seen when the bishop was at prayer or giving Mass. It seemed a strange contradiction, for churchmen like Deorlaf or the sadly deceased Bishop Heahmund, to seek violence so readily when their main function was supposed to be spreading God's love throughout the world. Still, love would not help them smash open the gates of Exanceaster.

'Come, my lord,' said Alfred, standing and lifting two cups from the table beside him. 'Have a drink with me. A toast to the success of this campaign.' He filled the cups with ale and handed one to the bishop who took it gladly.

'I want to be the one to kill Guthrum,' Deorlaf said as he sipped the cold drink.

Alfred shrugged. 'If we capture him alive, I have no problem with that. You can do what you like with him.'

'Then the sooner we start fighting the better,' replied the bishop, staring into his cup as if he could see himself there, seax in hand, slowly taking his revenge on the enemy king.

There was a sudden raising of voices outside the tent, and a thundering of hooves. Someone was shouting, and their words were being passed along through the rest of the men in the camp.

'The Danes!'

Alfred finally made out the words within the rising clamour.

'The Danes are coming!'

King and bishop looked at one another, surprised, but excited. 'It seems the battle will be joined sooner than we expected,' Alfred said, downing his ale and slamming the cup on the table. 'Guthrum must have grown tired of waiting and decided to ride forth.'

They went out together, drawing their cloaks up, for a stiff breeze was coming from the east. Alfred spotted Wulfric and Diuma hurrying towards them, dark looks on both their faces.

'What's happening?' the king asked, smiling in anticipation of the coming battle and a chance to get revenge for the hostages Guthrum slaughtered at Werham. 'Have the bastards come out of the town? Are we going to get a fight this time, instead of just chasing them as they run off like the cowards they are?'

Wulfric and Diuma stopped before them and shared a glance which made Alfred's blood run cold. 'What?' he demanded.

'Well, my lord,' Diuma said. 'We are indeed going to get a chance to fight.'

'Good!' Bishop Deorlaf shouted. 'Guthrum is mine, do you hear? Alfred promised me.'

'You can have him,' Wulfric replied, but his brow was practically V-shaped so deep was the frown he bore. 'But we'll have to beat them first, and that's suddenly become much more difficult.'

Alfred stared at him, but he did not need his captain to explain his portentous words, for he could see himself the mast of a longship sailing slowly towards them along the River Exe. And behind it, another.

'My God,' he groaned. 'How many are there, Wulfric?' He tried to remain calm, to remember the seven longships on the beach at Tweoxneam not so long ago, and how easily his West Saxon fyrd had managed to defeat them. His optimism was short lived.

'We're not sure yet, my lord,' Wulfric replied. 'But there's a lot more behind this first group. Many more still out at sea, on their way here.'

'What d'you mean, "a lot"?' Bishop Deorlaf demanded, his rage building again as he saw the chance to avenge his son's death slipping further away with each longship that hove into view.

'One hundred and forty,' Diuma said. 'At least. They've been docked at Polle Harbour, but messengers have just arrived with news that the fleet is on its way here.'

His words were met with stunned silence. Alfred tried to picture so many ships but it seemed incomprehensible to him. One hundred and forty ships, each with a crew of perhaps thirty men?

'That's over four thousand enemy warriors,' he calculated, mind reeling as he tried to imagine how their own meagre army might prevail against such numbers. It seemed impossible. It *was* impossible!

'More,' Diuma agreed. 'When you add the men with Guthrum in Exanceaster.'

'We cannot—' Alfred caught himself before the sentence was fully formed, but the other men knew exactly what he'd been about to say and it was impossible to argue with it. They could not win this time.

Wessex was doomed.

CHAPTER FORTY-ONE

Oswald, Alfred's priest and advisor, had been left behind with the main army at Werham when the king led his horsemen west, after Guthrum. He understood that the king and his soldiers had more pressing matters to worry about than him but, when the various fyrds had all moved on, either following Alfred as they were obliged to do, or returning to their homes, Oswald found himself with no clear idea what to do. Should he go with one of the ealdormen and rejoin the king, or would Alfred prefer him to return to Ealhswith in Wintanceaster?

In the end he decided to travel south, to Swanawic, an easy enough journey of ten or so miles on horseback. Oswald's parents hailed from the coastal town and, since he'd been given no orders from Alfred, it seemed a good opportunity to visit them. Besides, Oswald remembered the church in Swanawic from his childhood, and recalled it having a small, but well-stocked library. It was over thirty years since he'd last seen that collection of books, but he hoped it would still be there, and perhaps even have been added to in the intervening decades. Surely there would be something there he could take back to the king? Some volume not held, yet, in Alfred's royal library?

That would be his excuse should Alfred ask where he'd been during this time, but, to be honest, he doubted anyone would miss him. There were warrior bishops and other priests attached to the army so, if the king needed spiritual guidance he would have no shortage of advisors. Plenty of opportunities to hear Mass too.

His ride to Swanawic proved a pleasant one, despite it seeming to grow colder the closer he got to the sea, and his parents welcomed him into their home with happy surprise. His father, Ailric, was a thane of some standing locally, and his house was a large one, so there were no issues with finding a place for Oswald to sleep.

Over the next few days his parents entertained him with local gossip, and he told them all about his time as a priest and his elevation to the position of advisor to the king himself.

It was a relaxing period, filled with good food, good drink and walks with his mother and father by the sea. The town was quiet then, for many of the men had gone with the ealdorman to fight alongside Alfred at Werham and then followed the king east, leaving elderly Ailric to keep things in order in Swanawic.

Oswald did visit the nearby church and was granted access to the library by a rather grumpy old priest. Unfortunately, Oswald's childhood memories of the impressive collection of literature held within the old church proved quite inaccurate. There was nothing in the little library that Alfred did not already own a copy of, apart from one slim, heavily aged, collection of prayers. There was nothing particularly interesting about it, to Oswald's eyes, but he knew the king was fascinated by old books, so he bought it from the priest for a handful of silver pennies which were newly minted and stamped with Alfred's own portrait.

And then, when Oswald had almost lost track of how long he'd been in Swanawic and decided he should really make his way back to the royal household in Wintanceaster, news came that a great fleet of ships was congregating at Polle Harbour, just a few short miles along the coast.

With Oswald's father being the highest-ranking thane who hadn't gone with Alfred's army, it was left to him to rally the remaining men and prepare to defend Swanawic against the Danes. It soon became apparent, however, that the sea-wolves were not there to launch an attack on any of the settlements situated around Polle Harbour.

'They're just using this as a meeting point,' Ailric said, shading his eyes with his hand for, although it was still cold, it was clear that morning. The water in the harbour glistened in the bright sunshine although less of it was visible than usual, for the massive space was crowded with longships.

'I've never seen anything like it,' Oswald said in horror, trying to count how many vessels were there, but finding it impossible. 'There must be hundreds of ships!'

Some of them remained in the water, while others had been pulled up on the beaches which ran for some fifteen or more miles around the harbour. Their crews, even more innumerable than the longships, swarmed the golden sands like ants, while Ailric and other Saxon leaders watched with their fyrds from a distance. No fighting had occurred, yet, and, to Oswald's father, it looked as if the Danes had no intention of remaining there for long.

'I'd say there's no more than a hundred longships,' the thane said. 'Although my eyesight isn't what it used to be. And there will be more of the bastards coming with every passing hour. I don't think we have anything to fear, though.'

Oswald looked confused. 'Nothing to fear? With that many Danes here? Forgive me, Father, but I am feeling somewhat frightened!'

Ailric chuckled, a throaty rasp which pained Oswald to hear. When he'd last seen his parents they'd been much younger, less lined, more vital. It was depressing to see the ravages of age upon his once straight-backed, fearsome father.

'Oh, someone should be frightened,' Ailric said. 'Whoever ends up facing that great horde of Northmen. But,' he shook his head and turned away to walk to the small camp his men had set up a short distance from the beach. 'That will not be us.'

'It will be the king,' Oswald said, hurrying after him. 'Wherever he followed Guthrum to, he must be warned about this fleet, Father. And he will need as many reinforcements as he can muster. You must take your fyrd, and march west.' He turned back to look out across the horseshoe-shaped harbour, and threw out his arm, sleeve flapping, to encompass all the West Saxon warriors ranged around in small groups hoping to defend their own villages and towns. 'All of those men must go and join Alfred, or Wessex will fall! Father, you—'

Ailric grimaced as he lowered himself slowly onto a camp chair that was so close to one of the fires that Oswald worried the old thane might catch light himself. He held out his seamed hands and rubbed them over the flames, shivering as he did so. 'We've already sent messengers west,' he told his son, halting the priest mid-rant. 'And we'll send another when the ships depart and we have a better idea of their number. My job, like all the rest of the men gathered around the bay – be they from Werham, Lichet, Corf, Bere, or wherever else – is to stay behind and guard our homes.'

'But—'

'Oswald!' The grizzled thane slammed his hand down on his thigh. 'You are a priest. You must do what you do, and pray for the lives of Alfred and his men who will be forced to face the heathen army in battle. I am, or at least *was*, a soldier, and I will do my duty, which is to remain here. Or would you have us all march away and leave these settlements completely undefended? What if more Danes arrive and decide to take advantage of such easy pickings?' He gestured dismissively and stared into the roiling flames in front of him. 'By God, it's bloody freezing today.'

'Maybe a storm will blow up and slow down those ships,' one of the men, armed with a crude maul, suggested hopefully.

'That would be a miracle,' Ailric snorted.

'If none of you will march to help Alfred,' Oswald grunted. 'He will *need* a miracle just to survive!' With that, he turned and walked back across the loose, shifting sand he remembered so fondly from childhood and tried once more without success to count the ever-expanding fleet of enemy longships.

Four days later Ailric and his fyrd were still camped on the beach, and, as predicted, more ships had come to swell the enemy fleet. If their numbers had been difficult to gauge before, now it was just impossible, and made even more so as there had been a change in the weather. While it had been cold when the first longships had turned up in the harbour, it had been clear and sunny. They seemed to bring dark clouds with them, however – literally, as well as metaphorically – for it was now grey, and when it wasn't raining there was a perpetual smirr in the air. Ailric's men were soaked and in poor humour, openly wishing the Danes would sail away so they could return to Swanawic and sleep in a real house once more.

Oswald had spent much of his time with them on the beach, leading the men in prayer, or simply telling them stories from the bible or about local saints to try and stave off the interminable boredom. He also rode to the church where he passed many hours, imploring God to help King Alfred and the men of Wessex to hold back the heathen tide. It seemed impossible, but Oswald's faith was strong and he clung to it, using it like a shield against the dark daydreams that filled his imagination.

On that fourth day he loaded his horse with fresh cakes the baker had made to keep the fyrd's spirits up and rode at a leisurely pace to find Ailric and his men lined up along the beach, staring at the sea. The priest secured his horse, muttering an apology for the poor beast was drenched by the torrential rain that had started to fall again.

'What's happening?' he demanded, shoving his way through the warriors to stand by his father's side.

'They're leaving,' Ailric replied without looking at him. His gaze, like everyone else's, was fixed on the scene before them, as dozens of ships clustered together, moving through the narrow mouth of the harbour and into the South Sea.

'How do they not crash?' a young lad asked, gaping at the incredible sight before them. 'I mean, into each other? Or onto the rocks? There's so many of them!'

'If there's one thing the Danes are good at,' Ailric replied grimly. 'It's sailing.'

Oswald nodded. *They're also good at killing and raping and stealing and...* He silenced his thoughts and tore his eyes away from the harbour to look at his father. 'You've sent a messenger to the king?' he asked.

'I haven't but word is on its way, don't worry.' He waved a hand along the line towards a lean, dark man. 'Eoforheard is the messenger we sent when the ships first came here. He just returned today.'

'You've seen Alfred?' the priest asked hopefully. 'Is he well?'

Eoforheard nodded deferentially. 'I didn't meet with the king myself, lord,' he said. 'But I passed my message to one of his hearth-warriors.'

'Did you see the king though?'

'Aye, lord. He looked well.'

'Thank God,' the priest intoned. 'And thank you, Eoforheard. That's good to know.'

'There wasn't all that many men with him though,' the man said, almost apologetically, as if it was his fault the West Saxon army at Exanceaster was so small. He jerked his chin towards the departing fleet. 'They'll never stand against all those bastards. Even God can't save Alfred now, I fear.'

Oswald bridled at this casual dismissal of God's power, but he could understand the man's lack of faith. 'I will continue to pray for—' He broke off, buffeted by a sudden gust of wind so strong that he almost fell over. His father caught him, and then all the men gathered there averted their faces as the rain became so heavy that it actually stung their skin. As one, they ran, shouting and laughing in surprise, across the sodden sand towards their tents, some of which had been pulled out of position or even knocked flat by the sudden gale. Ailric's, being the grandest, and sturdiest, remained upright but the linen flapped loudly, buffeted upwards by the wind while simultaneously being battered down by the torrential rain.

'Where did *that* come from?' the thane cackled, drawing in ragged breaths and staring at the sky as they huddled within the tent. Outside on the beach the campfires had been extinguished, and any food that had been cooking over them was utterly drenched.

Together, Oswald and his father watched the weather turn the camp into a sodden mess, filled with the sounds of hammering rain, gusting wind and shouts from those men who were unlucky enough to have tents collapse and had attempted to right them. Ailric, still laughing, called on the struggling men, telling them to shelter with him until the squall passed and they could sort the camp properly.

As the thane shouted for his men to join him in the tent, Oswald squeezed past, heading outside. The priest walked away, towards the sea, rain bouncing off his tonsured scalp and running in rivulets down his cloak.

'Where are you going, you bloody idiot?' Ailric shouted after him. 'You'll catch a cold wandering about in that!'

The priest ignored him, and stepped right up to the water's edge, staring out at the longships. Practically all of them had made it out of the harbour before the sudden change in the weather, and, looking at the horizon, Oswald could see this was no mere squall that would blow over in a few moments. It was a full-on storm, and, if Ailric's troops thought they were being battered by it there on the beach, the longships were suffering much worse.

Vessels that had seemed so enormous just a short time ago now appeared small and insignificant as they were tossed this way and that by the roiling, churning waves. Oswald had seen longships up close; he knew how well they were constructed, with thick timbers, joined and crafted by master builders who understood wood better than any other men in the world.

Those ships seemed indestructible to Oswald, yet, as he looked on, squinting against the rain that lashed at his face, one suddenly splintered into pieces. The priest assumed it had been blown into rocks beneath the water, and he watched the whole thing sink beneath the churning waves as its crew was swallowed one by one, little black shapes in the distance. All that remained were shards of wood and cargo, tossed hither and thither by the maelstrom.

Oswald was torn. Did he pray for their souls? Should he pity those men whose lives had been snuffed out so easily? It was only natural to feel sadness while watching such a horrific sight.

And then another ship broke into pieces, and he watched a third collide with a fourth and they too shattered, emptying Danes into the sea, and another, and another. Tears filled the priest's eyes as he watched dozens of men drown and he knew that, if he could, he would reach out and help pull them ashore to safety, enemies or not.

He sensed a presence next to him, and turned to see Ailric and all the men of the fyrd lined up on the beach beside him, gaping at the carnage the storm was wreaking. They stood in silence, and Oswald began to pray, softly at first then louder, until he was practically shouting, arms outstretched although he was not even sure what he was praying for.

The storm lasted for a while longer, but at last the rain lessened and the wind dropped to a gentle breeze and, eventually the sun broke through the clouds, casting its light and meagre warmth on the soaking beach.

Already, the waves were depositing flotsam and bodies on the beach. On the horizon only a handful of ships remained afloat, and they soon disappeared out of sight to the east, continuing their journey to Exanceaster.

Oswald fell silent as he looked out at the limp, dead faces of drowned men. He had seen men dying in great numbers before, during battle – seen the horrific wounds caused by blades and hammers and maces. Somehow, this was more profoundly shocking, for these Danes had not been killed by any tangible enemy. No warriors had cut these men down. No human fist had wielded weapons that ended their lives.

God himself had stretched out his hand, and plunged those heathen raiders into the Southern Sea, filling their lungs with water, and ending their days as easily as Oswald had extinguished the candles during Tenebrae.

'I guess they won't be joining up with Guthrum at Exanceaster,' Ailric said, attempting to make a dark jest but speaking in such awed, stunned tones that his words lost any humour they might have held.

'We did ask for a miracle,' Eoforheard murmured. 'Looks like we got one.'

'How many ships d'you think were sunk?' someone asked.

'Dozens.'

'Fifty.'

'A hundred.'

'With about thirty men in each vessel,' Ailric said. 'That's a *lot* of dead Danes we're going to have to clear from the beach.' He brightened then. 'And a lot of plunder too! Many of them will be wearing silver or gold jewellery. They'll have arm-rings, torcs, swords…'

'Any wearing chainmail will have sunk to the bottom though,' Eoforheard noted darkly.

'Aye, but even most of them will wash up on the beach eventually,' Ailric said.

Again, silence fell over them and they continued to stare as body after body was carried in by the sea and left on the beach to rot.

'Who needs an army?' Ailric suddenly asked, and now there was real joy in his voice as the realisation of what this all meant sunk in. 'When we have Oswald with us?' He turned and embraced his son, and there were tears in the old thane's eyes too, of shock and relief and gratitude for God's holy gift to the people of Wessex. 'Your prayers worked, son! The enemy fleet is destroyed!'

The men cheered, and, like hunting dogs let off their leashes to chase a fox, they sprinted down to the beach and began stripping the drowned Danes of their weapons and valuables, laughing and cheering and calling to one another in excitement.

Oswald grinned, overjoyed to think Alfred would not have to face thousands of enemy soldiers. The tide had, quite literally, turned in the king's favour, and it was all thanks to God. Alfred would enjoy this proof of Christian supremacy and Oswald could hardly wait to see him to tell him about what he'd witnessed.

And then the reality of it all struck him like a hammer-blow and the priest collapsed on the beach, sobbing as if his heart would break.

CHAPTER FORTY-TWO

'This is your reward, Guthrum! You broke your oath to Þórr, slaughtered the hostages, and now… God has punished you for it.'

Once more Alfred came to parley with the Danes, and the two kings sat across from one another outside Exanceaster, small contingents of household guards standing silently behind each of them. The jovial smile that had seemed fixed to Guthrum's face on every previous meeting was conspicuous in its absence today, however, replaced by a deep frown and a haunted expression which told of the shock the Dane felt at this devastating blow to his plans.

Alfred did not know exactly how many of the enemy longships had been sunk, or how many men had been lost in that miraculous storm. Estimates put the numbers at one hundred and twenty vessels sunk, with around 3600 warriors drowned, smashed to bits on the rocks, or hacked to death by the locals when they washed up on the Wessex coastline.

'I told you your heathen gods had no power, did I not?'

Guthrum merely stared at Alfred, offering no denial, for how could he? Both kings knew this was a sign, be it from the Christian God, Þórr, Óðinn, Tyr, Njord, or whatever deity held sway over the sea.

'You should convert, Guthrum,' Alfred continued. 'Allow one of my bishops to baptise you, and become a Christian.'

For a long moment the Dane did not reply. He did not appear as confident as he usually did, which was understandable. 'Maybe another time,' he replied at last. 'You might not believe it, but what we did to your hostages has weighed heavily on me. Their sacrifice was for nothing.' He shrugged. 'I broke the oath I made, and the gods have punished me for it, but what's done is done. What do you want from me right now, lord?'

Alfred laughed, thoroughly enjoying the unusual feeling of superiority over his enemies. For once *he* held the upper hand, and it felt good. The West Saxons had superior numbers, they had Guthrum's troops still contained within Exanceaster, and the morale of the two armies could not be more different. One group was filled with righteous confidence, while the other felt like their gods had abandoned them. It was quite a reversal in fortunes for the opposing sides, and he could very well believe Guthrum had been worried about breaking his oath to Óðinn. The man looked visibly older, with heavy bags under his eyes and a haunted expression that had not been there at their previous meetings.

'What I want,' Alfred said harshly. 'Is for you to leave my kingdom, Guthrum. Properly this time.'

'I can do that,' Guthrum conceded eagerly, and the relief was plain on his face. He did not want a battle, not now, with Alfred's army greatly outnumbering his.

'I also want more hostages.'

'We can trade hostages again—'

'I did not say trade,' Alfred spat. 'You will take no more of my people, not after what you did to the others. But you *will* hand over more of your people, many of them, and they will be noblemen selected by us. Starting with him!' He pointed at the tall, athletic man who was always at these meetings between the two kings. 'That's your personal bodyguard I believe? We'll take him to start with.'

The warrior Alfred was pointing at gripped the haft of his axe, which was tucked into a brown leather belt, mouth open in surprise, eyes wide with horror.

Guthrum turned to look at him. He nodded sadly and the guard took out his axe.

Alfred forced himself not to move, although a thrill of fear ran through him when the axeman glared at him murderously. It seemed time stood still for a moment as the Dane contemplated his future, wondering if he should just hack the West Saxon king down instead of offering himself up as a prisoner to the Christians. The moment passed, though, and the guard thumped his weapon down on the table beside Guthrum with bad grace, before walking across to stand in the centre of Alfred's own guards.

'Search him,' Wulfric commanded. 'Then bind his hands.' Instantly, two of Alfred's men set about their task, as attention returned to the kings.

'My lord,' Guthrum said in a wheedling tone. 'We will leave here, gladly, and return to Mercia. You may take whatever hostages you desire to ensure our holding to the agreement.'

Alfred nodded, disgusted at the enemy king's obvious desire to save his own skin no matter what that meant for his followers. 'And you will return the silver you took from us at Werham,' he stated.

Guthrum grimaced. It would be a hard matter trying to get all that back from his warriors. They would be deeply upset. What choice did they have, though?

'Fine,' the enemy king sighed, before holding up a hand. 'In return for all of this, you must give us time to prepare for the journey.'

Alfred's eyes narrowed. 'How much time?'

Guthrum thought about it. 'Until harvest? We will leave before then, so the people of Exanceaster can gather in the crops without trouble.'

They stared at one another for a long time. Alfred could see no reason to allow the Danes to tarry in his lands, but, at the same time he knew he was demanding much. Guthrum's own men might even decide to rebel against his leadership if he told them they must hand over more hostages, and all the silver he'd just given them, and embark on yet another forced march through hostile lands.

'All right,' the West Saxon ruler agreed. 'I will allow you to remain in Exanceaster, on condition that you do not mistreat its people.'

'Did we harm the folk in Werham?'

'You murdered the fucking hostages, Guthrum!' Alfred raged, allowing his emotions to get the best of him. 'I saw their bodies! Trussed like chickens, throats torn open while they begged you for mercy! Even your own gods were disgusted by what you did to those men.'

They eyed one another in frosty silence for a time, and then, at last, Alfred said in a more level tone, 'Why did you come here? Why could you not remain in your own lands across the sea?'

'Why did you?' Guthrum countered. 'Your people came here hundreds of years ago, just like us, sailing in ships, raiding and slaughtering the natives. The Romans even had their Saxon Shore – a line of forts built to stop your people from attacking the coastal towns.' He gestured towards the green fields around them. 'Like us, your people wanted a better life and came here to find it. Why should you have all this fertile farmland, Alfred, while those who follow me are left to eke out an existence in places where the sun does not even shine for many days of the year? Why should you Saxons enjoy bountiful harvests, while we scratch at hard earth, desperately trying to grow enough wheat to feed ourselves?'

'Then settle down,' Alfred said levelly. 'You've taken numerous farms and lands in Mercia and Northumbria. Give up your lives of raiding and become the farmers you say you aspire to be. Give up your heathen gods, be baptised into our Christian faith, and live in peace, enjoying what this island has to offer.'

Guthrum stared at him and, for a moment, it seemed like the Danish king might actually agree with the proposal. But he looked at his guards, then turned back to Alfred and shook his head. 'Maybe one day some of us will choose that life but, for now, too many of my men are young and seek to win fame, renown, slaves, and, of course, wealth. To ask a warrior to simply become a farmer overnight would be like asking Sol and Mani to swap places in the sky. Impossible.'

Alfred could see there was no point continuing the conversation, and there seemed little sense in making Guthrum swear any oaths again, either on Christian or heathen relics. Guthrum might be regretting breaking his earlier oath, but such a man could not be trusted. So, the peace agreement was sealed, and the West Saxon delegation departed. Later, some of Alfred's thanes went into the town and personally selected a number of hostages who they judged to be of high standing. Of course, it was possible Guthrum had dressed lowly thralls in finery, but the West Saxons did the best they could.

A few days later, the four thousand pounds of silver, or most of it at least, was returned to Alfred, who gave it back to the noblemen who'd originally handed it over. The king, with his love for books and literacy, always kept meticulous records of such important payments, so he knew exactly how the wealth should be apportioned.

With that the great, gathered fyrd of Wessex was able to return to their homes. God had brought a very favourable end to the war for them. Yet, as usual, not everyone was happy.

'You promised me Guthrum!'

Bishop Deorlaf had been excluded from Alfred's councils since the news came in about the sinking of the enemy fleet. The wealthy churchman had been enraged by suggestions of making peace with the Northmen, causing such fuss and upset with his demands to attack Exanceaster that Alfred was forced to not only bar him from subsequent meetings, but also to confine him to his own section of the camp. The king tried to persuade him to leave, to take his troops back to Hereford, but the bishop had refused.

Now, with the war over, Alfred had gone to Deorlaf's tent, surrounded by his hearth-warriors, to try and reason once more with the old man. It was going predictably badly.

'You promised me Guthrum!' the bishop repeated, actually jabbing his gnarled finger into the king's chest. 'Now you're just going to let him live like a lord in Exanceaster for as long as he likes?'

Alfred was tired. Tired of dealing with Danes, and tired of feeling perpetually as if he was not master of his own fate. His arm shot out and he grabbed Deorlaf's wrist as the bishop continued to poke at him.

'You might not like it,' the king growled, squeezing the bishop's wrist and staring into his eyes. 'But that is what will happen. It is the best outcome for the people of Wessex. Your wish for vengeance must be put aside for the greater good, my lord. That is what I have decided, and the ealdormen agreed, so that is it. The war is over, and you must return home.'

Bishop Deorlaf bared his teeth like an angry dog and Alfred was glad they were within a tent so their soldiers could not see them. Noblemen should not behave like this, he thought. It was humiliating for everyone involved.

'I am sorry,' he said in a more conciliatory tone. 'I grieve for your son – he was a fine man, and did not deserve what happened. None of those hostages did. But you killed all the Danes we had taken as hostage. That act was an affront to God, for we had sworn to treat them with care, but I let it go in order to allow you a measure of vengeance.'

'Pah,' the churchman retorted, pulling his wrist from Alfred's grasp at the second attempt. 'You *let* me kill them because you wanted to send a message to Guthrum that you were not a weak king.' His voice dropped then, becoming a furious, accusatory hiss. 'But you are weak, Alfred. You, and all your dead brothers.'

Alfred gritted his teeth. He was physically much stronger than Deorlaf, being taller, broader, and four decades younger. He was also a proven warrior whose bravery was fast becoming the stuff of legend. It would be easy for him to reach out and silence the old man's insults and accusations; he would not even need to use the seax at his waist, his bare hands would be enough to shut the fool up forever.

The thought left his mind as quickly as it arrived, however, for it was not in his nature to behave in such a recklessly violent manner. Word of his deed would quickly spread throughout the kingdom and it would be greeted with uproar and a massive loss of support from his other ealdormen. Kings could simply not be allowed to murder those who disagreed with their policies. Wessex had not been built or governed on such principles.

'Go home to Hereford,' Alfred said, allowing his anger to drain out of him. 'We're done here. I thank you for your service during these last hard weeks and months, but your part is done now. Farewell, Bishop Deorlaf.' With that, he turned and stalked to the entrance, pushing the tent flaps aside and stooping to pass through them.

'You are a weakling,' the churchman called behind him furiously. 'And you will regret allowing Guthrum to live. He will betray your trust again, boy, and when he does, I'll not be there to help you. Plenty of us have had enough of your feeble rule!'

Alfred let out a long, exasperated breath and exited the tent, welcoming the fresh air which felt as if it was washing away the grubby taint of what had just happened.

'He didn't take it well, then, my lord?' Wulfric waited for him, tall and reassuring as ever.

'How did you know?' Alfred asked sarcastically. 'Of course he took it badly, as we damn well expected. Worse. It seems he's withdrawing all future support for me.'

'He can't do that,' Wulfric replied as they made their way back through Bishop Deorlaf's camp to their own.

'Maybe not legally,' Alfred said. 'But he can refuse to send his fyrd the next time we need it. And he wouldn't be the only one. How many of my other ealdormen did not support us here, or at Werham?'

'Yet we prevailed,' Wulfric said, and Alfred looked at him, smiling.

'It's not like you to be the cheery one,' the king said. 'I appreciate your positivity though, old friend. And you're right.

We survived this invasion, despite the odds being so heavily stacked against us, and now we can move forward with our reforms. Even if Bishop Deorlaf doesn't want to support me, it won't matter. Wessex will thrive, with or without him. God is on our side, Wulfric, and no-one can say otherwise, not after this!'

CHAPTER FORTY-THREE

Guthrum held true to his word for once, and led his Danes from Exanceaster that summer, before the people began collecting the crops. They were escorted to Wessex's northern border and disappeared into Mercia to cause trouble for the people there. Alfred cared little for that – he had his lands back completely in his control and that year's harvest was a bountiful one.

The king held one further Witan in the autumn, which was attended by many of his ealdormen and thanes and proved to be a raucous celebration of what had turned out to be an astonishing few months. God had not only smiled on the West Saxon people that year, he had actively participated in vanquishing their pagan foes, and most were keen to thank him by eating and drinking to excess.

Oswald, as was his wont, frowned on such gluttony, but Alfred merely laughed.

'God has allowed us to live when it seemed many would die in the war with the Danes,' he told the priest. 'Is it such a sin to celebrate life by enjoying ourselves with meat and ale?'

'If done in moderation, no, it would not be a sin,' Oswald had retorted. 'But too many see it as an excuse to gorge themselves, and act like fools when they're too drunk to walk straight.'

Alfred had laughed at the priest's stern expression, but he wished he'd followed Oswald's advice later, as another bout of his stomach troubles flared up. As a result, he ended up bed-ridden for almost a week and, when it finally passed, he'd lost weight and vowed never to drink again.

Winter quickly arrived, bringing heavy snows and winds which caused havoc across the kingdom.

Near the end of the Christmas celebrations, on twelfth night, Alfred sat in his hall in Cippanhamme, with the fire blazing, and surrounded by his family and hearth-warriors. He'd remained true to his vow never to drink alcohol again right up until Christmas eve, when it was only natural to enjoy a few ales. Over the course of the festive period, however, he tried his best to be sensible, limiting his intake of both drink and rich foods, and it seemed to be paying off.

'Your stomach pains have passed?' Wulfric asked him as they sat at the high table enjoying a troupe of musicians performing hymns on lyre, flute, drums and bells.

'They have,' Ealhswith answered before Alfred had a chance. She leaned over, speaking loud enough to be heard over the music. 'And he's even put the weight back on that he lost.'

The king smiled, leaning into his high-backed chair and rubbing his belly which, although far from being rotund, was nowhere near as hollow as it had been just a month before.

'I'm making sure he eats well, and drinks less ale,' Ealhswith added. 'Although, truthfully Wulfric, I think he's finally getting to an age where he knows himself not to get blind drunk all the time.' She grinned and pressed her head against Alfred's shoulder as he gave her a hurt look.

'That's good,' Wulfric nodded, a smile touching his lips too. 'You should be grateful, my lord. A caring wife is not always easy to find.'

'When are you going to remarry anyway?' Ealhswith asked the ealdorman, broaching a subject that was rarely, if ever touched upon. Wulfric's wife had died fifteen years before, after a decade of marriage which had borne four offspring, only one of which, his daughter, Deorwynn, had survived early childhood. She was grown now, and a nun in Ilminster. Wulfric did not like to talk about his wife, for they had been very close and her death still pained him. Ealhswith liked the bluff captain, though, and genuinely wanted to hear about his feelings – the wine she'd drunk during the evening's feasting made her speak more freely than usual.

'I'll not remarry,' Wulfric told her with a wistful smile. 'I'm happy enough as I am. And looking after your husband leaves me little time for homemaking.'

'Yes, he does need a lot of care and attention,' Ealhswith replied, winking at the ealdorman.

'You know, I am sitting right here,' Alfred protested. 'And I can take care of myself, thank you.'

The musicians finished the tune they'd been playing and there was a ripple of polite applause before they started another. It was still early evening, so they were performing softer, melodic pieces. Later on they'd switch to faster, more rhythmic songs and the entire hall would join in, singing long and loud into the night. When the wind howled outside in the dark, and the icy rain kept folk huddled indoors by the fire, there was no better entertainment than a rowdy singalong. Alfred always loved such occasions.

'How are the new building works coming along, Wulfric?' Ealhswith asked.

'You mean the king's planned system of burhs?' the ealdorman said. 'Well, we've started work on a few, but it's a huge undertaking. It'll take time.'

'We should have done it years ago, when we first paid Halfdan to leave,' Alfred said, shaking his head ruefully. His attention was drawn to the main door, where a thin, older man with a snub-nose was talking animatedly to an excited, and growing, audience.

'What's happening there?' Wulfric wondered, noting the thin man and the people listening to him, who were looking in Alfred's direction every now and again.

'Let's find out,' Ealhswith said, standing and gesturing. The group parted, made suddenly anxious by the royal attention they'd drawn. The thin man was left on his own, but he hurried over as Ealhswith repeated her gesture for him to approach.

'My lady,' he said, chewing his lip and fidgeting nervously. He had a thick, but understandable Irish accent.

'What's happening,' Alfred asked him curiously. 'Who are you, and why all the excitement?'

'The people were just interested in the news, my lord,' the man replied, rubbing his snub-nose and looking about the hall. 'I'm a merchant, from Ulaid, newly arrived here with fine wares to sell.' He looked around, even smiling as his natural instincts as a trader began to take over.

'What news?' Alfred demanded.

'About King Halfdan, my lord.'

Alfred glanced at Wulfric who appeared as baffled as the king.

'Have you not heard yet?' the man asked. 'I thought word would have reached here before me...'

'By Christ, man,' Wulfric broke in. 'Spit it out! What about Halfdan?'

The man shrank back, and swallowed before croaking, 'Well, he's dead, my lord.'

The hall had already fallen quiet as everyone listened to the conversation, but now it became as silent as the grave. Alfred simply stared at the merchant, wondering if he'd heard the fellow right. 'Dead?' he asked at last, before saying to Wulfric, 'Did you hear anything about this?'

The ealdorman was shaking his head, eyes shining in the reflected firelight.

'What happened to Halfdan?' Ealhswith asked in a kindlier tone, even handing the merchant a mug of ale which she'd poured herself. 'Tell us what you know.'

The Irishman took the ale and sipped it with relish. 'Well, my lady, Halfdan was king of what we call the "Dark Heathens" – newcomers to our lands. He and his men got into a fight with King Barid of Duibhlinn and his "Fair Heathens" who've been in Ireland for a lot longer.' He shrugged. 'Barid won.'

'Are you sure of this?' Alfred asked.

'Oh aye, lord,' the merchant nodded firmly. 'I sailed here from the very place where the battle happened. Halfdan's body was there for all to see; or what was left of it anyway. The gulls, you know...?' He winced, then looked at the king apologetically. 'I'm sorry, my lord. I assumed the news would have reached you already, or I would have come straight to you with it.'

Alfred knew what the man was after, and he was more than happy to take a large handful of coins from his purse. 'This is the best news we've had in a while, my friend,' he said, beaming as he gave them to the merchant. 'Take these, with my thanks.'

The Irishman stared at the silver before it somehow disappeared within his cloak, then he downed the last of the ale in the mug Ealhswith had given him, bowed deeply, and moved away towards the people.

'Did you hear all that?' Alfred shouted, standing and spreading his arms as he addressed everyone gathered in the hall. 'Halfdan is dead! God has wiped his heathen taint from these lands, and he'll bother Wessex no more. Drink up, my friends, for this is truly news to celebrate!'

Ealhswith and Wulfric were on their feet and Alfred embraced them both as cheering filled the hall and the musicians struck up a triumphant tune.

'God be praised,' Ealhswith said, sitting back down and raising her cup to toast the good news. 'Things really are looking up for Wessex, Alfred. Our fortifications are being expanded, our enemies removed. You have a lot to be proud of, my love.'

She kissed Alfred on the cheek, and he smiled boyishly. 'We all do,' he said. 'None more than you and Wulfric. I'd have been dead long ago if I didn't have your support, and I thank God for it every day.' He watched the lyre player deftly plucking the instrument's strings, although he couldn't hear the melody over the raucous singing of the people. 'This must be as close to heaven as a man can get,' he said, turning to look at his two companions. 'Don't you think? What more could anyone ask for on a winter's evening?'

Ealhswith gripped his arm affectionately as the song came to an end, then she gave him one final kiss on the lips before standing up. 'I'm going to check on the children. Save some of that roast boar for me, Alfred.'

He watched as she made her way past the benches and the people thronging the hall, nimbly avoiding collisions with inebriated revellers and the dogs that mooched around in the rushes searching for scraps of food. Still only in her mid-twenties, his wife had already given him three healthy children yet somehow retained her slim, lithe figure. Alfred felt truly blessed to have her in his life. The thought of losing her, as Wulfric had lost his beloved wife, terrified him.

What could happen though? They were safe in the heart of Wessex, their enemies either dead, or many leagues distant and neutered so they'd pose no threat to Alfred's people for a long time.

The song finished and there was a momentary quiet as the musicians took a rest. Alfred lifted his mug and held it aloft. Wulfric raised his too, and they clattered them together, spilling ale into the air. '*Was hail!*' said the king. 'Good health, and may the new year be as blessed as the last, my friend!'

Wulfric gave the traditional response of, '*Drink hail!*' and they supped their foaming drinks, both filled with a cosy, warm glow, and hope for the future of Wessex.

Shouts filtered through the sturdy timber walls then, ignored at first, until they rose in number and volume and Alfred glanced at Wulfric. Something was happening outside. When the shouts mingled with screams the king stood up, hand falling to his sword. He nodded to one of his hearth-warriors and said, 'Guard my wife,' then hurried outside with Wulfric and the rest of the men at his heels.

The cold air hit them immediately, sobering Alfred even more than the muffled screams had done. They could hear the sounds more clearly now, and the king started to run towards the gates, fear building within him with every step. Before they reached the town walls they saw a soldier reeling towards them, blood streaming from a gaping wound in his head that must have been inflicted by an arrow, or a thrown spear, or perhaps a stone shot from a sling.

'The Danes are here!' the soldier gasped, staring from Wulfric to the king, his panic-stricken features proving his words to be true. 'Hundreds of them, my lords, and more coming this way. Too many to hold off. Cippanhamme is done for!'

'Sit down, lad,' Wulfric said gently. 'And pull yourself together. You're a warrior of Wessex. We'll find you a healer to sort that cut on your head. You'll be back at your post in no time.'

From his beardless face and smooth complexion Alfred suspected the soldier was likely no more than fifteen summers old, and utterly petrified. But the boy took heart from Wulfric's firm, confident manner. He nodded, before slumping to the ground in a daze.

'Get your things, my lord,' Wulfric said, turning to Alfred. 'Get back to the hall and gather Ealhswith and the children, and head to the stables.'

'We're abandoning the town?' Alfred replied, astonished.

'For now,' Wulfric said. 'We don't have enough men to withstand a full-on assault, if there truly are hundreds of Danes approaching. The gates won't hold them for long, and then what?'

Alfred's head was spinning and he wished he'd not drank any ale, or perhaps had drunk a lot more. It might not help him think clearly, but at least he'd not be so frightened. His family were here, by God, and the Danes were not known for treating royal prisoners well.

'Find out what's happening,' he said. 'And come to me at the stables. I'll get everyone ready to ride. Take care, Wulfric.'

They parted, with the captain leading half of the hearth-warriors away towards the entrance to the town, while the rest went with Alfred as he ran to find Ealhswith.

She was in the hall, in their children's chamber, and had obviously heard all the commotion for she was hurriedly throwing clothes into a sack. 'There's trouble,' she said as the king came into the chamber. 'I know. I heard men shouting and screaming outside. A lot of men.'

'Danes are at the gates,' Alfred confirmed, and he too began pushing clothes and other necessities into a sack as Aethelflaed and Edward looked on fearfully. Little Aethelgifu was fast asleep, mercifully, and Alfred summoned the nursemaid. When she appeared, Alfred commanded her to quickly get the baby ready for a journey.

It did not take long before they were all outside and moving towards the stables, hearth-warriors guarding their steps. Horses had been prepared and Alfred helped Ealhswith onto one, her favourite grey mare. He gave her baby Aethelgifu and she secured the child's sling around her. Alfred lifted Edward onto his black charger and jumped up behind him, while Aethelflaed went with one of the king's loyal guards.

The sounds of fighting, and the unmistakeable thump of a battering ram, were growing louder now. Alfred looked at Ealhswith, terrified for her family's safety, and impotent rage flared in the king. Yet another attack during winter, and in the middle of a Christian festival. Even with Halfdan dead, the Danes could not leave them in peace!

Wulfric came running towards them. 'Fly!' he was shouting. 'We can't hold them off for much longer, my lord. There's hundreds of the bastards, they must be here for you.'

'We're ready,' Ealhswith replied. 'Hurry and get your horse, Wulfric.'

'I'm staying here, my lady,' the ealdorman protested. 'To lead the defence.'

'No, you're not, Wulfric. You're coming with us,' the queen consort commanded.

368

'Ealhswith is right,' Alfred said. 'Wherever we end up—' He had been about to say, 'if we survive', but didn't want to alarm his children any more than they already were. 'We'll need you. So, you're coming, and that's an order! Get your horse, and follow us.'

There was a massive thud followed by a terrific cracking sound which seemed to fill the entire town and Alfred knew the gates had been breached. He kicked his heels into his horse's flanks and started to move through the streets, fear and shame filling him as townsfolk came out of their houses and called to them, asking what was happening.

His head was spinning and he wasn't even sure where they were going – he'd only ever come into Cippanhamme by the main gates! Was there another way out? He assumed there must be, for his hearth-warriors were all riding in the same direction, as if they knew where to go. This shamed him even more, for he should have been prepared for an attack like this, knowing from bitter experience the underhand tactics Guthrum and his kind often employed. Yet Alfred had not been prepared, indeed he hadn't even thought to have an escape route ready in case anything like this happened.

Wulfric galloped up behind them and rode past, saluting Alfred and taking up a position at the head of the formation, bellowing at people to move out of the way or be trampled. He clearly knew where to go, and again Alfred thanked God that the ealdorman was his captain.

Men and women were running around the streets in a panic. Some seeking to flee, others heading for the gates armed with weapons. It swelled Alfred's heart with pride to see such bravery, but crushed him at the same time for he knew anyone standing in Guthrum's way would quickly be cut down. For a moment, he thought of riding back and surrendering himself to the enemy king, but it passed quickly. Guthrum would kill him, probably as painfully as possible, and Alfred had faith that, once he was safely away from Cippanhamme, he would soon be able to muster the fyrd and strike back at the murderous Danes.

And next time they met, he would not show any mercy. There would be no letting them linger within Wessex, and the leaders, especially Guthrum, would be slaughtered like cattle.

He tried to keep his spirits up by focusing on these vengeful thoughts and murmuring words of comfort to three-year-old Edward until, at last, he realised Wulfric had led them off the main street and down a narrower side road. There was a concealed gate in the palisade wall here, and two men guarding it. They saw the king's party approaching and quickly threw off the wooden beams that held it shut. Opening it, the pair hurried through, and there was the sound of more beams being knocked away.

When Alfred rode through after Wulfric and the others he saw there were actually two gates, one on each side of the main wall. This hidden way out was their salvation, for it led south, and there was no sign of enemy forces here. In contrast, Alfred could hear fighting within the centre of town now, and realised the area around the main gates had been overrun. The Danes were within Cippanhamme – hundreds, perhaps thousands of sea-wolves were killing Alfred's people and here he was riding in the opposite direction. It was shameful but – as he looked across at Ealhswith's galloping mare, and little Aethelflaed with his guard, and Edward on his own horse – the king was glad they did not have to suffer at the hands of the raiders.

'How did they manage to reach the town unhindered, and without us knowing?' he called to Wulfric over the pounding hooves and wind rushing past as they raced into the darkness, trusting to God that their horses would not break a leg on an unseen obstacle. 'They were in Mercia the last we heard!'

'They've most likely come from the north, and the east,' his captain shouted back. 'Probably through Ealdorman Wulfhere's lands.'

Alfred's blood turned to ice at the thought of his own noblemen betraying him in such a way. To allow Guthrum to pass, unchallenged, through his lands, without sending any word of warning to Cippanhamme? It was monstrous! Yet Alfred instinctively knew it must be true. Guthrum had surely paid Wulfhere to turn a blind eye as the Northmen marched through his lands.

And then another terrible thought struck him: how many more of his ealdormen would desert him now? He'd known for some time that he was not well-loved by the likes of Bishop Deorlaf and Ealdorman Wulfhere. What if they had turned even more against him?

'Where will we go?' he shouted to Wulfric, not wishing to continue down this depressing line of thought. 'If the Danes control the lands north and east of Cippanhamme, who knows where else they could have troops? Lundenwic is theirs, so they could have moved men from there across our eastern borders. And if Wulfhere has gone over to Guthrum, more of the enemy could be marching through Wiltunshire in the south right now.'

Wulfric nodded as his horse thundered across the ground. 'Agreed, my lord,' he said. 'I think we should head west, for now, until we can get a better idea of what's happening.'

'What about Brycgstow?' Ealhswith suggested. 'Diuma and his father, Ealdorman Wealdmar will give us shelter.'

'Excellent idea,' Alfred replied. 'We make for Brycgstow, Wulfric. From there we can send word for the fyrd to gather so we can retake Cippanhamme.'

They rode on, slowing their pace now that they were safely away from Guthrum's Northmen, saving their horses and making the chance of a spill less likely. The moon was up and Alfred looked at his family, tears streaking his cheeks for the slaughtered people of Cippanhamme. He thanked God for saving his wife and children, though, and looked forward to joining with Diuma in Brycgstow, which was just over twenty miles distant. They would ride through the night and be there before morning, all being well.

And then, Alfred vowed, he would set about killing Guthrum, as he should have done at Werham, and again at Exanceaster.

It amazed Alfred how resilient children were. All of his offspring somehow managed to sleep during the ride through the night, despite the motion of the horses they rode. There had been no sign of pursuit so, once a couple of miles had been put between them and Cippanhamme they slowed their pace from a mad dash to a gentler walk. Even so, Alfred found it amazing that anyone could sleep given their circumstances, and he sent a prayer of thanks up to God that the three children had found some respite from the night's terrifying events.

The king had no doubt they'd all come perilously close to a violent death in Cippanhamme.

By the time they reached the outskirts of Brycgstow the sense of immediate danger had faded. There were no signs of enemy activity here, the farms and steadings appearing peaceful and, when barking dogs warned the occupants of the passing riders, anxious faces appeared at doorways before bolting themselves inside once more.

That was reassuring.

'No sign of the Danes here,' Alfred said softly to Wulfric, keeping his voice to a low murmur so as not to disturb the children.

His captain shook his head, chewing his lip thoughtfully. 'I think we'll find that Guthrum has only attacked one place, Cippanhamme, and that for one reason.'

'To kill me.'

'Aye, lord,' Wulfric said grimly. 'Clearly some of our ealdormen have gone over to his side. The only thing that stands between Guthrum and total domination of Wessex is you.'

'Well, he missed his one chance,' the king growled. 'We escaped, all of us, and there's the walls of Brycgstow, where we'll find sanctuary and, more importantly, warriors to stand against the Danes and do as we always do by sending them scurrying for their lives.'

Brycgstow was a large town, with sturdy walls which had been expanded recently and Alfred felt an immense surge of relief as they grew closer. Even if Guthrum had sent men to hunt them down, they would never be able to penetrate this town as easily as they had Cippanhamme. The royal family was safe and, as a father, that was a crushing weight off Alfred's shoulders.

'Who's that?' a guard called from the gatehouse as they rode up to stand at the barred entranceway. 'It's the middle of the night! Piss off and come back in the morning like everyone else.'

'It's the king, you stupid turd!' Wulfric shouted back, although he refrained from using his loudest parade-ground voice for fear of frightening the children, all of whom had come awake now. 'Open the damn gates, or you'll get my boot up your arse!'

The guard stared down at them, squinting in the gloom as if somehow confirming Wulfric's words. At length, he grunted, 'Wait there,' and disappeared.

'Christ in Heaven,' Wulfric said in exasperation. 'It's just as well the Danes are *not* behind us, or we'd all be dead thanks to that useless prick.'

Alfred looked at Ealhswith and they shared a smile at the captain's usual ill humour and straight-talking manner.

The sound of booted feet clambering up wooden stairs on the other side of the wall came to them then, and another face appeared beside the original guard's.

'Diuma!' Alfred called, his smile becoming a wide grin. 'It's good to see you, my lord. We have bad tidings. The Danes – Guthrum again – have attacked Cippanhamme. Almost killed us before we managed to flee. That bastard Wulfhere must have let them pass through his lands without trying to stop them, or sending any word that they were coming. Thank God Brycgstow is safe! Let us in, my friend, and we can set about making this right.'

Diuma looked down on them, listening to the king's words, and Alfred's relieved grin slowly faded as the thane remained silent. He was no longer the wispy-bearded, lean youngster that had been embarrassed when he spoke up in Aethelred's hall years before – he'd filled out and his beard was dark and full now, while the battle scar he'd earned at Ascesdune was visible on his face even in the gloom. Despite all that, he seemed very young and uncertain of himself as he peered down at them.

'What are you waiting for, Diuma?' Alfred called, gesturing to the tired riders arrayed behind him. 'I have my wife and family here, needing a bed and some food after our flight. Open the gates.'

Diuma looked at his guard, then back at Alfred, and there was a pained expression on his face as he replied, 'I can't do that, I'm afraid. You need to move on, my lord. There will be no respite for you in Brycgstow.'

CHAPTER FORTY-FOUR

Alfred stared up at the walls in sheer amazement. No respite in Brycgstow? 'By St Albans' cock, Diuma, this is no time for jokes. We're exhausted, and we were almost killed by Guthrum's men. Cippanhamme is a smoking ruin by now, with hundreds of people murdered, and you would have us stand here while you play games?'

Diuma shook his head. 'My father, Ealdorman Wealdmar, has commanded the gates remain barred. You need to move on, Alfred, please.'

The king turned to Ealhswith, then Wulfric, all three shocked by the thane's words.

'No,' Alfred retorted, angry now but trying to maintain his composure for he was at a clear disadvantage here. '*You* need to remember who you're speaking to, Diuma. I am your king – you swore an oath to me, as did your father – and I command you to open the gates. By God, man, if nothing else, the ancient laws of hospitality demand it! Would you turn me away? My wife? My children?' He gestured at Edward in the saddle in front of him. 'It's the middle of the night and for all we know the Danes are hunting for us right now, so where would you have us go?'

His hearth-warriors were muttering angrily amongst themselves now, threatening to break Diuma's legs when they finally got inside the walls of Brycgstow, but the thane held firm.

'I'm sorry, my lord,' he called, and, in truth, he looked absolutely devastated by what was happening. He was like an anxious child standing atop the palisade wall and, as he opened his mouth to speak again, another figure appeared by his side. A much older person: Ealdorman Wealdmar.

Alfred had not seen Diuma's father in a long time – on the last occasion, Wealdmar had been bent and wizened, his joints practically seized up by arthritis. Now? In the gloom it seemed as if a shambling corpse had come to stand beside the young thane. Alfred wondered how the hell Wealdmar had made it up the steps; presumably someone had carried him, like an invalid, or a child. No wonder Diuma had been given command of Wealdmar's fyrd these past few years, it was incredible the old man was still alive.

'My lord!' Alfred greeted him. 'I'm glad you've come. Please ask your men to open the gates—'

The ancient ealdorman squinted down at him from rheumy eyes, but when he replied his voice was loud and clear. 'This has been coming for a long time, Alfred,' he said. 'You've allowed the Danes to ravage our lands for years now, and the thanes and ealdormen have had enough.'

'What thanes and ealdormen?' Wulfric demanded, eyes smouldering like embers in the darkness.

'Enough of them,' Wealdmar replied, waving a skeletal hand dismissively. 'They no longer support you Alfred, hence Guthrum's uncontested taking of Cippanhamme.'

They gazed at one another in silence and then Aethelgifu began to cry. The nursemaid came to Ealhswith and took the baby from her, then pulled down her tunic and began to suckle the child. Alfred looked at them, dread and fear filling him. How could he protect his children if his noblemen had deserted him? He needed their support to muster the fyrd; without an army, there was no way to oppose the invaders.

'My advice, for what it's worth,' Wealdmar said to him. 'Is to do what some of the other nobles have already started doing: sail for Francia, Alfred. Or Rome, like your sister. You could not stop the Danes, and your chance to do so has passed now. Save yourself and your family and flee Wessex forever.'

'Brycgstow has thrown its lot in with the Northmen, then?' Ealhswith demanded, her usually melodious, pleasant voice now bitter and accusatory. 'You'll allow Guthrum to become your king? Or to place a puppet on the throne of Wessex, as the Danes have done in Mercia, for the likes of you and your duplicitous son to kneel to?'

Diuma, still standing on the wall beside his father, blanched. He had always been deeply respectful of the queen consort. This was the first time Ealhswith had ever had a harsh word for the young thane, and it was obviously distressing for him.

'What difference does it make whether the king is a Saxon or a Dane?' Wealdmar demanded. Then he went on in a softer tone. 'This is the way of things. We've tried to hold back the tide for years, expending countless wealth, resources and men in the process. Yet we've never been able to make our borders truly secure, and now the powerful men of Wessex have come to realise the best way forward is to do as the other kingdoms have done, and stop fighting the inevitable. Guthrum has won, Alfred. And now,' he coughed harshly for a long moment before he was able to return his watery gaze to the king, who was glowering at him, teeth gritted, hand wrapped around the handle of his sword. 'You should leave, Alfred. Before your pursuers catch up with you, for if that happens there will be no help for you from the men of Brycgstow. Farewell, lord, may God protect you.'

He shuffled away and disappeared into the shadows behind the palisade wall, shouted curses and promises of retribution for his betrayal ringing out from Alfred's hearth-warriors, and only then did Alfred realise the town walls were filling with helmeted spearmen. Diuma stood, still looking at the king sorrowfully.

'I am truly sorry for this, my lord,' the young thane said in consternation. He looked down, hands moving behind the crenelated wall, and then he held something up and said, 'You should have this back. I don't deserve it.' His voice cracked as he spoke, then the object in his hand dropped with a thud onto the grass and he disappeared the same way his father had gone.

Alfred quickly dismounted and walked over to collect what Diuma had discarded, but the king already knew what it was: the seax he'd gifted to the thane for his service to the crown after the battle at Reading. Hurt, he stared at it, shocked by what was happening, despair filling him. He pushed the feelings aside and returned to his horse, holding tightly to his son, trying to reassure himself as much as Edward that all would be well.

'What will we do?' Ealhswith asked, looking from Wulfric to Alfred. There was no fear on her face, merely anger and determination. 'We can't break into Brycgstow, and we can't remain here.'

Alfred looked again at baby Aethelgifu, no longer feeding, but staring silently at him, and the weight of years pressed down on the king. He placed a hand on his side as he felt, or at least imagined he felt, a twinge of pain. Licking his lips, he met his wife's eyes and nodded. 'We'll move on,' he said hoarsely. 'But one day I will return here, and see the heads of Diuma and Wealdmar displayed on those walls they're so happy to cower behind!'

They turned their horses and began to ride south once more, away from Brycgstow.

'Where do you think we should go now, my lord?' Wulfric asked as they picked up speed. 'If Wealdmar speaks truly, and all the towns around here have thrown in their lot with Guthrum, perhaps we'd be better doing as the old bastard suggested and find a ship to take you to Francia for a time.'

'Francia?' Alfred demanded. 'I'm the king of Wessex. I'll not abandon these lands, Wulfric, not while I have you, and my hearth-warriors to fight at my side. Eh, Ealhswith?'

The queen consort nodded grimly, and Wulfric smiled. 'Probably not the most sensible option, my lord, but I'm glad to see you've not lost heart, despite the night's events. Where to then?'

Alfred's gaze swept across the countryside, beginning now to lighten as the sun was rising at last. In his mind he tried to picture the geography of these southern lands, and the topography. Where could he hide from the warbands Guthrum would undoubtedly send out hunting for him? Where could he rebuild the trust and support of his people and, ultimately, his kingdom? Only one place lay nearby that might offer suitable shelter for such a momentous undertaking.

'Athelney,' he said, speaking loudly so all his companions could hear. 'We'll hide within the marshes of Athelney and bide our time until we're ready to strike back at Guthrum and those of our own who've betrayed us. This is not the end for us, or for Wessex, my friends, merely another beginning. By the body and blood of Christ we will return one day soon, stronger than ever, I swear it!'

And so they rode south as the sun began to rise.

To Athelney, and a new dawn.

AUTHOR'S NOTE

Alright, I'll be honest – I knew basically nothing about Alfred the Great before I started researching this novel. Writing about him was my editor's idea and, when I started reading about the period, and about Alfred's life, I was amazed. Some of the events, like all those Danish ships being wrecked in a storm, were more incredible than the best fiction! At the same time, this was my first attempt to write about a real, historical figure and I was a little worried whether there were *enough* moments of excitement to fill a novel? I mean, if I feel a section is lagging when I'm writing about a character like Robin Hood, or my mighty warrior druid, Bellicus of Dun Breatann, I can just slot in some daring escape from a fortress, or invent a battle, or any number of exciting events. I couldn't do that this time: although I was not writing a biography of Alfred – or even what almost amounted to a hagiography, in Bishop Asser's case – I still had to stick to the well-known facts. Thankfully, I believe there was plenty to round out this novel and make it just as thrilling as my other, completely fictional, tales.

One aspect of Alfred's character that I found fascinating and really wanted to explore in detail was his poor health. Said to have suffered from piles, until he prayed God would cure them and replace them with something else, he ended up suffering from abdominal pains which many think were caused by Crohn's disease or irritable bowel syndrome (IBS). The idea of someone essentially making *themselves* ill was one I found both interesting and realistic. When I was doing my Open University degree I remember getting a strange headache which lasted, on and off, for around two weeks. It went away, then came back some time later. I only realised after the third year of this happening that the pain would happen just before I had to sit the annual end of course exam, and it would go away the minute I finished doing the exam! Similarly, during the COVID lockdown in 2020, I started to get some pains in my abdomen, rather similar to what Alfred suffered although not as extreme. When I eventually went to the pharmacist and told him my symptoms, he said it sounded like IBS and was nothing to worry about and, guess what, my fears, and the pains, disappeared! Just put yourself in Alfred's position: young, his parents and brothers all dead, and him thrust into the position of king while the Great Summer Army was ravaging your lands perhaps as some divine punishment for your own impiety. If a simple exam was stressful enough to cause me a headache, what kind of psychological damage would being King of Wessex around AD 870 do to a person?!

And yet, not only did Alfred somehow deal with these crushing demands, he went on to become known as 'The Great'. Truly, he was a remarkable man.

Speaking of remarkable, what about that Tenebrae service? In my youth I was taken to things like Midnight Mass around Christmastime, but I'd never heard of Tenebrae until I started researching this novel and I knew I had to include it. Alfred was famously religious and I imagine Tenebrae would have made a huge impression on him, as it would anyone experiencing it. So, although his brother, Aethelred, is said to have died AFTER Easter, I felt like it tied in so well to the Tenebrae service and its meaning that I had to bring the two events together, despite it not being entirely accurate, historically.

Again, I've not stayed completely true to the accounts of Alfred's defeating the seven shiploads of raiders in AD 875. It's possible that battle was fought, somehow, at sea. Trying to imagine two opposing groups of sailors, inexperienced in fighting from on board ships, conjured up some messy and not very exciting scenes in my head. So, I had the battle play out on land, avoiding any unwanted slapstick. Also, the West Saxons were said to have captured only one ship that day, with the other six escaping. I thought it made for a more powerful scene to have just the one enemy ship managing to escape though, so that's how I wrote it.

One final piece of artistic licence which I hold my hands up to is calling Athelney, well, Athelney. For every other place in the book I've tried to find the Anglo-Saxon name or at least the oldest version I can find, but I specifically made a choice to use the modern name of Athelney for those final, breathless moments in the novel. Why? Well, in the 9th century that town was known as Aethelingaeigge! Quite a mouthful, right? I thought using that name would take away from the power of the final scene and I will stand by that. I hope you can forgive me!

Now, it's onwards to the second book and the next few years of Alfred's life. Will they be as interesting and exciting as the first ones? I hope you'll join me to find out!

Steven A. McKay
Old Kilpatrick,
8th March, 2023

PLACES

Abbandune – Abingdon, Oxfordshire
Ascesdune – Ashdown, Oxfordshire
Athelney – Athelney, Somerset
Baseng – Old Basing, near Basingstoke, Hampshire
Bensingtun – Benson, Oxfordshire
Bere – Bere Regis, Dorset
Berrocscire – Berkshire
Brycgstow – Bristol, Avon
Ceodre – Cheddar, Somerset
Cippanhamme – Chippenham, Wiltshire
Corf – Corfe Castle, Dorset
Cornwalas – Cornwall
Dorcaestre – Dorchester on Thames, Oxfordshire
Duibhlinn – Dublin, Ireland
Englafeld – Englefield, Berkshire
Eoforwic/Jorvik – York, Yorkshire
Exanceaster – Exeter, Devon
Gegnesburh – Gainsborough, Lincolnshire
Grantebrycge – Cambridge, Cambridgeshire
Hægelisdun – Outskirts of Bury St Edmunds, Suffolk
Kennet – River Kennet
Lichet – Lytchett Minster, Dorset
Loidis – Leeds, Yorkshire
Lundenwic – London
Medehamstede – Peterborough, Cambridgeshire
Meretun – Unknown. Possibly in Winchester or Wiltshire
Muleforda – Moulsford, Oxfordshire

Polle – Poole, Dorset
Pydel – River Piddle
Ragheleiam – Rayleigh, Essex
Severn Sea – Bristol Channel
Snotengaham – Nottingham, Nottinghamshire
South Sea – English Channel
Strath-Clota – Strathclyde
Swanawic – Swanage, Dorset
Tamyse – River Thames
Theodford – Thetford, Norfolk
Tweoxneam – Twynham/ Christchurch, Dorset
Werham – Wareham, Dorset
Whistley – Whistley Green, Berkshire
Wichamtun – Witchampton, Dorset
Wiltunshire – Wiltshire
Winburnan – Wimborne Minster, Dorset
Windlesora – Windsor, Berkshire
Wintanceaster – Winchester, Hampshire
Valhöll – Afterlife of the Danes/Norse, later known as
    Valhalla